THE AMAZING MYCROFT MYSTERIES

THE AMAZING MYCROFT MYSTERIES

A TASTE FOR HONEY
REPLY PAID
THE NOTCHED HAIRPIN

Three Novels by

H. F. HEARD

New York
THE VANGUARD PRESS, INC.

Published simultaneously in Canada by
Nelson/Canada Ltd., 1980,
Don Mills, Ontario.

Library of Congress Catalogue Card Number: 80-52557
ISBN: 0-8149-0840-3
Printed and bound in the United States of America.
1 2 3 4 5 6 7 8 9 0

CONTENTS

Introduction

ABOUT MYCROFT HOLMES

Holmes, Mycroft, the brother of Sherlock Holmes. Seven years Sherlock's senior, he ostensibly audited the books in some of the Government departments[1], but in actuality, in Sherlock's words, Mycroft occasionally *was* the British Government: "The same great powers which I have turned to the detection of crime he has used for this particular business. The conclusions of every department are passed to him, and he is the central exchange, the clearing-house, which makes out the balance. All other men are specialists, but his specialism is omniscience. We will suppose that a Minister needs information as to a point which involves the Navy, India, Canada and the bi-metallic question; he could get his separate advices from various departments upon each, but only Mycroft can focus them all, and say off-hand how each factor would affect the other. They began by using him as a short-cut, a convenience; now he has made himself an essential. In that great brain of his everything is pigeon-holed, and can be handed out in an instant. Again and again his word has decided the national policy. He lives in it. He thinks of nothing else save when, as an intellectual exercise, he unbends if I call upon him and ask him to advise me on one of my little problems"[2].

Holmes insisted that his brother had even better powers of observation and deduction than he had himself, but that Mycroft had no ambition and no energy and would rather be considered wrong than take the trouble to prove himself right[1]. "Mycroft has his rails and he runs on them," Sherlock remarked. "His Pall Mall lodgings, the Diogenes Club, Whitehall—that is his cycle"[2]. He visited Baker Street only twice[2, 1], though he drove the brougham in which Watson rode to Victoria Station[3], and he was Holmes's one confidant during the Great Hiatus, providing his brother with money and maintaining the Baker Street rooms[4].

Watson was struck particularly by Mycroft's "sharpness of expression" and "far-away, introspective look," which he had in common with Sherlock[1]. "Heavily built and massive, there was a suggestion of uncouth physical inertia in the figure, but above this unwieldy frame there was perched a head so masterful in its brow, so alert in its steel-gray, deep-set eyes, so firm in its lips, and so subtle in its play of expression, that after the first glance one forgot the gross body and remembered only the dominant mind"[2].

—*The Encyclopedia Sherlockiana*

1 "The Greek Interpreter"
2 "The Bruce-Partington Plans"
3 "The Final Problem"
4 "The Empty House"

A TASTE FOR HONEY

TO CHRISTOPHER WOOD

A CONNOISSEUR,

THIS UNCLASSIFIED VINTAGE

CONTENTS

Chapter I

THE SOLITARY FLY

SOMEONE has said that the countryside is really as grim as any big city. Indeed, I read a novel not long ago that made out every village, however peaceful it looked, to be a little hell of all the seven deadly sins. I thought, myself, that this was rather nonsense—a "write-up"—devised by those authors who come to live out of town and, finding everything so dull, have to make out that there's no end of crime going on just behind every barn door and haystack. But in the last month or so, I'm bound to say I've had to change my mind. Perhaps I have been unfortunate. I don't know. I do know that many people would say that I had been fortunate in one thing: in meeting a very remarkable man. Though I can't help saying that I found him more than a little vain and fanciful and rather exhausting to be with, yet there is no doubt he is a sound fellow to have with one in a tight corner. Though, again, I must say that I think he is more to be valued then, than when things are normal and quiet. Indeed, as I shall show, I am not sure that he did not land me in one trouble in getting me out of another, and so, as I want to be quiet, I have felt compelled, perhaps a trifle discourteously, to refuse to go on with our acquaintanceship.

But I must also own that I did and do admire his skill, courage, and helpfulness. I needed such a striking exception to the ordinary (and very pleasant) indifference of most people, because of the quite unexpected and, I may say, horrible interest that one person suddenly chose to take in me. Yet, as I've said, perhaps I would never have known that I had become of such an awkward interest—the whole thing *might* have passed over without my ever having to be aware of my danger if this same well-meaning helper had not uncovered the pit past which I was unconcernedly strolling. And certainly the uncovering of it led me into great difficulties. I don't like being bothered. I like to think sufficiently well of my neighbors that I can feel sure they won't interfere with me, and I shan't have to do anything to them, and, perhaps I should add, for them. I must be frank, or putting all this down won't get me any further. I suppose—yes, there's no doubt—I came to live in the country because I wanted to be left alone, at peace. And now I have such a problem on my mind—on my conscience! Well, I must set it all down and then, maybe, it will look clearer. Perhaps I'll know what I ought to do. At the worst it can remain as a record after me, to show how little I was really to blame, how, in fact, the whole thing was forced on me.

As I've said, I came to live in the country because I like quiet. I can always entertain myself. When you are as fortunately endowed as that, mentally, and your economic endowment allows you to collect round you the things you need to enjoy yourself—well, then, persons are rather a nuisance. The country is your place and NO CALLERS the motto over your door. And I would have been in that happy condition today if I had stuck to my motto. I'm a Jack-of-all-trades, a playboy, if you will. I potter in the garden, though I really hardly know one end of a flower from the other; amuse myself at my carpenter's bench and lathe; repair my grandfather clock when it ails; but fall down rather badly when it comes to dealing with the spring mechanism of the gramophone. I'm no writer, though. I write a neat hand, as I hate slovenliness. But I like playing at making things, not trying to describe them, still less imagining what other people might be thinking and doing.

I have some nice books with good pictures in them. I'm a little interested in architecture, painting, and, indeed, all the arts, and with these fine modern volumes you needn't go traveling all over the place, getting museum feet, art-gallery headache, and sight-seeing indigestion. You can enjoy the reproductions quite as much as the originals when you consider what the originals cost, just to look at, in fatigue and expense. I like turning over the colored plates and photographs of my books in the evening, looking sometimes at a cathedral and then, with only the exertion of turning the page, at the masterpiece of painting which the cathedral contains, but which the photographer was allowed to see in a good light and the visitor is not, and then at an inscription which is quite out of eyeshot of the poor tourist peer he binocularly never so neck-breakingly.

I read a novel now and then, but it must be a nice, easy story with a happy ending. I never wanted to marry; and certainly what I have to tell should be a warning. But I like—or liked, perhaps I should say—to think of people getting on. It made me, I suppose, feel they wouldn't trouble me if they were happy with each other. I suppose I liked life at second hand—reflected, not too real. And certainly, now that it has looked straight at me, I can't say I wasn't right, though I may have been irresponsible.

Well, I mustn't waste more time on myself, though perhaps in a record like this there should be some sort of picture of the man who tells the story and how he came to have to tell it. My name—I believe they always start by asking that—is Sydney Silchester. My age doesn't matter—though I suppose they'd pull *that* out, if they were once on the track of all this; though what difference it makes whether I'm thirty or fifty I can't see. "Of years of discretion," is the description that occurs to me and seems apt. For certainly I am not of years of indiscretion—never, as it happens, was. "Old for his years," they used to say; and now, I believe, young. But am I any longer—"of years of discretion?" Certainly had I been discreet I would somehow not have become involved in all this! But my mind goes round and round like a pet rat in his whirligig. That's because I can't write and also because I am really considerably worried, shocked, and perhaps frightened. Getting it all down, I must repeat, will help. Get it down, then, I will, and no more blundering about as though I were trying to keep something back from someone.

As I've said, it all began through my breaking my rule—the rule, as it happens, of all village life of the better-off, of "keeping myself to myself." It was an accident, in a way, or rather two accidents coming on the top of each other. I'm fond of honey and one of the pleasant things about living in the country is that you can get the real stuff. But what was a little odd in my neighborhood, though I never thought about it, was that practically no one kept bees—said they couldn't make them thrive. Now I wish that I hadn't been so fond of it. Somehow I was too lazy or too busy with other things to try beekeeping myself. That was certainly fortunate. Bees always seemed to me troublesome insects—but how troublesome I never suspected.

I'd found, however, that there was one place where bees were kept and honey for sale, a house toward the end of the village. I found it because it lay on the way to the open country and you needn't go through the main street and run the risk of being stopped and being compulsorily gossiped. I never set out to be a recluse—only just didn't want friends, hadn't time for them. The couple who lived up there seemed quite as uninclined to make a small business transaction into a bridgehead for talk leading to a call. That seemed to me to be a distinct additional find. They were a Mr. and Mrs. Heregrove. When I called for my monthly supply, sometimes I saw one, sometimes the other. It wasn't a very small place, but they, too, never seemed to entertain. For all I know, they ran the house, gardens, and paddock themselves. They may have had a servant the first few times I called. Certainly I never saw anyone but themselves about the place later. If I had wanted to make friends they were hardly the people I would have chosen. I hate untidiness.

I saw Mrs. Heregrove first—or, to be quite exact, heard her before I saw either her or her husband. She had an unpleasantly penetrating voice and she was using it with such effect that she herself was evidently quite unable to hear the rusty doorbell I was ringing. Eavesdropping has never appealed to me. Other people's affairs always appear quite dull enough when one has to be told them and is expected to sympathize. I keep what little patience I have for such occasions. So when for the third time the unpleasant voice had asked of what was clearly a tense and provocative silence, What he meant to do about it and whether he was going to live on her money until they both starved, as the question was certainly not for me to answer or to hear, I rapped sharply with my stick on the door. That brought immediate silence, and a few seconds later the voice's face was before me. They matched.

"Well?" she said, with sharp suspicion.

"I want to buy some of your honey," I said at once. I was amused at the quickness with which the face changed, and the voice, too.

"Certainly; I have it both in comb and in jars."

I lay in a month's supply at a time. I also always pay cash—hate bills. I told the woman I'd take half a dozen combs and six jars and took out my purse to pay. She altered even more rapidly. I couldn't help noticing that the face became so lit with relief as to become actually good-looking. She hurried indoors and I caught sight of a shabby hall. In a few minutes she was back with the combs and the jars.

"I could lend you a basket to carry it," she said, and brought a large wicker thing mended with string.

"Thanks," I quickly countered. "I'll bring it back when passing again."

I feared she might make the retrieving of the basket an excuse for a call; at the best a bore, at the worst a beg.

But she replied, "Please do, and perhaps you'll be needing more honey or could recommend mine to your friends."

That was our first meeting. I did bring back the basket and got a second supply, and, as one is a creature of habit, one took to going up there as a matter of course. I never heard them quarreling again.

Once while I waited I caught sight of Heregrove himself. He turned and looked at me. Didn't nod: indeed, he appeared quite suspicious and unfriendly, although he must have seen me at the door plenty of times. I said nothing and he turned to go down the path, with his head bent, through the garden, which I noticed again was badly neglected. I watched him go out at the upper end and cross the paddock. There were some tumble-down stables shutting in that side of the field. I had been quite sure that the Heregroves didn't use them, but today I noticed that there was a horse in one of the stalls. Heregrove swung open the half door and disappeared inside. At that moment his wife came out to me with my order of honey. I remember distinctly turning over in my mind their having bought a horse. They had no trap, indeed, they were seldom seen outside their grounds. They clearly didn't like going into the village—owed bills, I suspected.

Then the tragedy happened. I was just running out of honey and was thinking of going up for more, in a day or two. The girl who cleans the house for me, who is a good worker and whose flowing tongue I had thought my icy silences had at last frozen up for a long winter of my content, began to trickle.

"Your honey nearly gone, sir."

I knew this was an opening. I plugged it unwisely with, "Well, I always order it myself, Alice."

"I know, sir." (I saw I had somehow opened the dam, not closed it.) "You always gets it at pore, dear Mrs. Heregrove's."

I recognized that "pore-dear" at once. It can only be used, like the Greek "beautiful and good," as a sort of Siamese-twin epithet; it means, of course, that the recipient is dead. I must have shown a flicker of interest or surprise. My enemy rose like a subarctic river in the spring.

"Not that the village c'd ever think much of either of them. Coming here and giving airs and then running bills and never paying. But, Lor, they was right out of heels, as you might say."

"I wouldn't," I interposed. "I don't want—"

But my wishes, commonly law, were now only the wishes of the living against the ancient right to proclaim the dead. The flow ran on.

"And that Heregrove: you could hardly call him 'mister' at the best. She was a lydy come down, but he—well, my dad said he never heard a fuller tongue, no, not in a barman. He'd spent all her money, they say, before the end. Why she'd ever 'a' married him no one ever could think, but parson was once heard to say that Heregrove had been a scholar of some sort and lydies are often queer-like, in that way—take a brain which can't even pay its way and let a figure go which c'd at least serve them—"

Alice saw that her tongue had got its head and was itself not only wandering but had reached the verge of "unlydylikeness." But with a magnificent pull she brought herself out of the tailspin, and before I could claim sanctuary of shocked bachelorhood, zoomed on. Mixed metaphors, I suppose—but an excited and talking woman seems to me to combine the characteristics of all the violent and rapid forces of nature and man. She zoomed into the vasty halls of death.

"Well, she's gone, and taken in the strangest way. Perhaps he'll feel it's a judgment on him, but none can say for sure. But we're all sorry now for her, pore dear lydy. Mrs. Brown, who has laid out 'undreds, you might say, and says she likes the doing of it, says it's a sweeter job any day than Miss Smith's, the monthly, for when we come we're all of a mess and go on giving trouble and needing to be changed, but when we go, we go quiet, don't mess our clothes, and can be laid so we look like statutes—Mrs. Brown says it was just a terrible sight, she—pore, dear Mrs. Heregrove—was that swollen and black. And she's right, for I asked Mrs. B. if I might have a look. Heregrove had taken himself off after calling and seeing Dr. Able—"

At that I did break in.

"Alice," I nearly shouted, "did Mrs. Heregrove die of something infectious? If so—" I said, drawing back and pulling out my handkerchief.

"Bless you, no, sir. She was as healthy as you nor me last night. She didn't die of a sickness. She died of a haccident, of stings. The bees got her. Though why, considering she'd been quite one of them for so long—but, then, you'd never know. My uncle—"

The main wave was past; the news was out. Only an ever-widening ripple of reminiscence would follow.

I turned to the garden door, saying over my shoulder, "When you have laid lunch you needn't wait," and myself waited for no more.

Still Mrs. Heregrove's strange end stuck in my mind, even though it wasn't infectious, and kept on passing through my thoughts as I occupied myself at various jobs. I've said I know little about bees but of course I knew they could, like most spinsters in crowds, become at moments temperamental and even neurotic. Perhaps that was one reason why I never had kept them. And now I would have to find another source of honey. Heregrove would have to destroy his lot. Even if he stayed on in the village he could hardly go on beekeeping. They'd be dangerous to him, no doubt, and hardly anyone would like honey manufactured by a homicidal horde. Probably even to call at the house would be to risk attack. I felt a strong distaste to being stung to death or going at all near where such a fate could possibly fly upon me.

The question was in my mind for some days, partly because at every meal I was reminded of it by seeing my honey stock run lower and partly because when I went to do shopping in the village I couldn't avoid hearing—like a sort of Handel chorus—the same phrases over and over again till I had the whole story. Ours is a compact little village, almost a townlet, so you can get most of the things you want and, indeed, quite a number I've no wish for. So I can do most of my shopping without having to send away for things. The story interlined my own business questions and answers.

"Dr. Able knew a case just like that before." "Dr. Able and the coroner talked it over in court." "Heregrove said the bees had been cross and quarrelsome with him lately and he'd told his wife."

"The coroner said it was a plain, sad case, an accident." "The coroner said the bees should be destroyed and Heregrove said he'd be doing that anyhow."

Well, that settled my concern, such as it was. I'd have to find another supply-source. That led to the second accident, my second honey hazard, which I now see was needed to bring the first, which I had already taken quite unconsciously, into play.

Chapter II

THE NEW BEEKEEPER

I HAD TO find another honey seller. Beekeepers were evidently very scarce, though I did not know how scarce. And, further, my dread of business dealings leading, if made with amateurs, to social entanglements, meant that I couldn't seek in the village itself asking all and sundry if any hive fanciers were known. I was determined to find a retailer who would not involve me in village life. And luck, as I thought, came my way at my first cast. But luck is a neutral word; it can be bad, just as well as good. This, after all, was bad. But perhaps I'd better leave luck alone. I don't like the word much. It has a superstitious flavor and I'm just superstitious enough, and clever enough, to know what a lot we don't know, and to leave superstitions severely alone. I'm not yet out of this wood or I wouldn't be so carefully retracing my steps in this account. Heaven only knows where it may all end. So I'll be cautious and say it was Destiny which took me along Waller's Lane.

It's a pretty walk, anyhow, and one of the least frequented. There are one or two houses along it, but they stand so well back and are so well screened that you would hardly notice them. I never had, beyond being vaguely aware that there must be some dwellings thereabouts. You couldn't avoid knowing that, for a small gate or two open through the high overgrown hedges here and there. I was wandering along, so much enjoying the quiet that I'd forgotten any purpose in my walk but the pleasure of taking it. For the lane dips after half a mile and there you are in a mossy sunken road which at that time of year, full summer, is like a garden. I don't care for big views. They somehow make me yawn. Perhaps I'm not long-sighted enough. But high, sloping banks covered with flowering wild plants seem to me the best possible scenery. Just at the right range, changing all the time and at the right angle.

I had, as it happened, actually stopped to look at half a dozen uncommonly tall snapdragon spires in full bloom, when, following their stalks to the top, my eye was caught by something beyond and above them. It was a small notice poking its head through the hedge at the bank's top. Seeing it, I noticed that there was a footpath gate beside it. The lettering of the notice was too small for me to read from where I stood, so, almost involuntarily, I mounted the steps which I found set in tussocks of grass. It was with nothing but amusement and pleasure, with no foreboding at all, that I read in quite beautifully spaced and shaped Roman letters: "The Proprietor has at present a certain amount of surplus honey of which he would be willing to dispose."

I think I've said that, although I'm not a writer and correspond as little as possible, I rather pride myself on my calligraphy. A scrambling age sees no discourtesy in illegibility and no gain in penmanship. But I do. I saw at a glance that the hand that wrote that notice saw more in handwriting than the surface sense of the words. "The style is the man"; very well, the hand is the gentleman. The lettering was, as all notices should be, based on the incomparable capitals of the Trajan Column, but anyone whose "caps" were so sensitive and whose serifs so assured would certainly command, I thought, an excellent italic. Then there was the intriguing fact that a notice, written with such care, should be posted in a moss-grown lane and, moreover, almost out of sight. And, finally, here was my honey—a supply as sequestered as I could require.

Three things like these coming together are some explanation—if the whole thing seems inexcusable—for my unprecedented precipitancy. Almost without reflecting what reception I might meet and what involvements I might incur, I lifted the latch, walked up a path which wound through a hazel thicket, and suddenly found myself, to quote "poor, dear" Mr. Yeats, in a "bee-loud glade." A lawn on three sides had dense herbaceous borders sloping up to thick yew hedges, over the top of which a fringe of hazel sprays could be seen. On the fourth side the lawn ended in a low white house with french windows opening onto the grass.

On the lawn itself, in tidy ranks, stood those miniature Swiss chalets which have taken the place of the romantic but I understand insanitary skep. The air was dense with the chalets' population. After our village tragedy, I stood with some apprehension wondering where these queer socialists might rule that trespass began, honey-making must stop, and all workers must unite to attack the exploiter. I was keeping my eye so carefully cocked to judge whether an air attack might be impending that I started with surprise when a quiet voice at my elbow remarked, "They are not militant workers, these. I get quite good enough results up till now, at least for my purposes, from the Dutch queens, so I don't continually disturb the poor things' temperament. They are nervous enough anyhow, without making them more excitable with Italian blood."

I turned to see beside me a serene face, a sort of unpolitical Dante, if I may so put it and not seem high-brow. It was cold, perhaps; or maybe it would be juster to say it was super-cooled, cooled by thought until the moods and passions which in most of us are liquid or even gaseous had become set and solid—a face which might care little for public opinion but much for its opinion of itself.

But I mustn't run on like this. I expect it is the fault of a bad writer—can't keep down to facts. Perhaps I didn't notice all this at once. But I was impressed, I know, because I remember saying to myself, "How like Dante," and then having to check myself (for my mind is always flighty, as anyone will see who has got as far as this) because I began to speculate whether if Dante were reincarnated today what he would do to get in his visit to Hell. Where would he find the cave opening? In modern war, maybe, or in a city slum, but hardly in the country or in a village.

"You are my first purchaser," he went on, evidently seeing that my mind was wandering and wishing to put me at my ease. "It is good of you to walk over so far from your place—"

"You know me, then?" I interrupted. "I don't go much into the village and have no friends there and don't remember catching sight of your face. You are a newcomer, aren't you? I often come down the lane but don't remember seeing before the notice which explains my call."

"No one else has," he replied. "It has been there a little while and considerable numbers of the village 'quality' have come down the lane, but none has troubled to go up the steps to see what is written on it."

That remark surprised me. It seemed out of character, somehow. I couldn't resist, therefore, saying, though it was perhaps a little impertinent, "You keep as close a watch on your lane and your notice as a fisherman on his stream and float."

"In a way, yes and no," he smiled, evidently not at all put out by my personal remark.

I thought, however, that it would be polite to put myself back into the picture.

"You come up to our end of the village and have seen my house?" I questioned.

"I must confess, no," he answered, again smiling. "You see," he added, "I have been busy settling in for some time and, like yourself, my reason for coming to the country was not for company but to be busy with all these incessant interests which the town, with its distractions, never really tolerates."

"But how, then—"

"Well," he kindly forestalled me, "there are so many ways of being wise after the event that I have sometimes thought during my life that if we would only act on that rather despised motto we would need to ask far fewer questions—which you and I agree are always, if only the slightest, infringement of that privacy we both prize so highly."

I could not help smiling at the way he had read my thoughts and he smiled, at least with the muscles round his keen eyes if not with his thin lips.

"No one," he continued, "who has taken some little care not to disregard things can fail to notice how much of our past and our settled environment we carry about with us wherever we go. I'm not a geologist, but soils always repay a little attention. This village, like many another in England, is a jigsaw puzzle of earths. That, by the way, tells us something about the past. Our ancestors planted these settlements in order to live off the soil, not to retire from town. So there have to be water and woodland and tilth: woods for fuel and the hogs' pfannage; good soil for harvests and, above all, good water. To get all that means living where the layers of soil have been cut by water so as to give man a selvaged slice of each of the qualities he wants.

"Now you live up at what was the clay end of the

village. I'm nearer the light heath soil. You have tiny patches of dried clay on your trousers. One clue helps another. I probably should not have been able to pick up that first clue which tells me where you live if it had not been able to give me the second indication—that you live alone and don't like being looked after too rigorously—in fact, can entertain yourself best when alone."

"But why—"

"The notice," he intervened, "which is well written, asking the passer-by to purchase and yet put just out of ordinary eye-range? An experiment. Village life, we agree, is a problem. Free, yes, but apt to lose its freedom even more quickly than town. A researcher does not need absolute solitude. Indeed, when I was working, I often found that it helped to talk over a problem with an interested if less absorbed mind. Some steps of reasoning can be run through and checked more quickly in speech than by writing them down, and often the listener, however inexpert, will see a slip oneself has overlooked."

A curiously simple and neat Naturally Selective trap, I thought.

"You'll be thinking I treat my neighbors as prey

and you sprung the gin. But I may want help on a problem which should interest the right man as much as it intrigues me. I'm not an apiarist and don't want to meet such specialists. You remember Henry Ford's dictum: 'A specialist is someone who is always telling you what can't be done.' In pure, as well as in applied science, I have found that to be true—someone who tells you that it has all been found out, that there is no further mystery, there is nothing more to discover."

"You're doing research in bees," I interrupted, "but I only want to eat their honey!"

"You shall; but hear me out. Then, if you become my customer and not my acquaintance, I can have the parcel of honey left on you regularly and you need not risk any further conversation. I came down here to study bees. Honey to me is simply a by-product I must dispose of. I'm not a Maeterlinckist! I believe he greatly overrates the intelligence of bees. Anyhow, I'm not interested in what intelligence they may have. All my life I have been estimating human intelligence not by its books or words but by its tracks. Now I want to study something else, but still by its tracks. I want to know about bees' reactions. After all, they are social beings given to living in dense towns. But, though like us, how different! There are no end of problems to be studied. There are the particular flowers they go to, the peculiar vision they have so as to pick out such blooms, and so the particular sort of honey they yield. We might get special brands of honey from certain broods—"

I was faintly interested, but began to feel much more strongly that I wanted to get my honey and get away.

"Yes," I said vaguely. "I expect a market could be found for super-honey just as for special proprietary jams and marmalades."

He saw my restlessness.

"If you will step inside I will make up a parcel for you," he remarked, leading me toward the house.

We entered a room on the left of the hall. It was evidently his laboratory.

"I will bring you the combs and the jars in a moment," he said. "I apologize for boring you. Yes, yes, and it was not—I must again beg your pardon—unintentional. You remember Oscar Wilde's silly remark, 'A gentleman is one who is never rude unintentionally?' I think, however, it may be more truly said that a trained mind is one which never bores unintentionally."

The boredom which had been growing vanished, and again I felt a not altogether pleasant surprise. One gets stiff when faintly startled.

"I'm afraid I don't quite understand, Mr.—?"

"Mycroft, if you will," he answered, with that quiet smile of his which was certainly disarming. "The truth is," he added, "I did first put up my notice as a sort of wager with myself as to whether in this village I should find a fellow curioso—not a specialist, not a conventionalist. I own I discovered, almost before you did, that I had lost my bet."

"Why, then," I acidly remarked, "did you continue?"

"Please step over here," came the quick reply, almost an order. He was standing with his hand on a down-turned glass bell jar. It covered a square of white paper on which lay a small object. The step I took, almost involuntarily at his command, brought me where I could see what it was.

"A dead bee?" I asked, somewhat challengingly. He lifted the glass bulb and handed me a large magnifying glass. As soon as I took it, with a pair of forceps, he lifted another dead bee off the window sill and placed it beside the first on the square of paper.

"Would you, please, examine these two bodies through the lens?"

"They don't look very different to me," I was just replying, when under the lens a forceps point advanced and pressed on the abdomen of one of the dead bees. The body cockled a little and quite clearly the saber-curved sting was thrust out, and retracted as soon as the pressure was released. Before I could ask what such an unilluminating experiment showed, however, the forceps point darted onto the abdomen of the second bee, depressed it in the same way, and out came the sting—but what a sting! It curved round until it seemed it would pierce through the chitin mail of the dead insect's own thorax.

The voice at my shoulder said, "There's a pretty problem here. The last is, of course, an Italian—fierce bees, anyhow, but I think, from comparing the body with some care with standard Italians, that this is a special variety. Certainly it was psychologically remarkable, even if the rest of it, except for that sting, is physiologically normal. It had the temper of a hornet. It attacked until it was killed.

Of course, it came in a troop, so I dissected a number of them. They all had these super-stings. That was remarkable enough to an amateur apiarist; but what was even more remarkable was the result of a small biochemical experiment."

Turning to a shelf, he took out of a rack a glass phial not thicker than a knitting needle.

"There are hardly half a dozen drops of venom in this tube," he remarked. "I have had to gather it from the stings of these bees. Perhaps I would have overlooked the necessity of doing so if it had not been that when my colonies were attacked—when I saw what was on, I myself donned bee-veils and gloves and got ready to defend myself with a special bee-smoker—my poor mastiff ran out. The invaders were not really attending to us, any more than we human beings, in a battle, waste our ammunition on the crows and vultures. But one of these miniature monsters swooped past us, caught the dog's smell, dived, struck, and my poor Rollo gave one howl and fell over. He struggled for some time when I carried him inside. I thought a camphor injection was going to bring him through, though his pain was obviously so great that I thought of putting a bullet in his brain if it did not cease. But suddenly rigors seized him, his tongue lolled out, and he was dead.

"I have had the opportunity of studying toxicology for some years. The only venom I can compare this with in strength—though, of course, its chemical base is the formic acids group—is the incomparably virulent secretion of two spiders—the small yellow which is found in northern Queensland and the so-called black widow of southern California. Even the giant ant lately found in Guiana, Paraponera Clavata, though one sting of it can paralyze a limb for some hours, does not approach the toxicity of this poison."

"But," I said, "what does all this mean?"

I felt, rather than fully recognized, a growing sinisterness in the atmosphere. I wanted to get away, wished I'd never come, but felt somehow that to go off now with the problem all vague and pervasive was only to carry it with me, like a swarm of bees trailing a man who can't shake them off his track! His next words confirmed my doubts and made my misgivings all too unpleasantly definite.

"I told you I put up my notice because, first, I wanted to carry out a casual experiment in seeing whether I could select a possible confrere, and then, after I had a more remarkable visit than I had counted on by what I think I may call in every sense of the word inhuman visitors, I saw I must signal for someone who had two characteristics—that he was a bit of a recluse, so that he might not gossip about what even then seemed as though it might turn out to be a business both ugly and easily driven out of reach, and also that he was a honey lover."

"Why the honey part?" I said, rather feebly and vaguely. My whole thought was bent on the unpleasant realization of how, like a fly limed on fly-paper, I was getting every moment more firmly embedded in this beastly business.

"Because you certainly have noticed that the Heregroves were the only people who sold honey in this place. They may not do well. It is hardly a millionaire's occupation, but they have had no other. So anyone who was a honey fancier and so would not buy the shop's stuff, could tell me about the Heregroves, for he would certainly be their customer."

"But why couldn't you call yourself," I asked with weak irritation, "or go openly into the village and inquire about the Heregroves? Why all this hokey-pokey and setting little traps for the innocent curious?"

I tried to make my remarks sound jocular, but the truth is that I was wanting to be as rude as I could with safety, for I was rapidly getting cross over the whole thing and, what was worse, felt that after being cross I might find that I had reason to be frightened. So I added, to smooth things over a bit, "Though I must own the trap has done its work neatly enough."

He smiled again kindly. There could be no doubt of that, and I could not help feeling that if I had to get into a mess with other people's business it might be hard to imagine a stronger and more capable man with whom to face a storm. Even now I still wish that I had kept clear of it all—but there's Destiny, of course, as I've already said.

"Don't say trap. Say my S.O.S. to which you have most generously responded." His voice was equally reassuring. "I couldn't go asking questions in the village because that might rouse suspicion and would certainly have brought me, whether or no correct information, undesirable allies."

Somehow I felt a certain quite unreasonable reassurance at being called by implication a desirable ally, though all that it really meant was that I was getting still more committed to schemes I did not understand and did most actively, if vainly, suspect.

"To visit the Heregroves themselves was, of course, out of the question, even more than making inquiries about them in the village. It is quite clear what he or they have done; though I must say it is so startling that it has shocked me back to a line of thought which I had told myself I had left for good. Heregrove has bred a bee to put all other beekeepers out of business. I confess it is an ingenious notion. I've confirmed it, though. I've already found that up till a few years ago there was quite a lot of beekeeping in this district. Now, as you know, you can't get honey anywhere locally."

"But," I broke in—for I must own my interest in this extraordinary story was getting the better of my self-concern, the whole tale was so mad, bad, and ridiculous—"but what an absurd amount of energy and ingenuity to spend just to corner the honey market of Ashton Clearwater."

"Yes, I thought that, too, and it puzzled me," he replied. "Of course, inventors are kittle cattle. For the sake of an experiment they'll ruin themselves, and to make a discovery they'll risk any number of people's lives, their own included. Still it puzzled me. Of course, after the attack on my hives I realized that a thing like this could and pretty certainly would grow. Apiarists are not used to suspecting people. Heregrove may have lit on this thing as a pure researcher and then have hunted about to see how he could make it pay. His super-bee may, indeed, have acted like a Renaissance 'bravo' or a Frankenstein's monster and gone off killing on its own. That may have put the idea into his head. 'Oh, Opportunity, thy guilt is great. 'Tis thou—' "

"Please," I said, "I prefer at this point psychology to poetry and facts to anything."

"Well," he smiled, "I can tell you the Heregrove bees came literally out of the blue. Fortunately they are so stupid that even if he did send them specifically they could not tell him that their expedition of extermination had failed."

"How did it fail? How could it?" I exclaimed.

"You want only facts," he chuckled, "and no theories. That, of course, is not possible if you wish to understand. But the fact remains, as your ears and eyes tell you, the home team survived."

"Then," I said, with a sigh of relief, "they are not so deadly as we feared."

"Oh, yes, they are," he answered, quietly. "I told you I drove off the first attack from myself and when my poor Rollo was dead and I could do no more for him, I decided to see if I could save at least my bees. Wrapped in bee-veils and gloves, I charged the smoke-thrower with a peculiarly strong smoke I used once when I was attacked long ago in not dissimilar circumstances: what I then took to be an accident but now suspect was a similar discovery being used by a man not unlike our present customer. Discoveries are generally made twice over and often fall into undesirable hands and even come into undesirable brains."

"But was the smoke enough?"

I wanted him to get on. Age and a long-practiced calm had made him more willing to view the past as equally interesting as the present than was I. I had spoiled my walk, missed my lunch, and had not even secured my honey. As a matter of fact, I was only staying on until I could learn how safe it was to go. I had no intention of leaving if there was any chance that in a quiet bend of the lane there might be a sudden hum and before one could even cover one's face one would be pricked to death with red-hot knitting needles. But I had no intention of staying, wasting more of my time, the moment I could be sure that the coast (or rather the sky) was clear.

"Yes, yes, the smoke worked. I mightn't be here if it hadn't. One crept up my leg and I smoked it only just in time. They're so devoted they'd work their way through anything. I doubt that gloves would be much protection for long against those super-stings. They are prodigious fighters, even normal bees. We'd have had no chance if they had been even a fifth our size."

He saw my dulling eye, went over to the door, and called out, "Mrs. Simpkins, please lay another place and call us as soon as lunch is ready." He turned back to me. "You will stay, won't you? Indeed, I don't want to be an alarmist, but I think you had better. I agree I have taken long in telling you how the land lies but cases such as these I have found can only be grasped—and caught" (he added after a pause) "if one understands much detail which at first sight seems irrelevant."

From the back of the house I heard wheezing but quite reassuring complaints.

"Lunch as soon as it's ready! And it's ready and bin ready this twenty minute and mor'n. Well, there's the bit of cold salmond. An' the patridge pie's warmed up none too bad. Couldn't have kept it waiting yesterday but today it's taken it nicely. Cold gooseberry tart with the whipped cream—never expected it to whip today—"

The inventory was as good to my eye as to my ear and even better on the tongue. My host knew about food and also about wine. He talked both, well and fully, as if he wouldn't touch on shop at mealtimes. I was hungry at first, fell to, and fell in with his mood. But toward the end it struck me that it was a grim little meal, really. Here was I with an unknown man who had already dropped a number of most sinister hints and had shown me also in the other room enough venom to make me die in agony in less than a minute—and, what's more, for the coroner's inquest to dismiss my death as though I had been only bitten by a flea and taken it badly. It was the thought of the coroner which made me push back my plate.

"If you have finished," my host said, rising, "I won't detain you for more than a few moments longer. We should, however, finish our discussion," he added, dropping his voice, "out of the range of any easily frightened ears."

Again I felt that queer, irrational disturbance

when pleasure at flattery is mixed with misgiving as to the flattery's motive. I was already alarmed and had good reason to be. However, I repeated to myself: "Better know the worst; ostrich tactics are little use when you may be fatally stung in the back."

Chapter III

ROLANDING THE OLIVER

BRIEFLY," said my host, when we were once more seated in the laboratory, with the phials and the dead bees to lend point to his words, "the more I thought over Heregrove's work, the more I was sure he had more or less blundered on this discovery while experimenting with bee-breeding."

"But how did you beat off the attack of his bees? Didn't they come back?"

"Yes, but by that time I was ready for them. That is why I think—deduction, I fear, yet often all we have—" (he chuckled rallyingly at me, and I feared a relapse into the past or, worse, into theorizing) "I think Heregrove doesn't know much about bees except their biology. Anyhow, I thought he didn't know much about bee psychology, about their patterns of behavior; though I'm not so sure even of that, now. It is pretty certain, though, that he didn't know that there is an answer to his pirate bee.

"I told you I was more interested in my bees themselves than in their honey. Come into my library a moment. I can best show you there. An actual illustration," he added, gauging my impatience, "often saves time," and then, with a glint of superiority which made me obey because I hate any unpleasantness, "especially when a mind, unfamiliar with a strange fact, must understand it unmistakably!"

By the window in the library hung a cage with a couple of small birds in it. I was going to walk in and take a chair, for I had been quite uncomfortably perched on a bench all the while in the laboratory, but suddenly my shoulder was held.

"Don't move," whispered my queer beekeeper. "Look at the birds and don't speak loudly."

"What am I to notice?" I muttered back, more crossly even than I had meant. All these antics vexed me.

"You notice nothing?" went on the level whisper. "Even when your attention is drawn to it?"

"I see two small birds," I whispered back, playing perforce this ridiculous game. "And one is sitting on the upper perch and the other on the lower."

Then the absurdity of being made to take part in an intelligence test like a backward schoolchild, by a perfect stranger, irritated me so that I wouldn't any longer go on whispering.

Aloud I asked, "Would you be good enough to tell me what we are looking at and what it is meant to convey?"

"Well, anyhow, that remark of yours has ended the performance," he replied airily. "And, for clues: the familiar passage, 'Look how the heavens' down to 'muddied vesture of decay' from *The Merchant of Venice*, contains the explanation." Then, seeing that my irritation was really mastering me, he stopped smiling and added, "Sir, you must pardon an old man. It is not senility, though, but something almost as out of date—patient thoroughness. When we entered, those birds were singing. At least one of them—the male, of course—was performing and the female was listening enraptured. No, you are not deaf—only a little unobservant with your eyes. One can see his throat swell and his beak open. No human ear—you get my Shakespearean quotation?—can catch one of those notes which his mate so appreciates."

"Yes, Mr. Mycroft, yes," I said, a little mollified (for it was a queer fact of which I had never heard before and I like queer facts). "But what have these birds to do with the bees? Are they to charm away the pirates?"

"You are pretty close to the truth," he replied, surprisingly.

"How on earth can a bird we can't hear, sing away a bee which is probably deaf? I've heard of bee-catching birds but—"

"We don't know of any bird as yet which can serve this purpose, but this inaudible songster was unknown to our grandparents. And we now know of a spellbinding singer which can do what you ask. More remarkable than a bird: it is actually a moth, a moth which sings a humanly inaudible note! I had to show you the birds because experimenting with them gave me a piece of apparatus which may be of no little use to both of us. They gave me my first records. When I had learned how to make these, and the hen bird had kindly shown me by her absorbed attention that I had indeed caught the note, I then went on to the harder task of recording a far more difficult voice and trying it out on a far more difficult and awkward audience."

We had gone back to the library. Mr. Mycroft, making me, I must confess, catch something of his interest—for I'm interested in gadgets—took out from an upper shelf what looked like a small home-made gramophone combined with a barograph. The drum had on it fuzzy lines like those I once saw on an earthquake chart. Beside the drum was a small hollow rod the use of which I couldn't imagine. He started the machine and the fine pen began its rapid scrawling on the paper as the drum slowly revolved.

"You are now listening to one of the most magical voices in the world," remarked Mr. Mycroft, complacently.

"You can say so," I replied, somewhat tartly. "But as you like quotations as clues to opinions, I can give you one from Hans Andersen's Magic Weavers: ' "The King hasn't got any clothes on at all," cried the child.' "

"Dickens will do as well," he chuckled. " 'There ain't no sich person as Mrs. Harris.' But there is a voice, even if, I regret to say, only a potted one, singing in this room so long as that needle pen trembles. Look."

He threw open a panel in the outside wall and revealed the back of a glass hive in which the bees could be seen thickly crawling over the layers of comb. Stepping back, he swung the horn of the gramophone until it was trained on the glass panel in the wall. In two strides he was back again. With a single movement, the sheet of glass was swung back, the comb exposed to the air. We heard the industrious hum rise to an angry buzz of protest. I was about to make for the door when the buzz was cut short even more swiftly than it had arisen. Not, though, to sink back into the contented working hum. What is more, complete stillness held the hive. It was a bee version of the Sleeping Beauty's castle. Mr. Mycroft's hand stretched back. The whirring stopped and, with the last scratch of the pen, the hive came again to life. For a second the bees hesitated, like an audience just before it breaks out of its spell into applause. I did not, however, wait for their ovation. Without asking leave, I clapped shut the glass wall. In a few moments they were as busy as ever on their obsessing honey.

"You could have waited a little longer," Mr. Mycroft remarked. "They are so dazed that they generally go straight back to work—work, for all workers, is the best escape from unpleasant questions and baffling experiences. Well, that is how I routed the invaders. We have air detectors against planes, but we have yet to find a note which will make enemy pilots forget they came to bomb us. When Heregrove's bees came back, I was ready with my bell-mouthed sound muskets turned to the sky. Down they swooped. As soon as they were in range —which I had found by experimenting with my own bees—I started up my inaudible order to desist. 'Heard melodies are sweet but those unheard are sweeter,' certainly if they save your hives. Already my bees and the invaders were fighting, but, at the first needle scratch on the drum, I saw them fall apart. My own dropped down to their alighting boards. Of the enemy, some lit on the flowers and trees; others settled on the lawn. It was then that I picked up enough specimens to make all the tests which I've shown you."

"One moment," I said. Up to that time I had

stood like an open-mouthed simpleton being shown an invention which might be magic or might be normal mechanism, for all he could decide. But now I was on my own ground or at least not far from it. "One moment. Isn't there something wrong about all this? I'm rather interested in gramophones in my way and I sometimes read about them. I've understood that the best gramophone today will not record even the highest note audible to the fully hearing human ear. How about these super-notes?"

"I'm glad you know about these matters," he replied, "for it makes it more interesting for me to describe to you this ingenious little toy. Perhaps you know that Galton made a whistle which blows a note which we can't hear but a dog will. That whistle set me on this line of research. You see the principle incorporated in that hollow rod on the far side of the machine by the drum. I won't go into details, but what happens is that air vibrations too fine and high for the ordinary gramophone recording or disk to render are stepped down when we are recording and then, through this simple but ingenious mechanism, stepped up again, so that the high, rare note is recreated. The same principle has been applied to moving pictures—to take through a filter a black and white film which would have all the tones, though not all the tints, of the color spectrum of visible light, and then to run this seemingly only black and white film through a complementary filter, when a colored film would be seen. The principle was tried out to photograph the Delhi Durbar of King George V, but until now synchronization has held it up. The difficulties with sound are not so great, so I overcame them without wasting too much time."

"Well," I had to own, "that is, I must say, peculiarly ingenious. But what happened when the gramophone stopped? You couldn't keep it on till nightfall?"

"I own I was a little uneasy. I kept it going the length of a full record and swept into a sack all the enemy aliens I could. But, apart from requiring them for purposes of research, there was no need. Dr. Cheeseman is right. When an insect's instinctive reaction has been completely thrown out, it cannot, as we do, recollect and carry on. It must go back to its original place, as a man after concussion often has post-lesion amnesia, sometimes of weeks or months or, in a number of well-known cases, of years. So, as they came to, those I hadn't bagged made off and my own broods were free to carry on."

"Did they never come again?"

"Once or twice, but it looks as though some kind of conditioned reflex were being built up in them."

"Well, you'll be free now. I don't know whether you've heard, as we haven't referred to the tragedy, but the coroner told Heregrove to destroy his hives. In the next week or so, at least, I presume the law will see that he has done so."

Mr. Mycroft looked at me.

"I know more of bad men than of bad bees. Heregrove will get rid of the present hives, maybe. But, mark my words, he will not give up beekeeping and the new lot will not be less malignant, but more, if he can make them. A man like that gets the habit, the taste for malicious power. It grows, and it is harder to break than an addiction for morphia. I know."

He evidently spoke with authority, of what sort I couldn't say. I was more anxious to clear up the bee mystery first.

"What is this note which cows them?" I asked.

"Well, as I have said," he replied, "I am sorry not to be able to show you an actual songster. They are harder to come by nowadays than those rare birds in the next room, and far harder to keep. I'll show you, however, a prima donna in her coffin. In fact, here is the form which uttered the voice that routed a thousand murderers and, as you saw a moment ago, can make the most fanatical of all the world's workers down tools and idle as long as her music holds the air."

As he took down a cardboard box which had evidently held note-paper, he added, "Queer, in the bird and animal world, the male sings and the female listens, but in these and some other moths—those, for example, like the purple emperor—with scent we cannot smell—" Suddenly he stopped. "*Am* I getting senile!" he exclaimed. "Would I have overlooked that twenty years ago? Well, this is just like the way a dream is recalled. Suddenly some incident of the day reminds us of a whole dream story which we would otherwise have clean forgotten."

I was completely at a loss as to what he was talking about and waited while he scribbled down a note.

"Forgive me," he said, looking up. "I think showing you this will have helped us more than all the rest of this valuable conversation."

He opened the box. Spread out, fixed with a pin

through the fat body, lay a very large moth, curiously marked on the head. "It is the biggest of all the British moths and now quite rare. I had great difficulty in getting a pair. The male is in another box."

"Queerly marked," I said.

"That gives it its name," he replied. "The death's-head moth. But its really odd characteristic is its inaudible voice. It uses that not merely to attract the male but for a purpose as strange as the instrument itself—so as to hypnotize bees, and, when they are so hypnotized, to enter their hives safely and gorge itself on their honey. Fancy holding up a bank only by singing—having to stuff the notes into your mouth all the while, and the bank officials ready to knife you to death the moment your voice gave out! When it comes to the fantastic, we must give the prize to nature every time. We poor creatures who try to imagine the strange are always beaten by the sheer, inexhaustible fantasy of the natural. Well, that shows how I beat off Heregrove's attack and, as I've said, he had no way of telling whether his aerial torpedoes took effect or not. He just guessed that no one else who kept bees would ever suspect that here was a challenge; still less, know how to reply to it."

"And now," I said, firmly, getting up and going to the door, "I am much obliged for a day's most interesting visit. May I have my honey and get home? I presume, now that the sun is sloping and your hives are closing down, none of Heregrove's harpies will be about, even if he has not destroyed them."

"Oh, you are safe enough," he replied. "They won't attack except to protect their hive or to rob another. That is why they came here. That is Heregrove's pretty little game. They root out all other rivals for him. It is really a very neat case of savage instinct being made unconsciously to commit crimes by savage intelligence."

I was nettled by his absorbed interest in his own wretched bees and then in Heregrove's supposed motives. I, obviously, came in only a bad third. Here he had detained me a whole day, under what, it was now clear, were false pretenses. Naturally I had assumed, when he said before lunch that I had better stay, that he said so because it would have been dangerous for me to leave.

"Why," I broke in, "have you then kept me waiting about all day if it would have been quite safe for me to walk home?" I own there was irritation, natural irritation, in my voice.

He showed no surprise or resentment at my rather rough interruption.

"I saw you would not stay simply to hear my explanations," he answered. "You have some of the impatience of a certain Proconsul Pontius who when in a famous, and, as it would seem, important interview, he found the discussion becoming abstract, terminated it with premature irritation, asking what is Truth and waiting not for an answer. So, as you chose to assume that I meant that you were in immediate danger of the bees and would not grasp that your danger really arose from your impatient unwillingness to understand the general character of the peril in which you stand, I permitted your misconception to serve your real interests and kept you here until you had had a fairly thorough demonstration of the factors impinging on your case."

He said this in such peculiarly exasperatingly quiet tones that I need hardly say that his explanation had the reverse effect from soothing my feelings, already on edge. The insult of coolly patronizing me by a lecture on my character was deliberately added to the injury of having used up my whole day. I held my tongue, however, though I felt quite uncomfortably hot. All this explains and shows how natural was my final and, I still think, inevitable protest. He paused. As I have said, I held my tongue with difficulty. And then he went on indifferently, as though there were nothing to apologize for, speaking slowly, as though he hadn't already wasted enough of my time.

"Since showing you that death's-head moth, I think I ought to qualify what I have said. I know how impertinent advice from elders and strangers always seems, and, unfortunately, I am both, but may I request that you do not call on Heregrove without me? I should be very pleased to come with you. Indeed, that was the final point I was going to discuss with you, after which I was not going to detain you any longer."

How could I fail to resent that? I had been treated like a child that has to be tricked to serve its elders' ends, and now, when I was highly and rightly vexed, as if the wasted time were not bad enough, this old dominie was going to force his company still further on me and, in fact, make an attempt to order my life. Who was this old stranger, pushing his advice on me and directing what I should do and whom I should see and in whose care? It was, of course, I felt, quite clear, that he had angled all the time to put me in a position in which I should be unable out of common politeness to refuse his request. He was a clever old crank of a busybody. I hate being managed and maneuvered. Even more, I dislike being made to change my ways and to do precisely the very thing which I live in the country just to avoid doing, taking strangers to call on one's acquaintance. I felt so vexed at this transparent stratagem, coming on the top of everything else—the silly old man with his senile sense of his own tactful finesse, thinking I shouldn't see through it (I was tired too, being kept waiting about all day)—that I felt a positive revulsion against him, and, I suppose by contrast, something almost like clannish protectiveness toward Heregrove.

What was this stranger, gossiper, romancer doing? Making all kinds of insinuations about one of our village—a man about whom I only knew, as a matter of fact, that his honey was always good and quite reasonably priced, and who, poor fellow, had just had his wife killed by his bees which kept me in honey. True, he might not have been very fond of her, but English law had decided, and rightly, that he was the victim of a horrible accident. Even someone you dislike, you can miss very much and be very sorry for, especially if he is suddenly killed in a horrible way. When I was a boy, we had a dog I never really liked. It used to bark and leap up on me—startling and dirtying. Yet when a car dashed over it and there it lay like a smashed bag, I felt not only quite sick, I was really sorry. These thoughts, of course, went in a flash through my mind. I was pretty certainly more tired than I realized.

Mr. Mycroft was standing before me with a rather assured expression on his face.

Before I had thought out the words, I found myself saying: "I'll pay for the honey. I'm a complete recluse and never introduce anyone to anyone else. As to my movements, I have never needed anyone to advise me on them."

I stopped. I own I lacked the courage to meet Mr. Mycroft's eye now that I was being deliberately rude, so I couldn't judge how he took it. All I know is that he passed out of the room without a word. He was away for a few minutes, came back with a neatly made parcel with an ingenious handle made of the string, and named a ridiculously low figure. I fumbled a bit, and I am afraid was a little red as I paid.

All he said was, "The string will hold quite securely. It saves the trouble of a basket being returned."

He held the door open and with a rather clumsy "Good day" I stepped out, hurried across the lawn, now in shadow, into the dusky path through the plantation and so down into the twilit sunken lane. My nerves must have been overstrung (perhaps I had been very discourteous). The whole place seemed unpleasantly still. Those silly, melodramatic lines from *The Ancient Mariner* kept running in my head:

> "*Like one that on a lonesome road*
> *Doth walk in fear and dread,*
> *And having once turned round walks on,*
> *And turns no more his head;*
> *Because he knows a frightful fiend*
> *Doth close behind him tread.*"

I didn't really feel at all comfortable until I was back in my own sitting room, with the lamp lit, the curtains drawn, and the door well bolted.

Chapter IV

FLY TO SPIDER

THE NEXT morning, however, I was quite cheerful. Only one thing seemed clear in the gay morning light. By observing my rightful impulse I had—at the cost of a moment's unpleasantness—escaped what might well have turned out to be a permanent invasion by a loquacious, opinionated, fantastic old bore—the very thing, I repeat, that one lives in the country to avoid, the special terror of town clubs and gardens. I was well stocked with honey. I put the whole question out of my head—even of what I would do when my supplies again ran out.

It seemed only a few days, however, before they did. It must, of course, have been a month, perhaps a little more. I remember that I evidently didn't want to notice that I was running low, for it was Alice who drew my attention to it and I was vexed with her. It was really her fault. She should have seen that it was quite clear I did not want to be troubled. But somehow the poorer people are and the stupider, the more they seem to expect you always to be reasonable and clear and sensible.

"You 'ave only 'alf a pot an' one comb now left, sir," was her opening.

"I know," I said, as a silencer. It was as ineffective as my effort to stem the obituaries of the late Mrs. Heregrove.

"An' you 'aven't, sir, rightly even that: the combs run so in this 'ot weather."

I grunted. Human speech of any sort, however astringent, seemed only to act as warm water to a hemorrhage. "An' where you'll be getting your new lot I can't but be wondering. There's never a hive now all round the neighborhood. 'Iveless Hashton, that's what my young man he called it the other day, an' he's right. He's a cure, 'Iveless Hashton."

This was too much, to have the cold and clotted wit of Alice's walker-out served to me after breakfast.

"Alice," I said, with a firmness which I don't remember showing for a very long time, unless it was when I broke away from the tentacles of Mr. Mycroft, "Alice, please get on with your work"—the breakfast table was half cleared, half the china was already marshaled on its transport tray for the kitchen, half still held its position on the table—"and I will get on with mine."

What that was, as I had been looking out the window when the attack had been launched, was not very clear, but I felt I must soften my rebuke by showing that we both had duties which forbade further waste of time. But Alice was wounded. I was being, I could see, not merely rude—that was an employer's right, but "not sensible," and that is something which the rustic mind finds far more upsetting than insult. The wound led to a further hemorrhage of words.

"Well, sir, I was never one to hoffer advice hanywhere, not even in the right quarters" (advice again!), "but I did think it seemed positively silly-like to get yourself with no honey—you being that fond of it and suspicious-like of shop things, as indeed I'm myself; an' all I meant, and no imperence intended and never was, that I'd 'eard that, maybe, you might again be able to be getting yer honey at Heregrove's."

I couldn't help starting a little. Alice was no doubt encouraged by this sign that her attack had made some impression.

"M'young man works up in fields beyond Heregrove's place and 'e's sure 'e's seen Heregrove tending bees as before."

I did want to know more but I was determined even more strongly to check Alice before after-breakfast conversations became established as a precedent.

"Thank you, Alice," I said. "I will look into the matter myself."

I was cold and stiff. I was rude. But I was being sensible. I was not being "simply whimsey." The stiffness, therefore, did not matter. It might wound, but the cut was aseptic. Alice was quite content. She had, of course, not had her talk out, as no doubt she would have liked, but she had made me do something. That was even more important. The gentry had been made to mobilize. I had been compelled to take command. Off she sailed, contented in her way, and soon the drone-drawl of "Abide with me" mixed with crockery clackings came through the baize door—a sure sign that Alice was enjoying that sentimental sense of having sacrificed herself to make someone else uncomfortable, which I believe bitter-sweetens the whole lives of the industrious poor.

But as I realized Alice's victory I was not so pleased. I should have to do something. I couldn't and wouldn't go back to my old bore in Waller's Lane. He, no doubt, would be glad enough to overlook my unavailing struggle to escape his hold. Alice's victory must not lead to a rout.

Then there was nothing left to do but to go and see whether what Alice had said about Heregrove was true—to spy out the land. And, after all, if he was again tending bees, there was nothing wrong in that. Of course he had got rid of the mad hive which had attacked his poor wife. If no one else could keep bees in the district, why shouldn't he? No doubt he was skillful—that was all, "bee-handy." These epidemics—foul-brood, Isle of Wight disease, etc.—were always wiping out hives. I had long ago dismissed old Mycroft's romances. All the demonstrations he gave me could easily, I concluded, have been staged by a clever eccentric. Probably he was the dangerous person to be in touch with—a borderline case. As to Heregrove, it was not my duty to boycott an unfortunate and skillful man. If other people chose to do so—well, it was an ill wind which blew no one any good and I should benefit by being his sole customer.

I went over all these points—small ones, they may seem, and no doubt are. "Why all this fuss," a reader might say, "over buying a few pounds of honey?" I have to own that my mind, far down, was far from easy. If I had not dreaded Mycroft's becoming a bore, an intruder, would I have dismissed all he had told me as mere romance and tried to convince myself that he was cracky? I crushed back the thought, but it was there, and the only way to get rid of it seemed to go and see for myself whether Heregrove was actually again beekeeping, and, if he were, to replenish my stock. So to escape one unpleasant train of thought—old Mycroft's speculations—I ran right onto the other horn of the dilemma—the very source of all these really rather unnerving suspicions.

When one has made up one's mind to hair-cutting

or being fitted by the tailor, I've found it always better to get it over. So that very afternoon I deliberately took my afternoon walk up to Heregrove's end of the village. Luck—no, I have decided to say Destiny—decided that the man should be coming down his garden path at the very moment that I reached his gate. I paused and we came face to face.

"I hear you may again be selling honey," was, I thought, a safe enough opening.

It was not very well received, though. He looked at me with a curiously expressionless face. He certainly was not what fashion papers call prepossessing. Dark, strong, resolute, and intelligent—yes, all these, and cold. Where had I seen a face as cold as that? Of course—old Mycroft's; but there it seemed to me that coldness came from detachment, this from hardness. When I was first taken with Mycroft's look I remembered thinking how quietly cool his face was.

This man's face was somehow not quiet in spite of its coldness. It went through my mind that he was deliberately making his features expressionless, not because he did not care what people thought of him but because he was determined to hide something.

That thought led to a still more disquieting one. I felt now sure that he was watching me with much more interest than he intended me to recognize. After a pause, which was becoming quite embarrassing to me, suddenly, like an electric light being switched on behind drawn blinds, the face lit up. I felt a queer, baseless, but quite definite conviction that he had suddenly made up his mind about something.

"I am sorry," he said, in a surprisingly low and accentless voice, "to have hesitated in answering. Since my great sorrow and loss I have been much of a recluse and long silences make for slow responses. Yes, I am again keeping bees." Then, after a pause, "My doctor, when I consulted him, said that after a severe shock the best cure is the hardest —to take up the actual thing most associated with the shock—men who have had a bad fall steeplechasing are told to jump fences as soon as they can again sit in the saddle. Of course, the actual hives have been destroyed, but I have a way with bees and am again thriving with them. I don't quite like to put my notice up again but perhaps I can breed queens and make a little that way." (A queer tremor of suspicion from the back of my mind shook me for a moment.) "But I would be glad to have you again as a customer as my poor wife had. I trust that while I have been out of business" (we were now walking up the path and I was aware his eyes had turned toward me though his head was not turned) "you have not suffered any inconvenience?"

"No," I said, evasively. "No."

I knew I ought to make up some story but, as I've said, living by oneself, one doesn't have to lie and gets out of the habit, at least of doing it convincingly. His next remark showed that I had been right.

"There are, I believe, very few other beekeepers in the district. As homemade honey is so different from the stuff most shops sell, I feared you must have gone without supplies."

I simply said nothing. I could hardly construe that remark as other than a searching question devised to discover where any other beekeepers might be lurking in the locality. However, he must take my silence as he wished. We reached the house and he showed me into the parlor, still as distressing a room as when I had seen it in his wife's day, from my casual glimpses through the door.

I heard his voice behind me continuing, "—Unless, of course, you went far afield hunting your honey?"

The chuckle he gave at this minimal joke did nothing to cheer me. The house, the man, my suspicions, all grated together. I turned around.

"I should like the same supply as I had before," I said.

He named the exact amount and then added, "Come with me. I store near the hives. It saves trouble when in the winter one has to feed them some of their own. Pure sugar is never enough."

Again I felt even more strongly the wish to be out of it all, felt a quite strong resentment toward Mycroft—why could he not have kept from boring me and just supplied me with honey?—and even a wave of irritation at Alice. Still, to refuse would be ridiculous. We left the house and went down the back garden path along which, I remembered, I had seen him, in his wife's time, going toward the stable.

Because that memory flashed through my mind and for the sake of saying something not to do with bees or honey and to break the silence on my part, I asked, "Do you still keep a horse?"

I own I might have taken such a remark made to myself by a stranger as impertinent, interfering.

But of course I didn't mean it as that. It was one of those pointless, stopgap remarks we make when we fear a silence may become too awkward. The remark did have a bad effect—there was no doubt as to that—a surprisingly bad effect. Heregrove stopped and turned on me. I looked round and confronted an unpleasantly searching glance. Another of those horrid pauses, and then the very commonplaceness of the reply only disturbed me more.

"No, I sold the horse some time ago. I couldn't afford to keep it."

"That's frank and obvious," I said to myself, but something in me told me I must have put a finger almost on the bolt which fastened down some grave secret in the man's mind. However, the thought that one is alone, talking to a dangerous fellow who suspects that you may know too much, is so disturbing that I chose, not unnaturally, the alternative, which had certainly still as good a case—that here was a poor creature who had had very bad luck (or an ill deal from Destiny) and whom I could help by helping myself to his honey. We seldom fear those whom we feel we can patronize. Fear is a beastly feeling, while patronizing always faintly warms one, though we don't like saying so. I needed warming, for I felt more than a slight chill of foreboding, so I changed the subject. The overgrown and bedraggled flower beds caught my eye.

"Even now that most of the best of the summer flowers are over," I prattled, "yet there are enough to keep the bees busy. Queer little creatures." I ran on, as my companion kept silent and I was determined that there should be talk, if only mine and only to reassure myself. "I suppose it's not color but scent which really guides them?"

Again I was aware I was being sidelongly looked over. But how could such babble do anything but reassure a suspicious character? Alas, I knew I was only fooling myself or trying to convince myself that my efforts had done anything of the sort. On the contrary, do what I would, everything I said and even my silences quite obviously heightened his suspicion, and, what was even more disconcerting, made him quite clearly resolved to hold on to me—I supposed to find out whether I was as innocent as I looked or as suspicious as I apparently kept on sounding.

We had reached the end of the garden and the beehives were now in view on the other side of a rather dilapidated railing. The hives themselves were in order. When we reached the fence, Heregrove seemed suddenly to change his mind.

"If you will wait here," he said, civilly enough, "I will fetch the honey. It is in that small shed alongside the hives. Most of the bees are already in but, you see, a few latecomers are still coming home. They might be a little irritable. Hard workers on returning home may get cross if they find strangers hanging about their doors."

He smiled as he said this; I was so glad of this sign of improving relations that I tittered rather foolishly in my effort to show my friendliness. He turned his back on me and in a few moments reappeared out of the shed with the load of honey.

"Well, that's done," I thought. "Somehow I shall have to find some other supply, or cure myself of the taste. For I don't think I can face another visit like this." But I spoke to myself before I was out of the wood.

As he came toward me he said coolly, "Before you go, we can just step across to the stable, as we are down at this end of the garden. I'd like to show you the place, as you expressed an interest in the horse I once kept."

The excuse for showing me the place was so

palpably inadequate that I was filled with a queer panic. Yet when I thought of how I could reasonably get out of going the fifty yards he asked me to go and looking into the tumble-down shed, I could see no reason to refuse, as there was obviously no possible peril in going just there, beyond what I might be exposed to in getting straight back to the road. Granted that he had some reason other than he alleged for wanting to show me the place, it was equally clear that that reason could not be to do me any harm. He would hardly wish to injure the first customer of the trade he was trying to revive. I made some sort of assenting sound and turned to follow him as he had already started walking toward the stable. I did this a little more willingly as I was slightly reassured to have him walking in front of me, not I in front of him, and as his hands were full of the jars and combs it was clear he would be a little handicapped if he did intend to assault me.

"Unless, of course," I said jauntily to myself, "he intends to turn on me, pelting me with honey, and so suffocate me. Clarence with his Malmsey; Sydney in his honey."

Joking with oneself sometimes works, but if it doesn't, you are all the worse off. I don't know whether it worked or not then. Perhaps it did, for at least I remember making aloud to Heregrove some little jest about last year's mare's nest when we stood rather pointlessly looking at the wisps of sodden hay that still lined the floor. I think my titter or chuckle did not sound too forced, though Heregrove did not join in. In fact, he seemed hardly to hear me. Where before he had seemed all too vigilant, now he seemed positively absent-minded. When he spoke he seemed almost to be speaking to himself and forgetting me.

"I used to fasten her up in this stall," he said, putting down his armful of honey and going over to the manger.

Out of courtesy I followed. Perhaps, I thought, he was really attached to the horse. Some misanthropes have to find an outlet for their affection. For myself, I don't dislike people—just don't require them—so I suppose I don't have to have pets.

"The little mare," he went on, "could look out of this window. I couldn't give her much exercise, and horses, you know, get bored if kept without anything to do; take to crib-biting and air-swallowing. But she had a nice view here and could look out at things and did, and used to whinny at birds and dogs."

The man was a sentimental recluse suffering from incipient brain-softening, I concluded. I must humor him and get away.

"Just look," he said, straining to see out the stall window, which was high and hard to see out of because of the manger underneath it. "If you look right, you see away to the road; straight ahead, meadows for quite a mile; and down to the extreme left, the road and the tops of the village roofs."

I stretched up to oblige him by looking out. To my relief he moved away.

"The little horse had a fine view, hadn't she?" he asked.

"Yes," I replied. "Yes."

After all, the man was only a fool and could become dangerous only if one insulted the memory of his dear departed mare (who perhaps in some way was, as psychologists say, "surrogate" for his dead wife). I would play the part he wanted me to play and as friends we would part—for good.

"Yes," I said, straining up again and looking all round the view. "There are the woods and the meadows and the village roofs. As pretty an outlook as one could wish."

I turned around; I was alone. Panic took me. I began to rush toward the door. I noticed the honey still on the floor. That would not have checked me. What did check me was to find Heregrove in my path. He must have seen my alarm, but he showed no sign that he did.

"Yes," he remarked, quietly carrying on the conversation, "it's a nice little view."

"Where did you go?" I blurted out.

He looked surprised. "I was only looking in at the other stall. There's room for a couple of horses here. The rats get in that side. I must set a trap there." And then he did something which surprised me and yet queerly reassured me. "I've cut my finger on a nail I didn't see down there when I was lifting a board to see the rat's hole better," he remarked, holding out his right hand. There was a piece of stained rag half wound round his index finger. "I always keep disinfectant about. Apt to get a nasty place if you don't dress it at once when you work in stables and gardens. I can't tie this up, though. Would you be so good just to knot it for me?"

The fact that the man had hurt himself and would put himself in my power placed me again quite at my ease. He might be cracky, pretty certainly was, but he was certainly harmless.

"Gladly," I said. I did feel glad with an almost unreasonable relief.

I am fairly deft with my fingers and wound the bandage neatly, but a lot of the dressing, which he had put on very clumsily, got on my fingers and even on the cuff of my coat. In fact, I suggested taking off the whole bandage because it was clear that owing to his gaucheness he had got more of the disinfectant on the outside of the lint than on the inside. He wouldn't hear of that.

"No, no, it will do finely as it is; don't bother."

"But are you sure," I pressed, "that the dressing has covered the cut? And oughtn't you have washed it out?"

"I did," he replied. "There's a tap in the other stall. The cut was quite small, though deep. And this disinfectant, though it hasn't a nice smell, is quite wonderful with cuts."

Well, he knew his own business best, and my job was to make a good getaway as soon as I could. Certainly the smell of the disinfectant was highly unpleasant; rank was the only word for it. I remembered as a child (smells bring back memories startlingly) being taken to the Zoo and becoming quite nauseated in the small-cat-house. "Small but strong," my father had laughed; but I was retching when I got outside. And the smell of this dressing brought back that memory so strongly that suddenly I thought I should vomit. I hesitated to ask whether I could wash my fingers, but as Heregrove did not make the offer and my own overmastering wish was to get out of the stable, out of the place, out of his company, I started incontinently for the door.

"But your honey," he said.

I had to bear being loaded with the stuff, had to fumble for my purse. But at last we were going down the garden path and I was headed for home and freedom.

As we reached the gate, Heregrove remarked, "I made a poor bundle."

"It's all right," I protested.

"Well, I think I can arrange it a little better in your hands, so it won't fall before you reach home." And he began to pat the paper and arrange my sleeve and pull out the lapel of my coat, which he said would get crushed.

I simply hate being pawed; and being pawed by a man who, however groundlessly, you mistrust, and who, with every pat, puts a revolting smell under your nose—all that turns an insult into an injury. Literally I broke away from him.

"Thank you," I stuttered, "thank you. Thank you. Quite all right. Will do nicely—splendidly."

I sidled off rapidly with my load, like a small crab which just scuttles under a rock before a gull gets a firm hold on it and pecks it to death. I glanced back in the dusk; the last thing I saw was Heregrove making his way again across to the stables.

I hustled on until I was safe once more in my own place. I had never come back so upset from anything. My return from my upset with Mr. Mycroft was child's play compared with this. Then I had been irritated and a little nervous; now I felt something beside which that had been almost amusing. For a moment I was so spent and foolishly anxious that I felt I would have been positively welcoming if I had heard that assured old voice at the door. It *would* have been reassuring and I needed reassurance.

Chapter V

THE FLY IS MISSED

STILL, just as after my upsetting visit to Mr. Mycroft, so on this morning succeeding my latest upset, I woke with every care off my mind. "Perhaps when you live very securely by yourself a little upset, even a little fright, is occasionally good for you," I thought to myself as I lay in bed listening to Alice laying the breakfast things downstairs. "It may stir the liver, or the glands, or something which needs a slight emotional rub-down now and then." Certainly the sound of one's comfortable life being got ready again for one to enjoy was particularly pleasant that morning. I bathed leisurely, the more to relish my enjoyment, and also in the hope that, if I dallied, Alice would have, in her argot, slipped up the village and popped in a little 'ouse'old shopping, and so I would be quite secure in the unadulterated pleasure in my own reserved way of life.

My plan worked. When I got down, the house *was* all for myself. The kettle simmered on its trivet with a sense of completely reassuring, comfortable patience. The toast was in the grate. I like my toast hard but hot. The eggs were ready to be put in the spirit-stove boiler, which was simmering also with well-bred efficiency. I dropped the eggs in, looking at my wrist watch, and brought the toast onto the table. Took from the hob the warmed teapot—brown earthenware—I keep my Georgian silver for afternoon tea—gave it the three spoonsful of Lapsang and poured the boiling water neatly onto the leaves.

It was, as it happens, the fragrant smoky smell, faintly tarry, but very refined, which brought back that abominable disinfectant of Heregrove's into my thoughts. I was (I always am) in my dressing gown at breakfast. I remembered now that on coming in I had put my jacket in the wardrobe, meaning to have it sent to the cleaners. I had carefully washed my hands, but I could, when I looked closely, still see a slight discoloration on the sides of my two fingers, and when I raised them to my nose I could yet detect very faintly, but still unmistakably, that smell. But you had to put your nostrils quite near to get it. I thought, though, I would see what another scouring would do. Landing the eggs, I ran up the stairs. After a rapid scrub, which I had to own did not diminish much that last, queer, clinging taint, I decided I must keep my head up and it must and would wear off. Passing through the bedroom, however, I thought that I had better see how the jacket itself had fared. I took it out of the wardrobe, with some apprehension, but there, too, the smell seemed mainly to have evaporated. It did smell, of course, if you put your nose right on it, but you wouldn't notice it a few inches away. As I'm very forgetful about dull routine details such as laundering, I took the jacket down with me and placed it on a chair beside the table.

"That will remind me," I thought, "to tell Alice, when she comes back, to have it cleaned."

Then I again marshaled the table, but a moment later I was again on my feet. Alice had put out for me that last running comb, about which she had spoken—as a mute reminder, I supposed, should I have failed to act. Her observations had been correct: nearly all the honey had gone out of it and, as she had neatly changed the plate, I was left with practically nothing but solid wax to eat. I am economical, but wax is not very pleasant or good for you. I had my new supplies, won with considerable discomfort. A few steps into the larder and there they were—neatly unpacked and stacked, each covered with a pyrex baking dish on white plates ranged along the slate shelf. I lifted one of these and brought a fine, sound comb with me to the breakfast table.

The windows were open, for though the day was not yet hot, it was clear and fine and the fire kept my feet warm. I was munching away in that quiet unthinking state of mind which is perhaps the nicest thing about meals by oneself, when one becomes like a placid animal chewing the cud under a tree in summer, so much at my ease that I was really not thinking of anything in particular. Everything seemed generally all right. So I can't say when I first became aware that this was no longer quite so.

Our hearing is said to be our most vigilant, unsleeping sense—last to go when we lose consciousness and first to come back when we regain it, even before we know where we are. I think it was hearing something without attending to it which gave me my first sense of undefined uneasiness. Humming sounds are generally reassuring, but this, for some reason, wasn't. Then a couple of bees flew in at the window. I thought at first they were wasps (though we have had few this year) after my honey. I held my knife ready to knock out the robbers directly they should alight. They zoomed above the honey but did not alight on it, and then suddenly swooped on the coat hanging on the chair. They settled on the sleeve and lapel, and at that moment the hum broke into full cry, as though a pack had viewed their fox. I saw a dense swarm of bees sweep down outside, wheel before the window, and come pouring into the room. They rushed, without a moment's check, to join the few scouts already settled on the coat. In a moment it was black with them. I started back, for I could see they were not investigating. They weren't even crawling about. Each was convulsively clinging to the worsted: they were stinging and restinging the cloth, piercing it through with their deadly little sabers.

Fortunately, the staircase was near me, and the chair with the coat on it at the other side of the table, or this story would have been written, if at all, by another hand. I scrambled toward my escape. My movement, however, must have given some alarm to the swarm, for quite a large group detached itself from the coat and swung into the air to investigate me.

I thought I could still manage safely to beat my retreat, when one bee, swinging past me, went within a few inches of my hand. Like a shot he threw himself on it. I knocked him off, trod on him, and threw myself up the stairs, flinging my dressing gown over my head to shield, if possible, my face and neck. This desperate stroke evidently made such a whirlwind in the small staircase that it momentarily drove down my flying attackers; but I saw, as I turned, that the whole swarm had now left the coat and were wheeling round to fling themselves after me.

A moment's wild scramble and I was through the bedroom, dashing over the furniture, had gained the bathroom and slammed the door. Rushing to the window, I slammed that down. Outside the door I heard the angry buzz and even the sinister little taps of the bees flinging themselves in murderous frenzy on the panels. A moment later I saw a couple come crawling from under the door. I stamped on them and felt an unpleasant glee as their bodies crunched on the tile floor. They were deadly as flying snakes, but my heel could still bruise their heads once they were forced to crawl.

I had begun to feel (very unreasonably, considering my actual situation) something of the thrill of victory, when, suddenly, a sensation like a mixture of an electric shock and a severe scald shot along my leg. Tearing up my pajama trouser, I saw a bee, its sting thrust into my shin a few inches above the ankle. I struck it down and crushed it and wedged a towel along the threshold crack of the door. I must have carried the brute with me into the bathroom. I remember looking over myself to see if there were any others, and then looking back at the sting, which had already swollen into a large black lump like a rotten chestnut. Then the pain, which had been rising like a tide, became so intense that I must have fainted.

The next thing I saw was that the door was open and the lock forced. That vexed me.

"The jamb is broken," I began, petulantly. "Who did that?"

I was addressing myself to someone I sensed was near me. Then I realized how odd it was to be talking lying on the bathroom floor, whether the lock had been smashed or no. I remembered everything in a flash.

"Shut the door!" I cried.

"It's all right," said a deliberately soothing voice. I was just going to try to get up when the speaker bent over me. "Don't move, just for a moment," he advised. "We've put a towel under your head. I'd just like to listen to your heart and have a look at that place on your leg before you get up."

It was young Jones, who, I had heard, was the new village junior medico—a smart young junior to help elderly Dr. Abel. Quite a bright fellow, I'd heard people at the post office remarking. He had his stethoscope sounding me in a moment, remarking, as he listened, "Um, all right now." Then to me, "Sorry to be so professional as well as intruding. Truth is, when your maid suddenly haled me in I thought at first sight she was right and you were in for something ugly."

I caught sight of Alice's face; she was standing in the bedroom wearing that expression of mingled woe and triumph, distraction and self-importance, which is the proper guise of those who have the distinction of having a tragedy in their house. That both amused and reassured me. I still felt a lot of pain as well as numbness in the leg; it was burning as though being scorched before a fire and throbbing as though it would burst. But I was apparently safe, for there was no menacing buzz to be heard and my two attendants seemed wholly concerned for me and unaware of any possibility of peril to themselves.

"How did you manage to wound yourself like that when you fell?" Dr. Jones asked, turning round from examining my shin.

"How did I manage!" I exclaimed. "Look at those dead bees on the floor! I was attacked when at breakfast by a swarm and only got in here just in time. That, thank heaven, is the one sting I suffered. Half a dozen and your help would have come too late."

"Attacked by a swarm coming into the house and

going for you?" he replied, with obvious incredulity. "Besides, I have never seen anyone react in that way to bee venom. You must be highly allergic to such irritations."

"Highly allergic to irritation!" I shot back. "Those bees were no normal bees. Those bees were sent—"

Dr. Jones turned to Alice and said, in the sort of aside voice which doctors use when they are getting a second opinion on a patient's statement, "Did you see any bees when you came in?"

"Well, sir, now you comes to ask me, p'r'aps there was a few about, as you might say, or maybe they was wapses, for we've hardly a waps till now, and of course we ought to be having 'em all along with the plums and such—"

"But you didn't see a swarm of bees?"

"I was just a-coming through the gate with me 'ands full up with parcels, for I'd slipped up to the village to pop in a little shopping before the shops get too full with the quality to get things quickly. As I say, perhaps there was a bit o' buzzing about, but what give me the turn was as soon as I'd put foot in the 'ouse to see the tablecloth all pulled awry, toast an' honey and egg on the carpet, napkin on the stairs, bedroom chair flung over and bathroom door shut 'n' locked, an' the 'ouse still as a death. My grandpa died of a fit just that way. Just flew off, you might say. So I rushed out to get 'elp and there by 'eaving's mercy were you a-going by."

It was clear that, however long Alice talked, this would be the substance, the sole substance of it. Dr. Jones would list me as a prize allergic, thrown into a seizure by a single bee sting, which any normal person would take with as little fuss as stubbing his toe against a table. Well, perhaps it was best. The bees, baffled for a moment, and losing close track of their prey, had evidently veered off as swiftly as a line-squall. And even if my story were told, who would believe it?

"You had better keep that leg up today, and, if you like, I'll take a look at it this evening. You certainly are intensely allergic" (there came that irritating, glozing phrase) "to bees. You should keep out of their way. Must say you seem to have chosen a spot where you can do that. Except for these few, that you say came on a special visit to you, I don't know when I last saw bees about here, except a few down Waller's Lane. Perhaps they were cross because they were lonely, or perhaps people who are highly allergic attract their allergy, if it's a living creature."

These speculations, evidently intended as pleasantries, did not amuse me. Obviously these bees could be no joking matter for me; on the contrary, they were nothing less than a matter of life and death. I was quite ready to keep indoors until I could think what to do, and the excuse of my stung leg was one small good out of what otherwise looked a wholly bad business. Dr. Jones and Alice helped me to the sofa which stands beside my south bedroom window. I thanked him and asked him not to trouble to call again unless I sent him a message. When he was gone and Alice was back, viewing me with a proprietary eye, I was able to effect another small stratagem.

"I feel chilly," I said. "Please close all the windows and keep the door shut."

"And I don't wonder you do feel a chill," she agreed. "Why, when my pore, dear grandpa was taken with the fit that put him off, 'e went as cole as a stone. You'd 'a' 'ardly thought it *was* flesh, so cold and clammy-like. Cold flesh to cold earth, I can just hear my ma saying, and she was right."

"Alice," I struck in, "my head is aching a little. Please go downstairs and make me a little tea and some toast."

"Mercy me, and you with no breakfast, all the time you've been lying here and lying there, as you might say."

"Alice, I need the tea *now*," I remarked, with all my weight on the ultimate word.

Alice was gone. Respect for command and pity for the wounded state acted as a double charge.

I was left to my thoughts. They could hardly be cheerful. Here was a desperately cunning man who, starting perhaps with some slight suspicion of me, now evidently for sport, if for no other reason, was set on killing me and in an abominably agonizing way, just to show off his malicious power and to experiment with an instrument of death, which, when perfected, he could employ with absolute precision and equal impunity. He had just missed, but only by bad luck (or Destiny). But the second shot would probably succeed; and there was no one who would believe my story or who, even if they believed, so long as they hesitated to act on it, arrest the man and destroy his diabolical bees, could give me any protection. I must skulk in the house, till the cold weather put my fiendish persecutors to sleep, dreading all through the summer every hum of a blow-fly—a miserable creature forced to hibernate all the warm weather and only able to go abroad and have any freedom and happiness of the slightest sort so long as the weather was raw and cold.

I heard Alice's step on the stairs. As I could not face more reminiscences of her ancestors' ends and the similarity of their fates to mine, I pretended to be dozing. I heard her come in, shut the door, and place the tray beside me, but after doing that she did not leave the room. I opened an eye warily and found her regarding me in a dubious way.

"Sorry, sir, to disturb you, and you 'aving 'ad such a morning. But downstairs, asking, as he can't remember, whether, 'as used to 'appen, he lent you a basket—you ain't a-going to faint again!"

My head was whirling.

"Alice," I said, in what I fear was only what novelists call a hoarse whisper, for I had no control of my voice, "Alice, go down at once and get that man out of the house. You know I never allow visitors. And see," I almost gasped, "he doesn't *take* anything with him."

Alice was electrified.

" 'Im a common thief! Well, I'd not put it pass 'im."

She whisked out of the room, closing the door quickly behind her. I strained my ears, heard some short sentences, and then her foot was again upon the stair. I positively welcomed it.

" 'E's gone, sir," she said. "I was too quick for 'im. All I said was, 'Master's lying up. I look after the 'ouse. There's no basket of yourn here,' and with that I shut the door 'n him and watched 'im through the winder go off down the path."

I lay uneasily all day upstairs. After she had served me my lunch, I told Alice to go back to her parents' house, where she lives.

"You can call in again about five," I said.

She went off gladly, no doubt looking forward to retailing all the details of my accident and both noting and hearing how well it agreed with a number of fatal precedents.

As soon as she was well out of the house and I had seen her hat bob its course above the hedge on its way to the village, I hobbled off the sofa and scrambled down the stairs. The room had been tidied, but my jacket was still lying on the chair and the chair was standing by the door of the living room which opened into the hall. Anyone waiting at the front door would see the chair with the jacket on it. A couple of quiet steps, while whoever answered the door was away on some bogus message—I snatched up the jacket. It fell from my hands. I remembered quite clearly that when I took it down there had been a handkerchief in the breast pocket. It was gone.

The door was locked, thank heaven. Not that my tormentor was likely to attack me with any instrument but the secret, horrible, agonizing one he had forged—and a taste of which was making my whole leg at that moment throb and burn. But the locked door gave me a little comfort, in knowing that I was screened from any chance of his looking at me or walking in on me to gloat on his helpless victim. If I had seen that cold face regarding me I think I might have gone out of my mind.

I dragged myself heavily upstairs. It was all too clear. The monster had come along, cool in his assurance that no one could suspect him, just to see how his bolt had fared; expecting, hoping that he would have found me a bloated, purple corpse. Finding, however, that his first cast had failed to kill, he had quietly walked in and taken something which would have my scent. It was obvious, he was hard at working out some new plan whereby—as he could scarcely hope to inveigle me within his pawing range a second time—he might manage to get his hell hornets on my track again by giving them my scent.

Alice came back, gave me my tea, my light early dinner (God save me from nightmares; I had now enough raw material, God knew), and then, after "making me comfortable for the night," as she put it (but which was a task beyond her, or anyone in the village, to effect), she went off. I didn't sleep much.

But why not send for Mr. Mycroft? Of course I thought of it again and again. But in a matter of life and death, such as this had suddenly become, might not any interference make it worse—only precipitate things? Could the old man really protect me with his gadgets? Wasn't the only safe thing to get right out of the village—go clean away—vanish quietly without telling anyone, leaving no address; just tell Alice one was called away on urgent business and then not come back?

Heregrove, I felt sure (it was, somehow, an additionally horrible thought) was killing me out of no particular spite, but just for fun, just because I happened, poor insect, to alight near him when he was trying out a new insecticide. "As flies to wanton boys are we to the gods; They kill us for their sport." It was not a comforting line to dwell on. Yet, I suppose, this kind of thing always does happen when men get the gods' power to kill with absolute impunity. But why should it have happened to me? Why should I be driven out of my house, and even then not be safe? This fiend, for all I knew, might enjoy hunting me with his demonic pack, all over England. Every beast of prey is additionally excited when it sees its quarry break into flight.

It was that thought that decided me. As the light came, I went to my desk and wrote a very apologetic, very humble note. When Alice came I gave it to her as she brought me up my breakfast, for my leg was still as stiff as a staff.

"Down Waller's Lane," she said, looking at the envelope. "Wait for a hanswer. I'd like to do that. They say that Mr. Mycroft's a perfect cure. Keeps himself to himself as others do and 'ave a right to. But he's an inventor person, they say. For 'is cook—"

"I want an answer as soon as possible," I said.

"Very well, sir. I could get down and back while you was getting through your breakfast."

I thanked her and watched her start on an errand which, obviously interesting as it was to her, was of far more moment to me.

Chapter VI

FLY MADE TO INTRODUCE WASP TO SPIDER

INDEED, I waited so uneasily that I only toyed with my breakfast. I saw that I was completely thrown out. The even tenor of my life, which I had arranged so carefully, was thrown into complete confusion. There was no honey on the table—that alone was enough to upset me and to remind me how completely my life had been invaded and overset. But of course it would have been madness to have brought the deadly stuff out into the air to betray me to my enemies. I felt sick at the very thought of my favorite food. That, I reflected, bitterly, is some measure of my misery.

I would have had the whole batch buried, only I wondered whether, while that was being done, it wouldn't attract those fiends. Besides, Alice might think I was going mad. She had remarked how stuffy the house was, with all the windows close shut, and indeed it did seem rather odd on a lovely morning to be keeping everything closed up as though we were already in the middle of winter—winter which, though I usually dislike the season, I had now begun positively to desire. And already she and the doctor she had foolishly called in were now secretly agreed that I was cracky and liable to fits and "uniquely allergic" and fanciful and subject to frantic illusions and God knows what else. It would need only another couple of false steps, which in my strung-up condition I might all too easily take, and there would be dolorously delighted, hysterical Alice and sharp master medico Jones together (and, of course, with the noblest intentions) landing me in the asylum!

I could hear Alice tearfully but triumphantly indicating to the two magistrates who would commit me, how much my case resembled not only her grandfather's but also that queer old aunt's, who first thought she was being eaten by cockroaches and then that all her family were cockroaches and so tried to extirpate the gargantuan pests by throwing quicklime in their faces. She would add no end of confirmatory details—my queer, secretive ways, my morbid distaste for talk, my little rules for having my things just so and for not being intruded on. I could see Dr. Jones nodding his head approvingly; giving some silly, impressive Greek name to every bit of behavior which Alice retailed. I was, of course, an acute case of agoraphobia, in an advanced condition of schizophrenia. That taste for honey? Oh, that was conclusive—oncoming G.P.I. They always have a morbid appetite for carbohydrates, especially for the sugars. No safer symptom. A typical paresia-seizure in the bathroom. A spinal puncture must be made at once. A stiff dose of one of the arsenical compounds—dangerous, of course, but might save us (not *me*, please note) from worse things. The patient (of course I had already lost any personality, let alone rights) ought to be put under the heat treatment without delay. Keep him at a temperature of 105° for some time and his sanity might return. No, he couldn't take any responsibility if the patient was left at large.

I saw myself made the most awful of convicts in a moment by these four well-meaning nincompoops. I saw myself taken off in a closed car, holding onto my self-control, knowing I was being watched as a certified madman and every move or remark I made being immediately interpreted as confirming my lunacy. I saw us arrive at that abominably misnamed place, the asylum, no refuge but the one place the sane must dread with an almost insane terror. I saw myself taken in charge, I who had always resented and avoided and lived to escape the slightest control or authority or being managed. I saw myself holding on ever more tremblingly to my last shreds of independence and self-mastery. I saw the quiet, convincing conviction in every face round me that I was mad and was only an incurably deranged machine dumped in this junk-house of broken minds. I saw myself making my last stand, saying to myself, "Well, they shall not have a shred of excuse for thinking I'm in the slightest way different from any of their stupid selves, too stupid to be mad!"

And then I saw, into the hard, white, prisonlike

room, through the hygienically wide-open window, right toward us, swoop one of those diabolical bees. I saw myself involuntarily duck and call out to them to take cover. I saw them (as in a nightmare but, oh, so inevitably) pay no attention to my actual words or to the bee. Even if one of the damned fools *were* stung, the rest of them would be so delighted at this beautiful little demonstration of my specific madness that they would have no attention for anything but my "seizure." I could hear them, in that clipped, conclusive, colloquial, group-assuring jargon, confirming one another's idiocy. "Typical case." "Trigger action." "Frenzy brought on by associative symbol."—Symbol! I could only hope that the stung medico was stung in some quite unsymbolic part—not that his pain would disturb their stupid equanimity and blind assurance. "Perfect example of hymenophobia." "Must study this for a clinical paper; a valuable demonstration. Old Singleton will be fascinated with such a complete case." And all the while they would be scurrying me along those long, high-lit passages; I, held in one of those oh-so-gentle-but-move-a-finger-and-your-wrist-will-break jiu-jitsu grips, and they talking of the bundle in their hands, of me, as though I were a corpse being lugged along to its autopsy!

I had just reached that pleasant climax of my all too convincing extrapolation of the remainder of my days; I was just imagining, with complete realization, night and day succeeding one another without feature or finitude, until I really fell in with their idea of me, until I was so persuaded by my unchanging situation that they must be right and I wrong that I would actually demonstrate for them. I would be brought into the lecture theater of the mental hospital and sit there amiably huddled in the demonstration chair, while students and their friends looked at the interesting specimen, the queer animal, and the lecturer told its history and indicated its peculiar points of interest, finally letting fly a bumblebee in my face. I would then obligingly go off into my seizure and be carted out by the attendants. But, just as they pounced on me, I saw, sitting high up in the visitors' part of the theater, looking down on me with a delight in this torture worse than death by poison, the face of Heregrove!

I had just arrived at such a pretty peep into the hell that seemed now all too likely to lie ahead, when

I heard not one set but two sets of footsteps on the garden path. Though I was well screened, for I always curtain my windows heavily—in my opinion, houses were not meant to be glass hives, as some modern architects seem to think—and though the path from gate to front door went round to the other side of the house (I always have my bedroom in the quietest place), I was so nervous now that I drew back and positively cowered in my chair. The front door opened and I heard muttered voices. I knew it was highly improbable, but somehow reason was no help and emotion only said with every pound of my heart: "They've *come* for you! They've come for *you*!"

Then there was a step on the stairs. I picked up a piece of cold, brittle toast. I must appear to be eating unconcernedly; I must make a last fight for my sanity and for being thought normal. I was hardly given time to answer the knock, and my throat was so dry I probably couldn't have said clearly "Come in."

"Why, and you've not even finished your breakfast now, and me gone ever so!"

It was very impertinent of Alice to make such a personal remark, but I was shattered by all that

I had been through and foreseen. I felt so strongly that her very "imperence" was a sort of semi-conscious suggestion that she thought I was already half certifiable and an intuitive test to see whether I would break out, that I answered in a positively demure, sub-acid voice, steady and quiet, though it shook a little to my feeling if not to her ear.

"Who has accompanied you into the house?" I felt that, though such a question to Dr. Jones would sound rank with agoraphobia and blatant with schizophrenia, to Alice it would be the best approach. She was still mainly my servant and I, at least for a few days more and as long as I was let be at large, her employer. Thank God, she reacted according to her type.

"Oh, please, sir, I was only sorry to see you'd not fancied your breakfast. No imperence was meant, sir. I 'ope I'd never forget m'place. And as for bringing in someone—well, sir, I couldn't 'elp myself. He's so quick and direct, is —" (I could not but feel my heart pounding even harder) "is Mr. Mycroft."

Somehow, at the mention of that name, my heart suddenly was free. It positively leapt. Bore or no bore, would not I have the old fellow every day, all my life, if only I need not be shut up. And now I felt certain he was the one man who would understand and could save me from one or the other of two frightful fates which I felt closing in on me.

"Please, Alice," I said, reprovingly, "don't keep Mr. Mycroft waiting downstairs. Go at once. Give him the paper. Offer him some tea. I suppose he has breakfasted. Say how pleased I am that he has called round. Tell him I will be down in a moment."

She went. I hurried with my dressing. I don't have to shave every day, unless I am peculiarly particular. It is more of a massage than a mow. So I was following Alice down the stairs in a very few minutes. Mr. Mycroft was standing by the fireplace as I entered. I must say he put me beautifully at my ease, and I needed it, I need hardly say.

"I have been away, Mr. Silchester," he began, quite easily and naturally keeping the talk away from me; "I have been over to Hungerford—still a nice, small town, with beautiful open country round it. I went for a few walks when I was there. You don't know it? And perhaps you do not care much for walking? I find I enjoy it very much, but, perhaps because I've always been rather a collector-hunter type of man, I find, to enjoy myself really,

I have to make some little objective for myself, some small sight to see."

There he was talking about himself, but somehow today it was positively a relief. All too soon we should have to come to my case and, as long as he was here, I felt safe. I felt that I ought to make some slight comment.

"Didn't that amusing writer Lytton Strachey live down there?"

"Yes; in fact, I passed his house, in taking my longest walk. But I wasn't on a literary pilgrimage. His house lies in the vale just before you reach the finest walking in England, the North Downs escarpment. I was bound for that. Right opposite that house's windows stands Inkpen Beacon. I walked there; really after I had done my little piece of hunting, just out of romantic interest." Looking away from me, Mr. Mycroft added, "There used to be a gallows on that crest. The last man hanged on it was a remarkable murderer. Indeed, I should have thought, at that date, more than a century ago, he would have got off. But they brought the charge fully home to him. I was reading up the crime at Hungerford. He was a small Hungerford farmer, living not far from Lytton Strachey's house." Then, turning to me, Mr. Mycroft said, quietly, "He murdered his wife with a simple ingenuity which I have myself not met with elsewhere in the records of homicidal crime: by upsetting her into a hive of angry bees."

I felt myself pale.

"But," he went on, "even at that date, he was caught. And, though time adds to all skill, even in devilry, it also adds to our defenses."

He paused. Then I summoned up my courage.

"Mr. Mycroft, it was extremely kind of you to come round so promptly. I don't expect to be able to conceal from you the condition I am in, a condition to which—"

"Yes," he said, with comforting confirmation. "I have seen plenty of men, who felt they were brave and tough, begin to go to pieces under the strain you have been enduring."

That kindness—what I would call the right professional or medical attitude (I felt now pretty sure the old fellow had been a doctor)—that steady understanding, certainly hit me pretty hard. He took the hand—rather trembling, I fear it was—which I put out and held it in a remarkably reassuring grip.

"You have been doing a useful and dangerous piece of work," he said—a curiously clever way of comforting someone who felt he had been only a bungling, impertinent fool, who had insisted, even when warned, on sticking his silly head all too literally into a hornets' nest, and now was frightened almost out of his wits.

"You have drawn Heregrove," he continued. "As we agreed" (that again was kind; it had, of course, been solely his diagnosis), "Heregrove is the typical murderer-with-a-bright-idea."

I shuddered at the word, but it was true enough.

"That type generally reads a great many detective stories and, as you are no doubt aware, detective stories, like many other of our modes and manners—if you will forgive what may sound like an old man's 'grouse'—have degenerated. They began with common sense and trained observation and perhaps a patient devotion to and belief in tidying things up, these three allied together—not necessarily to exact the law's penalty but to show the criminal he could not win; that the balance of intelligence and insight are, in the end, always on the side of order and right."

The old man was started, but again I felt only

relief. I thought of a long, plodding relief column, pertinaciously winding its way through narrow passes to raise the siege of a sorely beleaguered garrison.

"But now," he went on, "it is the gentleman cracksman who is the public's real fancy. Oh, I know the films have to show the G-man getting his gunman, but that is only a 'command performance.' The public has to see such pictures because it supposes they protect it from young, growing criminals. But the public really likes fancying itself in immaculate evening dress carelessly holding up the bank at Monte Carlo. Well, a few act on their day-dreams. They get a new idea, as they think. I have shown you that this one is not as new as our friend believes. They suffer from an old irritation—as old as the world, the returning to 'a dark house and a detested wife'—reverse the roles and the story is certainly as old as cyclopean Mykenae and the Trojan War, Klytemnestra killing her Agamemnon in his bath—older, if we only knew. They kill, and then, like most animals with the instinct to kill in their blood, having tasted blood, they must go on killing. Nothing else gives them such a sense of power—and this feeling they must have. All the members of the human race—proud, successful, hateful creatures—are in the murderer's hand. To them he may seem a failure. They had better beware! At his slightest whim, there they are—so much carrion."

It was all too obviously exemplified by my situation—the casual, nearest-to-hand neighbor following the hated wife into the oubliette.

"What are we to do?" I ventured to interpose.

"Mr. Silchester," he said, looking straight at me, "I am going to repeat a request."

"You needn't have any fear," I interrupted. "I shall never go near the place again."

"The request I made," he went on quietly, "had two clauses. The first, that you should not go alone, has proved to have been wise. The second—" He saw I had gone white. I now remembered it all too well. But he went on serenely, "Was that you would introduce me to your acquaintance, Mr. Heregrove."

"But I can't! It would be suicide for us both. The very sight of the man would make me tremble and he would be bound to make his brutes attack us, even if they did not do so of themselves. Can't you put all you know before the police? Can't you have him arrested?"

"British law is a noble pile," he replied ruminatively, "but, like most stately causeways, erected block by block, year after year for centuries, it has plenty of crannies in it. The liberty of the subject requires that the law should not lock too closely. For life and law are never very easy with each other and we must pay for our freedom to be eccentric by letting an occasional criminal get through and away." Then, with a sudden sharpness, "There's not a shred of evidence to go to a court upon. He's proved innocent of his wife's death. A court has said it was an accident. As for your situation: you were attacked in your house and no one even saw it happen. Your servant is hardly a mute. She does not ask to be questioned before she gives you both news and views. She sympathizes sincerely with you for having had some sort of shock. In her family, I gather, similar things have befallen. But she is certainly skeptical about the cause being other than, as she put it, 'in the family.' Indeed, Heregrove might turn the tables on you—he is certainly bold enough to do it—and say you were maligning him; trying to ruin him; either a blackmailer or a borderline neurotic. Remember, Mr. Silchester, an eccentric has few friends."

That so chimed with my own gloomy thoughts at which his visit had found me that I collapsed into a wholly apprehensive silence.

"But remember also," he went on, deliberately cheering, "Heregrove is also curiously helpless, curiously localized in his malignancy. He is like one of those slow-moving, stiff, poisonous lizards which, if you pounce and pick them up in a certain way, can't get their venom-spine into you."

He saw that I remained dolefully unconvinced. So he added, "Believe me, there is no safer place for you than in Heregrove's house. He's playing a game. He's perfecting his lovely, power-giving murder tool. He's not going to spoil all by striking at you when the corpse would fall on his hands."

I didn't like the phrase at all, but it did make the situation clear, if painfully so.

"No, no; in his house you will be under his guard. Some spiders don't recognize a fly if it is not in their web. Heregrove simply can't kill you unless you are outside his."

Still, I quite naturally hesitated. Mr. Mycroft looked keenly at me again.

"And unless we do get into that house we shall never get him off your track. I beg you to make no mistake over that. I have more knowledge of this particular psychology than, if I may say so, you are likely to have. At the proper range, with his perfect shot, he is as determined yet to get you, as a golfer who won't go on to the third green until he has holed out on the second. You are No. 2 on his score."

I knew all too well he was right.

"I must tell you," I agreed, "Heregrove came here, called here, the very day he tried to murder me, only a couple of hours after the attempt!"

"Yes, your Alice told me of what she, though ignorant of the fullness of his nerve, called his 'imperence.' She evidently has something of an animal's intuitive mistrust of malignancy, though she thinks your actual attack was a subjective experience: an interesting case, showing where intuition is sound but helpless, because reason is too rudimentary to argue accurately and attention too bird-witted rightly to observe."

"But, Mr. Mycroft, she could not have told you the worst. When I went downstairs, after he had gone, I discovered that, while he had sent her upstairs on a fake message to me, he had taken the handkerchief out of my jacket pocket, which was lying in sight of the door! Do you see?"

"You needn't explain," he interrupted. "I know I seem to you long-winded, but I won't waste your time on unnecessary details if I can help it, in this case. Time matters here. I'll tell you: the purloining of your handkerchief does not, I think, matter immediately by adding any instant additional peril to that in which you already stand. We have time there. Nor need you explain to me about your coat. When in one of my thinkings aloud, which grated on you so much at our first meeting, I suddenly called myself senile, or at least questioned myself as to whether I might not be becoming so, it was because I had not foreseen that move of Heregrove's. You remember?"

"Yes, we were talking about insects' being able to hear sounds that we cannot and how a number of insects track great distances also by smell."

"Well, that was why I begged you not to go to Heregrove's place alone. I was sure he would want you to come, and I was equally sure, if he could get you by yourself, he would try to put some mark on you whereby his bees could track you down. You played into his hands perfectly. Now, will you tell me exactly what he did?"

I gave Mr. Mycroft precisely the account which I have put down before. I saw his face light up.

"Fascinating," was his first and, I thought, rather heartless comment. He saw that my feelings were hurt and added at once, "I repeat, you did all of us an invaluable service by going there and taking the risk—making Heregrove show his hand before he was perfectly prepared. I believe you made the gun go off half-cock or half-charged. He wasn't quite ready, or he would have found some way of asking you up. But he could not resist when, as he thought (all murderers of that sort are megalomaniacs), Destiny had put you deliberately in his hands. He will know more of Destiny before he has finished. Meanwhile, we must not let our counter-preparations suffer from the same fault. You see now, we *must* call on him. The coat trick failed. As a precaution, have that jacket burned. Tonight put it well into the center of your weed-and-grass bonfire which I saw smoking at your garden's end. At night, mind you. Some virulent essential oils, like that of the pestilential poison oak of the south-western United States, actually become more pungent and irritating when burning, and that would simply mean that you were signaling to your vampires, asking them to come over and attack you again. Now for your hand."

I showed him the fingers which had been stained. No trace remained which even my nose could detect after all my scrubbings. But he insisted on getting some medical alcohol and rubbing the skin till it was sore.

"Now for something to throw off the scent, or rather to bury it under a load it couldn't pierce through," he remarked, drawing a small bottle from his pocket. "I brought this little mixture with me because I thought Heregrove would have tried some way of 'putting the doom on you,' as our ancestors would have phrased it, and quite accurately, too. I have noticed it throws out any animal's olfactory sense more completely than any one scent. It is citronella, valerian, and aniseed oils in equal parts."

Rubbing it on my fingers, which were almost inflamed by the alcohol, he added, "Now, please go up and wash. We don't want Heregrove to smell us, or he is quite shrewd enough to 'smell our rat.' We only want to be sure to put his bees off. They will certainly smell the anointing I have given you and be of the opinion that you are not the man they wanted so furiously, so little time ago, to kill. The voice may be the voice of Jacob but the smell will be the smell of Esau."

Quotations again; how the old man's mind ran on! I didn't want to attend to his sallies. My mind was in a most unpleasant whirl. It was all too obvious that he was pushing me, caparisoning me, I might almost say, as his mount, to go at once into action, to call straightway on Heregrove.

"I say," I began lamely, hoping, perhaps only to gain time.

He saw my tendency and was quite clear and quick.

"Yes, we must go at once. He must not gain a moment's more time, if we can help it. The fact that you come back again will be, to his cocksure vanity, final proof that you have not been able to put two and two together and so don't suspect in the least his designs. Even should you mention being attacked, he will show you a wondering sympathy, talk of the mysteries of instinct, of how, unless he's with someone they dislike, he's always safe with the bees—they are his friends, like his dear little mare (which, incidentally, he poisoned), and how he can sympathize, having lost his dear wife in the same strange way. The fact that you bring round an amiable if boring old gentleman, also anxious to purchase honey, will put the final seal on your ignorance. You hardly introduce fresh customers to a salesman who you know has just tried to shanghai you."

"All right," I said resignedly.

Only the feeling that I had no choice but to decide to go back to that den or to be driven out of my house and perhaps out of my mind or out of my body—only such a grim, clear decision made me agree to act. But even then, when I assented, that was not enough for my strange champion.

"No," he said, turning his head on one side and looking at me. "You must play your part a trifle more convincingly than that. As it is, you look as though *you* were the man with the noose closing round his throat. In spite of all Heregrove's insane self-assurance, that look of yours would raise doubts in his mind, and if he doubts, we are done."

I tried to smile, but it was a pale smirk of a thing.

"I'm sorry," said Mr. Mycroft. "You must *feel* that smile, if it is to be any good to us. You see, we shall be watched while we are there, not merely by a couple of very shrewd if deluded human eyes. We shall be under the instinctive surveillance of hundreds of little detectives who will be judging us, not by our look but by our smell, and who will try to kill us the moment we seem sufficiently, or rather smell sufficiently, suspicious. You've heard about the 'smell of fear'? It's the adrenalin which fright puts into our sweat when we begin, as we say, to get into a cold sweat of fear, and, indeed, long before we know we are even feeling clammy. It is this smell which all animals, especially bees, find intensely provocative, and, if it gets strong, quite maddening. The bees we are about to visit are sufficiently crazy already not to be given the slightest further excuse for feeling provoked. It won't be much comfort to us if we are killed by their attacking us a little prematurely, according to Heregrove's plans."

"Oh, let me out of this," I broke in.

"No," he replied. "This, as you know, is the only possible line of safety. We must grasp this nettle. And the more we delay, the worse it will be; quite apart from the fact that Heregrove may strike again, if we give him any more time." Then the note of command changed to one of constructive assistance. "But I thought this necessary initiative against our enemy might require more of you than you could quite command at will. Whatever you might wish, and however necessary you might see it to be, I saw it might well be impossible for you to get yourself to feel that this is a fine, boyish adventure. And as you must believe this, as your part in our act, if you are to convince the greater part of our audience—and if they hiss us, we are lost—just swallow this. It's only benzedrine hydrate. Does no harm. Not a thing to live on, but it does pull one through little scenes like this and makes one's acting convincing."

I gazed with some misgiving at the small white tablet. I hate drugs. If I get into a mood I stay in it until it moves off. I don't believe in making efforts with oneself; after all, does one ever know what one is doing and why things go on inside oneself? But I suppose every criminal going to the scaffold gulps down willingly enough his small regulation tot of brandy, even though he has always hated the taste up till then. I got it down, and Mr. Mycroft kept me walking up and down for some time while he ran over our final dispositions. As he talked, it seemed to me increasingly clear that he was a master mind,

Heregrove simply a malicious fool and that we had him in our grasp.

The mood held even when we found ourselves at his door and, if anything, grew even stronger when I listened while Mr. Mycroft took the whole game out of my hands and played it, I had to own, incomparably. All vestige of the leisurely old bore had vanished. He was as sparklingly vivacious and at the same time as charmingly ingenuous as a schoolboy. No doubt he was an amazing actor, but it was equally clear to me that he was really in high spirits, an old hunter, finding itself once again following a breast-high scent, a veteran adventurer looking once more into the bright eyes of danger. Romantic similes and well-worn ones, too, I know, but I must set down things as they happened, and that was exactly how I saw him then. It explains a little the extraordinary ascendancy he was able to have over me.

Heregrove, on opening, had not looked hospitable, though he pulled his face together and was obviously both determined to appear at his ease and uninclined to think that we looked dangerous or even suspicious. Obviously we did not. Here was that young fool who had already once put his silly head into the trap and now again, as stupid as a pop-eyed trout, which takes the same hook five minutes after it has got off it safe back into deep water, was returning for another visit to the man who was determined to murder him in cold blood. And he brings with him an old, capering zany, also after honey, and who also might serve well as Demonstration Case No. 3 of the perfect, trackless killer.

Mr. Mycroft was, as it happens, asking about honey. He had introduced himself and he had spoken with disarming frankness about his failure to keep bees himself. He supposed he hadn't the knack and was too old now to learn. His only wish had been to keep himself in honey. He had no knowledge of the strange insects and confessed that he found it hard to understand their normal ways, let alone their crotchets, their likes and dislikes and their complaints, of which there seemed to be no end and each one more mysterious than the last. Then his young friend here had told him that he had an acquaintance up at this end of the village who had kept him supplied for a long while now with excellent honey.

"Perhaps it's a breach of village etiquette for me

to call. Each community has its rules, which the outsider must learn. So I persuaded Mr. Silchester to come along with me this afternoon."

There was nothing very cunning in the opening, but it was delivered with an indefinable air, with that quiet, cheerful assurance which creates an atmosphere in which the other side simply has to accept your initiative and to believe at its face value what you say.

"Oh, come in, come in," said Heregrove.

He was obviously having to give ground, as a man with a weaker wrist, poorer eye, and less skill has to yield ground to a more powerful fencer. I was surprised to find myself feeling that we were the attacking party, and Heregrove in danger of us, not we of him. We entered that dreary living room, and he made an effort, having landed us there, to get away.

"I'll just go down and get you the honey. It's at the bottom of the garden, as Mr. Silchester knows."

That appeal to me, somehow, gave another fillip to my still rising courage. I certainly now should not smell of fear as long as I realized that our enemy, however consciously still unaware, was subconsciously so uneasy that he had to call me in to confirm his right to get unsuspected away from an old, effusive man and a dolt of a young one.

Mr. Mycroft, however, was as quick as a fencer taking an opening of his enemy's guard.

"I spied your garden as we talked outside. I think, too, I noticed that you have some uncommon stripings on your tulips. I wish I knew as much of bees as I do about tulips. I will take a modest wager you have a very interesting mutation there. Perhaps chance aiding skill? The chromosome study of tulips, I confess, fascinates me."

With his rapid conjuror's patter, Mr. Mycroft gently, firmly, irresistibly, forced his company on the retreating Heregrove. I followed, and so we three went down the garden path, up which I had last come so short a time before, little better than a fugitive and, as it happened, branded with the mark of death. When we reached the egregious bunch of late, mid-summer tulips—which, of course, I had never before noticed—Heregrove muttered something about knowing nothing about flowers, and indeed the flower beds fully confirmed him. But Mr. Mycroft would have none of this "false modesty," as he rallyingly called it.

"Obviously, my dear sir, you are not one of those

wearisome, prettysome cottage gardeners, but, whether by luck or no, here is a plant well worth an expert botanist's interest. I can't claim to be that, but I can claim to be able to recognize a remarkable sport when I see one."

He bent, examined the plant, looked into the rather closely folded petals, at the anthers or stamens or whatever botanists call that sort of tonsil things which flowers have in their throats.

Then, suddenly, "But we are forgetting our honey," he said, straightening himself up.

Heregrove had stopped, standing closely beside him. He was quite clearly taken in by his apparently bona fide enthusiasm and quite as clearly at a loss how to manage this lively old bore and keep him at the proper distance from places where his long nose might scent things less sweet and harmless than the faint, clean perfume of the tulip.

"The bees are apt to be a bit cross now; frayed nerves at the end of the season." Heregrove tried to make a little joke of it. "You had better not come too near."

I thought he glanced at me in a questioning way. The next moment he strode off to the little shed. Bees were coming and going in the air, just over our heads, as they went to and from the hives. But none paid any attention to us. The moment Heregrove had turned from us, however, my lively old companion was seized with another idea.

"Bless my soul," he remarked, making off quickly across the garden, "if that isn't purple Pileus growing by that stable door. Of course it's not rare, but in this locality, any mycologist would be surprised. I must have a glance at it; perhaps a local variant."

Heregrove had turned round with his hand on the latch of the honey shed, one foot already over the door sill. When he saw dear, old Mr. Mycroft skimming across the paddock something far more like terror than rage swept his face. I stood in between looking from one to the other.

"Mr. Mycroft," he shouted, "come here!"

"Just a moment . . . Purple Pileus . . . Odd locality," floated back over Mr. Mycroft's shoulder.

Suddenly Heregrove, leaving the door of the shed open, bounded across the garden strip, passed me without a look, and started running toward Mr. Mycroft. I thought all was up—that he would kill both of us on the spot. I stood, of course, stock still. Action, it will now be clear, is not my role. I am quite a good observer, though, in spite of what Mr.

Mycroft may think. I can see the whole of that scene as though I had a photograph of it lying before me now. Heregrove, as suddenly as he had begun to run, stopped and fell into a walk. That, I realized, must mean that he saw he would be too late. When he reached the stable door, Mr. Mycroft was coming out.

I heard his clear, vividly interested voice saying, "The spores have spread inside. The fungi are indeed the most interesting of all plant life. Of course, though, your tulip is the thing here. A high spot in my day. Thank you, indeed. Oh, you haven't yet the honey. You shouldn't have troubled to run over when I called. I'm always so excited by any plant discovery I make. Experts are too often like that, on their own subjects. It makes them bores, I fear. Ordinary, sane men can't understand all their enthusiasm—seems affected, indeed, almost insincere."

I could see Heregrove struggling with himself, but he had no chance of doing anything. Mr. Mycroft's ascendancy, the interpretation of our visit which Mr. Mycroft had forced on Heregrove's mind as the obvious truth, indicated precisely the same behavior which his own caution urged. He could not afford, I now saw, an outburst in front of two witnesses. I thought he would burst, though. As we parted, he was scarcely master of his voice, when, with the honey parceled up, we turned to go. He muttered the conventional courtesies and I could see the vein on the side of his forehead pulsing with its heightened pressure.

Out of earshot, Mr. Mycroft's first remark was not at all cheering, however.

"We shall have to call again."

"Couldn't you go alone, now you know him?" was my rather mean but really quite natural reply.

I was ashamed when I had said it and so quite a little relieved when, instead of taking me to task as he might, Mr. Mycroft's answer was merely, "The benzedrine hydrate is wearing off. You'll feel a bit let down now. As soon as we have buried this very dubious purchase in your garden, you had better turn in."

I felt even more ashamed when we went into the brick-walled part of my garden at the back of the house and Mr. Mycroft, with an energy I really could not command, proceeded to dig wide and deep the cursed honey's grave. When I wanted to stop, thinking we really had dug enough, for digging always makes my back ache, all he said was, "I have owed my life too often to not skimping jobs, to start doing so now."

At last, like bewitched gold, it was safe underground, and we were back in the sitting room, after washing in the kitchen.

"He's puzzled, and a bit frightened," Mr. Mycroft began. "But I'm puzzled, also, and if I depended only on the law to protect you and me, I'd be frightened too. There isn't a case against him, though of course he's as guilty as Judas and as dangerous as a cornered lynx."

"Didn't you get a clue in the stable?" I asked, almost irritably.

"A clue, yes," he answered. "But a clue is not a conviction, and the sharper you are at getting clues, the surer you may be that a jury will not see the strength of the evidential chain."

"But where are we, then?" I asked, with a growing sense of frustration.

"I'll tell you all I know. It may be more than you noticed."

"Of course it is," I said wearily. He bowed.

"Well, I hope you'll soon be comfortably asleep; but I must first clear your mind as to our present actual situation and our future action. First, I was determined to get into that house. Neither you nor perhaps Heregrove himself knew that that entry was forced. We walked in while talking and distracting him. If you keep on talking to a person who does not wish to talk, and meanwhile walk straight at him, as long as he thinks you are absorbed in what you are saying and aren't aware that you are walking him down, he moves back, thinking only how to stop you talking and so bring you to a standstill. So Heregrove, in spite of himself, had actually to say 'Come in.' Once we were in, Heregrove's next move, a fairly blind and unthought-out reaction, was to keep us from getting into the back premises, the outhouses, etc.

"The room itself was just worth the visit. In one corner I saw a familiar puce-colored piece of paper. It is the cover (unmistakable to those who know it) of a queer foundation in the United States, which has much money, some brains, little judgment, and less method. It lives on the bequest of a millionaire who was abducted and held for ransom by some kidnapers, left nearly to die (and certainly to get fairly unhinged) by the official police, and finally was saved by a private detective whom I once knew.

The detective's reward was a small fee, the foundation of this institute (the founding of which he, as far as his own interests were concerned, unwisely opposed, for millionaires even when sane *must* found institutes, as medieval barons had to found chantries and as hens must lay eggs), and the right to receive, all his life, copies of all the Foundation's publications.

"As I have said, I know that detective, and through him, I receive the periodical. The trust publishes research work for amateur detectives—a queer hobby, but more popular than you would suppose. And they have done some useful work—among a mountain of rubbish. As it happens, they were the first people to issue a description of the magnetized-dust test for fingerprints too faint to be picked up in any other way. They also published a very useful biochemical study of the animal ammonias. As we left the room I managed to see the number of the issue which he had. I will look it up when I get home, but I would take another wager that it is the issue which has that biochemical study in it.

"The next point, the tulip, was, of course, a bluff. His garden shows that he doesn't know enough even to know that I am fooling him. Naturally, I know sufficient genetics to counter him if he should try to expose me. He knows something about animal genetics and neglects plant genetics—the typical specialist; only in this case he has one confining aim—to perfect a new way of killing. No doubt he now does think he has got a freak tulip, and, as it happens, all these striped tulips are due to an interesting derangement of the chromosomes, as Hall has shown. But I turned to the tulip because it allowed me to examine not it but Mr. Heregrove at close and unsuspected range. A man changes his coat when he works in a laboratory but not his trousers. If he works long enough—and if he has no one to take his clothes to the cleaners, and it is obvious Mr. Heregrove has not—his trousers will get marked. Heregrove's trousers were within six inches of my eyes while I extolled that convenient but commonplace tulip, and I could see quite clearly a number of small stains and etches on the cloth which could be made by nothing but acids. So he makes his stuff himself. Next, I had to find out where."

"That's why you trotted off to the stable when he was almost in the shed?"

"Of course."

"But why should not his hellish laboratory be in the house? Isn't that more likely?"

"It is difficult to keep a horse in the house."

"I don't understand."

"It was plain to me directly you told me about the stable. Don't you know—we raised the matter before our visit to Heregrove, when we were discussing the smell of fear—that even amiable bees will often go mad if a sweating horse comes near them? You must never approach hives on horseback after a stiff gallop, unless you are looking for trouble. Heregrove's little research was naturally on the biochemical ammonias of horses. In other words, he has been looking for an essence which, when in full strength, will have just that quality which most rouses bees. He has (to put it in harsh Anglo-Saxon) been distilling and quintessencing sweats, like a medieval warlock, with all the witch-doctor's malignancy and far greater efficaciousness. His first simple experiment worked well enough to kill his wife walking in the garden. And now, like the first radio researchers, he is becoming ambitious to strengthen his transmission and to be able to make his messages travel over long distances. Your house is more than a mile away. It was just bad luck (or Destiny) that he didn't—well, shall we say, get perfect transmission."

"But you didn't find anything in the stable?"

I wanted to get down to facts. Mr. Mycroft could not be kept sufficiently interested in the real issue, that I was in danger and must somehow be got out of it. The problem, I could see, was to him one of general interest and my fate was only one feature in it. That was a point of view which perhaps I must understand but with which even he could not expect me to sympathize. He looked up, for he had been following his own line of thought, with his eyes fixed on the ground, and I expect he had really quite forgotten about me as a human being.

"No," he said, meditatively; "no, he has dismantled his laboratory. Not an uncareful man. I have known murderers as ingenious and far less careful—the two types do not necessarily go together. I could see where the bench and racks must have been. He was not lying to you when he said water was laid on in that stall. And after this visit of ours I am sure that a man who is as careful as that will take the precaution of clearing up again and even more thoroughly. And not only in the stable. The puce-covered periodical will go—would have gone already, but he was needing it right up to date and he did not expect we should get into the house, or if we did, that one of us would have such an out-of-the-way piece of knowledge as to be able to recognize that cover. All that remains, secreted somewhere, are a few small phials of a rather rank-smelling liquid marked 'Disinfectant'; certainly not healthy for microbes and certainly not very lethal, even if very nauseating to man. What good could a prosecution make of those, even should they be found?"

"Why," I shot in at this somewhat rhetorical question, for here I had direct experience he had not, "why, if the stuff was put on a piece of cloth and bees released near it, then you would see them go mad and bury their stings in it. Put a wretched rabbit in court with a smear of that stuff on its fur and it would be stung to death before the eyes of judge and jury! I can't think of a more conclusive demonstration and a more damning proof."

"You mistake our man," he replied without showing any interest in my contribution. "He's not so simple as that. In fact, I want you to realize that he is uncommonly clever, in his way—careful and cunning. No doubt he saw that was a way in which the noose might be slipped over his neck. I told you, at the beginning, that he bred special bees. True, he didn't know about their hearing and their curious limitation and ability to be controlled thereby. But that is just like nearly every specialist. Because he knows so much about their smelling reaction, he overlooks their hearing. He bred a curiously fierce and poisonous bee. You might expect *that* psycho-physical linkage—after all, rage *is* a kind of poison, and, no doubt, venom was evolved gradually by animals which, both weak and vindictive, were literally and bodily embittered by their sense of wrong and age-long yearning for revenge. There is, you know, a bee in Australia which, because it has no serious enemies, has yet to evolve a sting. The sting in all the bees and insects that we know is evolved from the ovipositor, the instrument first evolved just to insert their eggs into safe places. Venom is a late thing. There are, I gather, no poisonous snakes before the Miocene. It takes some considerable time and effort and brooding to be able to be as malignant as you wish. *Nemo repente fuit turpissimus.*"

"Yes, yes," I had to break in. "But we are discussing how *this* man got his diabolical knowledge and skill which today is making at least one of us go hourly in peril of his life!"

Mr. Mycroft did not seem vexed by my interruption, which, after all, considering his ranging interests, was necessary.

"Yes," he said," I was just coming to that. For though you might expect him to be able to blend fierceness with actual venom and to increase them together, I must own that his next breeding effort was remarkable and one which I might even have been inclined, offhand, to say was practically impossible. He refines animal ammonia, especially horse ammonia, until he gets a peculiar essence which wildly maddens a bee, but only a particular breed and strain of bees—in fact, his own monsters. No doubt his brooding mind caught that clue from what is known about those rare, but now well-noted and observed, peculiar specific affinities between the olfactory sense of one particular species of insect and the scent of one single species of plant—the best-known of which cross-alliances of insect and plant is, of course, the Yucca flower and the Yucca moth. But I mustn't say more tonight. You are dead tired."

It was true. I was having more and more difficulty in stifling my yawns when, however anxious I was to get out of the trap, he would give me long lectures on natural history. His next remark was, however, to the point and cheering.

"We certainly have at least one clear day for work, for Heregrove will spend tomorrow, every minute of it, re-extirpating every suspicious trace. I wouldn't wonder if he opened even the horse's grave and gave it another dose of quicklime."

That faintly awoke my interest to ask one casual question.

"How did the horse meet its death?" I questioned, as I showed him out of the garden gate.

"It was stung to death, poor brute, for demonstration purposes," he replied, and went off into the dusk.

Chapter VII

DOUBLE-CROSSING DESTINY

In spite of such a day, a day alternately too exciting and quite tiringly boring, I slept, nonetheless, quite well. I certainly was hugely tired. But I saw I could not let things rest as they were. I was like a criminal with only a short reprieve, and I must act if I were ever really to be safe and free again. So as soon as I woke I was up, had my breakfast, and hurried off to Waller's Lane—not without an apprehensive look up the road which led in the other direction to the dreaded honey-snare.

Mr. Mycroft was already out in his garden and greeted me with, "The first experiment is over and as we expected. Look, I'll repeat it." At the end of a cane he had attached a pair of tweezers in which was a speck of cotton wool, oily and brown. He put it toward one of the alighting boards of his hives. The bees scattered and the working hum turned to a buzz, but, on the cane's being taken away, only a few followed it, half-heartedly, and they soon returned to work.

"Is that the stuff?" I asked, rather scared.

"Yes," he said. "You see, my mild Dutch don't like it, but it certainly does not make them homicidal. Now look at this."

He stepped back through the open French window into the house, returning with another similarly tipped cane. He advanced it to the hive and immediately there was quite an ugly commotion—a squadron swooping out after the offensive ferrule. He thrust it into a pot of water and, after some angry rushes and swirls, the squadron also returned to work.

"That was a fairly strong brew of ordinary horse-sweat ammonia. You see how clever our man has been! His insect only goes quite mad over a special brand of distillation, a brand which actually affects the normal bee *less* than ordinary horse sweat."

"But how did you get the stuff?" I asked, excitedly.

"Even the coolest, most thoughtful criminal makes a slip if you follow him carefully enough," he replied musingly. "You remember those young murderers Leopold and Loeb, of Chicago? They planned quite coolly and, as they calculated, quite completely, to murder that schoolboy and get away with it. And all their plans run according to schedule, well enough. But, while they are disposing of their victim's body, one of these creatures, who think they are so superior to human mistakes and weaknesses, actually drops his glasses on the ground and there they are picked up, for they are plain for any passerby to see. Within a couple of hours the Chicago oculists are all rung up, the description of these distinctive lenses given. The oculist who ground them looks up the specification in his files and Leopold and Loeb's names are in the possession of the police. Part of their minds must have heard those glasses click as they struck the ground, part of their attention have noticed them lying there while they looked around, approving their silly, sinister skill, seeing how well they had concealed their victim's body. But they were betrayed by that deep part of consciousness which they had disowned. We reckon ill who leave it out.

"Heregrove has done much the same. I did not tell you last night, as it might have made you sleep badly had you known that I had the deadly stuff on me. But I had, you remember, taken the precaution to bury the honey deeply, and, I believe, without their own honey to trail them to their victim, the vampire bees cannot find you simply by this ammoniac stuff. Once they have found you and you are marked—well, I have told you how happy I am you are alive and how lucky I think you are to be so. Here in this garden we are, anyhow, safe, for, if they should arrive, I can turn my siren song on them.

"But how did I get any of the stuff? Well, I have told you—because the clever criminal is just the man who makes a complete, amnesic slip every now and then, so that you have only to dog him long enough for him to let an utterly damning clue fall into your hand. I have only a little of his precious brew and that under strict glass-and-wax stoppering. The smirched scrap I showed the bees a moment ago I am now going to drop into my electric furnace where it will be ash in a moment."

He suited the deed to the word and I could hear the damp speck of wadding hiss just before he shut to the miniature furnace's door. He returned, picked out the first cane, twitched off its tip of sodden wadding so that it was flicked over the hedge, upset the pot of water with his foot, and, while he watched the dry soil suck up the damp, continued.

"The piece I picked up was in the stable. I had, as you know, only a moment to glance round and to see that the laboratory had been liquidated, and was just turning to meet Heregrove, for there was no use taking unnecessary risks by letting him come upon me gazing at the site of his hell's kitchen—when I saw a scrap of whitish cloth on the dark ground. I stooped, picked it up, dropped it in my pocket, and walked out with my toadstool patter to meet our enraged but nonplused host. I guessed in a moment what it was—the sham finger-bandage which he used as his not uningenious way of tainting you."

"But why wasn't it covered with bees?" I questioned.

"That," he answered, "is one of those points of psychology where, as on a wavering border line, reason touches instinct—instinct which isn't mechanic reaction or clear calculation, the two processes we know something about, instinct of which we know, in actual fact, nothing. This is the converse of the Leopold and Loeb question—why did their senses betray them? Here we have to ask, why does that blind instinct which makes the bee sting, till it ruptures itself, an object which insults its nose, suddenly yield to a kind of reason which tells it a rag can't suffer or at least can't be killed? True, they stung your coat but it smelled human and they were looking for you. But, after all, our real problem is the Leopold and Loeb side of the question. What non-reasoning power betrayed also our careful, calculating Heregrove? Of course, as soon as he had seen you off the premises he went to the stable. The bees were in by that time and he was safe. But still, as it was only just dusk, a few loiterers might be coming home late and he knew well that even half a dozen stings are probably fatal. So he drops the rag, probably washes and disinfects his hands in the stable—and then why doesn't he come back and take the rag to burn it? Probably he does mean to come when it is quite dark, so that he can be quite sure all the bees are in and also that no one will see him burning anything. He is as careful as that, and his place can be seen from the road, and, you see, all this taking care only maneuvers him into the position where the fatal forgetfulness can be brought into play. What we do know is that he did forget to come back and so we have hold of this invaluable rag."

"I don't see the rag is much use to us," I said. "It doesn't tell us anything we didn't know and won't help get us a conviction, as the glasses convicted Leopold and Loeb."

"It will do more for us," Mr. Mycroft replied.

"How?" I exclaimed. "How can it?"

His face went graver than I had ever seen it. He remained silent for a moment.

Then he said, "I wonder, Mr. Silchester, whether you could bring yourself really to trust me?"

That is the kind of question I can't help profoundly disliking. It seems to me rhetorical, melodramatic.

"When a couple of people get mixed up" (I was

just going to say "by Destiny," but then that would make me also sound pompous and theatrical) "by luck in a mess with a lunatic, it seems rather silly to ask, when it's practically all over, whether one of them trusts the other."

"You take a far rosier outlook on the immediate future than I do, Mr. Silchester," he coolly replied, "if your considered opinion is that we are already almost out of this peculiarly tangled wood."

My heart sank. Before, it had always been he who had cheered me and I recalled with growing chill that though he *was* in danger, he was prospective victim No. 3 while I was No. 2 and No. 1 was long in her unavenged grave.

"We are," he went on, "at a place where two tracks divide. Our lives—I say it advisedly; I have often gambled with mine and I know something of mortal risks—our lives depend on whether the track which we decide to take is the right one. At the end of one of these trails there lies a peculiarly painful end for you and me, and" (it was this, I must own, that "put the screws on me") "and, Mr. Silchester, you have had a taste of this weapon which is now aimed at you as certainly as any gunman has ever aimed at and shot down his victim."

"Mr. Mycroft," I said in a voice which, though it may have expressed apology did express defeat, "I don't know why I am always trying to be difficult. I suppose it is because I am so frightened that I won't own I am, and so I try to get back onto that formal relationship which we should be on if this horrid secret peril had not forced us together."

How true that has proved—far truer than I thought even then. Mr. Mycroft evidently believed me.

"I don't want to frighten you needlessly, I think you realize. In fact, it is of the greatest importance that you should keep your nerve. Lose that and we may both be dead far sooner than we need be. But we must be quite clear about our situation and have no illusions over it. I have here the essence which, to put it frankly, even if it sounds melodramatic, puts death on people, at least in this locality. The law can give us no protection. But destiny has put this stuff in my hands. Fate made Heregrove drop the one thing which he could give us as an adequate defense against his attack; fate made him drop it and leave it where I could find it without his seeing me do so. Fate provided that I should have in the pocket into which I thrust it that small flask of the three strong essential oils with which I had anointed your fingers. No doubt that fact gave us an additional defense against any attack we might have suffered as I came back across the paddock with the stuff on my person. You must own that such an arrangement of events, although it would not have served us had we not been ready to avail ourselves of it, did make possible the present turn of events and that it does look as though, if a human may be so rash to say so, fate was, at least, not against us in this matter.

"Well, however that may be, and acting on the saw that Providence helps those who do not neglect to help themselves, when I got home I looked up my puce periodical. As I thought, it did contain that useful if recondite piece of work on animal ammonias—a piece of sound research which perhaps at present only two men in Europe and America happen to want—the one to commit, the other to stop an indefinite series of cruel murders. With these tables and the actual smearings on the rag, don't you see what we can do, what we can't do, and why I cannot do less than ask for your absolute confidence?"

I suppose subconsciously I suspected already the

position into which he was forcing me—no, that's not quite fair, and I must be absolutely fair—I ought to say the position into which Destiny was forcing me, forcing us. I played for time, again.

"What *can't* we do?" I asked evasively.

It seemed better to know first what couldn't help us, for I might find a loophole there; before facing what we might have to do to help ourselves, to save ourselves.

"I needn't labor the point," he said, eyeing me with an embarrassing steadiness. "To this man, the law is no more than a fence to a yellow-fever mosquito. The law protects us from the sudden, unpremeditated violence of the untamed blackguard. It is helpless against the calculating malice of a man who patiently and deliberately studies to get around its limitations. When you have really faced up to the fact—I know it is hard for those who have lived protected lives to face such an actuality—that the law, the magistrate, and the village policeman are helpless to protect you, then you will be free to consider fully the unavoidability of step two: of doing what we can do."

He waited; after some unpleasant moments of

silence, I must have showed some sort of assent, for he continued.

"I think you have been right in counting the cost and I am glad you have come to the same opinion as myself, only after mature thought. Right as it is, as well as wise, it is, of course, a very unconventional view. But we are, morally, precisely in the position that frontiersmen are placed when pushing out to the limits of a new country. We have to work the law ourselves and to make it run where, as yet, there are no rails. The law one day will catch up with this situation; then we shall simply tell the railway clerk where we want to be taken and he will see that we are conveyed. Today it is still, in such cases as these, a case of the sheriff's posse. We have to mount our own horses and under our own steam go after the criminal. It is, here, still the stage where every citizen must uphold and apply the law. You and I are the Western sheriff's posse. Fortunately we are adequately armed—"

"You don't mean that we have got to go like moonlighters and shoot through Heregrove's window some night?"

He saw that my protest was hardly sincere, in fact, only a prevarication, but he took it with perfect courtesy. I felt like a hooked fish making a desperate dash and splash, trying to get off on a false issue, and let by the fisherman, while it spends its strength, have the full run of the line, only to be hauled in when spent.

"My metaphor was clumsy," Mr. Mycroft apologized. "Of course, I only mean that we can and must counter Heregrove with nothing more than those instruments which he is attempting to use on us and which the law does not recognize as methods of murder—which, in fact, it dismisses as accidental, 'acts of God' and not of malicious man."

That was, certainly, put as reassuringly as possible. I could, and must own did, dismiss from my mind the Wild-West sheriff simile. It certainly did not appeal to me, the recluse, to ride about avenging murders which the law chose to overlook. I am not a Red-Cross Knight. But I am an easily scared individual, and the one fact which remained, boring down into my consciousness and pushing me to lengths which otherwise I should have thought absurdly desperate, was my actual desperate situation. I made a final twist, however.

"All right," I said, with an air of having thought everything out to the end and seeing exactly how much would be expected of me. "All right, go ahead. I promise you I will never divulge anything of this. Obviously I shall want, quite as much as you, to keep my mouth shut."

"Thank you," he said, a bit dryly, I thought. My heart began sinking to new low levels. "That means, of course, that you will collaborate with me, for, while I can manage the technical part of this problem quite well by myself, I shall have to require your assistance at the end, in the practical application. We shall, may I repeat, have to call on Heregrove again."

Those last words, which I had dreaded most, were like a knell.

"Now, Mr. Silchester," he continued, in the same level tone, as though we had been planning a picnic, "I must go back into my laboratory. When you arrived I had started a couple of experiments and I must go and see how they are cooking. You, too, will want to think over our conversation, no doubt. Perhaps you would like to rest or read in my library. The singing of my pet birds in there will not, as you have tested for yourself, disturb you. I venture to invite and advise you to stay here; not only because we shall have several more things to talk over, which we can best do as soon as my experiments are finished, but also because I honestly believe that today you are safer here than in your own house."

"All right," I said none too graciously but he seemed quite content. He knew that my resistance was broken. I was his pawn; a hateful position, even if you are to be used to checkmate a man who wants to murder you.

The morning passed slowly. I could hear Mr. Mycroft cluttering about, across the hall, in his laboratory. I couldn't read. I sat there dully, my mind slowly, like a mud-locked eddy in a stream, turning pointlessly round and round the events which had me snarled. At last my attention was caught by those silly birds as they hopped round their cage, stupidly safe, too stupid to know they were safe. As I looked, there they were, at it again, he singing silently and she listening enthralled. That soundless singing seemed to me all part of Nature's senseless arranging of things. Then, somehow, I had evidently gone too far in my disgust with everything. I realized how self-centered I was being, expecting the world to be made for me and to care for my fate; and how perverse I must be, for, after all, if I could have heard these birds squeaking away to each other I should only have been exasperated at the noise. I began to smile at myself. I got up, went over to the cage, and was agreeably surprised when the birds, instead of stupidly fluttering in dismay, both came at once to the bars, heads on one side, evidently expecting me to give them something or to play with them. I am not good with animals—they either bore or frighten me—but I must say, I felt a sudden reassurance that if I had to be wholly in the hands and power of a stranger, that stranger should have been able to make birds not only trust him but trust strangers also. I was musing on that; it was sinking into my mind, for it was a thought I was ready to reflect on, the only pleasant one I had had for some time, when the door opened.

Mr. Mycroft said, "Lunch is ready. I have washed. You know the way to the bathroom from your last visit."

Certainly, too, the house was very neat and efficiently run. That gave me almost as much confidence as the birds' confidence in me. And lunch was even better than last time.

"Last time," said my host as we sat down, "it was, I fear, a very scratch meal. Today, as I hoped I might persuade you to stay, there can be a little more design in living. Like everything else, a menu depends on foresight, in taking time in time." We started with borsch—a soup I love but could never get Alice to make.

"It is really one of the simplest of the great soups," said Mr. Mycroft in answer to some such remark of mine, "and, you are right, one of the best. The Russians are fine eaters. Primitive peoples often retain keenness in certain senses which we are too busy and hasty to have preserved. Taste and sound both are primitive. *We* have chosen sight, and so all our world is now hardly anything but a visual world, as far as we can make it. Our painting is better than Russian painting, in consequence. Their music and food are far richer. We have accuracy, neatness, tidiness. We treat smell as something disgusting, and it goes from us. 'You smell' is never praise in our mouths. Jacob's praise of his son, 'The smell of my son is even as the smell of the fruitful field,' makes us smile with more than a flavor of disgust. Indeed, 'you smell' is most often a phrase of the deepest loathing.

"We have order, but lack copious creativeness. We are scentless and are becoming very restricted in our hearing. Accurate but without flair (notice that word, set, by the logical French, over against logical thought—smell in contradistinction from reason). Precise but lacking intuition. And the narrowing and starving of our apprehension goes on apace. Already color—the side of seeing which keeps us most in touch with the warmth of actual living, is being banished as not quite nice. 'Loud,' we call it when condemning it—again a revealing word. We borrow it from our hearing, and we are afraid, anaemically afraid, of any volume, any width and size in things. Nothing must be too robust; everything must be muted, lower. We pick our way, creep about. We must at all costs be refined, even to the extraction of every flavor and vitamin out of life's raw juices. Plenty is vulgar. Well," he laughed, "we can actually and at this moment do something to correct that shrinking error. What a good color, as well as taste, borsch has! Loud, of course, and of course you know, in topical illustration of our point, that the word 'red' in Russian is the word for color itself."

So he prattled on. His obvious wish to distract and entertain me, and the excellent way his food was planned to match and support his talk, did give me quite remarkable relief. I think that was the first time that I realized that a wise, cool, calculating, and brave man can show (a fact which I had never imagined before) his coolness, courage, and considerateness by a gay and clattering amusingness and a wonderful and quite sincere interest in small and general things. I had never thought that a really powerful and strong and (I hate the word) good person could be gay and even foolish. I now began to suspect that only the biggest people, perhaps because they are at times as impersonal as life itself, can be merry and funny right at the moment of crisis, with their minds made up and their senses all alert as a marksman's. They don't even do it, I began to feel, even to cheer us, though perhaps that starts them. They do it because they are so free of everything but the actual moment. I don't know how to put it, but I suppose they are as timeless as an animal; perhaps more so, as timeless as a plant or even a rock.

I don't know, even less, why I have put all that down. I think it is to make clear how it was that my mood, which had been pretty bad, changed into a sense of security and gaiety almost like Mr. Mycroft's. Surely that is remarkable enough to need some explaining?

"This luncheon," rattled on the host, "is to be a salute to Russia: only red on the surface and at the dawn. Now we shall get down to the deeper Russia. Caviar, but not the cheap red. The sound black. This is also a pre-revolutionary way of serving it. I learned it when a Grand Duke of the *ancien régime* once wanted my company, hoping that together we might recover some rather indifferent pearls mislaid in a rather indiscreet way. That's a long story for lunch. Anyhow, I brought back this way of enjoying the sturgeon's black pearls. Cleopatra was right: most jewels would give us more real pleasure and do us in the end less harm if we could use them as crystallized cherries in a cocktail or a cordial, or as jujubes we could suck.

"Now for something more solid. These big Russian meat pies act as a pivot on which the meal turns, and they are wonderfully healthy if taken with their appropriate drink. This vodka was, I now recall, a present from that same Grand Duke who now, poor fellow, probably cleans boots in Paris or New York—so, I suppose, as I got the vodka, he must have got back the pearls. I hope they proved one of his liquid assets when the crash came. This is another sort of liquid which he certainly could not have got away with; so we need not mind using it ourselves. We will drink to his health, though, and to our success."

I felt now we could not fail, and drank to a success of which I was already unquestionably sure, though even that surety grew stronger as the warming stuff went through my veins. There followed a wonderful sweet: all of cream and almonds and honey. To a man as fond of sugar as myself it closed a banquet perfectly.

Chapter VIII

WASP STRIKES SPIDER

As we sat over our coffee, I therefore experienced no shock when Mr. Mycroft, without any change of his bright and almost careless tone, remarked, as though we had been discussing it all through lunch, "We'll pay that second visit to Heregrove this afternoon. The morning's work went perfectly—even quicker and better than I had dared to hope. Just come into the laboratory, and I'll be able to show you everything and how ready we are now to finish off this troublesome little matter."

One side of me knew that he was talking about a desperate and even illegal adventure. But that side was simply timid, calculating, bloodless reason. He had put his own mood into my blood, and that was surging about in a state of merriment which actually made (I must record it) the word adventure, to me, Sydney Silchester, have almost a ring of attractiveness in it, instead of the very warning sound which I have always connected with such a noun.

Mr. Mycroft closed the laboratory door, drew out a chair, cleared it of books, offered it to me, and himself perched, like a powerful bird, on the edge of the bench. Swinging round, he picked up a corked phial, drew the cork carefully and handed it to me. It contained, I should say, a egg-spoonful of liquid—quite clear but oily.

"Smell that," he requested.

I expected a shock to my nose and only sniffed as lightly as possible. I saw him smile, and so put it right under one nostril; then I drew a deep breath and finally almost touched the end of my nose on the test-tube's rim. Still I could smell nothing.

"Perhaps it's the vodka, or the garlic in the pie that has spoiled for the present my sense of smell,"

I said, a little apologetically, for though, or perhaps because, I hate all stenches, I rather pride myself on having a keen appreciation of scent.

He smiled back.

"I had noticed that you have an uncommonly lively olfactory sense. When we first came in here on your pristine visit you didn't like the laboratory smell, for you began to breathe through your mouth, though you made no effort to clear your nose, which you would have done had it been simply a little turbinal congestion which was temporarily troubling you. Then, when we went into the library, almost unconsciously, as we passed, in coming out, those Turgeniev novels bound in Russian leather—another reminder of my ducal devoirs—you could not resist just touching them and carrying your fingers immediately to your nose to relish the faint perfume."

"Then why—" I said.

"Because," he cut in, "there isn't any! That is just the point of my test. This stuff, I tried out on you. You have an uncommonly keen nose and you—scent is very 'suggestible'—expected to be able to detect, expected to be shocked by the strength of, a very rank odor. And you notice nothing. Try again, and don't touch the rim."

I snuffed until I must have vacuum-cleaned that glass, but not a ghost of a perfume rose to me.

"What does this mean?" I asked.

"It means," he encouragingly, if rather cryptically, remarked, "that we are far safer than anyone would have imagined that we could be. We have something amounting to the cap of invisibility."

"But what is it?" I asked again.

"Well," he said, "as it happens, it is that brown, pungent, so-called disinfectant, with which both you and I have been in touch."

"It isn't," I blurted out, "or, if it is, it has had taken out of it all the particular smell which made the original so dangerous."

"To us, yes, and that's half the battle: that's the defense, the parry. Your keen nose catches nothing. Mine isn't blunted. I have tried to keep my fivefold endowment sharp on every point of life's sacred pentagram. And scent, like taste, often outstays the present approved senses such as sight and hearing —on which our unbalanced age puts nearly all its weight. I, too, can smell nothing."

"But is there anything else to the stuff?" I prompted.

"We can't judge," he began.

"Then what's the use?" I exclaimed.

Having made up my mind to adventure, having thrown caution to the winds and with my courage seeming now unshakable, I experienced a sudden sense of impatience at all this caution and dawdling. But he cut me short.

"I didn't ask you in here simply to confirm my strong feeling that this essence is scentless. You must see that it is positive as well as negative."

He corked it carefully again, put the phial in the rack, anointed cork and glass with what my nose told me was his triple off-scent-thrower, the valerian, citronella, aniseed mixture. Next he told me to wash my hands as he washed his at the sink and then dabbed our fingers with surgical alcohol, rubbed them hard, and gave them also their anointing. That done, he went over to the other side of the room where there were some small drawers, their fronts covered with fine wire mesh, pulled out one, picked up a forceps, slipped back a trap, and brought out the forceps with a bee held by the wings.

"I captured it yesterday, in the early morning, before your Alice called for me. A few pirates were reconnoitering and a small squadron swooped. They'll never leave us alone, or any bees, as long as they are alive. I stunned them with sound, as you know, and picked up the few who actually fell on the lawn. They are now all dead except this one, though I gave them fine quarters and plenty of food. That, of course, is another mystery of the hive; it is what makes one of the greatest French apiarists say that the bee is not an individual, but only a loose, floating cell of that largely invisible organism or 'field' which we call the hive and of which we are able to perceive only its material core —the honeycomb and the queen.

"Certainly they will not live if kept from their swarm; and these are no exception. In fact, like most products of fancy breeding, they are evidently in this respect, as in others, more highly strung, more hysterical."

While he spoke he carefully carried the pinioned bee across the room. It, too, was obviously on the verge of death. Its legs moved slowly as if tangled in some invisible web. The antennae drooped. The bright, many-faceted eye already looked dulled.

Mr. Mycroft put it down on the bench. It nearly fell over on its side, and then recovered itself; it began to crawl laboriously, blindly ahead. But it had to stop, out of what was obviously sheer exhaustion.

"Yes, its minute, invisible pipe-line to its mysterious source of its general life is nearly severed," he said, looking at it.

"It will be dead in a few minutes," I concurred.

"Still," he said, "we are taking no risks," and, rather unnecessarily, I thought, he spent a moment in securing the wings, by slipping with a fine brush a drop of spirit-gum under each wing and so sticking the wing to the body.

So moribund was the insect that it did not even buzz nor seem to feel that its wings were now glued tightly to its back. Mr. Mycroft waited until the gum had set. The bee remained still. Indeed, the only sign of life was that it did not roll over. I was watching it with considerable curiosity and carefulness, so that I did not see what Mr. Mycroft was doing. What I did see was that suddenly, for no apparent reason, the dying bee literally sprang to life. It was as though an electric shock had struck it. Perhaps no electric current could so have galvanized it. The whole small body seemed to swell, the drooping antennae writhed like tiny snakes. A vibration of such intense energy went through it that the wings tore themselves free from their sealing, leaving the veined, transparent vans still stuck to the back. The stumps whirred wildly. Luckily for us, the possessed mite could not rise. The frantic tremor pulsed through it again. The body curled over on itself in a paroxysm of violence, and it was dead. The body still remained upright and humped as it had died.

I looked up. With rubber stalls on both index fingers and thumbs, Mr. Mycroft was corking the phial again.

"Why doesn't it fall over?" was all I could find to say.

He answered me by picking up the forceps again and taking hold of the dead bee. It required quite a considerable pull, however, to raise the body from the bench. When it came away, there, quite clearly, was the long murderous sting torn from the body and left deeply buried in the hard-wood.

"The master passion strong in death," he remarked, dropping the curled-up little husk into the ash-bin under the bench. With his free forceps picking out the sting from the wood, he dropped it into a small crucible glowing red-hot above a bunsen flame.

"One thorn of experience is worth a whole wilderness of warning," he continued, "and demonstration is always necessary. We both now know beyond any doubt that in that test-tube we have something which is precisely what we must have—a thing the essential nature of which is quite impossible to be perceived by us, while to the particular bee which we have to circumvent, it is as flagrant as a cup of vitriol."

"And now?" I said.

I realized that the time had come when we must go ahead, apply our knowledge and free ourselves and the world of a deadly pest. I knew that by an hour or so of resolute and obedient action I should somehow be delivered from a living nightmare and be able once again to go back to my quiet, secure, happy life, into the steady sunshine from under this hideous cloud. I felt also a curious sense of assurance, which the demonstration had at least given me reason for—the feeling, I suppose, that a hunter, concealed in a tree and armed with the latest sporting rifle, must experience when, all unconscious that it is covered, a man-eater strolls into perfect range. I felt that our enemy was as powerful, as malignant, and as stupid in his vain ignorance of what he was up against, as a tiger. So it was not any longer timidity which made me hesitate.

I was hunting for words, though, when Mr. Mycroft, who had been with great care drawing the clear liquid out of the test-tube by means of a pipette-nosed flask, his task finished and test-tube and flask shut into a hermetically sealed drawer, looked up at me, remarking, "The chemical interest of this experiment (and, I own, that has been quite absorbing in its way) has not made me forget that this problem, though now solved materially, remains morally a very grave one."

So saying, he went across the room, throwing wide the window as he passed, and opened one of the wire-covered drawers at the room's end. A dozen or so bees flew out. I ducked, but they made straight for the window. Looking out, I saw them swoop toward and enter one of the hives on the lawn.

"They are glad to get home," he said, looking after them. "I hate distressing them, blind and obsessed as all bees are, imprisoned in their fossilized dream of instinctive service to the hive. Perhaps I need hardly tell you that time and again while I was making this extract—eliminating the coarse essential oils, which alone our crude olfactory nerve-ends can pick up; finding the actual essence, partly by help of that odd article and its tables and partly by testing out my various refinings—by using that small caged party of my own placid bees as tasters, or smellers, by watching the the way they first reacted and then, as the brew became specific they became almost unaware, when the stuff, then crystal clear, brought near the pirates' detention drawer, made them nearly beat themselves to death against their wire-gauze bars—all that time the moral problem hung like a vast cloud on the horizon of my thought. Then, as the material problem was completely cleared out of the way, I turned on this other, and, to me, greater problem and found my mind as clear, as made up, and as convinced of its essential correctness as I am that the essence we hold is the stuff we need to fulfil our purpose."

"What's your solution?" I asked. I was myself so puzzled that I was really willing to take advice and act on it.

"I see," he said, looking at me, "you are kind

enough now to trust me, so I am going to ask you one more favor."

I must have registered some dismay, for he quickly added, "It is a very small one and between ourselves."

He's going to seal me to secrecy, I thought. Well, we are certainly in the same boat. I had told him I should be silent. I would certainly promise again. Even if I were an inveterate gossip, this was the one subject for which my silence could be trusted.

I was, therefore, surprised when he said, "I am going to ask you to trust me enough not to ask as yet how I have solved the moral problem, but to adopt my solution. It will, I believe, help the difficult and still quite sufficiently dangerous parts we have both to play if the man whom we have to *try* cannot see any signs, however involuntary, of collusion between us. I have to convince him again, after having shaken him badly, that I am what he still on the whole believes me to be, so that he will dismiss me as only a possible and peculiarly defenseless victim."

Well, it was a relief to follow, not to have to make up one's mind, to know that here was an authority who would accept the responsibility both for the material arrangements and the moral consequences. Perhaps I was too sanguine, too suggestible. Certainly my mood of physical readiness and mental acquiescence was not normal. I learned that later. It is, I think, a point of considerable importance, for it makes me far less responsible should any trouble arise in the future.

All the while he was talking, Mr. Mycroft was making preparations with a definiteness and a precision which, I must say, kept my sense of assurance from waning; for he evidently foresaw his moves (whatever these might be) as clearly as a chess player of champion rank sees, as the end-game begins, the exact positions his pieces will take up to bring about the checkmate. There was nothing unexpected in the flask's being taken out of its drawer now that all the bees were gone and the window was up again. He wiped the nozzle of the pipette duct with spirits, fitted its small cap on it tightly, and then slipped it into his pocket. The next move, however, was puzzling. He went to his filing shelves and collected from a number of periodicals a couple or so of loose pages, placing these in a drawer near the window. Then he looked at his watch.

"We are not rushed for time. We shall not leave

here until 5:30. Timing is, however, important. We must arrive when the sun is low, but it must not be dusk. Still, you always have to give these village craftsmen time. So I said three and, as I supposed, it is now four. I would rather none of us went down to the village. We ought not to be seen on that errand. I left my commission when I returned from you in the gloaming last evening. But though old Smith is slow, I think he will turn up. I am pretty sure he will have done the task I set him and I know he will be silent. He's the sort that likes a secret piece of fun, all the more when he has no clear idea what it is all about."

Naturally, I had no more notion than the unknown Smith as to the drift of these remarks. "A piece of fun" sounded almost the most inappropriate description that could be given of our adventure. Silence fell between us and while I was thinking of some way of trying to find out what he had meant, and beginning, even, to wonder whether he could have been so mad as to make a confidant of an outsider, I heard a limping step outside.

Mr. Mycroft went at once to the door, shutting it behind him; so I heard only a muffled word or two in the hall. The steps withdrew, and Mr. Mycroft returned, looking at a sheet of paper. I could just see that it was of quarto size and had a printed heading with a good deal of detail on it. After taking it and spreading it carefully on a drawing board which stood by the window, he turned it upside down so the heading, though well out of my eyes' range for reading, could now be seen running like a big footnote on the page. Holding it like this, with his free hand he opened the drawer in which he had put the loose pages and brought out what seemed a similar sheet, though with more writing on it; and this he placed wrong side up and a little above the first sheet. Then, taking a pen, he remained absorbed for some five minutes or so while he made what was, as far as I could judge, a small etching across what was now the top of the inverted sheet. He considered it a moment, compared it with something on the other sheet, and then went so quickly out of the room that I was unable to get a glance at it when he hurried by me. While I waited, I thought I heard the clack of a typewriter for a few moments, but was not sure.

He returned with his hands empty, simply saying, "Now we are ready. We have just time for a cup of tea. It is waiting us in the library."

We drank in silence. I knew I was at a divide in my life, but my mood remained curiously set, and, as I swallowed the tea—for, after all, tea is one of the most comforting of drinks—I actually felt the enterprising temper begin again to assert itself. When Mr. Mycroft said, "We ought to be getting on," I felt a curious mixture of two sensations. The one was like what I used to feel when taken by an uncle I liked to the Zoo. He knew one of the keepers in the lion house, so that we were let in behind the public cages and saw the keeper stroke a leopard. It was so pleased that it was both purring like a cat and at the same time tearing great splinters with its contracting claws out of the log on which it was sprawled. The other feeling I remembered experiencing when at school I was sent in to bat: everyone thought I should be bowled at once, but I actually hit a boundary and made twenty-three runs before I was stumped.

I do not recall what Mr. Mycroft talked about as we walked along, but a general impression remains that, like most powerful actors, he was building up his part. (I recall wondering whether that might have been his profession before he retired, and that after all he had not been a doctor. He certainly had a quite unusual and extraordinarily convincing way of taking parts.) I could not help seeing that now he was sinking himself into the character-mood he meant to impose on his audience; although that audience would only be two puzzled and more than a little uneasy men—one not knowing what kind of act he was going to put on but knowing that it was an act, and the other not knowing even who he was, but suspecting that he might be a fraud. I realized how much depended on his being able to put over that conviction of his actually being the part he was going to play—that this was so vital that even his play-acting must, in its detail, not be known even to me. For otherwise I would be prepared for his various actions, and my awareness of what was coming might destroy that sense of naturalness and spontaneity which he had to create, and which I, with my real ignorance must, and could only so, second.

I remember vaguely that he prattled about flowers and used a lot of technical terms. I don't think he intended me to listen. I know I didn't. He sailed up to Heregrove's door, seeming to pay no attention to the house, for he was apparently still engaged in a vivacious conversation with me, or rather pouring out an excited story into my uncomprehending ear. He would say frequently, "I was right. I thought I was—knew I was. And yet who would think it! I simply couldn't wait. Nor could he; nor would they; and you realize what that means! You don't surprise men like that into action unless you have a prize find—a perfect natural-history-museum piece."

We were at the door and he had rapped gaily on it, turned his back on it, and continued chuckling and repeating in a raised, excited voice.

"Yes, yes, Mr. Heregrove will be pleased at this; this means a tidy profit, if he cares for that, as well as no little distinction. The rights are all his. I have, of course, given him every credit, and I'll see he gets it. Most necessary to encourage amateurs, most necessary. The amount of good work lost by not doing so! Simply hopeless! Amateurs are always making discoveries and the professionals are too jealous to let the real finder have the credit."

He swung round in the middle of his stream of high-pitched chatter and struck the door again a couple of sharp raps. There was no reply. No pause came in his flow of one-sided conversation; no sign showed in his beaming face, as he scanned mine or played with an envelope in his hand, that he was impatient, that he was actually pressing to his lair a desperate criminal who was probably lurking within earshot. I do not think he had to keep the mask on by anything which I should have called self-control. All his surface self now *was* the amiable, excited old zany. Only, deep behind any detection, looked out the unsleeping vigilance which was determined that its prey should not escape it. I saw how right he had been not to tell me, an inexperienced actor at best (though I had taken quiet parts at school and once did quite a good Portia), and certainly not incapable of stage-fright on this awkward "appearance," not to let me know in any detail, the part he was to play. All the better could I fall in with my role, which, it was now clear, was to be the quite obviously mystified young man compelled to bring up again this absurdly eccentric old scholar. Collusion between us, not even a hunted murderer could suspect.

Suddenly, in the midst of one of these excited repetitions, he literally shot off at a tangent, skimming away from the door and round the corner of the house. Before I could follow I heard him cry, "Ah, you're here. Of course you would be. There were we, expecting to find you in the house. But you've guessed my news."

At that point I myself reached the corner of the house and could see down the garden. Mr. Mycroft was waving a piece of paper in Heregrove's face—a face in which quite clearly a very dangerous look was simply being forced off by what in any other situation I would have had to call comical dismay. Quite obviously he had thought he was trapped. He had seen us approaching—had lurked in the house and then had stolen out to the back. For what desperate throw I did not like to think, but Mr. Mycroft had been too quick for him, must have heard his careful steps on the path and had run round to meet and balk him. The sun was level, the air already cool, the garden still, the hives silent. The queer, desolate place in that quietude had a strange, resigned beauty, as of someone who has decided that death is coming and who no longer dreads or questions it.

This sense, however, was certainly not in Heregrove's mind. What I can only call a sort of exasperated relief was springing up in him. He could not prevent himself from believing in the story which was being forced on him and in the character of the story-teller, who, even in his play-acting, was so much more powerful than his vain, mimicking, murderous, megalomaniac self.

"Ah," said Mr. Mycroft, wheeling round as I came up, "I have given poor young Mr. Silchester such a time! He's my senior in the village and he said I simply could not go forcing myself on you again. You would call, and then I might return your call. If there was anything pressing I could write. But I simply could not wait. It wasn't fair to you. You must know. The big people hadn't hesitated; had been pressing. 'Why,' I said, 'why, Mr. Silchester, Mr. Heregrove would never forgive me for delay, and rightly, rightly.' Formal courtesy can be real unkindness, when good news is being withheld—simply for punctilio, for nothing else!"

I stood by, the picture of that confusion which I felt, though feeling it for utterly different reasons than Heregrove, when he eyed me, concluded. It was quite safe for me to look at him. I *could* only register what he *must* misinterpret. So I watched his face with a curious sense of my own impropriety, at the horrible incongruousness of the whole scene. I even found myself smiling in a sort of weak, sheepish way, which of course was the most convincing piece of acting possible in the circumstances. Yet it rose in me spontaneously while I watched Heregrove's face change from the desperate look of the hunted to the cruel assurance that he was, again, the hunter; that, far from confronting implacable hounds, he was faced by a couple of insane hares gamboling right up to the place where he, the fox, lay hidden.

By this time Mr. Mycroft had forced his piece of paper, so that Heregrove was actually holding it and being made to read it.

"Directly I got back last night I felt I must tell the big-wigs," ran on Mr. Mycroft. "So, though I dislike long-distance calls, I rang up Miles. He knows I wouldn't do that—at his home, too—unless I had real news. I told him exactly of your find. For, to tell you the truth, Mr. Heregrove, I shall never bring myself to believe that that was chance! I know chance is said to be capable of making monkeys compose all Shakespeare by simply strumming typewriter keys; but I never could believe that, and anyhow, even for that, I understand, it is postulated that they shall have infinite time. Well, well, *we* haven't that," he went on, breathlessly. "Nor did Miles think so. See, he wrote this note and ran out at once and posted it so I should get it this morning. Miles knows! And as he's been so long Secretary, a man in such a position can speak pretty definitely for the Council. He knows their mind and when they haven't one, he is it! And, see what he says."

He went on craning over Heregrove's shrinking arm and tapping the paper with his finger.

" 'Full recognition . . . Not only valuable but important' . . . very scientific that, very. Knows the *£.s.d.* worth of this, but the scientific prestige is, of course, the thing. *Tulpia Heregrovia* will be in all the catalogues in a couple of seasons. You will have name and remuneration. Well, I expect you will value both, and in this case both are comfortably considerable. The Dutch are being forced off our market by these virus restriction regulations. There's a demand now for really new mutations, a demand which makes bulbs fetch really big prices. A daffodil bulb raiser near Hastings had a sport worth £500. Tulips go higher, and once you have one, you may have many, if you have, as it is clear you have, the hand for that kind of thing. You see the Institute offers you all facilities. You know it, no doubt. No better place to work. They have sponsored many a brilliant amateur like you and, if I may so put it, set him up in a highly thriving way. Why I was so precipitate is that the Council meets tomorrow. You see, Miles mentions the date. He feels as I do. At this quarterly meeting they make the grants-in-aid for new research and offer their laboratory equipment and expert assistance, greenhouses, and planting-out plots to selected amateurs. If we can telephone Miles tonight that you accept, it will be a feather in both our caps—to have found a brilliant amateur grower who did not even think of applying to the Society!"

Mr. Mycroft ran off into asteristical chuckles—if I may coin an adjective—beaming alternately at the paper and at Heregrove's face.

"Dear old Miles," he ruminated, while evidently expecting at any moment Heregrove's affirmative. "You have, no doubt, seen that famous sign manual? It can do a lot, oh, quite a lot; though, as I always tell him, it is a hybrid sprung from an arabesque crossed with an anagram, and the only use of it is not to convey a name but to foil a forger. Well, I may telephone, 'yes,' mayn't I?"

Heregrove was obviously completely bewildered. The story, supported by the letter, he could not refute or reasonably doubt. But it was clear to me that though he believed the story, he was determined to refuse the offer, however profitable he felt it might prove and however firm he was convinced that it must be.

"You see, Mr. Mycroft, as I have told you, I am not interested in flowers. I am ready to believe you and Dr. Miles, that I have something valuable here. Perhaps—" (and here I saw lying creep across his face) "perhaps I did not tell you the whole truth last time and I have a certain knowledge and taste for flower breeding. But I cannot leave here or go up to London or attend the Institute. That is quite impossible. I'll sell the plant outright, if we can find an impartial opinion to decide its price. But I have other, more important interests than raising new varieties of plants."

I caught a certain contemptuous defiance and assurance in that last phrase. He was so certain of himself and his security that he was ready to tell us that he had more important work on hand than getting quite a considerable reputation and cash return. He was enjoying, even at a small risk of making us suspicious as to what that interest actually was, the tragic irony of telling us to our faces that killing us was more sport for him and of deeper delight than making new forms of life.

"I am sorry," said Mr. Mycroft, "I am indeed sorry that we cannot persuade you to take this line."

His voice expressed real regret. It convinced Heregrove, but, again, he was correct in judging the *expression* as being sincere, and hopelessly, fatally wrong in estimating the reason for that sadness. He thought he was faced by a fantastic, fanatical fancier, trying, all unconsciously, to make a tiger come into the house and play with a ball of wool. He was, in actual fact, face to face with his judge who was pleading with him to take a last chance—if, as it seemed to me, it was a spurious offer—to escape his doom. It was appallingly thrilling to me, this scene, which, with its tragicomic irony, seemed to me, as I watched it, to be more terrible than any trial scene, when the drymouthed prisoner at the bar sees the judge put on the black cap.

I could not foresee how it was to end in detail. But I could see that, however fantastic the dressing of the parts, perhaps because of that element of fantasy—because the doomed man thought himself to be the perfectly disguised and quite compassionless dealer of our dooms and that the man who pleaded with him could by no possibility be doing what he was actually doing—pleading with a murderer to turn from his way and holding over that murderer his secret and his fate—because the murderer looked with now obvious contempt at the man he was driving to condemn him, thinking that that man, his judge, was simply a helpless old fool and the murderer's victim No. 3. I could see more than the immediate crisis.

Because of this terrible ignorance, this complete, hopeless misapprehension of his situation, the scene suddenly filled me with an overwhelming sense of its general significance. Here in this grotesque play of stubborn misunderstanding, black hardheartedness dooming itself, and mercy pleading, as it only could, and maybe only can, in disguise and under symbols, in some way all our human tragedies, all mankind's doom, seemed to be performed before me at that moment in miniature. I was shaken more deeply than by this one savage and cunning brute's disaster. It shook me because I recognized suddenly, and terribly vividly for the moment, that this situation is in some way what we all confront in life: those people and events which we treat most contemptuously and thoughtlessly are just those which, watching us through their mask of insignificance, plead with us to understand and feel, and failing to impress and win us, have no choice but to condemn us, for we have really condemned ourselves. I own I cannot recapture that feeling, but in honesty I must record these thoughts which then went through my mind.

"Well, well." Mr. Mycroft's crestfallen voice broke a silence which cannot really have been long but which to me seemed to have been indefinite—a queer, timeless interlude between two acts of our dangerous farce. His eyes had been fixed on Heregrove, with an intensity which I could interpret as a supreme interest; scientific curiosity blended with a high compassion, and which Heregrove, as confidently, had to mistake for an unbalanced obsession with some trivial specialty. Heregrove took the first step, however.

"I am busy, gentlemen, and, as I can't agree to your suggestion, I must say good evening."

Then, grudgingly, and not to seem too suspiciously contemptuous, it was clear, he added in a perfunctory voice, "I'm obliged to you for calling my attention to the possibility."

He began to turn away, but quite easily and in character, Mr. Mycroft fell in beside him, ambling along down the garden path, carrying his way and imposing his company with that renewed flow of rapid talk.

"A real disappointment. Perhaps you couldn't accept, I realize. But I know *you* realize it was kindly meant and am sure you are interested in what I shall still call your achievement. Rewards you may neglect, but research, I think, you will permit? Ah, there it is! You will, I know, allow me one more examination. The last was little more than a glance—just enough to make sure, not enough to appreciate. We collectors and breeders, Mr. Heregrove, you cannot imagine how each minute variation and mutational clue thrills us. What the layman hardly remembers—indeed, scarcely notices—thrills us as a new star thrills an astronomer."

We had come abreast of the few tulips which Mr. Mycroft's skill had somehow turned into a pivot on which he made revolve his whole delicate and dangerous operation.

"As a breeder yourself, I need hardly tell you," he continued, addressing Heregrove, who stood by uneasily with obviously rising savage impatience, but unable to see how at that moment he could break away, "I shall take no liberties with your treasure, a treasure no doubt not less valuable than the ever-famous black tulip. But," and Mr. Mycroft bent toward the largest of the blooms, "I know you will permit. . . ."

He paused as though absent-mindedly engrossed in peering into the petals, but really, I could see, to be certain that he had excited and held the cupidity of the man, who, whatever his dreams of avarice and wealth won from murder, was still certainly very hard up. Heregrove, who, it had seemed a moment ago, would break clean away or at least stroll ahead, was caught, coming closer, lured and drawn as a trout is drawn in a curve by the fine line of the dry-fly fisherman, and himself also looking now, rather stupidly, I thought, at the flower.

I think that was the first time that I had realized, while I was up against him, that after all, with his considerable cunning, he was really a stupid man. One had only thought him terrible and all-knowing because one was frightened oneself and so could not put oneself in his shoes. Nearly all murderers, I began to see, are terrible only because we fear them and appear clever only because of the short start which breaking the rules gives them. We begin by thinking they are ordinary persons and won't violate the regulations of the game and so they get a lead for a stroke or two.

"I know you will permit me," Mr. Mycroft absent-mindedly repeated, "to study the plant closely."

Heregrove's eyes went from Mr. Mycroft to the flower and back again. Obviously he was getting every moment more confused. In his muddled mind the notion which seemed to have a small but unworking majority was that Mr. Mycroft was about to snatch the precious bloom from its stem and go skimming down the path with it. I, apparently, was cast by him for the role of the interceptor, who by blundering into the path of pursuit allows the thief to make a clean getaway. Mr. Mycroft added still further to the man's confusion by bending so far forward that he balanced himself by putting his hands behind his back. The rape of the bloom was quite impossible in such a position, a position in which Mr. Mycroft looked like a giant jackdaw as he turned his head and looked up with a keen eye at Heregrove.

"Yes," he said. "As remarkable as I thought.

But the light is failing and the petals are heavily contracted. I have seen enough to memorize the principal features for a brief account—which I shall, of course, submit to you. And, if I might advise, I would suggest that you register your find as soon as possible. If you don't by any chance know the address, I will give it to you as we leave."

This stroke evidently persuaded Heregrove that there was something to be got out of us, at practically no trouble to himself; that we might actually yield a little profit alive before yielding him the experimental interest of our deaths. So Mr. Mycroft prepared his next stroke until nothing could have seemed more natural and unsuspicious.

"The bulb is, of course, the thing, and as no one but ourselves knows about it, it is as safe in the ground as buried treasure. So I know you won't mind, so as to save a second visit to a busy man, if I take the one thing which is needed to make the full description of your wonder—a few grains of its pollen. They can, of course, be of no commercial value and are only of purely scientific interest."

I saw that Heregrove knew enough of flowers to know this to be true and that he thought he had better assent so as to conclude the interview. This would be the quickest way of getting rid of us. He may even have grunted permission. Anyhow, he stood still, looking down while Mr. Mycroft's hands unlocked from behind his back. His right hand was hidden from me, for I was on his left, a few yards nearer the house, and already the light was not of the best. I saw him put something into the bell of the flower and then heard him give a slight exclamation of annoyance.

"It's blocked," I could hear him saying almost to himself. Then, to Heregrove, "These patent pollen-extractors respect the flowers' virginity but I am not sure that the old toothpick with a speck of cotton-wool on the end wasn't better. It was certainly less trouble. These superfine tubes are always getting congested. I must blow it out." He turned and I could see in his hand the flask, the nozzle pointed down. Apparently engrossed solely in cleaning it, in order to make it create a good suction, he proceeded to squeeze the pump again and again. I heard the sharp wheeze and saw the tube, quite accidentally, it seemed, even to me, pointed at Heregrove's legs. Mr. Mycroft still shook the apparatus, almost straightening himself in the effort, and evidently so engrossed in getting it into working order that he did not notice that it was still pointed at Heregrove and now was actually in line with his body. Heregrove stood still, impatiently waiting for what he took to be a small air-suction pump to be brought into working order.

"*There* it is," said Mr. Mycroft, stooping again. "That's right. Now it is drawing. Only the slightest snuff does it, once it's working. Pollens are a wonderful study. Specks almost invisible to the eye, each has its very distinctive shape, telling you what genus it belongs to, giving you the whole history of a plant—indeed, with these wonderful fossil pollens, the whole ancestry of genera and orders of plants. But not the plant's copyright, in this case. So you are safe, Mr. Heregrove, from our taking anything from you even unintentionally. Our task in coming here," he continued, a less rambling manner coming into his speech, "was to make you an offer, an offer, which you, on due consideration, refused."

He straightened up. Suddenly the old flower enthusiast completely dropped from him, as a mound of ivy at a stroke may be stripped off and leave visible a gaunt tower which it has concealed.

"Good night, Mr. Heregrove, good night, and if in the night you should—I have done so myself and have found such thoughts well deserving my prompt action—wake and reconsider your decision, I do pray that you will come straight down to me without a moment's delay. I should really be grateful, more grateful than perhaps I can make you understand, if you could see your way to take the line I have been able to suggest. I know I must seem to you an absurd old man, fanatically fussing about what isn't his business and, you may even think, pleading with sentimental urgency for the protection and preservation of a queer and outwardly not important variety of life's many manifestations and mysterious forms. Is it worth, you think, being so particular? Why trouble to preserve everything that wants to live? Are things so important? Believe me, it is not the cash nor the reputation which I feel to be at stake. All life needs protection, encouragement, defense. We can't be indifferent or ruthless, can we?"

He trailed off rather lamely, and I was glad enough. Heregrove's patience was at an end. No shadow yet passed over his assurance that we were in his power, nor he by any possibility in ours. He turned rudely on his heel.

"I've wasted more time than I can spare," he remarked over his shoulder. "Shut the gate as you go out."

He swung off down the path toward the fields. Mr. Mycroft said nothing. I followed him as he walked swiftly past the house, reached the gate, opened it, carefully relatched it, and went down the road.

Chapter IX

FLY BREAKS FROM WASP

He kept silence until we were at my gate. Then he turned to me.

"I hope you did not mind being likened, together with myself, to a tulip of an odd variety. After all, the greatest poets have thought our lives are closely similar in their fates to the grasses of the field; and we have been asked by a high authority to consider each other, among other reasons, because of the moving, transitory beauty of flower life." Then, more gravely, "I had to give him every chance; even to taking that considerable risk at the end. I had to count on his dismissing as a chance coincidence (though the wise know there is no chance in life) that my concern for the plant's life and his indifference to it, pointed to, was a parable of, his terrible indifference to human life. I hoped this queer illustration might awaken him. It was a last hope. For a moment I suspected that he wondered whether I was aware of how apposite my words were in his case. But he is too sunk in that brutal self-assurance which is the final and fatal ignorance, that ignorance, that ignoring of appeal and warning which the most merciful and wisest of all the religions, Buddhism, rightly calls the chief and the one unforgivable sin. At least in this life. And that is all we poor men of action can provide for. The lesser of two evils here—and the hope that elsewhere, under other conditions, those who have found this life and body only a noose in which their struggles of greed and fear strangle them and make them in their blind strivings only a peril to all near them, may awake to their illusion, it may drop from them like an evil dream and they begin again to live and understand."

He was evidently moved, and though I was naturally disinclined to follow his rather extravagant speculations, I was quite distinctly willing that he should run on. I did not want to be left alone. The tension of action was over. I had come away from the drama. The curtain had gone down on the act. Now we had to wait on Destiny. My mind was being blown about, now that I was having time to reflect. I felt that, left to myself, I should hardly sleep and, if I did, my dreams all too easily might be worse than any wakeful worrying, however weary. I felt that I must retain Mr. Mycroft and keep him in my company by some means. It struck me that he might stay a little longer if I asked him to clear up a few points which in the last few hours I had failed to understand fully. Of course I had followed his main strategy, but certain details of his tactics had escaped me. I was too tired really to be interested, but I saw that by asking him to explain, his delight in showing one how clever he was would keep him hanging about and save me a little longer from the solitude which I now dreaded.

"I didn't quite follow," I said, in as abstract a voice as I could command, "some particulars of your behavior in the garden. Of course I grasped the main drift, but all that play with the paper, the letter, which I suppose must have been a sham?"

"Yet," he replied with a patience which would normally have irritated me but now was a relief, guaranteeing me a little longer human company, "yet you saw every step of those preparations. You saw me go to the door and come back with a piece of letter paper printed with official headings, a piece of official stationery, and you had every reason to arrive by induction at the fact that I had had that piece of stationery specially prepared for the work we had on hand. You then watched me while I took out a similar sheet, but with writing on it and, with the sheet I had had prepared turned upside down, you saw me copy something. Again, what, and what alone, could such an action convey?"

He paused, but I was not trying to think, only to keep his company.

"I gave you," he continued, when he saw that I was going to say nothing, "the full explanation while I talked to Heregrove. My actions could mean only one thing. I was copying, from a letter, which I had had from him, Dr. Miles's signature, and, of course, like all copyists or forgers of signatures or handwriting, I copied it upside down. That is the only safe way of preventing tricks of one's own handwriting from appearing in the letters and words which you wish to render facsimile. I didn't expect that Heregrove would know Miles's signature. But nothing must be left unprovided for and he might have seen it. If he had (for, as I said, that sign-manual is a remarkable exhibition of nervous vigor and display, if not of calligraphy), then my facsimile would have clinched his conviction that we were harmless. Only under a strong glass would suspicion be wakened, for then, as in all such slowly 'drawn' characters, instead of one or two small wobbles appearing at intervals on the dozen or so strokes, there would be visible quite a number of such regularly occurring little jolts in the lines. That fact has often caught forgers. These jolts are the records of the heart-beats. If you take half a minute to copy a signature and only a couple of seconds or so to write it if it is your own, you see, these tell-tale marks, giving your time and showing your amount of labor, must be much more frequent in the copy. But I took care to bring away the letter —you heard me type it after I had signed it—and I shall burn it now when I get home. I must be going. There are a number of such small things to do this evening."

I felt that I must make a straightforward attempt to hold him; just asking questions could no longer stave off my being left alone.

"I wonder," I said hesitatingly, "I wonder whether you would be so kind, Mr. Mycroft, as to stay with me tonight?"

"I am afraid that would not be wise," he answered kindly. "As I have said, I must clear up a few things at home, which you will recall need tidying up."

I understood. There was not merely the letter. The flask was still in his pocket and Mr. Mycroft, believing as he did in Destiny, left nothing to "chance." He hesitated.

"I would ask you to come to my place but, again, the less we are seen about together, the better, at least at present. In a village a recluse cannot change his ways and make friends without people asking why he has done so and even what enmity has driven him to seek allies! After all, do what we will, our neighbors are always forming opinions about us, and if we for a long time do not see any reason why we should care, we may be sure that the stories they tell about us will be more to their fancy than to ours."

"All right," I said, with a sudden, tired petulance. "All right. I am the most exposed. Nearer the danger; next on the list; leave me to face it alone."

All my restraint had gone I could not think where, but as I spoke the very words seemed to carry away that last crust of assurance and restraint. Mr. Mycroft's face was hard to see in the late summer dusk. His face was as difficult to estimate.

"You have gone through your ordeal and now you are in the reaction," said the even tones. "It would be wise not to fall into ignorance about your condition. It was not your normal self which carried you through today. Our lives would have been forfeit if I had taken the risk of depending on such power as you have at your command to make yourself behave reliably. I saw and studied your reaction to benzedrine hydrate. Like many of your type, you are extremely responsive to certain drugs. I therefore gave you temporarily the Batavian bravery which is not yours by nature. Now you must pay the cost in reaction. Perhaps not an exorbitant fee, considering that it is the only one charged for saving your life."

It maddened me that this old man had played with me, treating me as an equal while all the time he was only doping me like a race horse and forcing me into acts which I already saw had made me exchange the *possibility* of a danger, which anyhow was growing less (after all, who knows, as the first attack had failed, I might never be set on again), for a far graver one which well might dog me all my life. And then the complete disregard of my feelings, to speak to me in that insolent way when he owned I was tired out. Not the slightest attempt to make things easy for me, but a lecture which an old, angry schoolmaster might give a child before caning it.

"Good night, Mr. Mycroft," I said, sharply. I left him standing, slammed my gate, got into my house, went straight upstairs, and was safe in my bedroom before the energy given me by my outburst and the relief of being rude had worn off and I felt even worse.

I remembered that I had had no supper and it was quite time for it. But I couldn't even face going down to the larder. I felt that I should see Heregrove's face peering at me through the wire-gauze window. I took a warm bath, but the rushing of the taps made me dread I should not hear if there should come a step on the stairs. At last I was in bed, but if I have ever had a worse night I don't remember it.

When the light came, however, as so often happens, so provokingly, I did fall asleep. I woke, therefore, late, exhausted and vexed at hearing the disturbing noise Alice was making below. She might realize that this morning of all mornings, I reflected, I might be left, as she would say, to sleep it out. And then I realized that she could never know, must never know, must never have a suggestion of a suspicion. I must always be bright and cheerful and on time, for fear she and then others might begin to remark on how changed I was, how moping now: "Looks like he never slept a wink"; "And all since those days when he was all about with that queer Mr. Mycroft"; "Well, birds of a feather . . ."; "An' you know that was exactly the time when he fancied himself into a fit over bees!"

I flung myself out of bed, pounding down heavily on the floor. Alice would thus know I was up and full of energy. I splashed about in the bath—that, too, would show vitality and also give her plenty to do mopping up and polishing down—lack of work makes gossips. Then downstairs, making, I thought, a pretty good entry as an active, rested man, ready to take up his own interests and business and able to tell others to mind theirs.

But Alice was evidently not impressed. In fact, she didn't seem to notice my carefully prepared carriage and poise. She was full of something else and, alas, I knew it, before she began: "Pore"—I must own the "dear" was omitted, but the "pore," like a code-word, told me all. Yes, the milkman, she'd seen him herself as she'd been coming along and it was he who had found Heregrove. Stiff already, halfway up the garden path. Had called "Milk, O," and Mr. Heregrove (disaster, I could not help noticing, had given him a "Mister"), who was always early, hadn't answered. So Alf had thrown a glance up the garden path. Couldn't b'lieve his eyes; why, black he was as the earth he lay on.

"Alice," I said, "would you please make my bedroom now? I may have caught a chill and will probably go back to bed after breakfast."

She left the room with that stiff rapidity which indicates deep offense. I had cut her off retailing first-class news. She, the semi-sacred bearer of almost first-hand evil tidings, was silenced. Well, at least she did not suspect how horribly prepared I had been for her news. I did go back to bed after breakfast. I wanted to lie and think undisturbed. It was clear that Heregrove was dead. I was safe. But the clearer it became that he was gone, the more tenuous seemed the risk which I had run while he was alive and the darker loomed the possible danger which I must now watch rise and hang over me—perhaps never to be dissipated—certainly beyond the power of any private, well-meaning, but really busybodying old gentleman to deliver me from.

About noon there was a ring at the bell. Alice knocked and entered with a look of muted triumph which at once added to my misgivings.

"Please, sir, Bob Withers, the policeman, would like to see you for a moment."

I went downstairs, my heart sinking at every step. The village constable is not an awe-inspiring functionary. This one was as nervous as I, which was saying a great deal then. He had taken off his helmet and was passing it from one hand to the other, as though it were hot. He certainly was. After our mumbled good-mornings, he broke his message. It was about that there Mr. Heregrove. Perhaps I'd heard, perhaps not, but he was in the mortuary and as (here was the point) I had last been seen with him, it was wondered whether I could 'elp showing 'ow 'e came to his Hend.

It was preposterous that they should come to me when Mr. Mycroft had actually planned the visit and—but I must not ever even let my mind finish that sentence! Anyhow, I simply could not go through this alone. Only a little while ago in this abominable affair, I had foreseen myself driven into the lunatic asylum for life; now even such an end seemed an escape, a refuge, considering the alternative place where it seemed that a single slip of the tongue, a single thought aloud, would land me with—the best I could hope for, a life sentence!

My mind moved quickly, but I think my tongue was even quicker, for I heard myself saying, "Mr. Mycroft, of Waller's Lane, and I did visit Mr. Heregrove last evening. He had supplied us with honey. We spent a few minutes with him in his garden. He seemed quite well then."

"Oh, if Mr. Mycroft was with you, sir, perhaps you'd come along of me while I get 'is statement, too."

I saw that was quite the best thing in the bad circumstances and agreed. However much I did not want to see the old man, a time had come when he must carry us out of our common difficulty. It was his, really, more than mine, and anything which that cunning old brain planned to cover its own self and tracks would cover mine too.

On reaching his house we found him on his lawn. I felt as though he had been expecting us. He certainly showed no surprise, and nodded silently when Bob Withers told him that Heregrove had been discovered dead. We did not know whether he had heard the news before or not, and when asked for a statement, he simply remarked that he had seen the deceased the evening before and thought he seemed well.

Then he added, "I know, constable, you would like us to go with you to the magistrate to whom this case has been reported. Is it Colonel Treaves? Yes, I thought it was likely. He is generally on the spot. I can come along now."

He picked up his hat which was lying on a chair near him and without a word to me walked along with Withers, I at the constable's other side.

Ten minutes took us to the magistrate's house. We were shown in at once to his study. A lean, athletic man of about sixty, I judged, he rose from his chair as we entered and put out his hand to Mr.

Mycroft—he only nodded to me—saying, "It is kind of you to come over so promptly, sir. Always better to have a direct talk than get statements. But didn't want to trouble you, were you busy at the moment. I was informed that Mr. Silchester here and someone who accompanied him—and I suppose you were that person—last saw this man Heregrove alive?"

"Yes," replied Mr. Mycroft. "We visited him, for he had supplied both Mr. Silchester and myself with honey."

"Well, you probably know," remarked Colonel Treaves, "his bees caught him—like Acteon, wasn't it, and his hounds, what?"

"Do you mean to say that he was attacked by his own hives?" asked Mr. Mycroft, with convincing interest.

"Well, I don't think there can be a shadow of doubt on that point. You may not know—think it was before you came to the village—but his wretched wife died the same way and the coroner then told him to have the bees destroyed. He said he would, too. He either disobeyed the court's order or the Heregroves must have had something about them that bees can't stand. Never liked either of them myself—and the man! Well, *nisi bonum.* He was certainly stung to death; the body is swollen and black as a ripe mulberry."

That made me feel quite sick.

"All I would like to ask you gentlemen," he continued, "is whether, when you called on him, he seemed well and in a normal frame of mind?"

"Oh, yes," replied Mr. Mycroft. "I thought he was a queer customer and he was obviously a bit of a recluse, but he was certainly sane and healthy when we saw him, wasn't he, Mr. Silchester?"

"Oh, quite, quite," was all I could say, and all it seemed that I was expected to say.

"We took a turn or two with him in his garden," went on Mr. Mycroft. "It was impossible to judge on what terms he was with his bees, for they had retired for the evening. Perhaps we ran more of a risk than seemed apparent by calling on a man who was in such peril."

"Perhaps so, perhaps so," answered the colonel. "You never can tell. Bees are certainly queer beasts. In India I have known fifty people going down a lane. Suddenly from the sky will drop what seems a cloud of dust. It's a swarm of small, savage, forest bees. The swarm'll slump on one poor fellow, leaving unvisited everyone else. If there isn't a pool handy for him to be flung into, he may be dead in a few minutes and swollen like Heregrove's body. Some people say it's smell, but I don't believe anyone really knows. In India we say Bismillah—Allah's Will, and, after all, everything ends there finally."

Chapter X

AS WE WERE?

AND THERE, to my surprise, our fantastic mixture of adventure and persecution, of gratuitous attack and undetected counterattack, of scientific planning and Wild-West justice, came to an end. As suddenly as this typhoon had blown across the quiet track of my life, as suddenly it dropped. I live now in what I can only call a suspicious hush. We attended, more as honored guests than as summoned witnesses, the coroner's court. The coroner took the same view as the magistrate, with the added animus of, "Serve him right, disobeying my instructions." He also ordered, with the pointless pleasure to himself of just exercising authority, but to my keen though concealed delight, the destruction of the Heregrove hives.

As we left the court, Mr. Mycroft, who had, till now, abstained from speaking to me, strolled along at my side until the small crowd had dissipated itself. Then he remarked quietly, "Unpleasant associations are not the best foundation for an acquaintance, but an adventure shared sometimes is. I realize that you have had many shocks during these days and that once or twice I had to push you harder than you found agreeable, if we were not to be caught in the Caudine Forks, with results which would have been disastrous. I think now, however, you will realize that the wood is behind, the pursuers are scattered."

He seemed complacently assured. Perhaps it was the wish to find some adequate excuse for resenting his complacency and coolness, neither of which I could myself feel, that made me reply, "But what about our actual position? After all, whether we were really in such grave danger as we thought we can never be certain."

He looked as though he were going to interrupt, but I was determined to have my say out. Not only had I been treated like a child throughout this whole affair, as though I could not be expected to have a clear judgment on matters which did concern me more than anyone else, but when we went to see Colonel Treaves I had been hurt at the way both men had behaved, again, as though I were a child. Now I would assert my rights and he should hear my considered opinion.

"What we can be sure of," I continued, "is that we threw off what we took to be our pursuer by throwing him to his death. He may, at the worst, have intended to do no more than scare us. We certainly killed him. It is, I know, a nasty word, but it is better out and off my mind."

Mr. Mycroft allowed himself a short sigh.

"No law in any country," he said, slowly, "and I know something of the rules which men have made in attempting to save the innocent and helpless from the ruthless strong—no law would have given a cruel and calculating murderer the chances I gave him or would authorize the running of those risks which I took in order that he should have every opportunity, in fact, even a bribe, to turn him from his course. He was, you will remember, already a murderer and I was prepared, rather than take the line which all human justice has decreed, to treat his horrible, patiently-worked-out crime as a slip, as a bygone to be treated as something which had not taken place and not—as, alas, mankind is right in judging—as the fruit, and only the first fruit, of a long-nourished and now richly yielding root of evil.

The Romans with their legal minds were correct. I quoted the Latin judgment that day when we were discussing the evolution of venom in animals. It is certainly as true of us: *Nemo repente fuit turpissimus,* the murderer ripens more slowly than the saint—both are not accidents but achievements. Heregrove could not turn from his way, at the point where he crossed our path, even if the past were to be blotted out and the present to offer him a prize if he would only abstain from turning bloodshed into a business. He needed someone to bring home his crime to him, and that we could not do. We could only offer to deflect him. He would have gone on the same way in other fields."

I broke in there. "But your offer was a sham!" I exclaimed.

It was the only time I saw Mr. Mycroft nearly angry. His face didn't change color or the expression alter, but I caught sight of some slight alteration in his eyes which I own made me positively scared. Somehow I had never thought of him as someone who might be fearsome. Helpful, amusing, irritating, managing, boring—yes, all these things, but never formidable. Yet that gleam—I can't call it a flash—was certainly very disconcerting. It seemed not so much as though one were looking at a man whom I was trying to provoke and who I suddenly realized, might strike back at me, but rather that I was suddenly looking through a port-hole, through the eyeholes of a mask out onto something as cold, impersonal, and indifferent as an ice-berg emerging from a mist and seen bearing down on my ship.

"I mean," I rather stammered, "the letter was a fake. There was no offer for Heregrove, as a matter of fact, to accept?"

"You think then, that I did not really plead with that wretched man, caught in the toils of his own evil thought which had set until it became evil deed? Did not seek to make it possible, if it might be, that he should break out of his self-made trap? That I simply mocked him, pretending to hold out a helping hand and point a way out of the false dilemma he had caught and impaled his conscience on: 'Murder or starve'? That I put on a piece of play-acting the better to amuse myself and you with an exposition of the skill with which I had trapped and deluded a fellow creature, even though he was our enemy and mankind's?"

"Well," I protested, with my heart, I must confess, beating quite unpleasantly, for he was driving me onto the defensive when I had been sure I had a case against him. "Well, he could not have taken an opportunity which actually was quite fictitious."

"The offer," replied Mr. Mycroft gravely, "had to be—as are all life's offers—in a form in which he could believe and could, if there were no wish in him to serve Life and not Death, refuse. Do you suppose he would have been more likely and more able to accept had I said, 'You are, of course, a murderer whom the law cannot convict or even recognize. You are now planning to murder us and God knows how many more. If you will abstain I will pay you three or four hundred pounds and get you out of your financial embarrassments'?"

Mr. Mycroft waited a moment, but I was dogged.

He was certainly putting his dreadful and very awkward deed in a very clear light.

"Still," I replied, "I am sorry to appear stubborn and to be precise. The real fact that remains, when all is said, is that he could not have been given the alternative to which you verbally urged him."

"I am sorry," answered Mr. Mycroft—and I was alarmed to hear come into his voice actually something of that very same tone which I had heard when Heregrove refused the offer which we were now discussing and Mr. Mycroft used those same words with a curious, ominous conviction.

"Mr. Silchester, I am sorry that we have seen so much of each other and you are yet capable of thinking that I would lie to a man in mortal peril, offering him a spurious escape. As I have said, I could not tell him from whence in actual fact would come the resources which I guaranteed for his deliverance, would he but accept and turn, if only for a moment, from his way. We were his prey. Even if he could have faced the fact that we knew he was a murderer, he could not have believed in our *bona fides*. Man imputes himself. The fact that we were in possession of such knowledge he could only interpret as his nature could understand—that we would for the rest of his life do as he would do to such another who should fall into *his* power—blackmail him. Add to that fact that we come to offer him money, not immediately to extort it, and he can only be the more certain that here is a doubly cunning trap, beside which blackmail is aboveboard business. No; the disguise of form was essential for *his* one chance of safety, even more than for ours. But the substance, the firm offer was there.

"Because I have learned that expression of emotion is mere sentimentality, Mr. Silchester, I must ask you to believe that that certainly does not mean that I am without feelings, still less coolly irresponsible. By every possible means, I was determined to rescue that murderer and to spare him from the fate he was drawing on himself, if I could. I was as set on that as on saving *your* life at the cost of compelling you more than once to act, when you would much have preferred to procrastinate and dally.

"The offer made Heregrove was a real one. I had arranged that, should he go to the address I would name and which I should see he would think was that of the registered offices and the legal adviser of the Society where he would receive his grant-in-aid, he should be received by a long-trusted solicitor friend of mine, given £200 with his ticket and any other expenses paid to any place he should choose to go, and with a firm offer of another £200 when he arrived at his destination. My friend was to be sufficiently (but not too fully) seized of the case, being told that Heregrove was a blackmailer against whom a charge would be difficult to present and who should be given this chance of clearing out. This friend of mine, as have many fine solicitors in the course of their practice, has dealt across his quiet, brief-covered table with more than one such dangerous man in this effective way. What the large forceps of the law cannot pick up and must leave lurking under our feet, often the steady hand of a wise solicitor can lay hold of and drop out of the window. The plan would have worked, had Heregrove assented, for I have so broken the news—if I may use that phrase—to several unconvictable criminals, that I knew their record and would give them one more chance, and quite a number have made good. But Heregrove was by nature not one of these. I repeat the question, and must ask you to reply, 'Was not he self-doomed?' "

He was right, just, and generous, I had to allow,

but still I could say nothing. This last display of such courageous, thoughtful efficiency, I know, ought to have swept away my last timid considerations and have made me apologize as handsomely as possible, urged by a not less generous trustfulness. Awkward as it was for me to recognize, I could no longer avoid seeing—indeed, I had forced him to prove to me—that he was a wonder, a man ahead of his age in skill and also in justice. His attempt to save the murderer was no less wonderful, patient, and daring than his success in saving the designated murderee.

Yet, somehow, the very supermanly quality about it all put me off, daunted me. I don't want to have to live with mental or moral geniuses. They may always be expecting you to be heroic, and he certainly had landed me in a position which might quite easily at any moment become dangerous.

"I don't know," I said. "I really don't know. I shall never be sure. Right or wrong, the thing, as it has actually happened, or been made to happen, will always be hanging over me. It might at any time come out, and then in spite of all the fine motives which I don't doubt prompted the actual deed, where shall we be, what will be my position?"

He looked at me again as though he were making up his mind whether to say more or no, whether to tell me something further or to leave things as they were. As I did not believe that there was any answer to my question and so felt pretty hopeless about the whole matter, I really didn't care whether he went on trying to console me, or left me alone. Evidently he decided, in the end, that he could do something for me.

"As to your position," he said, "I think I can reassure you by telling you one more thing. It, too, is a secret. Mycroft is only one of my family names."

I could not help wondering, on hearing this opening, to what fresh freak of vanity I was to be introduced. This sudden emphasis upon himself showed how his egotism had to peep out even when the matter in hand was my safety. How could his family names matter to me, much less protect me? We were not in the Middle Ages and he a big baron.

"I have used Mycroft," he complacently continued, "because my full name was once pretty widely known, and I wanted, when I retired, to be quiet and unmolested. You have been served, and, I may add, if you so wish, you are still under the protection" (the man seemed quite self-assured that I should so wish)—"your case still has as its defense—"

There! I have forgotten the name he gave himself. It was something not unlike Mycroft—Mycroft and then another word, a short one, I think. But I was too bothered to memorize still another set of names, especially as it was quite clear that they could really be no defense to me. I had known him as Mycroft, had known both his capacities and limitations. I could not see how the one would become the greater or the other less by calling him by another name. As Mycroft we had struggled along together through this upsetting business. I suppose he or Destiny had got me out, but only at the cost of leaving me under an abiding apprehension. I could not feel that there was anything magical in either of his names. It came over me again, and this time with complete conviction, after seeing this last proof of what he thought to be adequate defense, that if I were ever to be safe I would be safer and more comfortable by myself.

"Thank you, Mr. ——"; I think I called him by the new name he evidently so much prized, but which awoke no meaning or association in my mind. "Thank you. I am obliged, and you must forgive what may seem perhaps an apparent churlishness. But I think I will again retire into my shell."

He took my breakaway, I am glad to say, with composure. We were parting without a scene, and I was grateful for that.

"Very well," was all he said.

I thought, then, that perhaps I ought not to leave it quite there but might give some sort of explanation of my action, of why I could not think our continued alliance would add to my safety.

"You see," I said, "now that I do know your real name, I have to own I have never heard of you before."

Then, I must own, he looked amazed—perhaps the only time I had seen him profoundly surprised, and he turned away without a word.

For a moment I felt an immense relief. The feeling grew. I had not anyone to interfere with me any more. I was once more my own master. The relief lasted a couple of days. Then the other darker shadow, the shadow of apprehension, that I was an accessory to murder, if only to counter-murder, settled down on me. That is why I have been driven to write all this. If the worst comes to the worst, after all, Mycroft did it, not I.

REPLY PAID

TO CHRISTOPHER WOOD

ANOTHER BOTTLE FROM

THE SAME BIN

Chapter I

WHEN the flyer, whose flight is not through air, sitting in his cage stretches his wing toward the left.' I've read it a hundred times. It just gets under my skin —not being able to figure it out. I put it away in a drawer after the first few dozen attempts. Then suddenly I'd be sure I had it, snatch it out and start counting the letters, changing them, trying all the tricks. Even the simple plan of alternate letters, you see, begins by promising something—'We tel'—just tantalizing enough to make one wonder if one wasn't on the trail and some further variation of the letters might yield a straight message. Why bother? Well, because that's only a beginning. Because after that picturesque gibberish there's something that follows.

Yes, it isn't plain sailing, even then, but it's all the better reading for the eye which has picked it out. There is something here, mark my word, though the casual reader would have dismissed it when he saw it in the paper in which I found it printed, as first to last all one piece—either crook's code or just one of those pieces of perverse silliness with which the over-leisured amuse themselves. So, you see, I need a start. Now do you tumble to what I'm driving at? I need to get my hand under the edge of this code. I'm asking for bearings."

The man who had shot all this off at me hadn't given me a chance to reply. He hadn't even sat down on coming into my office. He hadn't even waited for my secretary to show him in or even knocked! What he had said should show I had little chance of understanding what it was that he wanted. So I spent my time, while he ran on, in looking at him. Though his tone was pretty excited, it didn't seem to fit his appearance—a quiet sort of little fellow. Big head with black hair which I suppose he rumpled whenever he was puzzled; nervous hands with those knobbly wrists which look as though constant twisting of them had made them get enlarged. He'd a knobbly nose, too.

I had just reached that point in my inventory, when, without waiting for me to give my guess as to his line, he continued: "You're a decoder, aren't you?"

"Well, yes," I answered. "Codes have always interested me."

"I know; I've followed you. That's part of modern prospecting."

"What do you mean?" I asked.

"Like everything else today, it has to be teamwork and, worse, teamwork against time. Name your fee and I'll tell you what I want. I've got to find this thing and I've got to find it fast. I think you're my man, and if you're not—well, I reckon I've only time to make one mistake and then this chance may be gone for good."

"Mr. ——?"

"Intil," he added.

"Mr. Intil," I said, "you have come to call on me without making an appointment. What exactly do you want me to do?"

"I've said; I've told you," he replied. "Have I come to the wrong place? You *are* Mr. Silchester, aren't you?" Taking my nod for enough, he rushed on: "First you wrote that little book on cross-word puzzles and their setting and solving. Then you made that study of the Roger Bacon stuff—whether there was really hidden Greek information in the twirls and twists of the tails of the letters in the actual manuscripts. And I know you're the author of a dozen articles in *The Decoder*. I know your style even when you don't sign. Yes, I know about your lot. You're just like the chess-champions—they can look and be as dumb as a dolt till you put a board in front of them. Then they just go through it like a water-diviner following a buried drain."

I let his compliments rest. "You want me to decode that piece of paper?"

"Of course! What have I been saying since I came here!"

"Then hand it to me."

He hesitated, then put it carefully down on my desk in front of me. The passage which he had copied out, maybe from a press-cutting, ran as he had read it.

"It's usual 'agony column' stuff," I was remarking, when he cut in, "That's the disguise—put your sense and your secret where only fools look for fun."

"Mr. Intil," I said decisively, "please sit down! As you know my work, you know my method is aboveboard as chess."

He drew a chair and sat on the edge, watching his beloved copy.

I went on, "You know, therefore, that there are a number of basic tests to make. Anyone can work these out, but, as in chess, some people have a natural knack for eliminating at once the blind alleys."

While I was saying this, I ran my eye through and across the lines. The born decoder, I've found, keeps his mind open, taking in the whole text. Then, if there is a clue, suddenly he'll see certain letters almost as though they were of slightly different type. These letters generally give him a start on the message. None of us, I believe, ever gets the code message straight off —it glimmers through too briefly and is gone. Any strain or pull and it sinks away. But that diagnostic dip has shown if there is a message, running through and under the disguised surface-sentence—just as a chess master sees there's a middle game and a "mate" standing out, if he can keep the path clear among all the possible other moves that lead nowhere.

But nothing came through to me—not a hint. To stop strain and keep fresh I raised my eyes. My visitor was looking to and from the paper, glancing at it and then at me.

"Haven't you gotten a clue?" he questioned.

I said nothing, but again gave that quick total glance. Then I was sure. Of one thing there could be no further question.

"Mr. Intil, this is no word code."

"How do you know?"

"Why do you come to me unless you think I know?"

"But you haven't tried!"

"That's just what I have done."

"You haven't worked at it!"

"How do you work to find if a bell is sound? Ring it. I've rung this. There's no letter code here."

Before I could say more he'd reached over and pocketed his precious paper. "Then you're just a fraud," he snapped, "Mr. Sydney Silchester!"

Yes, I'm Mr. Sydney Silchester, whose sole distinctions were that he liked honey and being left alone, and so, quietly living on the rim of life, was nearly pushed over the edge by his honey dealer. How, then, did I get into the position where Mr. Intil thought it worth while to call on me, and I to receive him? I suppose that concerted bee-drive must have roused me. They say ordinary bee stings are good for rheumatism. All I know is that after that escape I'd had from being stung to death, I found myself unable to settle down again.

Not that I moved at once. Like those prickly sea-urchins, I'd not only kept people at bay, I'd actually sunk right in and become embedded. But though my daily round went on outwardly undisturbed, my mind was steadily dragging its anchors. The first sign was that I began quite methodically to do puzzles. Indeed, I've several times since noted, that may be the first symptom that a mind is going to come out of its shell. It's a sort of attempt, I believe, still to keep asleep. We feel that if we thought about anything real it would be too hard and sharp. So when our minds want to think on anything for long and tire of being distracted, we try to put them off with artificial problems. We give them knots which people have tied on purpose for them to untie—for fear they might otherwise start untying the knots which would let the cat out of the bag. Then, of course, as all puzzles go according to plan, it gets more amusing to be the knot-tier. That leads straight on to teaching knot-tiers, to writing guides to disguises. When you reach that point, you begin to look about for more material to work on. You want a lock meant to resist any but the secret key. You become a decoder.

So, by steps almost unnoticed by myself, I found that my mind had bored its way out of the shell I had built for myself. I was still careful enough not to make actual local acquaintances, but I did enter into correspondence on my special subject and became, in that special world, fairly well known. Much of my work began to lie across the Atlantic. Finally there came a conference in the States which I was asked to attend. There I should meet several experts in this queer little field in which my mind seemed determined to stay and feed, and, maybe, grow. The long and the short of it was that I crossed the Atlantic and, as one might say, while my back was turned Europe blew up.

Several riddle-colleagues pointed out that as money could no longer reach me I had better make some; what is more, that I could quite easily. So, with a little good-will, or interest, or whatever one calls it, I found myself with a small office and quite a considerable and growing mail-and-personal-visit business. I had been advised to settle in some place where money was freely made, where odd fancies could be cultivated and odd interests congregated. Those three requirements are not frequently found combined. Maybe no place in the world combines them to quite the degree to which they may be found in the wide district called Los Angeles—" 'The largest city limits in the world,' and certainly an urbanity which tolerates more variety than any other town," I was told. So to "L.A." I went and found the forecast accurate. I became quite a busy man, seeing sometimes as many as a dozen or even a score of clients a day and keeping an amanuensis who was mistress of my mails and helped me with postal inquiries and the placing of my interviews, and so on.

Perhaps some people will say that this sort of work not only improved my prospects but also mended my manners. I don't know about that. All I know is that, if a client interested me, I would stand a great deal more from him (both for the fee and also for the interest) than I'd ever have stood from anyone before. That is why I stood Mr. Intil's onrushes. Why I did more is perhaps harder to explain. In itself, maybe, it was a hunch. Perhaps it was being rapped on my professional knuckles—perhaps the fact that we who use *both* hunch and analysis are always a little ashamed of our "starter," prevented me from bowing my rude intruder out. He was pretty certainly a bit crazy, but then what about many of one's clients, what about my own profession and the way my gift works? And he certainly somehow held my attention.

"No," I said, "not a fraud. For, first, you have been asked no fee and, secondly, instead of disguising from you my primary method and wasting your time, I told you straight away I couldn't help."

His reply was odd: "But who else can I go to—I must——"

"All right," I said. "You've seen my method. I tell you there's no code here that a word-decoder could unravel. But I'll tell you something positive as well, which you'll believe because you already believe it. Though there is no regular code here, I am equally sure, as sure as you are, that there is a real meaning and message in this. It's not a cipher but it is a cryptic communication." I didn't add, "And something which I believe is a bit uncanny," but that was the reason for my next remark—that, and the equally queer feeling that having shown that my method was, at least to start with, un-rational—a hunch—I must justify the hunch method.

My visitor was standing up already, uneasily eyeing me.

"Mr. Intil, if you are as anxious about this as you

appear, I will give you one more piece of advice. I've let you see my main method—hunch or 'integral thought' or what you will. That's the way, after all, any artist immediately estimates whether a picture is really a work of art. First he gives a look, and knows if it is a masterpiece, in a split second. Then, if it is, he settles down and gets the reasons."

His only reply to this very reasonable approach was, "Can you, then, tell me someone who can see what this is?" He held his precious slip of paper up in his thumb and finger.

"That was precisely what I was going to offer."

"Well, you're honest, in a way," he ruminated. "All right."

So in ten minutes we found ourselves walking together.

"I'm taking you," I said, "to a friend who goes one step further than I along the 'traceless track' of detection."

I'd first met Miss Brown at the Decoders' Conference when I had first come to the country. We included there a pretty wide spectrum—from the infrared of the physicists and the chemists with their X-rays and their reactions and their analyses, right up to the ultraviolet of dowsers, psychometrists, and the like. Miss Brown was well up in the "u.v." But she was uncommonly sane in spite of it and I'd seen her do some decoding which went far beyond my gift. It was chancy, her work, of course—all hunch and no deduction. But it was, after all, only an extension or extravagance of mine. And, as I couldn't help feeling there was something in Intil's scrap of paper, I wanted to see whether her queer gift would confirm my suspicion.

"If there is something in your find, the person I'm taking you to will scent it, if anyone can," I told Intil as we went along. For I have found that if you can build up confidence you often get results you never would otherwise. A discouraged detector, I believe, couldn't see a haystack. Mr. Intil, however, made no answer to my attempt to excite his interest but scanned with some doubt the small front of Cortegna Cottage, when we stood waiting in front of its door.

"Miss Brown," I said, when the owner had answered the bell, "you told me last week to come along this afternoon. I've brought a visitor who, I think, will interest you."

Miss Brown, like most experts, was as noncommittal, as "out of character," as one could wish. I saw Intil look at her and I saw that he saw exactly nothing. "Medium height, eyes light, hair brown, complexion fair, age—youngish." Yes, she was the living image of those descriptions which the poor police have to issue but which of course never lead to an identification—or worse, can lead to almost anyone being identified.

Miss Brown, intelligent, healthy, no doubt "compos" in every way, nevertheless was one of those creations which leave no clear impression—perhaps because she looked in every respect so normal that you couldn't recall her. There was no apparently outstanding feature, still less abnormality, by which to catch hold of her and pin her to your memory. Hers was one of those nice, accentless faces no cartoonist can caricature. That, I need hardly say, was her crowning equipment.

"Come in," she said. And, of course, the voice was as clear, kindly, and commonplace as her looks and was equally hard to "place" and memorize. You couldn't have mimicked her. Her tone woke no reaction. I led Mr. Intil into her sitting room. She followed, and kept going that pointless conversation which is so much more noncommittal, so much more silent than silence. For, after all those gentle clichés—not only is not a single phrase of them recollectable, it is even hard to remember that they filled any time or what one did as the soothing sound went on. Perhaps it is all part of that mysterious by-play which conjurors, I believe, call "patter"—a kind of verbal massage under which stroking and patting our suspicions lie down and our clenched minds open up. So she settled us in, and when we were seated, in order to inform Mr. Intil what she was, I began to inform her of what he had told me.

"My visitor here brought me an interesting specimen to classify. . . ."

"He failed outright. Now, can you make anything of it?" Mr. Intil had hopped up and, while still poking in his pocket for his precious scrap of paper, advanced on Miss Brown.

"No," she said, laughing, getting up, too, but moving away from him. "No, Mr. Silchester can't have told you anything about my method if you think my looking at your evidence would help to find out its secret."

"Are you collaborating lunatics?" he exclaimed. "One says, 'There's no code, but come along and we'll show it to my female colleague'; and she remarks 'No, please don't show me anything!' "

Quite unruffled, Miss Brown continued, "If you will sit down and keep whatever is your clue in your pocket for the present, I'll explain, or perhaps it would be better if Mr. Silchester did."

Mr. Intil didn't sit down, but he did take his finger from his vest pocket and turn on me.

"Miss Brown," I said, "goes beyond me. I confess I have to use hunch to start me, but I then, as I've told you, have to work out the sequel by sheer searching, going up every likely turning. I make a first glance and then know if there's a case for further searching—a sort of grand jury stunt. Miss Brown *doesn't* glance and then gets the picture."

"You've brought me to a medium, then!"

"Oh, labels are libels! A medium's only someone who has a gift he doesn't understand. Miss Brown is as much a medium as a water-diviner is."

"Um, I've seen them work. Yes, and saw one who could spot metals—saw him do it. Yes, that's within the range of the new prospecting, I guess."

"All right, then," I said, for the little fool was exasperating me, all the more as I couldn't get out of my head that he had hold of a secret something that could be highly interesting—otherwise I'd have turned him out before this. "All right, then don't be a fool. Did you ever see a dowser who could work and find water if you kept on cutting capers round him and flipping his rod out of his hands?"

He didn't answer, but went back to his chair.

Miss Brown looked across to me. "Shall we now begin?"

"I think we can get going now," I answered.

I drew down the shades while she turned her chair to the fire. It was a warm day but she added a few small logs to what had been a low smolder and in a few minutes the hearth blazed. The room quickly became uncomfortably hot. Mr. Intil panted and started to mop himself with his handkerchief, but, thank heaven, kept quiet. Miss Brown, however, her chair drawn up to the fire, spread a handkerchief over her face. And in this attitude, beloved of old gentlemen on winter afternoons, brisk Miss Brown, on this hot, bright day, fell into stertorous slumber. I don't like the adjective—it's journalistic, alliterative, and unladylike—utterly unsuited to be applied to a neat young female. But this is reporting—not an essay on style and in taste or vice versa. Miss Brown went heavily to sleep. She breathed to the very limit of not-snoring, and then, as do heavy sleepers, she twitched and jerked her body, muttered a little, gave a small gasp or two and stirred, rousing herself. The handkerchief fell off her face. She was in trance. She was, evidently, already carrying on a rapid, affable conversation but not troubling to enunciate her words—it was a sort of impressionist sound-picture of a conversation. The tone was clear enough now but the sense was sadly to seek. And then, as in those old days, when we used to develop our own negatives, the photo in the red light used to begin to emerge and finally, out of the yellow fog, there was visible unmistakable detail, so in her "blur" of patter clear sentences began to emerge.

It was, of course, the usual stuff. "Oh, there are such a *lot* of people here" (grammar is seldom a prophetess' strong point). "Oh, there are so many persons who are just longing to say something. There's an old man, such a lovely beard, he says his name is—oh, it's something that has to do with something you put round the cord that brings the electric light, something black and sticky, a kind of tape."

"Yes," I interrupted, for I knew from past experience that this "fishing" and splashing in the telepathic shallows could be abbreviated, "Yes, that's very good, very good, and you see, don't you, as well as the insulation tape—for that's not quite right, but you're getting warmer—another object? Don't you see a cash-register and something being put into it?"

"What are you doing?" almost hissed our clue-seeker. "Are you trying to spoil everything?"

His whisper was drowned in the trance-personality's gleeful cackle. "Why, if that isn't it, just as you say, Mr. Sydney!"

"Good again, Elsie, you've got our visitor's name and he's ever so grateful for your bringing his dear old father along."

"My father!" came a sotto voce snort. "With a beard! Here, stop this fooling!"

But now, of course the sitting was hatching out.

"Mr. Intil, Elsie, has in his pocket, you know, a weeny piece of writing. He is so puzzled what it means."

Like a shot the mawkish voice answered, "It's a cage. I see a cage."

"It's a frame-up!" I heard Intil snort.

"But what an odd cage. It's round—quite round—and where's the bird? Oh, I see, but he's so thin I nearly missed him."

I could hear Intil draw himself up out of slumped contempt to attention.

"So thin?" I queried. "A queer bird, then?"

"Oh, *so* queer, I don't think, Mr. Sydney, I'd very much like to have him for a pet. His beak, it's so very sharp, and he has it right against the bar of the cage, this side." The medium waved her right hand. "He *could* peck."

"Is he pecking?"

"No, he's not pecking, leastways not now. He's sitting right in the middle of his cage."

"Yet his beak is touching the bars—is he trying to get out?"

"No, no, his beak and head are out that way 'cos that's the way he goes—all pollies do—when they want to stretch their wing in a cage. He's sort of yawning with his wing—he's stretching it."

Intil was completely quiet now.

"Elsie, can you tell us anything more about this bird? It interests us quite a great deal."

"Well, I've told you, he's so thin he's all point," the "control" giggled childishly.

"All point?"

"Thin as a rail, thin as a pointer."

"Pointers aren't very thin, Elsie. They aren't birds. They point at birds—they're dogs."

"Oh, don't be so stupid, Mr. Sydney."

"Oh, you mean a pointing rod," I remedied my false cast.

"Of course I do. Well, I don't think there's much more about him. He's so thin. . . ."

The voice began to trail off. This was bad. If the "secondary personality" lost interest and dropped the thread, it would probably never catch on again, and here we were right on our clue if only it could be held. The next remark confirmed my fears.

"Oh, the dear old gentleman does so want to speak. He wants me to stop looking at that silly polly."

I heard Intil breathe a devout "damn."

"Oh, it's naughty to swear!" said our exasperatingly infantile informant.

"Yes, dear Elsie," I hurried into the gap. "Of course it is, and of course if we swear the pretty polly might pick up the naughty words."

That served its turn: it revived the interest of the imbecile but gifted layer of Miss Brown's mind in the subject we needed its odd gift to be turned on. "I wonder," said Elsie with provoking slowness, "I wonder whether that polly *could* learn to speak? I rather think not, Mr. Sydney. It has such a tiny head and such an unparroty beak. It just pushes it on one side as far as it can to let its wing stretch just as far as *it* can the other way."

Well, here we were back again at our caged bird, though we didn't know anything more, really, than we knew when we started.

"Will he let you scratch his head?" I volunteered in desperation to keep "Elsie's" idiotic interest on the clue. Again the cast got a rise.

"If I thought he wouldn't peck—perhaps, perhaps —it would be easy." Evidentiy the dream mind was seeing some sort of cage and bird. "It would be easy 'cos the cage—what a queer cage. Why does he stay in it?"

"What's queer about it?"

"Why it's a sort of circle thing with no bars, only this hoop thing."

"Well, many pollies are sometimes kept in cages like that. It gives them more freedom."

"Yes, but they have a perch, don't they?"

"Of course; hasn't this polly?"

"I can't see what he's sitting on. Now, isn't that queer!" (Thank heaven, the infantile curiosity of the subconscious was now roused.) "But I can see one sort of thing—a number of them. Round the hoop of his cage are little knots." The medium's hand rose. "There's one, quite bunchy, at the top." Her finger pointed up. "And another, not so bunchy, right under the polly." She pointed down. "And just under the point of his bill is another, rather a squiggle than a bunch, that one. Oh, I can see them so clearly. There are twelve of them." Then, with a sudden failing of interest: "But I don't know what they are. And it's such a silly bird sitting there yawning on and on, with his wing. Oh, it makes me yawn. Oh, I'm so tired and sleepy. No, I don't want you; go away."

And, suiting the deed to the word, the medium yawned widely and then began to breathe deeply once more. She settled back in her chair. Her head fell to one side. It wasn't much that she had brought through, but it was something definite. I felt pretty certain that as far as it went I had caught an answer. Intil stirred; I waved him back to his chair.

"But—" he began.

"Be silent," I hissed, so successfully that he was.

Miss Brown began to stir. She muttered, almost whimpered. A questioning note came into this low whinny. Her body again jerked once or twice. She cleared her throat, sighed and sat up.

"Well," she said, "how long was I away?"

"A short spell."

"Did anything worth having come through?"

"Yes, quite enough."

"What!" interrupted Intil. "You give her a lot

of hints and helps and then she rambles on, romancing all about birds all made up. . . ."

"Mr. Intil!" I shot in. "If you're as stupid as you're ill-mannered you'll never find anything."

"Oh, it's easy to be abusive when you want to cover up failure," he sneered, and so got right under my skin. I hadn't intended to tell the boorish fool anything. But the sitting *had* been a good one, and I had got from it my clue, I felt sure.

"There you're wrong, as usual. How you can be a prospector and so blind beats me!"

"Oh, so you, who couldn't discover anything yourself, you're going to flatter yourself now by pretending that you understand this mummery!"

I rose and opened the door. "Please leave the house! And let me tell you that the answer to your question *was* given! The initial passage of your message really runs: 'When the hands of the clock stand at twenty minutes to three!' "

I meant to surprise him but never expected quite such a success. He looked at me for a moment, then turned and literally ran through the door, through the hallway, plucked open the hall door, and slammed it behind him. And we heard his feet as he scampered off down the road.

Chapter II

I WENT back to Miss Brown.

"Don't tell me what happened," were her first words. "That little fellow interested me. There's more in this, I fancy, than my 'control' gets at. If we find ourselves back on this trail again it will be all the better for me to know as little as possible, or my surface mind will interfere."

I knew her method—the rule of all authentic "mediums." Otherwise the surface mind interferes, tries to make premature sense of what has come through from deeper levels and all's spoilt.

"Well, you know," I answered, "that you did get onto the question which was bothering our queer client;

you know that you gave me the answer which earlier, on my own, I failed to give him and that he was—well, one can't say content, but obviously struck with our joint effort."

She smiled, "You'll let me know, then, if he turns up again. There's certainly some very odd business he's mixed in."

My own hunch told me with just as much emphasis that this was so. I took leave of Miss Brown, telling her I'd certainly call her should our queer little whale that had just sounded, spout again in our waters.

Several months passed, however, and I recalled Mr. Intil only when on my half-yearly check-up of my case-file I saw the one-line entry under the IN's—"Intil: by self, no result: collab: Miss Brown. Clue found. n.f." The case had evidently closed itself and when n.f. comes at the end it is usually a signal of finality. For n.f. means "no fee."

My work all that time was routine stuff. Once or twice my mind did go back to the man but mainly because I was still feeling a distinct pleasure at the way that I had caught hold of the clue which Miss Brown threw out in trance. And soon that little success was buried under others. I enjoyed my life in my quiet way. Puzzles that pay—it was a lucky stroke that put me where I could still amuse myself and at the same time earn a living.

Then one day I was going down the street with my mind, I believe, actually turning over the solution of a set riddle when automatically I stepped aside, not looking up, so as not to disturb my train of thought. Someone was in my path, I was vaguely aware. But when I shifted, the figure I wasn't looking at, by trying to avoid, shifted too. I looked up pettishly. It was one of those silly little subconscious duels in courtesy—each of us was giving way so spontaneously to the other that we managed to keep in each other's way. That pedestrian double-stutter has always seemed to me the best demonstration of the need for intelligent selfishness. Then I saw that I was mistaken. My vis-à-vis was not trying to get out of my way but into it. He was a man, distinguished I am sure he knew himself to be. He was old: white but very—not erect, there was nothing military about him—but limber, I think, is the word, lithely loose—odd, I thought, in an old man. He had heightened his remarkable appearance by a short, sharp white beard. I looked then at his eyes. They were on mine. He was blocking my path deliberately. But where had I seen those eyes? Surely one knew them, and surely, as he was not a hold-up man, surely he must think he knew me, too?

"Mr. Silchester," he said.

"Mr. Mycroft!" I exclaimed. "Where did you drop from?"

"As you see—" what a familiar opening, always asking me to see what was of course obvious and of course overlooked by me—"I am on your track."

Somehow the tone he used, and the slight start I had had, put me on the defensive. After all, I was not the helpless fellow that I had been. I was a bit of a detector, now, as well as he.

"Mr. Mycroft," I said, pulling myself together, "I know when we last parted I was, perhaps, a little discourteous in my wish to get back to my retired life. Well, Life has kicked me out of my soft seat and somehow I have managed to fall on my feet or to get a footing."

"Yes, yes," he said, with that knowing lightness. "I can now call you confrere, and," he added rallyingly, "if occasionally I fall into the old habit of saying, 'Don't you see?' take it as a compliment, not as a criticism."

"A compliment?"

"Because we are now colleagues."

Yes, of course, as of yore I was flattered. So when he went on to ask whether I could spare him half an hour, for he had an interesting story to tell me and stood in great need of my advice, I asked him along to my place.

"Yes," he commented as we entered, "yes, if you will forgive a personal remark, I thought when we last met that if Fate really made you fly you had feathers which would carry you. I'd heard of your work and seen it. The flair will out, Mr. Silchester. But now you will want to know why particularly I am today your client. I am out here on a very peculiar trail. I don't think any of us detectives"—I felt like Queen Victoria when Disraeli, fresh from the success of his histrionic novels, remarked to the authoress of *Leaves from a Highland Journal*, "We authors, Ma'm"—"have ever been given, if I may use a modern phrase, a stranger assignment. I want to be quite frank with you, Mr. Silchester, and so will start at once by saying that I cannot be wholly. This is, I say it advisedly, the biggest and," he paused as though reckoning, "yes, the most curiously and many-facetedly dangerous thing I have ever been on."

That second part of the description, I own, made my rising curiosity begin to yield before the cautious sense of letting sleeping snakes sleep on.

He continued, though, "But one thing we can be open about. It is the point on which you can help me. It is the reason why I came to ask your aid. There is a man somewhere in this quarter of the world that a few men who are respected or to be reckoned with in most quarters of the world—and for whom I am working on this assignment—want above everyone else to be able to contact. And the last man to see and talk with that man was, Mr. Silchester, you. Do you know, and if so, will you trust me with the information as to where a Mr. Intil may be?"

I couldn't help feeling a certain trust in the old fellow. With that trust there sprang up, too, a sudden revived interest in that queer little broken-off piece of a case. For answer, then, I stretched over to my filing cabinet, took out the slip I'd looked up a few weeks before, and placed it on my desk in front of Mr. Mycroft.

"Clue found," mused the old sleuth.

I told him the story frankly, though I was a bit nervous as to what he'd think of the Miss Brown incident.

His reply, "Neat, very neat. And we'd all do better if we used the subconscious more," pleased me. "I wonder whether I would have pounced on that clue without a collaborator?" he added. "Some time, if you would be so good, I'd be obliged if you would introduce an old-fashioned reasoner to one who has evidently made flair really follow a special scent.

"And now to our muttons. There is one thing I may and indeed must tell you about Mr. Intil. You two collaborators were right in sensing something of more than routine interest in him; and what you have told me puts me greatly in your debt. It falls into place: we are a step on. Briefly, as you may well have guessed, though Intil may be more than a little mad and—well, I'll leave my further suppositions for the present—he *is* on the track of something big. Perhaps I should be more exact and give you a better sense, too, of the bigness of his quarry if I say he has tracked, I believe, someone who has a trail leading to something beside which pirate gold is nursery stuff. Now that's all I ought to say. To repeat your quotation from Miss Brown, 'One can easily know too much to find out more.' But I want to be quite definite as far as we have gone. I am asking you, Mr. Silchester, to come in with me on this hunt."

He saw my hesitation. "Frankly, I need your help. You have met Intil and you could point him out. I don't think he suspects you. I do think he suspects me—or that someone from my clients is after him. He is one of those who prefer business by mail and no personal contacts with those who might surmise the full nature of that which he believes he has to sell."

I was still humming when he added, "Honestly, I would not have asked your help before you became what you are now, a trained researcher, and, of course, neither would you have accepted." (Oh, that frank, sensible, kindly flattery!) "Besides, and another of course, as we are both professional men I can speak openly to you. Secretive men are not unseldom trustworthy. I don't want to make one unnecessary mystification. I want to tell you that our game is not only dangerous. It is dangerous enough, no doubt, but it is far more valuable than it is risky. As I have said, and said advisedly, it is a treasure hunt, and a treasure hunt beside which Potosi silver, Inca gold, and Eldorado itself, all rolled into one, would be so much waste-product."

Even when I had mistrusted Mr. Mycroft I had to own that he was highly accurate. This must be a serious proposition and, equally, it must be a very big one. My old caution still retracted me.

"Why me?" I questioned. "You want a bloodhound, not a truffle-hound, for your job."

He smiled, "I'll do the heavy old dog on the trail if you will play the dog that smells the hidden root. We'll need both types, I believe."

"My work . . ." I was putting up my last defense. I felt the humor of it, I who had idled nearly the whole of my life. But leaving my office was leaving now my home and my hobby—and my livelihood.

"If this search reaches its goal you won't have to think too much about costs. I'm making you a straight offer. I am a businessman and have made businesslike arrangements with my clients. Money is really no matter to them—nor need it be. I am prepared to offer you one-third of the fee that I am promised. I am not being quixotic in this. It is one of such a size that it does not mean much to a man of my age."

I knew there was really little use opposing Mr. Mycroft once he wanted a thing. I realized also that he made ample provision for whomever he employed. Business was, I knew also, just now none too brisk with me. Of course I yielded.

As he left he remarked, "May we meet tomorrow morning? I have a few preliminary inquiries to make and then we can start on our hunt."

"But," I said, "I have no idea where Intil is. I have seen him only once—months ago, and then he literally fled."

"Oh," replied Mr. Mycroft, "it is not quite so blind a chase as that. I have more than a suspicion along what track our man is moving and so where we may hope to catch a glimpse of him if we can recognize him when he passes. That is where you can yield your first important service. And these facts rule our rendezvous. You know the little Church of the Angels after which this amazing but not specifically angelic town takes its name?"

"The little old building by the square?"

"Very well; be in there at ten-thirty tomorrow morning. And now, if there is a back way out of your office, it would be no harm if I took it. Blessed are the inconspicuous, for they shall not be asked why they were where they were."

I showed him how he could get to the back of the quiet block in which my small office stood, and I had hardly finished pointing out the way before he was gone.

At ten-thirty the next morning—I was always punctual even when leisured—I slipped into the shabby little church. Dark and poor inside, it was an excellent meeting place. A few Mexicans were at their prayers. Every now and then someone looked in but, finding nothing to see, went out. It positively smelled commonplace and unsuspicious. When my eyes were used to the rather dismal dusk—from the glare outside—I found myself a seat and after a few minutes someone sat down beside me.

"When I leave here," said a whisper which just reached my ear, "don't follow for two minutes. Then go to the stone seat at the other side of the square. As you approach it you will see a man wearing a wide-brimmed straw hat and big sun-glasses move off, going toward the city's center. Don't come up with him—follow him till he goes into a drugstore. Go in and take a seat near the window. Immediately opposite the drugstore is a shop with scientific instruments in it. Keep your eye on that. It is a big shop and plenty of people go into it. Should you see Mr. I., put your hand up to the back of your coat collar as though you were adjusting it. Then go back to your office and I'll call you."

That became my drill for some days. I never sighted Intil, though I watched until my neck had a crick in it from looking sideways. After some two hours Mr. Mycroft would walk out and I would follow at a respectful distance. After the first day, the first and second acts were omitted, the meeting in the church and the trailing from the square, but the watch in the drugstore seemed all the longer for that. I forget how many times we had gone through this ritual—I up in the window and Mr. Mycroft, in true spider fashion watching his web in the background, when on getting off duty and meeting in my office I asked him why he thought that Intil would ever turn up and, if so, why at that spot and time.

"It's a guess-deduction," he said, "like most detection. But part of the reasoning is evident enough. I don't want to irritate you as I used. I know you have sharpened your powers of observation. But you have not as yet given them a cutting edge in the direction of criminal detection. So have patience with me. I believe we are right over the hole our big fish will visit and one day he'll slip along about the hour of our vigil."

His assurance kept me going, especially when, at the

end of the first fortnight, I think it was, as we met in my office after the usual blank watch, Mr. Mycroft produced a check—quite a surprisingly large one. He did the whole thing in that quick, businesslike way which makes one feel one isn't just being paid. Here, anyhow, were results. He must think, and those who employed him, whoever they were, that there was a big fish to be landed, if they were so generous with the ground-bait.

Then one day while I was scanning in a routine way the customers going in and out of the store opposite my coffee-bar coign, I saw a man coming out carrying a largish case. He was dressed in leather jerkin, "blue jeans," and cactus boots, and under his big hat I thought I saw even a bit of whisker on his face. It was the typical turn-out of the High Sierra hiker, a uniform without which nowadays an ordinary businessman would no sooner go calling on the Desert and the Mountains than a New Yorker would be married without wearing a high hat. The man turned quickly down the street, and then something about his walk—I put my hand to the back of my collar and saw, in the glass facing me, Mr. Mycroft move quickly out of the door and across the street. For a moment I watched the two wide-brimmed hats, drawing closer together in the street crowd. Then a streetcar came between and both were lost.

I went back to my office and waited. Finally I did a little routine work. I had already told my typist secretary, whose efficiency was disguised under an appearance made up to establish the right to be called Miss Delamere, that she needn't wait. I had myself decided to stay on only another half-hour. Then Mr. Mycroft walked in. He looked pretty tired, I thought.

"We've got him and lost him," were his first words. "You were right, I'm sure. That was the man we want, Intil. And we'll get him yet. But he's left town."

"Then how do you expect to get him?" I asked, perhaps a little irritated. "This is a very big country, Mr. Mycroft and, hereabouts, an empty one."

"That is why," he replied, "trailing will be easier."

"But he could hide out anywhere for, literally, a thousand miles."

My acquaintance with the huge Southwest, though slight, made me feel that I must impress my superior knowledge on a fellow countryman who, as it were, had maybe only just stepped out from the close, inch-measured confinements of our native isle.

"That man of ours," said the old fellow, "isn't hiding out. He's going to a hiding place, maybe, but not to hide himself. All right, I'll give you some proof to go on. Why did we watch that instrument store all these days and why for just those hours? Have you ever heard of the Etvos Balance? It was the first and father of a number of superfine detectors. There are the electromagnetic detectors which are so sensitive to electric currents that they can record an addition to the general earth-current when they are above streams, above water running at great depths, water which is showing that it is in touch with ore because a current is being so given off. There are the gravimetric detectors which will show the presence of a mass of ore or a coal seam a thousand and more feet down, by the slight change in the gravitation-field made by the buried mass which weighs a little more—or less—than the main mass of rock around it."

I hadn't heard of these super-gadgets and didn't very much want to. To hurry on the story, I asked, "Granted that Intil was buying one of these, why should he not get it at any hour of the day?" "That's why," said my old dominie, the "step-by-step" and "you mustn't be in a hurry" lecturer coming back on him, "that is why you must first understand the nature of these new detectors. Some people think that instruments supersede men. That is just the reverse of the truth. The finer the instrument, the more skilled must be the user. Indeed, some of these machines are almost human in their delicacy and intuitive power. Some are too sensitive, like great scholars, to work save at night; and one of these superfine gravimetric instruments has actually taken its own initiative in discovery and found things which we had never asked it to find, for we never knew they were to be found."

"Yes, yes," I said. "But what about Intil?"

He chuckled. "We have time, Mr. Silchester. Let an old man refresh and unbend his mind by glorifying his profession. 'What a piece of work is man.' I have had so often to look at him misusing his gifts and all toiled and snarled because he let the net of his own cunning (a noble word once) wrap him round. Let me stretch up my mind and give thanks for an intelligence which is so clean and clear and lovely in its instruments."

The outburst did touch me. After all, the real detective, I realized, how often he must despair as to whether in all this coil and riddle, cross-hatched and double-crossed, there can be any sense, any drift, any goal.

"I see you relent. Will you go a step further? Will you be British with me and have some real China tea?" He drew from his pocket a small pouch. "I carry always a little Ichang with me. Tri-methyl-xanthine—that is the tonic for detective minds. Alcohol for obvious action; caffeine for common council; theine for thought."

I boiled some water and soon we were more at our ease than any other drink can make the high-strung.

As he sipped his cup Mr. Mycroft went on, "You'll

see quite soon why all this has to do with Intil and why we can, in consequence, let him have a little rope. As I've said, there's an instrument so sensitive that it has discovered something about which we only know that this instrument records it! So superfine that it will only work at night (seeking the night's screening out of the day's magnetic disturbances), it won't work even all night. In the middle, generally somewhere about the witching hour of one A.M. it just gives a series of, at present, indecipherable signals. Why? We don't know. All we can think is that at that hour in the unseen world around us, some force or tide goes by. This may be a wave from the new ocean of discovery, breaking on the narrow, land-locked beaches of our senses. Its bearing on Intil and us"—I own I looked my relief over my cup—"is that such instruments, I need hardly tell you after that, have to be learnt. Beside some of them a violin is obvious.

"Salesmanship in this department has to be scholarship. In brief, that instrument store, as you must have gathered, stocks all geological prospecting instruments. This great state of California is a state founded on minerals, from gold to oil. The ordinary gear can be sold straight away without directions. But the latest scientific instruments must be demonstrated. When I came here to track Intil, the first thing I did, of course, was to find the first and finest geological detector instrument store. I discovered that they had had an inquiry for a very peculiar instrument, one which has only of late been on the geological market, a detector specifically for radioactive ores. Fortunately, they had not as yet received one from the scientific instrument manufacturers. But they had that week received an advice, from what is here called the East, that it was about to be dispatched. At the same time I discovered, to my relief on your behalf, that the only man who could demonstrate the finest instruments they stocked attended only for a couple of hours every morning. They pay him to be on duty for a few 'advanced' customers who will want this advanced stuff. His own principal job is in a natural history museum.

"I was therefore as certain as I needed to be that Intil would go to that shop at that hour. He did; he took delivery of the instrument and had it demonstrated to him the day we saw him. Further, I trailed him to the railway depot, saw him take ticket and where to, and that he did get on the train. Then I went back to the instrument store and had a friendly word with the manager, who asked me to call in three days' time, for he hoped to have another example of the 'balance' in stock by then. It was kind of him to wish to show me the instrument, but I had to say that I'd have to come in later. For in three days' time you and I, Mr. Silchester, should leave the city behind. With your leave, we are bound for the wilderness—the trackless desert."

"To find a man when you only know the station he's getting off at, or, maybe, only changing trains?" I protested.

"No, no, I have my clues and have made some plans. Will you come?"

I felt none too sure, but I did say yes and we parted.

Chapter III

"THE train doesn't go till two P.M.," said Mr. Mycroft as he came into my office when I was cleaning up things preparatory, as he warned me, to perhaps a fortnight's absence. "But we have some shopping to do. And do you mind if I still behave with a certain secrecy? Do you mind putting yourself in my hands to that degree—so as not to ask questions?"

A slight cloud of irritation, I know, crossed my mind. Was the old man just putting it on, putting me in my place, or was it really necessary? Well, I'd give him the benefit of the doubt. He handed me a list of things he wanted bought—the usual stuff for a hiking trip—sleeping sacks, camp-cooking kit, some food purchases, etc.

"Meet me," he said, "in the railway waiting hall at one forty-five," and I trotted off obediently enough.

His bundle, when we met, was smaller than mine. I felt I had done the major labor. When we were in the train, which was largely empty, he unpacked and rearranged part of it. I remember that I caught sight of very heavy waterproof gloves.

"I thought," I said, "we were going to the desert? It's cold often at night, but this isn't the season when we'll have even a shower, or find a hole with any water in it."

He looked up. "A shower?" he said. "A gusher, then, maybe?"

I felt the remark might be aimed at my talkativeness. It hurt me and I resolved I would ask the old man no questions, not even when we should arrive, wherever it might be.

We rumbled on. I read. Night came. We slept. He read too. Well, I could keep up silence quite as well as he. The next day also began to wear. I was then idly looking out over a landscape which now had become nothing but a huge-scale chart of geology. The train had paused—it was a pausing train, falling into meditations in places which seemed made for that and nothing else. This pause place was precisely like the last half-dozen. But Mr. Mycroft got up.

"We are getting out here," he said.

True to my resolve not to ask questions, if he wished to be noncommittal, I looked out and down from the carriage window. A small shack was standing quite close to the line. Already my packages were being unloaded. Outside we stepped into a heat which made me for a moment cease to look and only feel. The huge landscape, with its unscaled perspectives, seemed much more like a close, suffocating room, than the air-conditioned train we had just left. This large black cylinder of civilization, within which we had been introduced into this inhuman desert world, now snorted, jerked itself violently out of its temporary torpor, gave a sad wail and drew off. We might have been marooned on the moon, at full-moon midday. I'd tried to give Mr. Mycroft the impression that I knew this country. But in fact I had never been actually dipped into the full desert before. I had just passed through it in the train, which is really like taking a short trip in a submarine—you peer out into another element but you are never actually in touch with it. And of course I had made a trip or two in favorable weather to one or two of the desert parks. Now, I felt I was far from home.

Mr. Mycroft was, however, in careful conversation with a man who had emerged from the shadow of the shack. As I, having pulled myself together, came up to him, he turned to me.

"Mr. Silchester, this is Mr. Kerson," and, the introduction over, "Step one is taken, and, as far as I can judge, in the right direction. Now for step two."

He, Kerson, and I, when I saw their drift, lugged our parcels in the heat and glare to the other side of the shack. There a car was waiting. By now the train had diminished to a black spot with a dark blur above it, both shrinking as you watched. How one used to hate soot and smoke and soot-stained iron. Yet now that I was surrounded by a world of hard clear color —an earth of fawn-yellow, framed by mountains of amethyst and lapis and shut in by a sky of unflawed sapphire—I looked longingly after the one rapidly shrinking stain on the whole vast landscape. Now nothing was left but the frail parallels of the tracks stretching away until they became a fine black thread—all that united us with anything human.

"Everything's in," said Mr. Mycroft's voice; and, irritatedly ashamed that I hadn't helped, and at my own misgivings toward the desert, I followed him into the car.

"Where are we going?" I could not help asking. For now I noticed that there was no road and we were pointed away from the railway line.

"Mr. Kerson is right," Mr. Mycroft replied. "The surface is excellent and he tells me that it is so for many miles. We shall be running along the edges and floors of a chain of dried-up lakes."

The heat was terrific, but after the first shock of it —like standing in front of an open oven—I found that I began to adapt. It was absolutely dry and that, I understand, keeps you going, though, I must say, after a while, I began to feel round the nose and lips rather like a lizard. I don't know how far we drove; pretty fast going it was, on those flat floors of hard sand. At last I noticed the shadows rimming hills or mountains (you couldn't judge their scale without a living thing to help the eye form a judgment) beginning to make big bays of blue cut out of the fawn-yellow. As we crossed the next rib of rougher ground, which separated these fossil lakes, I heard Kerson say to Mr. Mycroft, "Back of that tumble of stone to the left I've made a dump."

We drove up to it. He switched off the engine, and a silence, which one guessed had hung above our little buzz of self-made sound, suddenly swooped. I suppose it wasn't more than a few seconds, for neither Mr. Mycroft nor Kerson—a man who looked as desiccated as the desert itself—seemed to pause. They got out and I followed. It seemed a second step out and down—the first out of the train, and now out into something more distant and deeper. After a few steps Kerson turned sharp to the left and disappeared. So clear was the air in that place that he might have stepped right through the flat painted sheet of scenery which seemed to have no depth. When I came up I saw that there was quite a fair-sized ravine at one's feet; but, though it was some fifty yards across, one had, till one stood on the brink, no idea that there was this gap in the earth. Under some huge boulders which crested the rim was a cave into which Kerson had gone. Inside were set out some stores and it looked as comfortable as a log cabin—more so, for it was cool and spacious. Our guide set about getting supper ready.

"Come with me, Mr. Silchester," said Mr. Mycroft. "We'll cover up the car and bring in the luggage." I followed him out. While we carried out these details he said, "Kerson is one of my trade, gone eremite. The tracker, of course, is the prehistoric detective. This man has a small trading-post some fifty miles from here for serving the Indians—we're not far from a big reservation. As soon as I had made my preliminary studies for this case—with which I need not bother you now—I knew that I would have to keep an eye on the desert. You could tell me, I soon learned, of Mr. Intil himself; but someone else I should need to tell me of his goal."

"It's a pretty large target."

"But marvelously clear and empty."

"Still, here a man could be lost for good and no one know."

"Yes, he might be lost; but I'd take a large wager that though all this seems so vast and empty, some eye, though it might not see the moment of his perishing, would have noted him going to his doom. The Indians are natural watchers, onlookers. They won't interfere, if they can help it. They won't even tell what they have seen, unless there seems good reason. But one of them will have seen. Of his nature, he cannot help noticing. He doesn't like strangers, still less trespassers. So he'll generally leave them alone even when they have got themselves *in extremis*."

"But has Kerson any news of our man?" I asked a little impatiently.

"I'd have hardly brought us out here, if he hadn't."

We had finished shifting our baggage and as we passed behind the boulders and picked our way into the cave, Mr. Mycroft spoke to Kerson, who was sitting on the smooth earth floor cooking with a pressure stove.

"Would you please repeat to us two your record of the stranger's moves three days ago?"

Without turning from his work and in a flat drawl the trader recited, as though he were reading off a ship's log, "Blue Feather saw man with two burros—he may have gotten 'em off that old prospector Sanderson. *He* used to be all over this once. Not been seen for quite a while now—perhaps he's lying up somewhere. Being Scotch, off and on he takes a rest just on 'Scotch.' Blue Feather watched burros and man 'way along this trail. They went on from here quite a bit. 'Course that outfit (if he can keep not too far from water and knows his trails) can go from here to Canada. We'll be able to follow the start anyhow. Blue Feather says they're clear a good way on from this."

Mr. Mycroft made no comment, but started getting coffee ready on another stove. As I was, I supposed, meant to fit in, I unrolled our bedding and spread it on the broad sill or platform which ran on either side of the cave. When I turned, Kerson was forking out fried bacon and eggs onto battered tin plates and Mr. Mycroft had collected an equally weather-beaten fleet of mugs. The fact that the dinner service looked like the salvage from a refuse heap did not "put me off my victuals." The smell was excellent and I was hungry in that rare air. What made me feel, if not distaste, at least a slight hesitation over this highly fragrant meal was its main setting. Through the cave's mouth one saw—as it seemed, almost close enough to be touched—a mountain of solid amethyst. It looked as though it were made of one immense crystal, too smooth and steep ever to be climbed. The sun had sunk on the other side of it, but one felt that one ought to be able to see the level rays, dyed purple, pouring through the wall of rock, so glasslike it appeared to be. Above the knifelike edge of the summit-ridge the sky went up in bands of orange, lemon, green, to blue and purple-violet that was almost indigo. Right down into the green belt the embroidery of first-magnitude constellations was already visible, a stitching of gold. Somehow eating one's fill—and I was ready for it—and that utterly serene emptiness didn't seem to go together.

"The coffee's ready," I heard Mr. Mycroft say, however, and once I had started drinking and eating my queer scruple left me.

Yet when we had cleared up—Kerson had already rolled himself up; Mr. Mycroft was also laid out, only making some notes by an electric torch—I took one more look at our super-surroundings. The sky was now all indigo, but so dense with stars that it seemed hard to believe that there could be much space in that cosmic blizzard of suns. Overhead in a complete arch they had become a belt of luminous mist—one was looking up into the Galaxy, the disk and wheel of our own island universe. There seemed no air. The stars stood right on the edge of the mountain range one fronted, as clearly as they stood right up above one's head. Every moment, like distant lighthouses, they blinked down behind this sharp western wall, while another watcher flashed up from behind the eastern range. Suddenly starting out of the dark a meteor made a perfect curve of light, left a faint glow for as long, and vanished.

"That's one of our clues," said Mr. Mycroft's low voice at my shoulder. "Don't think, Mr. Silchester, because we are after a man and two asses in this immense wilderness—'All geology by day, all astronomy by night,' as Mr. Priestley put it succinctly—that we have got things completely out of proportion. Literally, we too follow a star, so real that I'd rather follow it than hitch my wagon to it. Further, and, indeed, more to the point, what we are searching for and what we are attempting to prevent going wrong if we can prevent it, is something which links us with the nature of things. Go to bed, Mr. Silchester, and sleep well. The 'eternal silences' need not 'affright' us, for, if we choose, we can speak what they would say."

What all that rhetoric meant *I* was at a loss to say. But I felt that the old man felt he had a goal worth getting at and saw his way to get there. And certainly I began to feel rapidly that nothing now could be better than sleep. I slipped into my sack and was gone before I could turn over.

The other two had already begun to get breakfast ready before I woke—woke with an appetite that saw no reason for not eating everything it was offered, however fine the view. Mr. Mycroft and Kerson had evidently already made their plans. They had assembled the baggage we were to take with us. So, when I had eaten heartily, I sat outside admiring the view which was, in the early morning light and cool, not so fine as the evening before but perhaps even more attractive. I began to feel that the desert and myself might get along. There was a light air moving; the sun was low enough to cast plenty of shadows which brought into relief all the scarps and colored rocks. The place was more a fantastic garden, hereabouts, than a desert. In the crannies of the colored and carved stones grew, I now noticed, queer little plants which almost seemed stone, carved into stout leaves and stalks. I thought, "It only needs an animal or two to make a perfect composition of its sort," and at that moment out scampered a lithe gray creature rather like an elongated squirrel. With a quick scurry it was over a boulder and onto the ground again. I waited still, watching its easy movements. It was making for a small piece of crust I had thrown down a couple of yards away. It darted out and caught hold of the bread, then looked round, giving the food a relishing bite or two—and was knocked into a small bundle of bleeding fur. My left ear was singing as though it had been boxed. I swung round. Kerson was standing a few feet back, his automatic in his hand.

"You brute!" I exclaimed hotly. I was startled, and shocked, too, at this cool killing. I turned and bent over the poor little corpse, the bread still in its teeth.

"Don't touch it," said Mr. Mycroft's voice; "otherwise its blood may be literally and mortally on your hands. We're not so far from Tulare County, now sadly famous as the spot where tularemia was first noted, though it's spread now for thousands of miles. If you have a small cut on your hand and the animal's blood meets yours you're in for it."

I shrank back. In the desert, the sterile desert, still deadly infection dogging one!

Kerson added carelessly, "Don't want those little brutes all over our stuff. Tularemia's not so bad, for it's only in the blood. But a ranger told me other day the gophers and ground squirrels have plague now through them. Get bitten by one of their fleas and you're worse off than if a rattler bit you."

I drew back even farther—already I could see with disgust a little procession of brown dots moving off the still gray fur.

"They won't settle on you," said Kerson offhandedly, "unless they have to. But if those fleas were all over the cave, like as not one would bite you casually like and whatever his notion for doing so, you'd be a casualty." He chuckled at his unpleasant pun. "No, if one kills 'em at sight and leaves 'em to dry, one's fairly safe. The mischief would be if ever anthrax got among 'em. A ranger did tell me, not long back, he thought he'd seen a case of that among these damned rodents. But of course he just poured gasoline on the body and cremated it. He wasn't going to risk a post-mortem."

We finished our final arrangements and went off in silence. I was upset and sat without speaking a word. We followed the edge of the next dried lake floor and could go at a fair pace, for always, like a neat stitching in the selvage of hard level sand, just before it broke into a fringe of pebbles and rocks, ran a precisely indented pattern. When we first sighted it, Mr. Mycroft and Kerson got down. I followed.

I heard Kerson say, "They'll remain sometimes for years." Mr. Mycroft replied, "In the Bactrian desert Aurel Stein, the explorer, visiting a site he'd gone to a few years before, saw a track of a man and dog going in front of him. It was his own years'-old trail."

"These are fresh, though; look at the edges. Bet Blue Feather meant this chap."

We climbed into the car again and purred along while the tracks went uncoiling ahead of us. Round headland after headland we went, where once, I suppose, tree-crowned knolls had been reflected in still cool water—a painful thought to some pioneer. Then suddenly my reflections and perhaps, I thought, Mr. Mycroft's hopes were cut short. The lake floor of hard sand ended—we had reached its upper shore.

"This is the last of the chain," said Kerson. "It's no use trailing like this any further. There isn't any more sand, only rocks and scree."

Mr. Mycroft didn't seem much downcast. "We've been lucky, with your aid, to have made such a good start. I think we'll reconnoiter a little further on foot and look round the countryside. If you will leave some of the provisions here I don't think we'll need anything else, and if you come back for us to this spot in the evening we will plan our walk to meet you at this spot."

"O.K." was the only answer, and in a few minutes even the sound of the car was lost as it rounded one of the rock promontories. We were sounding a new deep of solitude.

"Now for some real detection," was, however, Mr. Mycroft's reaction. "That breast-high scent is all right for those who want only a morning gallop but not for true hunting." He went to where the eight little indentions and the two broader prints left the sand and passed up onto the shingle. Once or twice he cast his eye, turning his head on one side. "It's fortunate," he said, "that the sun isn't yet very high. Look, you can just see in the shingle the hint of a trail."

So, stooping and starting, we covered, I suppose, the best part of a mile. The lake, evidently, long before it dried up, had had a shallow end of pebble beach on which the waves broke on rough days, making a rough foreshore. It was exhausting going, for the sun was getting up, the surface was unpleasant walking, and we were at an altitude which already made me feel more out of condition than perhaps I actually was. All this made, perhaps I need hardly say, little, if any, impression on my companion. The trail was everything. He made two concessions only to climate and environment: strong leather boots and a light, big-brimmed hat.

"Why," I asked, mainly to break the silence and gain a pause in our scurry forward, "why didn't we bring the baggage?" Besides, then we would have had to have a burro, and being able to hold onto one then, seemed to me, would be a great relief.

"We won't want our gear yet," he said. "This is a trial cast." After another half-dozen quizzes and scurries forward, he stopped. "The sun's getting to be no use."

"You mean it's getting to be a confounded nuisance!"

"Oh, this isn't heat," he smiled. "We'd have to go on if it were only that. There's not enough oblique shadow to show the tracks in the shingle now."

He looked round him and then, very much like an old but lively goat, began to scramble up a huge boulder which lay in the shingle, thrown there, I suppose, by some earthquake. He saw handholds and footings in it as shrewdly as he had seen in the shingle the faint blurred traces of the ten footsteps which we were pursuing. Gently and without strain, he worked his way up until he stood on the top, some twenty feet above my head. Taking small binoculars from his pocket, he swept the desolation ahead. In a couple of minutes more he was beside me again.

"You sometimes can find a lost track again if you can get a little above it. Fifty feet above water you'll see much deeper and clearer than when looking down immediately above the surface. I think I can see how the trail goes over the further shingle and I'm pretty certain that on beyond, on another sand stretch, I can see marks going forward as before."

Another panting, stumbling advance and we were at the sand. Sure enough, the trail went on clearly once more. It was only a short spell, however, and this time it ended not in shingle but in hard ground on which not a shadow of a trace remained.

I must say that it was with relief I remarked, "Now we shall have to stop."

"Well, you wait behind this rock out of the sun while I scout around." I lay down and watched the indefatigable old figure turning and dipping just like some great stork looking for small frogs under stones. After some ten minutes of this he paused for a little at one spot, bent down, then turned and called me. Unwillingly I got up on my feet and went over.

"You see"—that familiar opening, but I was quicker now.

"Yes, a small bush of desert holly," I answered, "and it's been pulled about quite lately."

"Right; one of the burros took a bite at it. Hardly a refreshing leaf, that ghostly prickle. But look, he took it in his mouth and it acted as a kind of chewing gum. He turned it over and then"—all the while we were again scudding along in the intense heat—"bit by bit he let the chewed fiber fall from his lips."

That desert holly trail took us much farther than I had feared, but at last it, too, gave out.

We had reached a sort of low saddle. Behind us we could look back, for the ground I now noticed had been gently rising all the while, along the whole chain of dried lakes. In the next wide and shallow depression, I suppose, once had gathered the streams, torrents, and headwaters whose overflows filled the areas below. The opening in our forward view gave us a welcome pause, for Mr. Mycroft again swept the area with his glasses. He had climbed another boulder and, at last convinced that there was nothing ahead, was taking a last sweep of the landscape well away from our direction, far out to the right. I was watching him with some impatience, for I felt that he was just refusing to give up, trying to find excuses for not going back and so looking in directions where there could be nothing, just to waste time.

I was, indeed, about to call to him that obviously nothing could be expected in that direction, the rocks sloped right up and ended in a mountain wall, when as I rose to catch his attention I saw that his sweeping gaze had become fixed. He was, through his glasses, attentively studying something. A breeze quite strong, but anything but refreshing—rather like a draught from an oven—was now blowing up from behind us. Through it he called down to me, "From here I can see, I'm sure, something fluttering." He took his bearings carefully. Then he scrambled down and set off in the direction he had sighted.

Of course it was farther than I had imagined. I'd thought, I'd hoped he'd seen some clue comparatively close. In the end, though, after dips in which we lost sight of the place where he said it lay and rises in which the rocks to which he pointed looked no nearer, we saw clearly across a small canyon. It couldn't be, now I caught a clear look of it, withered leaves on an old branch—but it was that color. It dipped and wavered in the wind, which now was unpleasantly strong. Mr. Mycroft stopped and looked. He didn't raise his binoculars.

"Careless," was his only description of what he made out. He then looked carefully onto the ground from where we stood toward the waving branch. "No clues here," he remarked. "Walk carefully and notice anything on the ground that might be a trace."

As I was trying to do this and following him, I did not notice that we had reached the foot of the canyon and had come some distance up the other side. Mr. Mycroft had stopped, we had evidently reached our objective. Even now, looking down on it, I couldn't for a moment see exactly what it was. It wasn't a branch. It stuck out from under some stones. A second look and I glanced up to see Mr. Mycroft watching me.

"I said 'careless,' didn't I?"

It didn't seem to me the time to draw attention to one's "dicta."

"That," I said, drawing back as I said it, "That's —that *has* been a human hand and arm!"

He was already kneeling down. I gingerly approached again.

"It was said of a desolate land, 'In that place there is not water to drown a man, a tree to hang him on, or earth to bury him in,' " he remarked over his shoulder. "Well, it's even harder here to dispose of your dead. And here, you see, death is an embalmer."

He took the poor withered limb. After the first shock of recognizing what it was, I saw that there was nothing really repugnant in it. It was beautiful almost, this bone, wound about with shrunken sinew and perfectly desiccated flesh. To and fro it waved in the wind, a gesture attractive in a growing tree. It was as flexible as a spring. Mr. Mycroft had already removed the greater part of what, it was now clear, was a hastily made low cairn. I helped, and as we uncovered what it had almost hidden, I felt strongly the need to be friendly with the only living man in this desert of death, which here, for us, centered in a dead man, a man turned into a desert thing—more desiccated than the desert holly, his flesh drier than well-cured parchment.

"Why did you say 'careless?' " I asked, conciliatingly.

"Well," he replied, not looking up from his final task of taking the last stones off the dead man's feet, "it is careless not to bury more carefully when you have murdered."

"You're sure?" I asked.

"Look at the skin. It's perfectly unbroken anywhere else. But there is a tear in the chest and I think that darker color on the piece of shirt is pretty certainly blood."

It was hard to deny the unpleasant deduction. But still, this was not at all my notion of a murdered man. I'd never seen such an object and now it lay before me. The skin was stretched to the tautness of a drum over the sinews and bones. The whole creature was the barest outline of a man. I had never imagined anything could be so withered, desiccated. But save for that hole in the chest, the skin was unbroken.

"It's horrible and unbelievable," I said.

"Yes," he replied. "Whoever killed that man who once filled out this shell at our feet didn't know enough about the desert. It's life that abolishes history and records and traces. Death is the preserver—the Keeper of the Records. This man was killed. We'll go into the how and the why later. Let's now try and understand why he was let signal to us searchers. He's shot," went on Mr. Mycroft, evidently reconstructing the conditions in his mind and so working back from what was present to what had happened, "he's shot probably by someone who followed him, by someone who perhaps relieved him of his burros and of other things and then a considerable time after, when what has been taken off him has been studied (for even the desert takes some time to do as fine a piece of tanning and curing as this), the burros with their new master pass again near by, seeking their old master's trail and goal. But here we are only at the day of the murder. The dead must be buried. Well, as we are agreed, burial here is a difficulty: cover him, then, with stones. But desiccation here is quite unusual. A body, our bodies are some 68 per cent water. If you can dehydrate such a sponge—well, it goes as hard and springy as a well-cured sponge. That is what this desert did. It put the evidence immediately into its perfect preservative —air, super-thirsty for any drop of damp. Our killer goes off, having packed his limp victim, with arms huddled across the breast, under the heap of small stones. Then the desert got to work and, as it carried out its embalming, limp and soggy muscles coiled and shrank like wet rope; lax sinews twisted like spring wire. The arm on the upper side curled itself round—the pebbles rolled off—the springy limb waved its macabre au revoir to its enemy, its summons to us."

"You know who killed this man!" I interrupted.

"No, I don't, for certain."

"Why, it must be——"

"Mr. Silchester, you know now as well as I that it is just as important never to run ahead of one's actual evidence, never to make a leap, as it is never to miss a single signpost that it offers us. I have said it is certain that this man was not killed by the last man who passed this way."

"All right," I said, vexed that he should still be the old master when, after all, I had now graduated. "If guessing is out, what does your detective deduction give us?"

"This man, we agree, has been shot; murder probably, manslaughter certainly. The next thing we can settle before we attempt the why and 'by whom,' is the fairly simple question of 'when.' The desert works quickly hereabouts, but, as I've said, it needs a certain time. I've used dehydration several times for preserving specimens, severed limbs, and the like," he said casually. "I know the rate. The air here is peculiarly favorable"—that detachment, as arid as this forbidding wilderness, calling this fatal desolation "peculiarly favorable"!—"a steady hot wind all the daylight hours and practically zero humidity. And there is a final and peculiar feature in the air of this place. If we had approached from the other side, I should have been puzzled. But those dried lakes gave me the clue, as we came along, though I did not know that we should be needing it. Those sand beds are so well caked because they are dense with natron salts, so common in these desert lakes. When at night there is a slight humidity and this salt-laden air rises and is borne over this ridge, then this drying body would take up these salts and so become, as it is, literally pickled—a natural tanning process. The same sort of thing can take place under a number of circumstances, wherever the same balance, though in different proportions, is preserved. In the vaults of the old church of St. Michan's in Dublin, there the bodies exposed simply to the right mixture of air impregnated with the gases from an old, marsh-engulfed oak forest are just like this, pickled, tanned, quite cured and flexible. Yes, the process would be quick here, quicker than there, quicker perhaps in this one spot than anywhere. Therefore a most unwise place to commit homicide and hope that nature would clear up your traces.

"Yet even here," he bent down and touched the springy limb which wheezed gently as it swung, "even here, I feel sure, there must be quite a considerable time before the weather-curing required for this extreme of dehydration could be attained. So this man met his end by shooting some months, perhaps half a year ago. Now, who is he? Well, he *is* someone that someone wanted to murder or at least to rob. I suspect what clothes he had, beyond this shirt and trousers, were taken and, after searching, burnt. You see, a search, a hasty one, was made. The trouser pockets have been pulled out, so as not to miss an inner pocket, and not put back." Mr. Mycroft was kneeling close beside the shriveled cadaver. "Um," he said, "hurried but not unthorough. That nip out of the shirt was to remove the sales tag, I suspect."

"Well," I put in at that point, "we can't find out anything more. Hadn't we better get back and notify a sheriff or someone?"

The whole thing was rather too gruesome for my liking, and the longer we hung over this really horrible twist of what had been a man, the more Mr. Mycroft seemed to become absorbed by it. He positively brooded over it like some huge bat. The situation had become positively eerie for me and I was just trying to raise my spirits by reflecting that, after all, a vampire could not have chosen a less productive victim than this sorry bundle of sinews and shriveled skin, when, looking down, I was—well, horrified and disgusted. For Mr. Mycroft had taken hold of the object. He had raised it so that his lean, hard, white face looked into its face, dun-colored and chapfallen. But that was not the shock. It was what he did with it as it lay on his knee. He had slipped his left hand round the back of its scrawny neck until I could see his long fingers squeezing its jaws. He was manipulating it like a hideous ventriloquist's dummy. And, sure enough, to my alarmed disgust, the mouth did open. I saw the withered tongue come forward as the muscles at its base were squeezed in the neck.

"What are you doing?" I cried.

He made no reply, so absorbed was he in his beastly task, whatever its purpose. For a moment my fear made me think he might have gone mad—too much heat and exertion and, no doubt, shock—all that coolness was only cover and pretense—and here was I alone in the desert with the corpse of a murdered man and a lunatic playing with it. I couldn't take my eyes off that terrible pair. But the next thing which the living did to the dead, reassured me. It was only my panic which had made me believe that he was trying to make the cadaver speak. No, he was examining not the play of the tongue but the line of the teeth. With relief, I felt sure he was looking for any dental work whereby, maybe, an identification could be made.

"But why not look at the finger marks?" I suggested, anxious to show myself that we were still the right side of sanity and, gruesome though our actual occupation was, it was really only part and parcel of a routine inspection any policeman would be expected to make.

"The skin has stretched away all its natural markings," he said without turning round. "No, it's here we'll find a reference, if anywhere."

Curiosity overcame my disgust. I bent over his shoulder and peered into the dead man's mouth, opened now just the way a strangled rat's will gape. No, there was no dental plate or bridgework or indeed anything but a few noncommittal fillings and a gap or two where a few of the middle teeth had been lost.

"Nothing to report," I said, glad to have joined in the inspection and not to have winced. Now, at last, we could go.

But a last and worst shock was in store for me. Just as I thought we could leave this wretched shred of mortality under its rearranged pebbles, for some official to take or leave, I saw Mr. Mycroft, instead of putting it down, shift his hold. His left hand forced the mouth to open still wider until the horrid thing seemed laughing at us. Then quickly his right hand darted into the mouth. There was a sort of tussle which was one of the most nauseatingly ludicrous things I have ever seen—a ghastly sort of Punch and Judy act—as the thing wobbled and struggled and Mr. Mycroft wrestled and hung on. At last there was a tearing sound which really nearly made me sick. Mr. Mycroft let the corpse fall on the ground and slipped something into his pocket.

I was so upset that when he said, "That is all we can do now. Help me, while I cover this over again with the pebbles," that I hastily joined in scattering shingle over the withered thing (the waving arm, I'm glad to say, Mr. Mycroft made rest by putting the body face down) and followed him dumbly as we turned back toward our base.

I think Mr. Mycroft knew I was shocked, but perhaps he was just indifferent to what I felt. Perhaps he was completely absorbed in his puzzle, treating that horrid object with the detachment I should treat such a word as *cadaverine*, for instance, if I knew that it was really a code-concealer. I should be quite indifferent to the fact that that word stands for one of the most terrible of stenches, and so I suppose Mr. Mycroft regarded what we had found as just so much evidential material. I was tired and really exhausted by the time we reached our base. He, with his easy reserve of energy, poured out cold coffee from the flask and offered me cigarettes though, I noticed, he did not smoke.

"Kerson won't be here for another couple of hours. I didn't expect we'd net such a fish in our first cast. It made going farther not worth while, at present." He sat back and now was evidently enjoying the austere scenery with complete appreciation. There was nothing else to do and, with his usual power of attention, he did it.

At last, as the pools of blue shadow began to fill up the shallow fawn-colored cups of the lake-beds, we heard the motor's purr in the distance. Before night fell we were back in the cave camp.

Chapter IV

AGAIN I slept heavily, waking to find Mr. Mycroft and Kerson already bundling up all our goods. "Are we off?" was my natural but not very detectional remark. I own I woke in that mood which my nurse used to call getting out of the wrong side of the bed —though the "bed" I had slept on, the broad ledge round the edge of the cave wall, had of course only one side for alighting and I had slept well enough. It was the strain of yesterday. I wasn't fit to trail treasure with corpses as ambiguous signposts. I should stick to cross-word puzzles. Yet, with natural perversity, when Mr. Mycroft said, "Yes, we're going back," that too offended me.

"Back when we've found nothing!" Then I paused. While we drove back the evening before nothing had been said to Kerson about our find. It was hardly to be called a treasure, but it was certainly a discovery. Had Mr. Mycroft told the trader? Caution did not overcome my irritation, but it switched it to more open issues. "Without breakfast?" I queried in a challenging tone. I was hungry and needed food. Yesterday had been very heavy going for me. Kerson looked round in an offensive way. I knew he thought I was a tenderfoot or greenhorn or whatever barbarous term he would use for a nature more sensitive than his own.

Without turning from his baggage wrapping Mr. Mycroft said, "If we are to catch the late afternoon train we have time if we start in the next ten minutes. It does not stop where we got off coming up."

I bundled myself out and pulled on my outer clothes. I had slept the last two nights in my underthings. I hate doing this, indeed, had hardly ever before in my life done such a thing. And now there wouldn't be time even to shave. My mood was, then, hardly communicative when we climbed into the car. I would not, even to satisfy my curiosity, ask why all the luggage was not on board. For a moment I cherished the unfriendly hope—so vexed had I become by all these repeated scratches—that they had forgotten part of their stuff (a silly illusion, as far as Mr. Mycroft was concerned). But in any case I was not going to unbend. I felt stiff with unfriendliness and the futility of our desert escapade. I wanted to be free of the whole thing and back in my own neat office with my neat work neatly served by my neat secretary. Nor did the long drive in the blinding glare of heat supple my mood. It grew more crusted. Under the high sun all color and relief went out of the interminable landscape. It was simply a tumbledown furnace—everything crumbled away by repeated calcining. How could I have ever found anything beautiful in it at any time of the day! Mr. Mycroft read my mood and in silence handed me some cold coffee—of course it spilled as we jerked over some stones. I swallowed a little, but the rest dribbled onto my clothes, staining them. The next offering—a sandwich of stale bread with pieces of perspiring cheese as the middle term—after a nibble, it so disgusted me that I frankly threw it out of the car. One of those poor little infested rodents could have one last good meal!

I spent the next few hours expecting we should miss the train and the hour after that—for we did arrive in ample time and the train was forty-five minutes late—in wishing we had not jolted along without more than five minutes' pause in the whole run. Certainly, my temper had deteriorated through the day and, disobeying the Proverbial advice, I let the sun go down

—which it did when we had settled ourselves for some time in silence in the soot-covered train—on my wrath. We had no sleepers engaged. We jostled on through the night. When the dawn and the city appeared together I had made a resolve—no more desert detection for me!

I gathered my last stale, desiccated crust of courtesy and said to Mr. Mycroft as we stood together on the platform, "Thank you for a remarkable trip. I think, though, you realize now that I am hardly cut out for real life-and-death detection. I am glad to have been of use in setting you on your way and I am sure that you will not need my small services any further."

As usual, nothing that I could say seemed really to penetrate down to his full attention. It was as though it were dealt with by some automatic secretary, while the chief himself was never even told that you had called.

"Perhaps not, perhaps not. But one can't be sure, can one? It's a peculiarly rich case already and a number of apparently side issues may come in again."

I don't think he was thinking of me, but still, even by allusion, I don't like to be referred to as a side issue. After all, everyone must be central to himself. Indeed, I thought of saying something more, just not to be brushed aside like a ticked-off shopping list. But already the old bird had turned, called a red-cap, and was collecting his things. I called another, as my only possible reply, and our respective bearers led us off, the crowd separating us.

After a quiet day in which I cleaned myself up and felt supple and smooth again, shaved, washed, properly fed and slept, the morning after I was at my office. My secretary had quite a large amount of interesting work for me to look over. There was a number of new inquiries. The next few weeks I was perfectly happy. This, I said to myself, is my right life—interested but not involved—unraveling riddles, as it were, in a riddle laboratory, but not like a silly, excitable terrier rushing down rabbit holes and getting oneself stuck fast at the bottom of one of them.

After a month I felt I had, for the moment, everything in perfect running order. So one day, when I had signed all my letters and seen my last inquirer, I looked at my watch and it was still only three-fifty. "I'll go," I thought, "and ask Miss Brown. There are two cases I'd like to ask her whether it wouldn't be worth her while giving a sitting to. And anyhow, I haven't seen her for an age." I hadn't any doubt that my reading of those two riddles which I was taking over to her, had been right, but I knew she would appreciate my talking them over with her and she had a very nice way of appreciating my hunches—an approval which did, I knew, make them work better. There's nothing like encouragement for the subconscious. A telephone call told me that she was at home and also had no more appointments for that day.

After a cordial greeting, when we were comfortably settled over tea and she had approved my two interpretations and said that she did not think that a sitting with her "control" would help any further my clients, I asked her about her work.

"Oh, the usual thing: 77 per cent wanting evidence that Aunt, Uncle, Ma or Pa, Hubby or Wifey is 'happy, oh, so happy, over there.' Well, it may be as they wish. I don't know, as I'm not here when they are trying to use my subconscious as a long, long-distance line or super-world radio-beam. Then there's the lost luggage department—'Where's the will, or the cache of notes or coin?' " She paused. "By the way, did you ever hear again of that queer little fellow whom you brought round when you were last here? He's been in my mind off and on. You know, I felt about him there was something more than met the eye. That's the worst," she went on, "of being an honest medium. You miss all the fun. You're like a child who has to be sent out of the room as soon as its elders begin to exchange confidences."

I wanted, anyhow, to talk about my adventure, now it was over and evidently safely closed. So I had little difficulty in persuading myself that I owed this kindness to a colleague.

When I had finished, Miss Brown, after a minute's silence, remarked, "That was an experience. And I have a hunch, for what it is worth, that this adventure isn't closed. I believe it won't close until you help close it with your colleague."

"It's not my business. Whatever help an outsider could give, I gave . . . at least you and I," I added.

"Well," she said, without pressing a point which she saw that I wanted left alone, "well, wait and see. You have a better conscious-hunch mind than I. Maybe you're right and there's nothing more to turn up."

But, though I didn't tell her so, that precisely was my feeling and not a very pleasant one. Anyhow, I had been rude to Mr. Mycroft and so didn't want to see him again; and my hunch was that behind my rudeness was, as usual, fear.

There is no doubt, though, that her words helped forward what followed. Perhaps it was three days—not more—after my tea with Miss Brown that my secretary said I was wanted on the phone—by Mr. Mycroft. I think that without Miss Brown's gentle urging I should have said, "Say I'm out and he can leave a message." But as it was, I took the receiver.

"I should like your opinion," said the familiar tones

—and the simple formula worked, of course. I was, with a phrase, made ready to listen. "I should like your opinion on a very interesting result of our trip. I have something to show you which I believe will be of interest to you."

He wanted me to go round to a place which he said he had rented. My cautious side could only say, "Well, better get it over." Whatever my real reason, the fact remains that I went. As I might have expected, Mr. Mycroft had made himself very efficiently comfortable. He offered me tea; it was, of course, excellent; chatted genially about our trip as though we had parted with perfect agreeableness and then, remarking that he did not wish to waste my time, led me out of his sitting room to a small room behind it which he had fitted up as a laboratory.

"Here is the little matter on which I wanted your judgment," he said, pointing to his microscope. I peered down it obediently. I saw in the lit field a white disk covered with concentric rings.

"It looks," I ventured, "like a cross section of a tree trunk with the growth rings just showing."

"A very good diagnosis," replied the voice at my shoulder. "It would, though, be a very dwarfish tree at such a small diameter to show such a wealth of growth record, for there are far more lines there than with this magnification you can see. One moment, if you will let me." He took my place at the eyepiece and twiddled some rib-edged screws at the side. "Now?" he questioned me back to look again. The lit field of vision showed a number of lines which covered all the space I could see. "The higher magnification shows the lines clearly and, moreover, you will see, it discloses that most of them are different."

"One," I replied, "is so different from the rest that it looks as though it were drawn by a clumsy, excited pencil. In contrast, the others are almost mechanically perfect." I paused in my reporting, trying to think what record this could be. "Then there's almost as badly drawn a one up in the corner. What is this—is it a root or stem?"

"Yes, your observing is good. Now, with a little deduction, I believe you'd discover what it is you are looking at. But I don't want to waste your time and I do want your opinion on another specimen."

The slides shifted under my field of vision and when it was clear again I saw the same pattern.

"You've put back the same slide by mistake," I reported.

"No," he replied, "that is a different one of a second specimen."

"But I see exactly the same patterns of thin lines and the few ill-drawn ones."

"Thank you; that is what I hoped you'd report.

Now may I tell you what that broadish ill-drawn curve is? It is a birthmark. And what appears in a corner of your vision, that's a serious illness at six and a half years."

"What do you actually mean?" I asked, taking my eye from the eyepiece.

"A few words will explain," he said, offering me a stool and perching himself on the edge of a table. "What you have been kindly reporting on are fine cross sections of two human teeth. A few years ago a discovery, very useful to detection, was made by a biologist. While studying the effect of fluorine discoloration on rats' teeth, he fell upon the fact that if you took cross sections of rodents' teeth, under proper magnification—it has to be high, for each ring is only some one-fifteen-thousandth of an inch—you could see growth rings, exactly like the growth rings in trees. He found that rats lay down a new ring every day throughout their lives and that these rings are quite as accurate records of the rat's growth and health and accident and disease as are the tree rings of the individual tree's history. Nor did he stop there. He went on to human teeth and found the same thing—though we lay down a new layer only every four days. But we, too, chronicle in ivory-inlay all our major events. I said that broad, 'badly drawn' line, which you drew attention to, was a birthmark. That's precisely what it is. Birth is a severe shock to us humans, comparable to a considerable illness, and our distress at our first eviction is registered so."

"But if that's so, each tooth in one's head would carry a similar record?" I questioned.

"Precisely; you have confirmed my opinion—that these two teeth, cross sections of which you have examined, belong to the same man. They have identically the same pattern—the same illness mark at six and a half, then a fine run with a flowing variation of years of good growth and years not quite so good. The man whom we have been questioning through his teeth, was a fine, healthy specimen. Then at fifty-four he died without an illness."

"Do you know more?" I questioned. I was sure he was on a hot scent, if one might so describe these two fine slivers of that very dry object, a tooth.

"Yes. You were disgusted at my handling of that desiccated body. But I saw at once that it was our only chance. And if the Greeks are right, then the one wish of the ghost which sits by the corpse is that its murder should be avenged. So I was acting, if strangely, with nothing but ancestral piety. For in this way I could hope to find out who murdered this man by first finding out who the murdered man was. Some dentists—there are one or two of them in this part of the country—are now making tooth collections. They ask their colleagues to send them their extractions, with name, age, and any other relevant details of the patient. They prepare these cross sections and then correlate the ring-recorded growth with the personal information. It is the rise of a new science, and that is always a thing to be watched and used by detectives. The second I called on was a true enthusiast. He had a fine collection, beautifully tabulated. Like fingerprint matchers, we sat with my slide thrown on one screen and he running through his, throwing them on a screen just beside. We hadn't done a few hundred before we both exclaimed, 'That's our man.' He took the serial number on his slide over to his card-index, raised the slip and read out, 'Sex male, age fifty-three: additional information given by dentist-donor: extraction: upper bicuspid; patient's name: Samuel Sanderson.' "

"Sanderson," I interrupted, for I'm good at remembering names, "Sanderson? Didn't Kerson mention that as the name of a prospector who used to be seen about in his country?"

"You are correct, and you will recall that neither Blue Feather nor others of the Indians had sighted him for some time. They missed his departure." Then, with a pause, "We saw him for the last time under that too-carelessly made cairn of stones."

"But how will that help? Granted we know," I was

in my excitement associating myself with the hunt as a quiet cob will suddenly break away and leave the road when the pack crosses it in full cry, "granted we know the name that—that thing carried when alive, does Kerson know where he lived, and if he did, would that put us on the track of his murderer?"

"No, Kerson couldn't help us, and anyhow I don't want to interest him much more in our researches. He couldn't, anyhow, be of us. These prospectors are queer creatures—close as a crab. They wander for hundreds of miles over this immense Southwest territory, more than a third of which is yet waiting to be properly mapped. If they find a lode—and that I gather is not nearly so uncommon as the world imagines—their one wish naturally is to conceal their track to it. Kerson told me he knew of one who, when he found he was being trailed, doubled back in the night and, finding that his pursuer had only a day's water and had shown that he had no knowledge of that terrain, led him into an area where you must have three. Perhaps it isn't actual murder; certainly no blood is shed when the desert withers an intruder. But it is a pretty terrible defense. Of course I don't know whether Sanderson would have used it, and you may say he showed the danger of not doing so. What I do know—from an address which it was not difficult to find with the assistance given me by the expert who loaned me this specimen" (he held up the slide which he had borrowed)—"what I do know is that Sanderson led a double life—which again is not uncommon. In the wilderness he seemed a fanatical waif. In town he had a very comfortable address. I have it here."

"Then you think Intil was—what do they call it—hijacking?"

"We don't have to think yet. If we are willing to act, we can, I believe, get much closer to proof positive before we have to argue and deduce."

I confess I was intrigued. Somehow the whole thing—the way Mr. Mycroft had literally snatched evidence out of the mouth which its murderer was certain he had silenced forever, the fact that we were obviously on the track of a first-class mystery—made me able to believe him when he said that at the end lay a first-class prize.

"What is the next step?" I asked, with, I know, undue curiosity.

"Obviously we call at Sanderson's residence."

"But will anyone be there to help us?"

The answer, "I hope not," gave me both a sense of our self-sufficiency and also of adventure.

So when Mr. Mycroft said, "Will you come and pay a call this evening at 10272 Chellean Drive?" I didn't say no, and he added at once, as a sort of sealing of the pact, "Then we'll dine first."

And dine we did, excellently, at a little restaurant he had found and I had never heard of. When dinner was over I then stepped with him into the taxi with no more than the sense that we were about to pay an after-dinner call, or, if no one was at home, get a glimpse of the kind of property the lost prospector used to frequent when "on shore."

The roads wound away, however, and we climbed as the light faded until square miles of "the largest city limits in the world" lay like an illuminated carpet at our feet. Finally the car stopped.

"That's as far as I can take you," said the driver. "The realtors pushed this road up here in '29 and then the rains of '38 cut the road to ribbons. But I guess 10272 lies somewhere along this contour. I couldn't take the car along it, but you'll be able to walk this bit."

"You'll get a fare back if you'll wait half an hour," said Mr. Mycroft, paying him, I saw, a handsome retaining fee.

"You bet," evidently signified assent, and we turned to follow the road. It had been engineered round the contours of a very steep bluff: the concrete pavement had mainly stood, but a deluge of rain had cut the soft, disintegrated granite on which the road itself had been laid, almost clean away. It had become a very isolated spot and, when we had picked our way round the bastion of the hill, we found ourselves at a dead end. The concrete curb, silted over with sand fallen from the cliff which had been carved so as to give the road passageway, here came abruptly to an end. The great boom of "permanent prosperity" had driven its path as high as this, and then suddenly the slump came. The fluted concrete street lamppost with no light stood marking a "high" in real-estate development perhaps never again to be touched.

"He chose a quiet spot," Mr. Mycroft commented. "That dark mass above us is, I judge, the house."

We clambered up some concrete steps also nearly hidden now under silt and sand.

"Talk of building on sand!" I exclaimed. The house stood out on a sort of bracket of concrete struts.

"Well, you can see who is approaching," he answered, "and a prospector may be excused for liking wide horizons." We had reached a small platform which ran round the house front. "No one at home," was his next remark. "And if I know anything of American homes, they put more trust in mobile than in rigid defenses."

To my alarm, while he said this, Mr. Mycroft was looking over the place with too professional an interest, and I began to say, "Well, we have seen all we can."

"Oh, I wouldn't have brought you so far for just

that," he politely hastened to un-assure me. "We can certainly see considerably more if this catch is the kind I think it is." Of course it was. A panel of a window swung open, the whole window swung back and, with perfect courtesy, Mr. Mycroft was holding out his hand, inviting me to join him in a little after-dinner housebreaking. As I hesitated, "You'll be less conspicuous inside," he told me, and it was true enough. I slipped over the sill and was fatally committed to larceny or some such legal trap.

The lights from the city below made, through the large, undraped windows, enough illumination for us to see our way about.

"He meant one day to make a splash when he'd collected enough specie," commented my leader into temptation, as we stepped through the kitchen and passed into a wide living room. "See here, he has already indulged in a certain amount of collecting. The way to get an appetite for luxury is to have wandered, literally, in the wilderness."

The room was bare, but standing about in it was quite a collection of furniture—big antique chairs, a sofa in the same full Venetian style, even a couple of heavily framed pictures. Two fine carved bookcases with glass doors proved to contain, when we looked with the aid of an electric torch into their interiors, a number of rather incongruously bound books, almost all on archaeology.

"Perhaps he was trying," I suggested, "to educate himself up to his new acquisitions."

There was also a table with massive gilt legs and scrolling wreathed round its under edge.

"Yes," remarked Mr. Mycroft. "That's the reaction from desert austerity. They always go more rococo when their ship comes home. No severity in his home for the man who has been homeless, but craving for comfort in the homeless waste. That buhl table, even by this light, I judge to be a genuine piece, and this desk—yes, already he must have made a pretty piece to purchase that. I expect he used to come back here, adding an object after each trip from the sale of his quills of gold dust. Why didn't he stop?" Mr. Mycroft was now mainly thinking aloud. "Because he was on the trail of something really big—making all these siftings and nuggetings mere nugae." While he talked he was running his hand over the big pieces of furniture, judging their nature and quality as much by his keen touch as by sight. "Yes, genuine enough, and so—" he suddenly stopped this rapid sotto voce monologue, but his hands were still running over the table. Next moment a small spot of light from his pocket torch threw a little circle on the table. One saw the gleaming squiggles of ormolu-brass writhing round the darker curls of the carved tortoise-shell.

"A hideous form of decoration," I let my thought express itself. "There's nothing to keep us longer here looking at such objects."

"Hideous, maybe: *de gustibus non disputandum;* but the old man certainly had another idea besides decoration—at least in this piece. The decoration was a very helpful disguise, like the conjuror's patter when, if he were silent, you'd be more on your guard. Ah, I have it," he said, stretching his hands apart as though pretending, it seemed in the dusk, at piano playing on the table top. There was a small rasping click. "That did it," I heard him say. "Now we have only to find where it did it."

The spotlight appeared again, tracing its way over the massive table, while a running commentary gave me some idea of what he was up to.

"These fine pieces—for they are magnificent technical work, even if you happen to hate the style—were made for the offices of ministers of state, men who had to seem elaborately urbane on the surface, their conversation all in the grand manner with florid compliments and empty eloquence, as pointless as these never-ceasing arabesques and—ah, here we have it," he was running his hand down the back leg of the table; "a capacity for perfect concealment under all this camouflage of decoration. Here's the code drawer which these tables often contain and which can be found and opened only by knowing precisely where to press on a couple of points concealed in the decorative carved foliage." Suddenly his voice rose a little, "*And* what I was looking for."

I saw, in the pencil of rays, that his lean index finger was working into a small cleft now apparent, where the table leg swelled into big scrolls with which it supported the table itself. The light snapped out.

"We shan't have kept our driver waiting beyond our covenanted time." And indeed, ten minutes short of it we were back with him.

"Anyone at home?" he queried. "No," said Mr. Mycroft. "But the view was worth the journey. Certainly night is the time to visit this drive."

When we were back in his house he took from his breast pocket a small squill of paper. It had been folded, I judged, and refolded. As it rested in his palm it was a small band, perhaps six inches long and a quarter of an inch wide. When it was unfolded it was perhaps little short of a yard in length. On it, however, there appeared to be nothing, but at the edges I did notice some little touches and tips of ink, as though someone had been trying a pen but had, in the end, written nothing.

"We've found nothing," I said. "That is only a

chance piece of paper, perhaps with some measuring check points made by the carpenter who made the table and left by him in that secret cleft."

"No," said Mr. Mycroft, who had been looking at it through a lens, "that is modern paper, for one thing, and I'd wager that is modern ink, too." We bent over it together. "Look at it," said he, handing me another lens. "Don't some of those touches look like bits of letters?"

I bent closer. They certainly did. I passed my eye from one to another, scanning up and down the ribbon of paper. But the marks refused to yield any clew. Gradually, however, as I worked on it, determined to show Mr. Mycroft I could scan as carefully as he, the paper began to curl. I was so close to it that inadvertently I was breathing on it. I put out my hand to smooth it flat again but my hand was held. Mr. Mycroft was not only restraining me, but he too was breathing on the paper and, as he breathed, it began to buckle itself up quite definitely.

"Don't touch it," he said, and then, chuckling to himself, "Well, Scotchmen are called laconic, and our old Gael was evidently scholar enough not only to know what that word means but how the Laconians capitalized on their speech-parsimony."

While speaking he had plugged in a small electric kettle; when it began to simmer he brought the spout near the underside of the paper ribbon, which he had turned over so that all the marks were now face down. He lifted it gently and ran the steaming spout along the underside. The curling of the paper became very distinct and, helping it with his finger, the strip began to turn itself into a corkscrew scroll.

"I've got the pitch," he said, replacing the kettle. And taking up the paper, which was now like a little snake, he slipped it onto a narrow round ruler which lay on his desk.

"It's not a perfect fit," he remarked, "but, with a little shifting, it's near enough. Look." And, sure enough, the pitch of the curl brought each little pen touch near enough so that complete words began to be made by them. "It is the old Spartan way of sending code messages. They have to be short. This one is. And they should be on a paper which when untwisted does not retain its curl-torsion. This did. Otherwise, unless you have the exact duplicate of the original stick round which the paper was curled when the message was written on it, you have little chance of reading it." He took the paper-wrapped ruler to the light. "This, I think, will sound familiar to you," he remarked, and read out, " 'When the flyer whose flight is not through air, sitting in his cage, stretches his wing to the left.' "

"Of course," I exclaimed, "it's Intil's clue which I decoded for him."

"With Miss Brown's help," he added before I could, which I thought was discourteous.

"She only gave a picture; it was I who found out what it meant."

Of course it was silly of me to justify myself, but we had been scrambling about and housebreaking and after a heavy dinner the excitement and strain had brought on indigestion and that always makes one touchy. I was cross, I confess, and Mr. Mycroft's slight tone of superiority put a match to my mood. And he didn't let it pass. He actually teased me further.

"Then, no doubt, you'll be able to help with the rest of the message now we have it in its entirety? I have, I think, done my bit and here we enter your field. I can tell you, if you have not followed the track so far, that Samuel Sanderson was remarkable among that remarkable crowd, the prospectors, and, in keeping with their tradition, he kept very quiet about his prospects. The one thing he seems to have feared—as he was getting on—was that he might get forgetful. I am sure he, too—perhaps the first of us—knew that there was something worth finding somewhere in the unmapped desert. He has set the rest of us on this trail. Perhaps he actually found the thing himself, but he had to find it again. If my supposition is true, he couldn't handle it himself, or at least without the most careful preparation. A number of visits would probably be necessary. He carried, then, one clue with him, one verbalized map, I believe it to be. That was taken off him after death. For fear he should lose it he made this duplicate, and not only put it in code, but, using the ancient Spartan method of disguise, having hidden it in a secret place, he was able to make the actual *aide mémoire* look worthless should anyone stumble on it. Yes, we are tracking a 'verra careful mon' as his cautious compatriots would say. Indeed, had I not combined, with a taste for what you call ill-taste furniture (and a knowledge of its craftsmanship), a good memory for my Thucydides and some of the out-of-the-way information which classical studies give—well, we'd never be where we are now."

This self-congratulation, all the more because it was true and couldn't really be answered, vexed me further; and when with that badly timed raillery Mr. Mycroft added, "Now all you have to do is to read what I have put in your hand," I became angrily nervous. I must try, though nervous anger is, of course, the worst of moods in which to try and summon your hunch to start you on a line.

"Well," I said, "the first part runs, 'At twenty

minutes to three o'clock in the afternoon,' or we can say, if we like, 'At two-forty P.M.' " Then I paused.

"Yes?" said Mr. Mycroft. "Yes, we are agreed about that. And now for the rest."

It was maddeningly like an old schoolmaster taunting a boy who hasn't had time to prepare his translation.

I read on, "Cloc Friar's Heel. AP. 20111318 — 3." That was all. "Short inscriptions are the mischief," I said.

"Yet even the Etruscan and Hattitic yielded results," he answered—showing off his learning in order to be able to provoke me more.

"Well, I've done work on the Roger Bacon clues," I retorted.

"I doubt if they repay study," was his gratuitous answer. I felt he was trying to show that I was no use. I made a last effort.

"Cloc," I said. "Well, obviously that has to do with the time-reference which I've already decoded. He left out the *k* to save space. 'Friar's Heel,' yes, that's a reference to the old mission trails. You know the Franciscans opened up much of this desert Southwest."

I looked up. I was doing far better than I had hoped. My hunch *was* working. The old fellow who thought he knew everything, would have to admit I could be of use, and on my own, without any wise-woman to help or start my native skill. I looked up, but there was no encouragement on his cold old face. Didn't he know how much a gift such as mine depended on the spark not being quenched! He was jealous, that was it. But just to know that didn't help.

I stumbled on: "AP. 20111318 less 3, these of course are bearings. I suggest, just as a line for further research, AP stands for Latin *Apud*, 'near,' or 'approximately,' or even, broadly speaking, 'at.' Then some measurements which a little figuring could work out: the total sum or direction to be corrected by three."

I stopped. I knew I was getting out of my depth. But, hang it all, I had a line and the silly old fool, the jealous old dominie, was just determined I shouldn't score and take from him any of the praise. Pope's bitter but just line flashed into my head: "Bear like the Turk no brother near the throne." Here, as always, was old crusted authority crushing out young promise.

I struggled with my temper and managed to say, "If, Mr. Mycroft, you will give attention to the suggestions I have been able to make, I feel sure I have been able to provide you with some further information which is pertinent to our search."

"Codes of this sort," was his indifferent reply, "don't have spare words in them; if they do, terminal letters are not omitted to save space. 'Friar's Heel' is not uningenious, I own, just here, but not in its wider context. As for the letter-number references, I own I'm still quite at a loss as to the important ending—minus 3 is especially obscure. But taking into consideration what I have found out already about our man (and codes and men fit like saddles and horses), I doubt if AP is at all what you think. Without knowing something of our late prospector's nationality one might be utterly at a loss. As it is, I have a faint feeling that it might pay me to revive a knowledge that I once had of a book I ceased to study before I took up Thucydides—a book once much loved by riddle-raisers."

"Riddle-raisers." At that last, almost openly contemptuous phrase, and the whole out-of-hand dismissal of my consistent suggestions, my patience snapped.

"Mr. Mycroft," I said, "it is clear that my particular assistance is nothing but a hindrance to a mind set as yours." I thought of trying to use Dr. Johnson's grand slam, "Sir, I have given you a reason, I cannot give you an understanding," but I hadn't the nerve quite to venture on that. I would have probably provoked a painful rejoinder. So I simply went on, "I have done my best and given you, I cannot but believe, some useful, essential information. Your attitude, however, persists in being . . ." I wanted the sentence to be just, balanced, ironic, final, but it wasn't going any better than the code. "I can't do anything more," I stumbled on. "I'm tired and I think you're deliberately provoking. I am going, and want to drop this unpleasant business."

"I apologize," he said. "I think aloud too much. I have to keep my own mind clear. You were muddling my line of thought."

A nice apology, to say your colleague is worse than useless!

"Very well," I snapped. "I can, at least, prevent your clear mind from being further contaminated." And I walked straight out of the house.

Chapter V

AND I found myself back in my well-proportioned life, again busy with problems, neat, adequate, remunerative. Mr. Mycroft made no motion to reopen our acquaintance. To close the matter definitely, I even returned his check, though I felt I had really more than earned it. There was no reply. For all I knew he had left the country, having failed to find a real clue. After all, even that old dead fellow—well, one was always seeing in the papers about some hobo found dried up in a gully after wandering off and getting lost. The Indians often put a few stones on top of them and don't tell anyone, not wanting to be pulled into court and questioned. I'd had pointed out to me several such cairns when I visited Death Valley and Cactus Park. And as to all that tooth business—I've always had my doubts about all this fingerprinting. The patterns are too simple not to be repeated pretty often; and tooth-rings—well, they're even more unreliable, I should wager. About the clue hidden in the table's secret drawer? That was odd—at least that it should start with the very words I had decoded. But then, who knows, there might be some silly-solemn confraternity Ku-Klux-Klanning round these desert states and playing at being hooded, barefoot friars—all that New Mexico "Penitente" business taken up as a new thrill by whites from the Indians and the Mexicans. Anyhow, I was determined to dismiss the whole story, and as I was judge, dismissed it was.

Once again the whole matter was shelved. When, right into my office, right past my secretary, without check or warning, in walked—Intil! Of course I had made up my mind that Mr. Mycroft was foolishly wrong. Therefore, of course, I had no reason for being startled at seeing a man suspicions about whom I had decided were groundless. Yet he had undeniably behaved very oddly with me and Miss Brown. I could and would take a stand on that—demand an explanation.

"Well, sir," I got in first, and threw myself back in my chair—always a strong position with a fine desk in front of you, "your behavior needs no little explaining. I give you a perfectly successful reading and then you bolt off without a thank you!" It was just on the tip of my tongue to add, "The rest of the passage is obscure but I believe . . ." when caution suddenly said "Wait."

He took my attitude, which was, I flatter myself, quite magisterial, very well. That was clearly the right way to deal with this sort of excitable creature. Anyhow I should pocket that long-overdue fee. I was right here, too.

"I have come to pay what I fear has been unpaid very long."

It was perhaps not the real reason for such a return, but a good enough one as a start, for me. And it would also give me a nice little opportunity to test his sincerity.

"As I gave you to understand," I went on, not asking him to sit down as yet, "I don't charge for a mere interview. Unless I obtain clear results I expect nothing. But when they are obviously obtained and a second opinion has made the finding undeniable," (I was acknowledging Miss Brown's assistance, which in my mind, whatever Mr. Mycroft might imagine, I had never minimized) "then an adequate remuneration is certainly due. The professional fee"—that always sounds better than "my charges"—"is fifty dollars."

I had named a fairly big price mainly to see his reaction. Again I was pleasantly surprised.

"Very moderate," he remarked, "very. And may I add a similar sum as due to your assistant?"

Again I allowed him. I wanted to be sure that Mr. Mycroft was wrong, and here, in a most pleasing and substantial way, my belief in human kind—as being if not good at least not dangerous—was being established against the detractor.

"Very well," I agreed, with a judicious attitude toward the whole thing. "I think that may settle quite satisfactorily all outstanding claims."

He paid the notes straight onto my desk. I own I was thawed, and thaw may always lead to a little gush. I couldn't now bow him straight out.

"Well, is there anything further I can do?" I asked. It was little more than putting "your obedient servant," as lawyers used, when signing their letters. Though it still seemed odd that he should have called, I really never quite thought he would reopen the old question. After all, whether he was a Kluxer or a New Penitente or just an eccentric on his own—though I had decided that Mr. Mycroft was wrong—yet this man was hunting something; he'd never have bought that equipment and somehow furnished himself with a couple of burros if he hadn't been out after something other than a hike. These thoughts had run through my mind. Nevertheless I was more than a little surprised when, after he had turned back and shut the door, which was still standing open between the office and my sanctum, he picked up the "interviewee's" chair, put it on the right side of my desk, sat down, and spread a scrap of paper in front of me. A glance, and my surprise took on a keener edge. There was no doubt about it. Here was the full clue—as I had seen it when Mr. Mycroft put it together. This one was, however, copied out straightforwardly on a sheet of paper the length of a bank check. It was, I felt sure, a copy of some original, an original—I could not rule out this one supposition, though there could, fortunately, be ones less disconcerting—which had been possibly on the body of a man when he had been killed. And for which he had been murdered? That question was too unpleasant, in my actual immediate situation. Anyhow, I must and would gain time. And certainly, when I sidelongly looked at the little fellow beside me, he didn't look dangerous—not in a comfortable office with a competent secretary within call.

And he was speaking quite reasonably. "Your remarkable success with the first part of the test I made with you, leads me to hope you might be equally fortunate with the rest."

That was all aboveboard, at least as far as it went. I did believe that I already was on a line which might lead to solving the conclusion of this cryptic sentence and that Mr. Mycroft's crude and superior behavior had just thrown me off the scent. It was really no concern of mine what use—or none—sense or nonsense—my clients made of the readings that I gave them in reply to their riddles.

"Yes, I think I can help," I said, glancing at the words which were more familiar to me than he imagined. "The time-reference we have already settled, and that part of the clause undoubtedly governs the next word, 'Cloc.' " I thought he became a little restive at that, but I wasn't going to have my hunch ruined again, and this time by a highly remunerative client. "All that remains, is, then, to settle the last few words. The next two are plain and helpful. Here is obviously a reference to a trail—a mission trail, no doubt. One of those outlier Gospel-raids probably, made by the first Franciscans here. . . ." (Did he know that I knew that he had gone to the desert?) "I should then freely translate this part of the passage as, 'On the track of the mission trail.' " I could feel that he was watching me closely. "The remainder of the message gives precise bearings. We have, then, given: one, a definite time, two, a definite route, and, three, the actual spot on that route." He was dead silent. To relieve what I felt to be an awkward tension I added with some conscious carelessness, "Of course, I'm no seer. It is for the client to apply the reading. I have no idea what the message means but I am glad to be able to tell you that that is what, in point of fact, it says."

I turned toward him. Yes, he was watching me with a curious nondescript expression—puzzled, I felt, and if certain of anything, then . . . ? Well, perhaps not so friendly as I could wish. He'd been friendly enough till he knew enough? That was my vague, not very reassuring feeling. He remained watching me until I really became quite nervous.

"Well," I said, rising to break the tension, "that, I think, concludes the matter."

"No," he replied with a curious and none-too-pleasant intensity. "You're wrong, every word of it—'cept for the first words you did long ago. I can't have clever theories. I must have facts."

I was a little frightened, but I was also a good deal more angry. He had hit me where quite a large bruise remained from Mr. Mycroft's unpleasant handling. He was just wanting to get out of paying—well, he could get out. I was sick of the subject, a nauseating mixture of the sinister and the silly—a beaten-up white of egg silliness over some horrid little smear of peril. I heard myself say, "Get out of this office." I felt it quite out of character but again—as earlier with this odd customer—it worked. He had stood up, looked at the door, then, holding his precious scrap of nonsense in one hand, he rubbed the fingers of the other hand smartly up and down the bridge of his nose till it was quite red.

"Mr. Silchester," he said, "will you take me along to Miss Brown? Didn't mean to vex you—always was a bit hasty—have a good deal on my mind—can't help feeling that, back of this, there's something worth all whiles to find. Honestly, know enough to bet the reading you gave—very good, I say, very subtle—still it's just not the thing. Do let's see if Miss Brown can see."

So he really didn't know more than I did, and, on the other hand, he and I shared his feeling that there was really something worth seeing at the bottom of this puzzle. As long as he'd behave, why shouldn't I give the thing one more chance? Then caution and comfort both urged: Leave the whole thing alone!

"No, Mr. Intil," I said. "I've done my bit and my best. You can again decline to pay. I don't expect you to. Perhaps you can ill afford it. Certainly if that is so you should not bother Miss Brown."

"You think I can't pay?" he said. "All right; all

right." He was turning over something in his mind, I could see. He looked at me and then I could see he had come to some decision, something, I judged, which cost him some effort. But now that his mind was made up he seemed at his ease, more than I had ever seen him. "I'll trust you," he said, "if you and Miss Brown will keep my confidence. I have a feeling that people are on my track. I just must get through before I'm forestalled. I can't get this clear by myself—have everything right but can't quite get the precise bearings. I'll promise you two a big fee." He hesitated. "Two hundred and fifty dollars apiece?" he looked up at me. I bowed quietly and noncommittally. "Five hundred each." Yes, he evidently had gone very near some goal if that was a serious offer. "If you'll really put yourselves into this decoding. Well, I've trusted you. Will you close with my offer?"

I must say I couldn't get the feel that he was really trusting. But I did get very strongly that he was in a fix and had his finger very nearly on a big thing—just out of his reach.

I made a frontal attack. "What precisely are you, Mr. Intil?" That should bring him out into the open if he really intended leaving cover. And it did, with a rush.

"What am I?" he answered, quite melodramatically. "Well, in a phrase, I'm one of the queer crowd called prospectors. Prospectors, you'll say, why that old '49 stuff? There are none now except those poor crackpot old fellows you'll see off in the Mojave and other of the deserts trailing about behind a couple of burros. There, though, you're wrong. Individual mining days over? Not a bit of it. Though perhaps it's best the public should think they are. Truth is, they're only beginning. Frontiers closed? Nonsense. They're opening as never before. Gold? There you go again down the old trail. Mining's only beginning now, I tell you. But if that's so, what am I doing with a slip of worn paper, trying it over and over? Why am I not out with pick and shovel? Why, there are two good reasons. In the first place, we're in the New Prospecting age. In the old-time mining there was just copper and a hope of tin and, of course, always the silly lure of gold. But the really precious metals or minerals were just coming over the horizon. The really precious metals, haven't you read about them? About Big Bear, colder than Klondike and far richer. What was there? Something that looked like bad coal. What was it? Pitchblende so shot with radium that literally you burnt your seat if you sat on your precious find. Talk of hot money—what about that! Price of radium still makes all the old 'precious' metals look like junk. And there are"—he paused and eyed me carefully—"bigger and better deposits than Big Bear." He paused again. "I'm nearly on the track of such a lode and Miss Brown (I have it now firm in my head), with what I give her, can get the line. Now will you take me to her?"

So this was the real story. Well, it fitted in fairly closely with Mr. Mycroft's speculations. And as he had declined to give me his full confidence, I could not help feeling a certain justifiable satisfaction at finding out what he had kept from me. Besides, paying him back was a wrench; and here I should not only "turn a pretty penny," but I should find what he had held back from me, and, more, what he himself didn't know. I, despised Sydney Silchester, would be there first. That decided me. To be able to write to Mr. Mycroft, in quite a friendly way—I supposed he'd have his mail forwarded to him—and just as a casual piece of news give him the whole story, clue and climax! I own that tempted me too much. Intil was out, it was quite clear, after some rare ore. It wasn't at all likely that it would pan out as he dreamed, any more than it was likely that Mr. Mycroft's dramatic detective rendering of the story was the right one. Intil might well be crazy, but if so, he was the sort that has enough money to be worth humoring. I didn't doubt that Mr. Mycroft might have been sent by some interests which were concerned about getting some sort of new ore. I'd heard that minute amounts—such as of tungsten—could change the quality of steels. There was no need to swallow all the embroidery with which either of the men gave their particular trimming to the tale. The thing was to find the main thread under it and to see that that at least was "a thread of gold"!

"All right," I said. "If you will provide an advance payment of, say, 50 per cent, I'll see whether Miss Brown and I can again work the oracle."

He did not hesitate. "I'll have the cash here tomorrow for you if you can make the appointment for then."

I picked up the telephone. Miss Brown was in. "If you will wait in the outer office I will have a word with my colleague. I can give you your answer in five minutes."

As meek as a schoolboy he said, "Thank you," and went out, closing the door gently. I certainly had established an ascendancy. The last misgivings in my mind shrank into the background. I felt I had the initiative in quite an entertaining adventure.

"Miss Brown," I said, "do you remember a Mr. Intil who never paid a fee for the very remarkable sitting you gave him?"

"So the little fellow who bolted has come back?" she answered.

"Yes, he wants another sitting."

There was silence at the line's other end. If Miss Brown would not help we were done. And though she was stable enough, as good, unpretentious "extra-sensory" people usually are before they are spoiled, she of course had to respect what she couldn't control—her subconscious temperament. I knew that, by myself, I couldn't get another word of that damned Scotch-locked code.

"By the way," I added, "he's already paid us both handsomely—capital and interest—indeed, one could say damages for our past neglected services. And he's prepared to come cash in hand—which is better than 'cap in hand'—for further help."

"I wasn't thinking of the pay," her voice replied, and I could agree that she certainly was not mercenary. "I was thinking whether *I* could produce."

"Oh, you can; you've done it already," I said encouragingly. She had; and I felt sure, if I gave her the assurance she'd do it again and we'd get the whole tangle clear and beat old Mycroft at his own game, and perhaps, who knows, cash out even more handsomely than our present payment promised.

"No, it's not so simple as that. Don't you see, your man interests me—my surface, Miss Brown self too much. That interferes. As soon as I try to make any sense of what comes through, or, if it has come in trance, then even if I find I'm feeling a recurrent interest or faint curiosity about what may have come through, I'm just fouling my own deep-sea fishing lines."

All I could do was to answer, "Do try; I'm sure you can get it again."

"All right," she said hesitatingly. We settled for three the next afternoon and I went to tell Intil.

"It's touch and go," I said. "Naturally, sensitives don't like being treated as you have treated Miss Brown."

He took my rebuke properly enough, only anxious to know whether I'd any hope for him.

"But I think I have persuaded her to give you another chance." He brightened like a child, and I felt quite the wise elder and not at all unfriendly as I added, "Of course, I must impress upon you that nothing can be guaranteed. On the other hand—" I was pleased to see how judicial I was, and it shot through my mind that it would do Mr. Mycroft no harm to see me carrying out so successfully this role. "On the other hand, I am equally convinced, and I speak with no little experience, that it is highly improbable, most highly, that you will find any other combination"—I smiled at my choice of word—"which can hope to unlock your riddle." He nodded. "I would then further impress on you to be here precisely at two forty-five

P.M. tomorrow and to bring with you the necessary remuneration."

He rose quickly. "I'll be here," he said. "I'll be here and you'll have nothing to complain of this time." At the door he turned round. "You see, you just see, you get the clue clear and I promise you you'll never have another word, not another word to say again against Thomas Intil."

The last words were said with such conviction—how shall I put it?—with such unnecessary conviction, that I remained looking at the door after he had gone through it and it had snapped sharply behind him. I felt, in a way, quite sure I had made an impression, felt that he wasn't going to try to shake us off again. He evidently had realized that we were quite essential to him. And then some other line of thought, some further hunch was trying to rise up into my mind. I couldn't think he could be dangerous to us here in a big city, even if he wished—which I didn't believe he did; why should he? After all, Mr. Mycroft's mind ran on murders and mysteries. I knew, now professionally, that many people like their little bit of mystification who'd never dream of violence, far less murder.

All that about old Sanderson was really complete supposition. We really didn't know even that anyone had shot him, that the withered thing we had seen had really been shot or really been Sanderson. I ran over these points again in my mind and the more I thought of it the more likely it seemed that if a hardy field prospector had met poor little Intil plodding after him in his new stiff cactus boots in that hell of a heat it would have been Intil who would have become pemmican, not Sanderson or any pioneer. "And the clue Mr. Mycroft had found in Sanderson's house?" my mind asked me in this final check-up. That, I had to own, was far queerer than coincidence. But even here the simpler hypothesis—the anchor of all scientific deduction—was that both Sanderson and Intil could have come upon some record of a cache in the desert—they've often been found and traced before—some deposit left by an old miner, or even a Spaniard's hoard. All the talk about the new prospecting which Intil had shot at me, that, I now concluded, was simply to save his final disclosure for himself. He had to get our help and so put us off with this fantasy about a new mineralogy. That was it: Sanderson, Intil, and maybe the desiccated unknown (who knows?) were all on a common track and they had all, or at least two of them, kept their clue, naturally, to themselves. Neither, I concluded, had found his objective, and probably, too, neither knew precisely what or where it was. Sanderson was at present out of the running. Mr. Mycroft owned that he was stumped by the clue he had furnished himself with from that source. And how funny it would be if, while he was fumbling at it, Sanderson actually came back! A nice point in morality for my magisterial Mycroft: "Go ahead; use someone else's information to lay hands on someone else's property—or own you've been housebreaking and have purloined the owner's title deeds or something near enough to that to make no moral difference."

This reverie ran rapidly through my head, and, I'm glad to say, cleared the last misgivings out of it. At the very least, I was going to make a handsome fee; I felt somehow fairly certain that I was going, also, with Miss Brown's help, to make another spectacular interpretation—I suppose something of the feeling which Joseph must have had when Pharaoh asked him about his cattle dream, or Daniel when he went in to guess the writing on the wall.

I turned back to my secretary. "A nice little fellow that," I volunteered. My secretary is one of those competent girls who disguise hard, technical efficiency under a deeply laid bloom of glamour. She replied by tapping with her dictation pencil on her "smile-proof" teeth. It was her dot-and-dash signal for "I do not agree."

"He was upset last time," I continued, for I was wanting to have my revised opinion confirmed.

"Um . . . that sort's better when upset."

"What do you mean?"

"I saw him while you were phoning and when you came back. He can switch. He just didn't think from my appearance I was worth keeping up appearances in front of."

That is hardly the kind of English sentence I like. Miss Delamere's (I have already mentioned my secretary's unconvincing name) handling of prepositions was as loose, out of verbal carelessness, as her appearance was of deliberate intention. But in both cases—of ear and of eye—she knew quite well the effect she wanted to make.

"And your verdict?"

"He hasn't become any fonder of you during the absence."

I felt that this conversation might well destroy all my new initiative if I let it go on.

"That's interesting." I always close by finding Miss Delamere's last remark interesting. It generally is—quite enough to let the question rest and to let her know that I value and shall turn over her opinion.

"And here are those inquiries you ought to settle today," she remarked, knowing the signal and raising from her "To be answered" basket half a dozen letters. "I've already answered for you in the polite negative the invitation to the A.B.C.—the Anagram-Bacon Club; two requests to cast babies' horoscopes; an offer of partnership with a dowser doctor; and a request to speak to the Five Featured Fundamentalists."

We settled down to a good afternoon's work and when it was through Mr. Intil had taken his proper place—a client among clients, all a little odd, rather interesting, fairly remunerative.

Chapter VI

THE next morning's work was also equally perspective-giving. So by two-thirty I was feeling no more trepidation about the oncoming appointment than I would at any routine visit of a normal client. Nor, when he entered, did Intil seem in any way abnormal. Even Miss Delamere's searching look at his back, as she left him with me, only amused me with the reflection that a woman bears a grudge against any man who is absent-minded enough not to notice her.

"Will you," I said, "if you have not done so, put your clue or code or whatever it is, in an opaque envelope?"

He hadn't, and I handed him one from my desk. His

hand, I noticed, shook as he inserted the thin single slip of paper into the envelope. Then he raised it to his lips to seal it, but paused, looked over the top of it at me, and then, evidently forgetting that he hadn't sealed it, slipped it into his pocket. It didn't matter, so long as he kept it there. Miss Brown's surface mind would catch no clue with which to confuse her deeper consciousness.

"I've brought the cash," he volunteered.

"Very well; you can make the payment to Miss Brown at the conclusion of the sitting and I will, at the same time, pay over to her the balance of the joint fee for the last."

"Can we start now?" he queried.

"We have plenty of time," I answered, determined to keep the initiative. "I have a few things to collect. You should be provided with a firm pad of paper and a pencil so as to take adequate notes and I will have another." I handed him these items. "If transmission is good, the speed may at times be considerable and much valuable information may be lost. It is often difficult to remember quite outstanding information which comes with much, the relevance of which, at the moment, is to seek."

I felt that I was preserving exactly the tone which I wished to impress and that my hearer was, at the least, not unimpressed. In the outer office I paused to give

Miss Delamere a number of small instructions and reminders about things which she had pretty certainly not forgotten. She made, though, small pencil notes and I closed the scene by asking her not to wait should I be detained beyond five. It was a thoroughly sound exit. Why couldn't I have walked straight out? To that Intil-like question I can only answer that I suppose deep in my mind I wanted for some unknown reason the reassurance that I was directing the entire incident in all its details and at precisely the pace I chose. Then, at any moment, should I wish, I could terminate the proceedings.

It was seventeen minutes to three, exactly the time I had calculated that it would take us to get there, when I stood on Miss Brown's doorstep. I glanced at my watch and, seeing the hands, into my mind ran that curious beginning of the clue, "When the flyer . . . stretches his wing to the left." Well, I reflected, in another swing of his wing we may know more about what that date was meant to specify; we shall perhaps have read the entire message.

I looked up; Miss Brown was standing in the doorway. She had already stoked up the parlor. It was almost like a tropical hot-house with a big fire burning and the shades and curtains drawn. The fire and the light which came through the shrouded windows made it easy enough to pick our ways to the two chairs she pointed toward. Then, without a word, she took her seat in a chair close to the fire, threw a handkerchief over her face as before, and one saw her form, quite relaxed, sink back into the cushions. For two minutes the breathing grew deeper and quieter; then came those odd little twitches and a whimpering murmur like a dog in its sleep. The breathing became normal again. The far-too-bright voice of the little infantile "control" caroled "Good morning." It was, of course, well on in the afternoon. But one must be amiable if one is going to be informed.

"Good morning," I said, with avuncular benevolence. "Good morning." I looked across to Intil who was scribbling away, his pad slanted to get the light from the fire.

"Say 'Good morning,' " I whispered. He looked up.

"Oh, he needn't if he doesn't want to," said the spook-child-prodigy. "But you're nice and friendly, Mr. Sydney. I like you."

I didn't at all want these blarneying compliments and was familiar enough with this sort of exploration to know that if once the silly little "guide" wandered off on my side line of nursery sentiment, we should never get any results.

"I've brought such an interesting man," I began.

"Oh, I don't like him. I like you. He's that rude stranger. We're friends, you and I, aren't we?"

"Of course," I said. "Of course."

I wondered what the mischief could be the splinter of intelligence which can actually give a confused but copious mass of otherwise unknown information and yet not know that I doubted even whether it was a person and, if it was, disliked it and its mawkishness intensely. Fortunately, at that point Intil realized what was required of him—that he must blow this odd spark until it shone in the direction in which he needed to see. And he came up to scratch surprisingly.

"I'm so sorry. Please forgive me, little lady," he started off in a voice as copiously sentimental as the "control's." "I was so busy getting ready, so as not to waste your time if you were able to come along and help us, that I just didn't realize that you had come."

"That was very stupid of you, Mr. Instill. There's a word like your name but I'm too young to know clever words but it's like Instill, yes, yes, they say to me it *is* 'instill'—you should instill—that's it—into your mind more readiness. It's rude not to answer when someone says good morning."

This dreadful patter—and now it was started it might run on, a series of self-generating echoes!

But Intil again surprised me with his readiness. "You're right, little lady; you're plumb right, and I wish you a very good morning. I offer you also my apologies and I thank you heartily for turning up."

"That's better," said the childish martinet.

"Thank you," Intil answered immediately, with that effusiveness which evidently warms the cockles of the subconscious. "For that was such a wonderful message you brought last time——"

"What was it about?" said the voice vaguely.

"All about the queer birdie sitting in his pretty round cage."

"Oh, yes, oh, yes, oh, yes, the round cage with the dots on it and why the birdie could sit in the middle when there wasn't a perch for it to sit on at all!"

"That's it, that's it, little lady. Well, you knew all about the cage and the birdie."

"Did I?" the voice hesitated.

"Oh, yes, you did. You're so cute and you made all so plain to us. And you know, of course, it's just the beginning of a wonderful fairy story—a real fairy story. You see the cage now, don't you?"

"Yes," rather slowly. "Oh, yes. He's still stretching his wing."

"Right you are! And then, beyond his cage, the further side of it as you might say, there's something else, isn't there?"

"Yes, but I can't see it clear at all. It's all fuzzy."

"Could it be an old hobo in a brown robe?"

"What you saying, Mr. Insul? No, you're all wrong. Old man in long frock! No, *that's* not it. No, it's not a thing at all a hobo'd have. It's a thing kings have—a sort of crown."

"A crown, little lady? That's wonderful."

" 'Tisn't very wonderful"—said with a sort of finger-in-the-mouth speculativeness. "Crowns should be ever so bright. This isn't; but it is a circle with prongs sticking up all round. Now, what would you call that, if you wouldn't call it a crown, Mr. Sydney?"

My sudden summons into conclave almost caught me as much off guard as the initial "good morning" had caught Intil. "I think you must be right," I gagged. "It does sound like a crown, doesn't it?"

"It doesn't sound," snapped back our little precious. "It looks. I've told you what I see. Mr. Intil, Mr. Sydney is just not trying. What do you think it *can* be?"

I didn't demur at the transfer of affection, and sat back content to let Intil spend his breath blowing on the queer little smoldering spark of "vision."

"Well, it's a circle anyway," he ventured.

"Yes," with great child's play of judiciousness and of viewing the subject from every angle. "Yes, it's a circle, it is that, you are right, Mr. Instil. You think faster than poor Mr. Sydney. He's slow and doesn't want to attend—perhaps he's getting old."

Fortunately, Intil was as unwilling as myself to seek through the mouth of this suckling further revelations as to my age and "actuarial expectation" of life.

"Yet," he tactfully steered back the wandering attention to its first interest and vision, "yet the circle has prongs."

"Ah, that's what I said. That's why I said it was like a crown. But a dull, gray crown! They're gold always."

"What's near the crown?" That was really a neat cast by Intil.

For at once the asinine little angel said, "Why, there's another prong! They all stand round like candles round a birthday cake. And he stands all by himself."

"I see, he stands looking on?" prompted Intil.

"He stands in the way. Oh, I see now, it's all level and bright that way and he stands right up in the way of it. Leastways, the bright path is just swinging on to him. You see, don't you, Mr. Intil?"

"Oh, yes, oh, yes," he lied encouragingly. I was sure he was just as lost as I. "And the prong that stands outside is now just getting into the way between the circle and the bright?"

"That's it, Mr. Intil, that's it, and now he's right in the way . . . Ooh, something flashes . . . Ooh!" The medium broke into a regular yelp as though her toe had been stamped on. We all started. She was whimpering now.

"We'll have to stop if she gets miserable or frightened. That's a common 'fade-out,' " I whispered to Intil.

"I'll try now with the next clause," he shot back. "Little lady, that was fine. You've gotten it, there isn't a doubt, and you'll get the rest. Do you see anything more?"

The whimpering stopped. "That was getting horrid," said the mincing missy voice.

"Yes," agreed Intil. "But the next will be fun. If I say slowly to you, 'AP. 20111318,' don't you see something?"

"Stop," she squealed. "You mustn't mix it all up. I've got to tell you what I first see and then what comes after. Now first, just the first part, mind you, it's ever so big and, oh, it goes up." Miss Brown's hands rose with a waggling wave like a baby trying to catch an air-balloon. "And everything, every teeny thing is in front of it. That *is* all. It's just that."

"You can't tell us anything more?" he questioned, almost sharply.

"No," said the voice with equal sharpness, "and you're a rude man to speak in that tone of voice."

He was quick enough to salve the sensitive's hypersensitive feelings: "Oh, but I was only so pleased, so excited. It's all so wonderful the way you work. Oh, it must be lovely to see so much and to be able to help so much all us poor blind people."

The slick sentiment worked. "I love being of use to all you poor people who can't see. But you mustn't be impatient, Mr. Impul," the voice cackled with delight at its alliterative skill.

"I won't be. You've been so good, so good and helpful. Yes, we'll leave that last picture alone and just think it over. I only wish I could see it like you. It must be wonderful!"

"Oh, some day you will, if you're good."

Intil no more than I, perhaps less, wanted a talk on sugar-plum-fairy heaven.

"You've been so good to us," he positively crooned. "We won't tire you. But you said that there was something more you could see—just one more picture? Won't you tell me a little more about those little numbers?"

I was sure the childish intelligence, under that suggestion, must see a car complete with license plate. But nothing was said for quite a minute. Then I noticed that the medium's body had raised itself in its chair. The face with closed eyes—for the handkerchief had long been discarded—seemed to be staring at some object in the far distance. "Sea," it said.

"Sea?" queried Intil.

"Don't interrupt," it snapped back, as a dog snarls at someone who tries to draw it from watching a distant cat. "Sea—oh, and it opens just like a whale coming up. But it isn't a whale. Oh, he's horrid! He's all spotted, but his paws are all furry."

I feared she was again going to put herself into one of her self-imagined terrors with all this fairy-monster stuff. But, as suddenly, and of herself, she sheered off, and said with her excessive self-composure that grated on me perhaps more than all her other poses, "But the horrid animal really doesn't matter. It's all because he's got a number."

The mind had evidently skidded back from its hectic delirium imagery to the numbers that had been mentioned to it. I felt it was time I took a hand and closed the sitting. Though I had to own Intil had done wonders, utterly unsuspected wonders, in keeping things going and in encouraging the wayward hunches of the ungeared mind, nothing had come through. Well, that was the way with this sort of questing. You had to draw a bow at a venture. Most of the arrows went into limbo but every now and then one struck a real object, an object well out of the range of any other kind of insight.

"Thank you," I said. "Thank you; yes, we've already got the number."

I thought this would close the sitting. But the little pet, instead of falling into lullaby inanities—which is the end of most sittings, good or bad—suddenly spurted up, "There you're wrong, Mr. Sydney.

You're so smart in telling us what we're seeing, when you can't see a thing! That's just it. That isn't the number—the number is . . ."

Intil had become quite credulous. I had, of course, often seen that—the solemn, priggish, hard-boiled skeptic attending one good sitting with a few undeniable telepathic "hits," suddenly, his front of superiority crumples and there emerges the pathetic "it's-all-true" believer. Intil sat forward in his chair hanging on her every word.

"Oh, I can't see them clearly; you've made it hard."

Intil, I saw in the firelight, shot quite a venomous look at me. I was highly amused. "They're all little quiggles, one just like the other."

"Yes, yes," he encouraged. But it was quite time Miss Brown was let come back, or come together again, or whatever happens when a trance state clears off and normal consciousness is resumed.

"Thank you," I said with quiet finality. "That's all we'll need, and thank you again. Good-bye."

"Oh, it's not," came with a second flash. "You're so silly. I was just seeing it come clear. Serve you right, slick Mr. Sydney, serve you right!" and the medium's tongue was stuck out to express a small schoolgirl's past-all-words contempt. I chuckled again as Miss Brown's form settled back into its chair and the reverse process—of drowse, slumber, twitch, half-sleep, yawn—was run through.

While it was going on I turned to Intil. I thought I'd make a "sounding" half-apology, just enough to suggest that the sitting had been all that I knew it had been—quite empty wanderings. He was making some rapid notes but he looked up as I turned to him. The fire was still bright enough for me to be able to see unmistakably the expression on his face. But, though it was clear, it was such a mixture that I was at a loss to interpret it. He was clearly interested, interested profoundly, moved, one might almost say. But if he was moved, that was not to say that he was melted. On the contrary, he looked particularly set—satisfied and at the same time defiant, hostile even. Of course I had upset him by closing in when he had been making all the going. But, after all, he must trust an expert in a field in which he'd owned that till that day he had been, save for one previous occasion, an ignorant stranger.

"It was a sitting with a number of interesting points for an expert," I began. He waited. Miss Brown snoozed on, taking her own time in coming back to the solid, adult world. "I shall be glad to work on them from my record here." I tapped my writing pad in which I had taken an adequate record. "And when the clues are ordered, I'll show you the results. I can well understand that you found it pretty confusing. But that is so often the way and why it is so important to have an expert with one." I felt sure I could write up a number of suggestions out of this rigmarole we had listened to and the very extravagant senselessness of the dream imagery would quite possibly stimulate my mind to pick up a real clue.

His only reply was to ask me a question. "You're sure it was a bad sitting? Nothing clear to you in it at all?"

"Well, nothing that does not need considerable decoding," I said, feeling that I was surely on firm ground there.

His next remark puzzled me more—startled me, I might even say: "Are you a clever man?" It was said more to himself than to me—an unfinished sentence, the second part of which was, of course "—or a fool!" He was a bit mad and evidently indifferent as to what one thought of his manners; but I was determined, however disappointed I might be in him, he should remain outwardly *compos mentis* until the fees were paid. And as he pulled himself together I left the question as though he had never made the impertinently intended remark.

"Yes," he went on as though he had said nothing else, "yes, that would be very helpful to a beginner. It is so puzzling, this method, these flashes. Don't trouble too much about working on the report; I too have my record. And, if I find myself in a fix on a particular point, I'll come round to you for elucidation." He was obviously trying to be affable and Miss Brown, emerging into full ordinary consciousness at that moment, I just nodded affably myself, turning then to her to tell her how well things had gone, for certainly, as journalists say, copy hadn't been lacking and the client was apparently far from unsatisfied.

Intil rose. "I'd like to settle my financial account now," he said, and drew the notes from his wallet, counting them out on the table, as I had drawn back the drapes. He was evidently going to leave at once, and I felt that the interview should be closed with some kind of conventional courtesy.

"Thank you," I said. "And may I congratulate you on your perfect sitter technique. Many sitters seem never to learn that particular and vital attitude—that stimulating interest. Miss Brown, your control found Mr. Intil far better company than her erstwhile friend Mr. Sydney."

Miss Brown smiled, turning to Intil to say, "It does make such a difference if the sitter can keep the 'control' interested and amused without giving anything away."

A flash of some sort of triumph appeared on the little man's face. He was evidently susceptible to praise from specialists. Indeed, he seemed disproportionately pleased—a sort of suppressed exultation, for which just knowing how to handle a medium in trance seemed hardly sufficient cause. Yet he evidently thought it was.

"You see, Mr. Silchester, that a prospector is more widely adaptable than perhaps you thought. He can tumble to a new trail and pick up a new way of tracking and stalking quicker than most."

So that was it: under his meek phase he had resented my rather magisterial handling of him and now was pleased to be able to show off that at the very first time that he really took a hand he could make a better sitter than I. Stalking, I thought, rather a melodramatic word for just keeping amiable and expressing interest while an infantile part of one's hostess's personality gave "free-association" tests and suggestions. But he was particularly pleased with the term himself.

"Stalking's really the heart of the matter," he informed us. "Getting within reach while the quarry plays about. Then you simply have to put out your hand, knock off the flies, and help yourself." His curious tongue, of which I'd had more than a taste already, was evidently getting its head again. But to my relief he realized that of himself. He suddenly shut up, didn't shake hands, hardly bowed, turned on his heel, and walked out of the house.

"Not quite so precipitate an exit as last time," remarked Miss Brown as he disappeared down the street. "But he is certainly an abrupt type and how I wish I could question my own subconscious and ask it (or her) why I feel so oddly about him!"

"And I," I exclaimed, "have lost the opportunity of questioning him as to his address. I can't send him the edited script!"

"You didn't want very much to do so, did you?" she smilingly questioned. "I don't think you and Mr. Intil are meant to be client and professional adviser. It doesn't need for me to call up the wise-woman side of me to know that you and he are '*non simpático*.' "

She was getting out the tea things while she spoke, and certainly, soon the atmosphere was so "sympathetic" that any undefined cloud which Intil might have left behind, dissipated itself. What he had definitely left, the very large fee, remained comfortably and firmly in our pockets. As we parted, I remember saying, "I feel quite balanced about this business. If he never turns up again we end with a substantial balance in our favor. If he does, we may learn more and make more." As I went home I reflected that I had failed in my main purpose, to settle whether there was really anything to the code and, if possible, to beat Mr. Mycroft at his own game. But on second thought I concluded that I'd probably never again see either of these oddities. It was mere chance that had brought them across my tracks.

Yet in a fortnight I did hear an echo. The telephone rang. "Will you speak to Miss Brown?" said Miss Delamere's demure voice from the outer office. Of course I would, and Miss Delamere knew it, but that was just part of her "doubling of parts," as actors say. About an ordinary appointment with a complete stranger she would take all control, tell me what the applicant wanted, was like, was likely to pay, what time she had settled as best for the interview, even what I had best look up before. And it would all be done with her gazing at and turning over the letter and her notes —she always had notes which she made and consulted, but once or twice when I managed to find crumples of them in the wastepaper basket all that was on them were not unclever cartoons of the visitor and sometimes of myself. But when it came to a casual talk with Miss Brown, then the part of the hard-boiled secretary and adviser was dropped. The frontier between business and the greater unmapped territory of Private Lives had been crossed. The shadows of possible romance blurred all the hard outlines. Miss Delamere lost all decision; she was nothing but discretion. I knew her little game, but still it could vex me.

"Of course I will," I replied, not that the "of course" would make any difference next time. "Put her through." It was a relief to hear the sensible voice of the so-called "sensitive" after my very valuable, very hard-boiled, but very film-fanned secretary's.

"I thought I should ring you up," she said, "as there's a small point of professional etiquette. Intil has just asked for another sitting but, you see, he wants to come direct to me."

"I shan't object to that," I answered quite sincerely. "I own that he vexes me, we certainly don't suit each other, and, though I don't want to spoil your muse's inspiration, I own I could make nothing of what came through last time. Please have him and you're welcome to the gift."

"Very well," she replied. "I agree I don't think he is the kind of man you aboveboard—or above-the-threshold—decoders can help. I feel, for what my surface feelings are worth, that he hasn't really an ordinary code to puzzle with."

I wondered whether I'd tell her all I now knew but decided that it might only disturb her deep hunches. "You're probably right," I contented myself with answering. "If he's got anything, you can get it, and if he hasn't, well, as I've said, you're welcome to him as a client. He seems now inclined to pay and I'm letting out no secrets of the confessional if I repeat that your 'control' and he seemed to like each other strangely."

She laughed. "You mustn't be jealous. I know you

have really a low opinion of my poor little 'familiar.' I expect she likes people a shade less grown-up thar you."

"All right," I said, "and good fishing."

I was just going to hang up the receiver when Miss Brown cut in with, "Oh, by the way, you were sorry you didn't get his address. I've got it now: it's on a letterhead. He didn't phone, he wrote."

She gave me the name of a small hotel somewhere in the city. I didn't take it down because I didn't want to see Intil again; he was an irritating of-no-interest, and I can never carry in my head those four-figure numbers ending with a street named only by *its* number and a point of the compass. It's as bad as trying to recall longitude and latitude directions on a sea chart. So the reference was out of my mind as soon as it went in.

But Miss Brown rang up once again; again it was about Intil. I was busy. I didn't very much want to hear. It was a week after her last call. Miss Delamere made the usual courtesy-delay. When we were in contact, "Yes," I said, a little hastily I fear, "yes."

"I'm sorry to interrupt," she began. "I only wanted to say that Mr. Intil sent a second note to say he was suddenly called away and was sorry he'd have to postpone our appointment."

"I'm sorry," I replied, for I was sorry that my tone at the beginning had been sharp.

"I'm not," she replied. "He does interest me, but the last two days I've felt as though I had influenza coming on and my hunch collapses the moment my temperature rises."

She didn't sound too low, so with "Well, it's an ill wind . . . and I hope you'll be all right soon," and a small joke about Sleuths being linked sometimes with Bromo Quinine for all colds, I hung up.

Chapter VII

THE next development—well, it gave Miss Delamere a part she felt made for her. Perhaps it was a week, perhaps even less; we had gone through the mail and settled our answers. I was sitting back getting ready actually to dictate the first. Her cigarette held off at the correct angle by the raised fingers of her left hand, her pencil poised in her right, her legs crossed to balance on her knee her shorthand pad, Miss Delamere was poised in the precise display-angle which she had long studied, at last perfected and strictly preserved. It was as detailedly stylized as the "caress-the-child-and-bless-the-worshiper" carriage of a Byzantine Madonna or the fan-flourish and hip-twist of a Bali dancer. It was the high point of finish, detachment, hard-boiled elegance, I realized. And so, I suppose, I ought to have realized that it was the precise and chosen moment when, with an easy air of just filling in an odd instant before we were well under way, Miss Delamere would be likely to give me a surprise. Nevertheless, I gave her a far more satisfactory reaction than I should when she remarked with deliberately slurred casualness, "Oh, by the way, poor little Miss Brown's dead."

I was swung back in my desk chair, my hands behind my head—it helps dictation, that stretch. I came forward with something almost of a crash. Of course Miss Delamere's drooped and curled eyelashes kept their slant of semi-bored, almost drowsy indifference. Had I dictated, "Brown, may my body lie by thy cold corse," she would have flicked down the line with a neat pencil flourish, perhaps asking if I liked "corse" with or without an "e." As it was, she flicked off a neat little cast of cigarette ash into the small lacquered tray which always stood on my desk's outer corner to serve her need of occasional gesture.

"Dead," I said with that silly mental echo which the shocked mind will give. It was most highly improbable that Miss Delamere would ever spoil an effect by a false climax. No, Miss Brown was dead, never a doubt of it—the source was unimpeachable. "How?" I said, almost as stupidly as I'd said "dead."

"She wasn't well last week, y'know. Good deal of flu about. Reckon she'd a rocky heart."

Well, I shouldn't get any further by simply gasping like a landed fish. I swallowed the words, "Why, only last week . . . She did say she was a little off color . . . The last thing I said was a joke about taking chills seriously. . . ."

I knew my shock was meat and drink to Miss Delamere. I was doing the sentimental Britisher—that dear, mellow nineteenth-century spontaneous, gentlemanly stuff, with which Aubrey Smith has made the whole screen world familiar. She was just waiting for me to cough and blow my nose and pull myself together with a fine assembly pull at the old school tie—while she, in the hard-boiled good taste of the New Yorker, might go so far as to allow, with another neat contribution to the ash tray, that it was a queer deal for the old girl. Well, I wouldn't play my part in her little "two-period" piece.

"In reference to your inquiry I can give you an appointment at three-fifteen on Monday the thirtieth. It is important that you should bring with you adequate specimens of the code in question (period). The examples with which you have provided me indicate that the system employed is (comma) pretty certainly (comma) one of that class in which for purposes of decodification it is necessary to detect the repetition of a series of letters or transposed words (period). In these circumstances . . ."

I rattled it off at such a pace that, to my delight, I forced Miss Delamere to put down her cigarette. I couldn't hope to drive her to cry for quarter with, "I'm sorry, I didn't quite get that." But the abandonment of that careless, casual, only-need-half-of-my-attention-and-must-fill-up-the-rest cigarette—*that* was making one's opponent give ground, if not drop her point. Indeed, I felt that all the ground which I had lost had been regained.

Victory must be confirmed, though, and I worked away all through the lunchtime till every letter was complete. Miss Delamere never even grew tense. If I chose to stick it and so disprove her casting of me in the role of the all too easily touched Englishman who lets business come second because an acquaintance has had to leave business for good, well, then, I had proved my unspoken contention. But I must prove it to the hilt. It must be no mere temporary rally, but a fixed attitude. The hilt, I think, really was reached about four. We were both tired and both with our wary admiration of the other restored—maybe heightened.

"I think," I said, "you needn't type all those till tomorrow."

"It won't take me really long," she said.

"No; do those four important ones about appointments and the two long ones giving readings and references."

"Would you like flowers sent to Miss Brown's address?"

I knew now that she was the fully co-operative secretary. The hard-enameled glamour girl had had her innings and, if not the human-hearted, at least the more natural-skinned secretary was taking her place.

"I don't think she had any relatives, as far as I know. So I don't see the use."

There, I knew, I was gaining another point, for we old post-romantics, when we jettisoned crape-and-jet mourning, left obsequies to become part of sub-hygiene; while, to the young hard-boiled, a funeral had, by good business salesmanship, become another essential social function. It was an opportunity for another style of sartorial smartness and a muted wit—another chance of showing oneself able, even with Death, to chat lively across even that super-silent Presence.

"I think, though, you might inquire if there is anything we"—I used the plural—"could do to help in tidying her affairs. She may have left some things unarranged."

"I'll see," was answered with an emphasis that made

me sure that the inquiries would be properly made and that my secretary-observer was glad to be able to serve in this way.

I was therefore able, when it was collected, to be given information without its seeming food for sentiment. It was simply reporting back on a minor business arrangement: "Yes, Miss Brown had sent for Dr. Innes, who thought she was faced with a pretty sharp attack of flu. There had been some about for a little while, but this was evidently the first—at least to his knowledge—of the second wave which is always considerably more severe and can easily have complications. Sure enough, on the second day they did turn up: high temperature, considerable discomfort, inflammation. Condition was acute in another twenty-four hours. Patient had evidently lived on rather a low diet and pretty certainly had a tired heart. She was one of those unlucky cases sulphanilamide doesn't seem to help, and, for one or two of them (of whom she might have been one), it's now and then actually contra-indicated. She had a really bad day. Then, the fight given up, she went out easily enough."

Well, that was all there was to it. I'd liked her in an easygoing professional way; should certainly have never known her but for that. It was the suddenness that jarred—like leaning against the back of a firm little chair and suddenly it collapses. My work went on, and, even in real losses, I've heard that work, at least when one's at it, makes one forget. There was plenty to do and at the same time, in all the cases, not one in which I could have needed to ask her opinion. I didn't, of course, forget Miss Brown. It's silly to say that, I think, of almost anyone you've known—at least for years. I just got used to knowing she was dead.

A month must have passed and then I was given a small opportunity of doing something for her memory in quite an unexpected way. I certainly would have declined, had not what I was asked to do seemed to be a slight act of acknowledgment of our acquaintance and her general niceness. One morning, going through my mail, there was a bulgy unopened envelope left on my desk by Miss Delamere—resting like an egg in a nest of neatly opened sheets. Miss Delamere had left it intact because, written on two corners of it in heavily "printed" letters was the "keep out" word "PERSONAL." I put it aside until, with Miss Delamere, the opened letters were all adjudged and decided on. Then, when she had withdrawn to begin the answers, I turned to my personal correspondent. I slid a little steel spatula (I hate poking my finger into an envelope; it's just the way to get hangnails) into the tightly sealed flap and cut it open along the top edge. The spatula flipped out what had made the envelope bulk. It fell on my desk. It was, besides a letter, another envelope that had been folded inside the outer. Before retrieving it I dropped the outer envelope into my wastepaper basket. I then picked up the letter and looked at it.

On it I read, "Dear Mr. Silchester: I must ask your assistance. I am at a loss. After the help you have already given me" . . . so he acknowledged I had been of use . . . "on two occasions" . . . so he was able to appreciate now that I had helped the last time also . . . "I feel sure you will a third time solve my problem." Well, he couldn't turn to Miss Brown, poor lady! But what was this! Here she was becoming the mystery herself. "Where has Miss Brown gone? How can I find her? I was hoping just to finish off, with her aid, the detail of some of the clues you two had provided for me" . . . a none-too-neat way of saying he'd been by-passing me, trying to save "toll" . . . "I applied for an appointment and was given one. Unfortunately a sudden business call compelled me to cancel that. I wrote, the very next day, apologizing, and asking for another, and enclosing my fee as evidence of bona fides. I received a reply naming a date a week ahead. I waited impatiently, I own. Miss Brown's gift is surely not in such great demand!" (That vexed me: who was he to judge!) "Then I arrived at her address, only to find the house closed and that she had gone." Yes, that was indeed a fact, though he evidently had no idea how far. Then my mood, which had been shifting from impatience to vexation, suddenly, like a boom on a yacht, was flung right over into full-blast indignation by the sentence which concluded this increasingly complaining letter: "I'm a poor man. I know I did once keep her waiting for her fee" . . . no reference to his treatment of me . . . "But I did pay her and you" . . . now I was included when it came to his praising himself . . . "handsomely enough, didn't I? So" . . . and here was the astounding impudence, "she shouldn't have bilked me. I suppose you know why she has gone off and where, and I will ask you, as the man who introduced me to her, to let me have her new address. I enclose a stamped and addressed envelope, as the matter is urgent."

Had Miss Brown been a bad woman, I thought, how gladly would I have given you her present address and told you to go there! As it was, wherever she was, she was away from the irritation of this little self-centered fool. I hesitated, about to tear up his impertinent note. Then the chance of giving him a piece of my mind seemed the better choice. I snatched up a pen and wrote rudely on a scrap of scribbling paper, "Mr. Silchester presents his compliments to Mr. Intil and begs to inform him that Miss Brown is buried!"

There, I thought, he won't believe me; he'll have to make inquiries and then he'll find that it's literally true—as true as of John of that ilk. I read it again: there was quite a little punch in the phrasing. Yes, he should have it. It might jar him a bit. And I'd send it to him in his own make-haste-please reply-paid envelope. He'd then see his own writing, think I'd risen all anxious to please and try for another fee, and then inside would be this neat smack in the face like a jack-in-the-box. I folded my note carefully. I reached out my hand and picked up the still folded envelope he had enclosed. Yes, it was correctly stamped, and addressed—this time to a box number, not to a residence. I tucked in my note so that till the last moment he shouldn't see what I'd written, and think he'd gained his point.

I was actually raising it to my lip to moisten the flap when I paused, hearing Miss Delamere's voice raised in rear-action barrage: "No, Mr. Silchester is engaged—is busy. Please wait here." It *was* a rear action, for her voice was coming closer to my door. She was yielding ground to someone who was evidently not even troubling to reply to her. The door swung open. I saw her to the side. She had failed to act "Bar Lass" and to keep the gate. In the doorway stood another figure—Mr. Mycroft.

My surprise at the intrusion was, need I say, great. It kept me gaping, with the envelope raised to my lip as if I were blowing a kiss or doing something equally idiotic. But the first shock, considerable as it was, was completely obliterated by a second. He didn't say "Good morning," or "The reason for my intruding"; he simply snapped, "In time!" and strode across to where I sat behind my desk, and pointing at me, almost shouted, "Put that down!" My anger flared up, as fire will out of a whirl of smoke. The intolerable insolence of the old intruder suddenly rushing in from God knows where! I suppose it was a kind of involuntary defiance that made me do it. Under the transparent excuse of going on with what I had been doing before this intrusion—moistening the envelope—I stuck out my tongue as far as I could until it nearly touched the gummed flap. The effect of this gesture led to an action far more outrageous than anything he had done so far. Mr. Mycroft literally swooped and, shooting out his long, skinny left arm, caught my wrist, while with his other hand he snatched the envelope out of my fingers. Surprise made me speechless, until I heard him saying, "Go and wash your hands at once and thoroughly."

Those words, after the snatch and grab, brought back so vividly my nurse relieving me of candy and sending me off to clean my fingers, that I broke into laughter.

"Here we are again. It's like a pantomime farce. The old dominie drops from the ceiling and the bad boy is hurried off to be birched. But, joking apart, Mr. Mycroft, to what do I owe the honor of this visit, where in the name of heyday have you dropped from, and what the mischief do you mean by dashing in and snatching my stationery practically out of my mouth?" My tone showed I was roused. His answer showed, though, that my irony had been misspent on him.

"It's not your stationery," was his queer reply. Then, taking a small box out of his pocket, he gingerly dropped the envelope into it.

I could only think to say, "Kind of you to mail my letters in your private box." I added to rouse him, "It's no joking matter."

"You wholly mistake me if you think I imagined it was."

"Then why the devil——"

"Yes, it's quite diabolic."

"Mr. Mycroft," I cried almost in despair, "where have you come from? What are you up to? Are you mad or am I?"

His answer was certainly methodical: "I have been hereabouts a considerable time. I am up to my old game. There is a madman—not you nor I, but the cause of our meeting—and the cause of your death, had I been a moment later, a second more ceremonious over my entry."

Yes, he was sane enough. So, when with increased emphasis he said, "Well, if you won't wash your hands, I must," we both did so. And when I saw the thoroughness he used, I followed suit, for I have a real fear of infection. When a man whom you have known to be brave and careful takes from his pocket a small bottle of that horrid creosote disinfectant, makes a wash and scours his hands with it—well, when one has been handling the object he just touched so carefully, one is inclined to imitate. That small purification rite somehow eased the ridiculous tension between us and I listened, I must own, eagerly to what he was telling me.

"You have just escaped a curiously clever death."

It was an unpleasantly professional way of talking of my possible demise. But by whatever epithet anyone names one's own death hardly matters—that noun is so dominant that any adjective scarcely counts. I was convinced that here was a case I should have to listen to. However much the old man grated, if there was any shadow of truth in what he said I should have to ask him for any aid he could give. We returned to my sanctum; Miss Delamere, realizing that the citadel had capitulated, made no attempt at a relief expedition.

As soon as we were seated, the old man remarked, "I'm not going to give you theories. I know they rouse your suspicions. I will, therefore, bring you proofs, facts. To provide you with these I must leave you for an hour or so. I would ask you to accompany me so that you might follow every step. But not only would you, I am sure, prefer to be left quietly in your office to complete a morning's work which my intrusion may well have deranged, but it may, as probably, be safer for you to stay here till I return. I promise to keep you waiting no longer than is absolutely necessary." He rose. "I may leave, may I not, by the back way? I don't see any danger, now, that we have not"—he paused—"under our hands. But you are right, I may overlook some things just because I see and attend carefully to others." He spoke quietly, considerately; made a gentle, old-fashioned bow and was gone.

Miss Delamere sailed in and posed and poised in amanuensal readiness—watching me, I knew, to study another angle of English reaction-behavior. My tired mind would only reflect, not on the mail, but on how very wrong she was to think of going into the films—she should be a novelist. "Women Prefer Weaklings," I thought would be the sure-fire title of her first, or "Ladies Prefer Loons" or "Ladies Like Loonies." No, I must stop this wandering. I picked up the letters of the day's mail which she and I had shared, trying with them to make a screen against the one which she had not seen. Somehow I dictated a few further corrections and replies, though I noted that this time I never gave the cigarette hand a moment's uneasiness. Indeed, it carried on, keeping far more than half of Miss Delamere's attention. It de-ashed, stubbed, selected, lit, yes, and even offered the cigarette so often to her lips that Miss Delamere's head swung on an easy rhythm—almost each line of dictation by the right hand being balanced by a slow inhalation from the cigarette offered by the left. I was becoming hynotized by her easy rhythm, as birds, I believe untruthfully, are said to be hypnotized by cobras swaying in front of them. I had to break the spell.

"You can type what is done," I said.

"And if your visitor returns?" she questioned as an over-the-shoulder exit.

"Why, show him in."

She nodded, not so much an assent as a confirmation to herself of her foregone conclusion. She had won this round and I might as well admit it and be counted out. Nor did it matter much. I really wasn't very much interested in keeping up "face" any longer. My uneasiness was sufficient to make me indifferent as to what appearance I gave and whether I could or could not upset the picture Miss Delamere liked to have of me as foil and background to her patient, lifelong presentation of herself.

I waited until it could not be any longer merely my impatience which made the time seem long. Then I allowed myself to look at my watch—I won't have a clock in the office; a clock often makes clients think they are not getting a long enough interview. I was right; it was late; Mr. Mycroft had well outstayed his own leave of absence. I waited again, trying to work on a code which I had been constructing, off and on, for some time. At least it served as a screen while Miss Delamere swung in, deposited the final letters I had given her, all typed, and remarked that if I wasn't inclined to go on with further work, she would go out and get some lunch. I agreed, telling her gratuitously that I had had some new ideas about the code, and thought, while they were fresh in my mind, I had better try them out. When she was gone I didn't go on with the code, gave up all pretense. I started a little, with a sort of half hope, half fear, when I heard, after a considerable time, at last a step in the passage outside the office. But it was only my all-too-efficient secretary back from an all-too-slimmed lunch with an all-too-interested wish that we should get on with our work. Yes, I was thoroughly upset. I didn't, I wouldn't put my feelings into thoughts but I own I couldn't help feeling something hanging over me.

At last another step was outside; I heard the outer door open. I heard two voices overlaid, talking at once, and once again Miss Delamere and Mr. Mycroft appeared together at my door. And again his conduct was as disconcerting (and of course deliciously bizarre to my secretary) as before. Again he swooped, but this time not to snatch my letter out of my hand—I wasn't holding one anyhow; I was just waiting. But his action was just as extreme, and this time I noted, with a queer added discomfort to my anxiety, that Miss Delamere, though she was actually not looking on and treating us openly as a show, at least had allowed herself the liberty of leaving the door open. Mr. Mycroft, though, didn't say anything. He simply dived under the knee-hole of my desk and took the wastepaper basket from its kennel.

"First out of my hands and now from under my feet," I thought with that anaemic fun that seemed all that was left when one fell into such a searching grasp.

Emerging, like some sea-god playing with a monster shell, Mr. Mycroft, over the brim of it, questioned, "No one has touched this since I left?"

"Not even a discarded stamp has been added," I answered.

"I'm late because Intil made a mistake," was the way he disregarded my reply.

"Am I supposed to ask what you mean?" If he simply wanted to snub me, let's get it over, and then, maybe, he'd do whatever he thought of doing in silence.

"I said I'd bring you proof that my behavior, though odd, was rational and your position, though it seemed safe, was one of the greatest danger." I waited while he scanned the contents of the basket which he'd carried to the window, for all the world like a giant jackdaw looking into a little bird's nest before deciding which of the eggs to purloin. "That's it," he said to himself. He set the basket on a small coffee-table and, taking a pair of long surgical forceps from his pocket, fished up an opened envelope. I had risen, and could see it was the once-bulky one marked "Personal." "Would you," he said, "ask your secretary to be so kind as to bring in the small box I left in your outer office?"

He had not finished before Miss Delamere came in carrying a polished wood box with a paper parcel tied on the top of it. He watched her till she withdrew and closed the door, then laid both forceps and the envelope it still held, down in the fire-grate—I like an open fire in the cooler months. Unpacking the parcel, he drew out surgical rubber gloves and put them on. The parcel also contained long-handled surgical scissors. Next he opened the brown wood box and lifted out of it a microscope, selected a slide, set it in place, and asked me to look.

"Nothing of particular note, as far as I can see," was my report.

"So I believe, and that was the reason for my delay."

I had given up any hope of making him explain by questions. The old fellow must be allowed to exude his knowledge at his standard, one-drop-per-minute flow. I suspected there was some real danger about, and so stood clear and silent in the offing, only doing a "super" part when called on. He turned then to the fireplace with the surgical scissors now in his left hand, picked up the forceps—which still retained the envelope in its jaws—and proceeded to snip into the top of it, finally cutting out a small disk from the center of the back flap. Disengaging the envelope and leaving it in the grate, the forceps then picked up this fragment—about the size of a piece of confetti. Placing it between two fine slips of glass, he clipped it into the field-platform of the microscope. Then he was still, for a little while, save for his long fingers twiddling the focus screws at the side. Finally he sighed, raised himself, and said, "May I trouble you again?" pointing to the lens. I stepped forward obediently. "You should be able to see some small objects, almost in the center of the field of vision," he said. I did. "Those," he said, "are perhaps the neatest packets of poison a murderer ever dispensed."

Instinctively I took my hands away from the table, putting them behind my back and began to breathe through my nose. I knew that such defenses would be of little use really, but one reacts like that to remarks of that unsettling sort. It was, therefore, naturally irritating to hear Mr. Mycroft saying, "More careful precautions than those would be needed if the enemy were really loose."

"Loose?" I queried.

"Yes, though of course we are taking no risks with such a monster, still I think we can say he's held at present. Now if you will be seated, may I explain?"

Such questions are, of course, rhetorical. I waved him to a chair and sat, rather heavily, down in mine.

His opening was good: "I need not now, I believe, take much of your time in striving to convince you that you have very nearly been murdered in a very ingenious way." Well, I suppose a decoder ought to feel a little comfort in that—that the bump which bumped him off was given with a curious grace, a pretty skill. I smiled wanly. "Until I had proof I was not going to take your time and, as you see, even this morning, when I thought I had everything unraveled, there was a last twist. But that really, as you will see, put me at my ease. I knew we had time then, and then I realized a little later, not only that we had time but that time, in this matter, no longer counted. May I then begin from where we are and work back?"

I touched the office bell and Miss Delamere sailed in. I hoped she thought Mr. Mycroft was anything but what he was, my savior. I knew I should fall forever in her estimation if she suspected I had been such a dumb-bell that though I lived by decoding and detection I'd all but been murdered in my own office by one of my clients.

"Miss Delamere," I said, "please don't wait. I may be kept for some time." She nodded and in a minute or two I heard the outer office door click.

Chapter VIII

"You received a letter this morning, marked 'personal'?"

"Yes," I said. "There it is," pointing to it lying in a tray on the left of my desk.

"It is safe to handle," he said, "and as I am sure of the drift of the contents, perhaps you'll not mind reading it to me or letting me read it?"

I handed the tray to him and he picked it up, carelessly enough. He read it twice and then smiled. Certainly his reactions were a little inhuman: his sense of humor had, I could only suppose, become highly specialized.

"It's well done," he remarked. "I'm sure you noticed

the skillful appearance of clumsiness? He has to get you to answer. It is quite likely you won't. He must provoke you, so that, perhaps against your better judgment, you'll dash off a reply, an impatient retort—a few lines and then fling them into the envelope put ready to your hand—and so send the bearish fellow off with a flea in his ear. You react as he planned. Now for my intrusion. Until 'by-passed' you to Miss Brown. So, I confess, did I. You and I had fallen out. I fear I grate on you, do what I will. You had awakened my curiosity about Miss Brown and her gift. Besides, I was still trying to work out the mystery on which you began by helping me, and especially the code. Miss Brown, a charming woman, kindly gave me a sitting—odd, how specialized we are, Mr. Silchester. Here's an old detective and yet till then, believe me, I'd never had a sitting with a good medium, or, indeed, with any of that sort. It was, as far as I was concerned, a brilliantly successful attempt." He sighed, "A great loss."

I thought I ought to say something, I suppose to show that after all here was territory in which he was the tyro, I the proficient. "Didn't you find the so-called 'control' pretty exasperating?"

"No," he answered complacently. "I have never required of my informants intelligence or critical acumen—only that they report fully what they see. And, in this case, that, my one demand, was copiously met. But of all that later. Fortunately, I have enough information. That, however, does not make the tragedy any less regrettable."

"Yes, she died very suddenly of acute influenza."

"No," he contradicted, "she died of diabolic poisoning.

"First, how did I find out? Casually, as we were having tea after my sitting and sedulously avoiding the topic on which I had come to see her (and, ten minutes before, I had been obtaining ample clues from her alter ego, her other mind), she, making conversation, mentioned you. I had, of course, when asking for an appointment, said that I had known you and now she said simply that she had seen you last over a client you had brought into her.

" 'We mediums, Mr. Mycroft,' she chuckled, 'are supposed to be unstable. I suspect, though, our instability, were it compared with that of many of our clients, would make us look a sober lot. The little fellow Mr. Silchester and I tried to help—beside him I feel as phlegmatic as a policeman. His first visit was absurdly amusing. I'm afraid he upset Mr. Silchester, but he interested me. I'm breaking no professional confidences, for, as you realize, I don't know what goes on once I have made whatever this long-distance connection may be. I'm out, as long as "it" is in. His second visit intrigued me, for he acted up to character, though he was perhaps a little less abrupt. And now,' she said, 'I've just had a third demand that I consult the oracle once more for him. He won't telephone.' Pouring me out a second cup of tea, she looked up smiling. 'I think that is rather nice and old-fashioned. Don't you think it's a point in his favor? That though he's so impatient when he's on the spot, he can control himself in trying to get one to join him there?'

"I asked, 'Is he really capable of courtesy?' For you know, Mr. Silchester, I am—I have had to be—no detective is really any use unless he is—interested in human nature *per se*. We have to face the puzzling fact (which will always make our work an art and deny its becoming a science) that human nature can be extremely inconsistent. At the same time, though we deal with a far wider spectrum-band of behavior than that narrow belt of the commonplace, with which conventional characterization deals, in novel and in film, we have to know that it *is* a belt. There are no leaps and gaps. One state of mind passes into another. The angry man can be very brave and very brutal—up or down. But he can seldom be sensitively sympathetic or diplomatically subtle. My estimate of Intil was, and remains, that if he ever showed virtues—and of course he might—they would not be those of delicate considerateness."

I suppose it was because I knew that I was in great danger and, even worse, did not yet quite know what it was, knew it was near and yet didn't still see precisely where it lurked, that I heard him out. But his detachment was pretty exasperating. My fidgeting, though, did not accelerate his processes. He was evidently waiting for my opinion of his generalization.

"I suppose so, I suppose so," I said, letting, quite willingly, some of my impatience show.

"I wanted to know whether you agreed," he went on, "because on this judgment of mine depended my succeeding actions and"—he paused and looked over at me with a look which I did not quite like—"the steps I took for your safety. So you must understand why and how I arrived at my conclusion that *you* were in the greatest danger."

He was a shrewd, delicately manipulating old bully. When he wanted me to move, out came his hypodermic tongue and gave me that shot of flattery I couldn't resist. When he wanted me to stand still, to stand at attention, that same sharp tongue gave me a stab and sting of sharp fear.

"I may then resume my explanation?" It was again one of his closure questions, rhetorical questions, just flourishes of an arrogant condescension. For he never waited for me to reply—indeed, turned away and looked out of the window as he continued.

" 'Why shouldn't he be capable of courtesy?' Miss Brown then asked me. 'He gave, surely, a small sign of it when he sent a stamped and addressed envelope?' 'That might well be impatience?' I questioned. 'No; he left me to name the date of the appointment.' The subject seemed anyhow a trivial one and, after the conversation had turned to one or two other small topics, I left. I had work to do on the information the trance-personality had given me and I remember thinking, also, that Miss Brown looked tired. I know little of these abnormal states of consciousness and thought that she might be wearied by the long trance-spell she had lately undergone . . ."

Glad again to be more experienced, if only for a moment, I interjected, "No; on the contrary, Miss Brown, as is the case with most good mediums, is very little affected by her work."

"I came to that conclusion," he resumed, "when we parted." (Of course he had to be right!) "As we shook hands I was sure she was in for a slight feverish attack. I could feel it. How I wish," he went on with a really human regret that I own touched me, "how I wish I had risked being officious and begged her to see a doctor—but even then!" He paused. "Well, I suppose," he said, turning back to me, "that you now see the procedure?"

"No; not quite; I mean, I see, of course, that perhaps. . . ." I stopped.

"Very well, then, let's go back a little."

I groaned inwardly. Why couldn't I be sharper and avoid this endless lecturing which, at the slightest hesitation on my part, slid back, like a badly opened spring door, back to the beginning, so that the whole case had to be reopened *de novo!* My fears were right.

"Do you remember when we were in the desert you were a little startled—startled into a momentary impatience—" he smiled. Oh, I thought, if only my impatience now were but momentary. "—by our guide's killing a ground-squirrel which was coming near our camping site?"

"Yes," I said dully.

"You don't know, however, what I discovered later in talk with that trader, that he'd shot another of those poor little beasts in the presence of another 'tenderfoot' in that district and that that tenderfoot's reaction was even more amusing to the trader than was yours. 'The one,' he said, retailing to me his piece of gossip in a place where, you may imagine, gossip is almost as rare as gooseberries, 'the one greenhorn gets all gooey over the poor dear little vermin. The other also asked why I shot 'em if they come near. I told him as I told t'other. And what does he do? He makes a note of it! Day after, I was up along that way and saw his tracks again (he was all over that country then, before and after your visit). But what tickled me was the timid little fellow (as timid but different from your dude) had, would you believe it, shot, I swear, every ground-squirrel he'd had in range. There were their bodies. It tickled me, so that I'd stop every time I saw that piece of bloody fur. Sure he'd killed them—no one else'd waste a shot on 'em out in the open. He must have stopped and knocked 'em out as soon as they showed a nose. Must say he's a fair shot. But Lord, what a timid fellow! Afraid of infection, I guess, until it's almost a mania. Well, I've heard of people who couldn't just stop washing for the same reason.'

"I checked him there. 'Did you look at his tracks when he stopped to shoot?' 'Well, now you ask, of course I did. Yes, and he didn't only stop. That's sure enough, I remember. He'd walked up to each of his kills and inspected it. Well, perhaps he was crazy public-spirited—wasn't so afraid of being infected as wanted to clean up the desert and make it safe for the Indians!' Then our guide's interest changed. 'But what the hell, sir, was he after at the end of it all? What's he really tracking? I've been out here for twenty year. The old prospectors, 'course, just scrape up a bit. But sure, he's after something bigger than that? He's not the old pick-and-shovel type?'

"I didn't tell Mr. K. my—our?—expectations. I didn't want his interest aroused there. I did want his attention referred back to the first subject—what he took to be Intil's hypochondriac notions of preventing infection. 'Tracks went right up to the kill?' I questioned. 'Yes,' he added with professional interest in noting every character of a 'trail.' 'Yes, would you believe it, with a stick, or something, he'd actually turned the bodies over. Do you think he's so crazy he wanted to make sure they were dead?' Then, Mr. Silchester, I allowed myself a small comment. 'Perhaps,' I said, 'he wanted to make sure whether they were really infected?' The vagaries of hypersensitive greenhorns had, however, by then ceased to interest my informant.

"Well, at the time, I felt there was here either monomania or a skill I ought to understand, a method in madness which might quite easily come back into our lives in some queer way. But unfortunately my mind was up along the other track, trying to decode that cipher and trying to think out where Intil would have reached in his converging trail on the common goal (hence my repeated visit to the desert), a goal neither of us actually knew but both of us suspected was so big as to make all side issues insignificant. You see I was doubly lulled. I thought there was no danger anyhow. I couldn't see a red light along that track. And even if there was, Intil himself, I felt, was so engrossed in his search that he would have no time left to plot. A more active mind than I thought.

"But mine suddenly cleared—a very unpleasant clearance—when, ringing up to ask Miss Brown how she was—I was, I suppose, subconsciously uneasy, and the excuse was to tell her that her sitting was so successful that I felt I had the clue quite clear, thanks to her. And, of course, getting the clue off my mind and the goal fairly in sight, made me run back and check along the side lines which had not been fully explored."

"Oh, please go *on*, Mr. Mycroft!" I cried. "These parentheses! Do, please, tell me what you found that has put me in such danger?"

"All right," he almost shot back. "Miss Brown; dead: one. Doctor's opinion: acute influenza: two. Really, anthrax: three."

"I'm at a loss," I had to own.

"Then, please, let me give you, as I wished, full proofs."

I subsided once again.

"Look," he said. "Miss Brown suddenly dies of a general infection. She falls ill just after receiving and sending off a reply-paid envelope. That envelope is sent to her by a very ingenious man who has lately learned that ground-squirrels may often now be found infected with anthrax, who has acted on that information and killed and examined a number of such ground-squirrels. All this we know.

"Now, what do we know of anthrax itself? First," he tapped off the points with methodical swiftness, "it is a spore infection and so, like all such fungus growths, immensely resistant. As you know, when a farm beast dies of it, the agricultural authorities have the carcass cremated. If a sheep so infected dies and is simply buried, it has been known that other sheep which simply ate the grass growing from the earth under which the animal lay buried, have contracted the disease. 'Badger hair,' made in Japan into shaving brushes, years later gave anthrax to users in Europe. Spores are the most vital forms of life: they are unhurt by immersion in liquid helium—the cold of outer space. It may be that life reached this earth in such tenacious form. Second, to return to our deadly muttons: we know that, though farm-animal infection of this most dangerous kind can be combated, we can do little once such diseases get loose among the small wild rodents. Thirdly, you will say, well, anyway, anthrax is a well-known, well-marked disease."

I hadn't said so because I didn't know. That, however, did not prevent him from replying, "But, though that would be a natural mistake, you would be wrong —pardonably wrong, but wrong as a matter of fact and, sad to say, nature knows nothing of nonculpable, pardonable mistakes, but only of matters of fact. In many cases of anthrax attack, the patient, especially, as in this case when the person and the society he lives in have never been exposed to that type of infection, dies straightaway. Having no resistance built up against these toxins, they have a free run. The mark, the symptom which gives the disease its Greek name is, like most symptoms, a body-reaction, a defense, if a desperate one, being put up by the organism against the attacker. That is shown by the fact that the anthrax, the 'coal,' the black nodule under the skin, appears most frequently in the groin—in other words, in those glands which protect the main organism from infection, contracted in the limbs. No doubt if a doctor made a careful examination, and suspected from the start that some such infection was present, such an examination would lead him to see that the groin glands were in a queer state. But, as usual, much can be overlooked if our suspicions are not aroused. The number of people murdered is, I am convinced, always far higher than the number so certified."

That was so uncheerful a thought for me that I did not venture again to hasten him back to my own acute predicament. "You've made the anthrax information quite clear to me. But I still am puzzled how Miss Brown was killed."

"It was beautifully simple." Again that gruesome,

detached interest! "These spores live indefinitely. In the desert Intil collects bits of the skins of the animals he shoots. You need only a scrap if the animal is thoroughly infected. That explains why he seemed a good shot. He was a far better naturalist than a gunman. He reserved his bullets for those ground-squirrels which ran badly, not because he could shoot them more easily but because they were so obviously ailing and therefore possibly dying of what he wanted, anthrax poisoning. Then, taking his spoils, as carefully, no doubt, as I have handled your correspondence, he brings back all his specimens. One or more *are* anthrax cases. That's all he needs. It's ample.

"His next step? He makes a mucilage, a gum. Into this he introduces a number of the spores by just dipping a little of the skin and hair into the fluid. Next, he paints this 'doctored' gum onto the gum on the flap of a stamped envelope. All he has, then, to do, is to let it dry. That seals up the spores—till anyone should moisten the gum. Then, should they do so—a natural reaction—with their tongue or lip, they have poisoned themselves. He simply writes his name on two of these envelopes with his address and mails the first to Miss Brown. The success of that you know. He waits, watches, learns with quiet satisfaction, and then mails his second message of death.

"The success of the second cast I, with my precipitancy, just averted. I had just concluded my deductions—that Miss Brown had been murdered, calculated that her murderer would be striking again, now in this direction—can you wonder that I infringed the rules of general courtesy and your office regulations?" He looked up smiling, and this time I did answer the rhetorical question.

"No," I said. "No. You were right, quite right, in fact, very kind. Indeed, I'm really sorry . . ."

He was as unresentful to my slights on his feelings as he was indifferent to the way he hurt mine. "Very well," he said. "That's settled. I was in time, and so now I may ask you to admire the beautiful simplicity of the beast of prey's action—at your leisure. He kills—he makes you fall into his trap, put your head in the noose and, as it is a delayed-action noose, having fatally strangled yourself, you have still sufficient time to hand back to him the very tool with which he has killed you! The mere chance that the letter might be found and tested—a very slight chance—even that he avoids and guards against. The only thing which can be found is a letter partly friendly—in Miss Brown's case, wholly so—partly concerned with another person. This is alibi raised to a further range of art, this is the true boomerang—indeed, it is the boomerang of boyhood's dreams which strikes and kills the prey at which it is aimed and then returns itself to the hand of its sender."

He paused. "It is really, in its way, a perfect case. Everything is present. A simple but wonderfully sound idea carefully carried out; then man himself making a masterly cast. That is all as one would expect. But there is something more, that excites my admiration much further."

Was the old man, could he be going to make full amends and say that the way I had stood up under the strain was the really fine thing about it, the way I had taken Miss Brown's actual death and my own terrible risk?

"Mr. Silchester, you know I am deeply interested in human motive. Without that interest I could never, I have told you no detective could, be successful. But the trade itself would be too depressing to a man who was not callous—and a callous man becomes too clumsy and blunted to be a good detective—unless there was a deeper interest, an interest in the disclosure of a vaster design, a huge counterpoint whereby a basic harmony continually 'resolves' these surface discords."

It was a very long-winded compliment—if, indeed, it was ever going to turn into one.

"This case, I am thankful to say, shows both features, and the really remarkable cunning is overscored, overruled, shall I say, by an intervention far more remarkable, indeed wonderful."

So he was falling into nothing but a delicious reverie at his own skill and the opportunity the cunning of a murderer had given him to display his overruling powers! I knew I ought to have nothing but gratitude for my deliverance and to my savior, and that my behavior had not been that of the rescued overcome by gratitude. Yet really this complacent enthusiasm for the masterly murderer and for himself, as though they were duet players, was a little unpleasant, with myself left as the mean instrument on which they had shown their wonderful techniques. It was hardly moral, I reflected, so to regard crime, and that made me bold again to interrupt, for I was evidently once more right out of the picture. After all, my safety was part of the safety of the state, of society.

Mr. Mycroft remaining silent, lost, I suppose, in abstract admiration of still a new nicety in assassination, I plucked up my often-sat-upon courage: "Oughtn't we do something about Intil?" I questioned.

"Well," he said coolly, "you're out of danger now." He rose and, taking the slide out of the microscope, put, with tweezers, the small disk of paper in the metal specimen box. Next he went to the fireplace and, picking up the forceps, which still held in its jaws the deadly envelope marked "Personal," he made the instrument place it, with the piece cut from it, in the box, which he then snapped shut.

"But," I stammered, "he might try that beastly trick on other people, on you."

"Well, even if he should be so silly," he dryly replied, "neither of us is likely to be quite so absent-minded as again to oblige by licking a stamped and addressed envelope sent us by Mr. Intil. That reply has been paid—I believe once and for all."

"But won't he try to kill me in some other way?"

"Yes, undoubtedly, undoubtedly, if he had the chance." He said this as reflectively as someone might say that there was a good chance of a heavy dew falling that night.

"But he may," I insisted. "Evidently he still would want to kill me—though why? I suppose it's all because he somehow knows I let myself into trailing him with you. Oh, why . . ."

"Gently," he said in a quiet but hardly gentle voice. "Your panic, which I have told you is groundless, is, like all fear, preventing you from seeing the actual situation."

"You mean," I stammered, for fear and anger were making a sort of oil and vinegar emulsion inside me, little globules of sickly fear spinning round with clear drops of indignation (I had been far too long under the strain of uncertainty), "you mean that it is not clear that I am in danger from a man who wishes to kill me?"

"First be just, if I may not ask you to be generous," was his sententious reply. "I think I shall, I know I shall, be able to prove to you that Intil wanted to kill you not because you accompanied me on that trail, but for another reason. I have good reason to suppose that he never saw our tracks. He has reason to keep off that particular path where his dispute with Sanderson left after it a piece of evidence which, who knows, might be brought home to him. He went once again along that trail. Then he avoided it. Anyhow, he soon learned that his actual goal lay far from there. I have even better reason to suppose that he flattered you—fear nearly always overrates a foe—by thinking you had knowledge which—an awkward compliment, I allow—he was prepared to kill you if you were clever enough to have guessed."

I was going to interrupt, but he raised his hand and his next sentence made me listen, made me swallow the previous impertinences.

"Are you in danger, in any danger now? I shall know that in four days' time, and I am prepared to forestall Time's verdict—I say no." There was a refreshing certainty in his voice which so reassured me that, fear subsiding, indignation became my dominant mood.

"And now I would like to ask," and my tone was quiet and quite sarcastic, "I would be obliged if you would indicate to me in what respects I am failing to comprehend the situation we are in?"

"It is that your intense interest in the foreground, in the intended action, had blinded you to the over-arching 'surround,' to what has actually taken place. You have missed what thrills me—the intervention of —well, what I have ventured to call the element which makes detection worth while."

"Oh, stop being obscure and superior!" I cried, my self-control nearly all gone.

"I will," he said. "But if I am to be quite brief and conclusive, we must wait for four days." He rose quickly. "I will return then," he said, "and by then your tension will, I hope, have abated—by the time my proof is clinched."

The door closed on him almost before his sentence ended. I was left to calm my feelings as best I could.

Chapter IX

"FOUR days," I said to myself, as I went to my office the next morning. I had to admit that I had been quite unable to banish "dead yesterday" from my mind. Indeed, I had slept very poorly. If only I could have been reasonably angry with Mr. Mycroft and reasonably sorry for Miss Brown. But I was, I had to own it, not merely sorry for myself but vexed. Why couldn't I have let the domineering old fellow have his way, have it out, however he liked, and have it finished for good? After all, even if he had gone on praising himself and providence, drawing attention to his own skill and how it was approved by the nature of things, at the outside the whole business would have been closed in four hours. And now I had to wait four days, wait until I'd positively welcome another long lecture! My natural irritability had made me only postpone and extend punishment which, had I sat out the first dose, would have now all been over.

As I entered the building I tried to pull myself out of my reverie and be ready to meet Miss Delamere's drooped but darting eye. My "Good morning" as I passed into the inner office was nevertheless, I felt, very unconvincing. She would know I was upset—poor, soft-boiled Britisher. She might even say something, ultra sub-acutely sympathetic, out of the side of her mouth, while her cigarette and its black holder bobbed a kind of semaphore accompaniment. The rest of her face would be as blank as a wax model—which indeed it was. Well, I had better call her in and get it over and into the day's work. I pressed the buzzer, and then remembered that I hadn't even looked at the mail which she had opened and stacked on my writing pad. Her shadow was, however, on the frosted glass panel of the door, so I snatched up the wad of letters, hoping to look as though I had run through them. Yes, she was going to be superiorly kind, I saw. She wasn't going to let me not know that she knew I was—what do they call it—a "stuffed shirt," I believe—anyhow, a horrid phrase.

The cigarette and the cigarette holder began to bob

and, from a small aperture between the two perfect curves of carmine which showed where she wished the world to believe her lips extended, her ironed-out voice said huskily, "That's a new one on the top. Suppose you'd see him at three—spare hour then—gives his number——"

"Yes," I said, "yes," hastily running my eye down the page which I was supposed to be reading but not a word of which penetrated my mind. "Three is a clear hour?" I asked, to gain time.

"Don't know what else you'd think of doing then."

Of course three was, almost as a rule, kept for visitors, and, as Miss Delamere said, it was vacant today. I should have remembered. But first I must find out what the client wanted, who he or she was. A man—yes, Miss Delamere was right, there could be no doubt about that, it was John. John what? John—what vile hands people wrote who always typed and were never taught to hold a pen!

"Have you deciphered the signature?" I said. It was a better opening, for it looked as though I had read the letter and was simply graveled by the illegible name at the foot. "It's a K," I prompted.

"Took it to be Katton—might be Karton," the cigarette signaled. "Can I get him on the phone and tell him to come along if you wish to see him?"

"Yes, do that," I said, and she had gone, with one

of those short-skirt, long-leg sweeps which I suppose they practice as part of polished poise, a sort of sharp slide.

I heard her making the call before I began really to read the letter. None of it was typed—all was in penmanship, if one may so describe a hand which surely must have had no fingers, simply a fist. What Miss Delamere had picked out was fairly clear. He wanted an interview that day, if possible, and gave a telephone number at which he could be called. Next I began to make out of the squirms and skids which the tortured pen had made, that he wanted help with a clue. Well, most of my work, I had to own, did not lie with the highly intelligent and cultured. I had better see him and see what I could do. In a small business, a client is first and foremost a cash payment and all other interests must be secondary. Miss Delamere was back. Yes, she had made a contact. The client would be here at three.

The day had settled down into its routine. I was grateful to my illegible visitor-to-be. We went straight on with a number of straightforward riddles, etc. Miss Delamere was fixed securely in her major part, the efficient secretary. Even I began to give nearly all my attention to the present. My mind ceased to be engrossed as to what would happen or wouldn't happen in the next four days. I could wait; surely I should know that most things just peter out, don't come to anything. Even my dramatic Mr. Mycroft had bet that I wouldn't be troubled further. So I soothed the back of my mind, while in front I worked away with the safe little riddles people spin for themselves because they find most of their lives such plain, unrelieved sailing or sewing. And it worked. I felt myself becoming calm and content and the time slipped away. Miss Delamere lunched; then I lunched; no, not even going to the drugstore, for stopping work started unpleasant reveries. I read, as I munched my sandwiches and drank my milk, an ingenious work on double-code—the familiar book-code enriched and made far harder to detect by the actual meanings made to depend not on finding the actual word but by knowing how to calculate by an arithmetical progression where the real word would be "displaced."

It was then almost three when I got back to my work. I saw that someone was waiting—the outer door was ajar—so I slipped round to the second entrance to our small suite, which led directly into my own room. Miss Delamere heard me and I was not settled before she was in and saying, with her hand holding the door closed behind her—this half-turn was another of the "photogenic" poses, "The three o'clock client has been in since two forty-five. Shouldn't be difficult—a simple type—small fee, though—will you see him now?—practically three."

"Very well," I agreed, and splayed out a few papers on my desk. It is always better to be brooding—Archimedes and the Roman soldier—when an inquirer enters. So I heard the door close behind my new client, and Miss Delamere was gone before I looked up. I was glad she was—for I found myself looking at a face I knew, but certainly hadn't expected to see here or perhaps ever again. My "reaction" was not very ready.

"Oh, of course," I said aloud but to myself, "I ought to have guessed—of course it was 'Kerson'!"

"Yes," said my visitor, taking a seat without being invited. "You're the guy was out back by the reservation. The old fellow said you were a detector of a sort—read codes and that sort of thing . . ."

I was just going to begin to feel pleased that Mr. Mycroft had named me as the detective, when I realized that naturally he had done so to draw attention to me and away from himself. My face must, then, have remained blank, and I can only hope that he took it for a poker-face of noncommittalness.

Anyhow, after a pause, he did go on. "Living a bit of a lonely life as I do, I get to figuring out the fancy-stuff riddles and that sort of thing which people put in the papers and the competition stuff and what have you. Gotten pretty cute on it. But queer how it gets you! Can crack open most puzzles of an evening now. But when you get one that won't split—" he paused, "Why, then, it sort of gets *you!* Just can't get it out of your brain-pan. I say, not many of 'em can get you so fixed but when one does—well, you don't seem able to let the darned thing drop. Sometimes, after a week or more, you get it. If you don't, why, then, you just have to have it out. Now, you're an expert. The old fellow says you've just the hunch for this one sort of thing." I bowed; I suppose he was also conveying that I was no use at anything else. "So when I got fixed a fortnight ago with a small puzzle I found in a little old book of puzzles—when I got myself quite mad with this one—had all the others cleared out and up—as anyhow I was coming up to the city, I thought I'd drop in on you."

"To what book do you refer, Mr. Kerson?" I asked. "Often students, if they know the volume, can give the answer straight out of their reference files."

"Funny," he said. "Can't remember the book's name—*Old Puzzles*, or some such term. And I left it back at the store. But," with rather abrupt cheerfulness, "I did copy out fully the one that had me stuck. Worked at it all the time in the train. Thought—" he gave a wry smile "—if I can get it before I get to his office I shan't have to pay. I'll have extracted the acher myself."

Well, he intended to pay. That is always an encouragement. I honestly believe one guesses, or hunches, or whatever it is, with far better aim if one's subconscious knows it's up to real business. It puts it on its mettle. I know that there are fine fanciful natures who feel that any thought of gain would tarnish with the foggy breath of avarice the fair mirror of their vision—or so they say. But I am certainly not one of those up-in-the-air seers.

To seal the proffered contract, I said, "Ten dollars for a consultation and twenty if the decoding is immediately verifiable."

"That's a lot," he said dourly. And that just put my "dander" up.

"Very well," I retorted, "take your code to another expert or let it stay aching in your mind. It makes no difference to me." That worked.

"Not so fast. I didn't say I wouldn't pay."

"Very well," I snapped, following up the advantage. "Time, too, is valuable. Hand me your deposit and your copy of the code. I work fast."

Sure enough, he laid a ten-dollar bill on my desk and a long slip of paper. My mind had need to work fast—but it didn't. I looked up at him. He was looking at me. But, as far as I could judge, with no suspicion—no suspicion, for example, of why, when the slip of paper began to curl, I put a ruler on it to keep it flat. Now that reaction was right. I should have left it there—should have said, "This isn't a code, surely? Perhaps it's a message partly in invisible ink. Those little dots and flourishes may be parts of the ink which have come clear. The whole might yield to chemical treatment—but that's not my specialty. Go to a chemist. I advise . . ." etc. Of course this thing could never have come out of a puzzle book. I hesitated—and compromised.

"You know," I said, "this isn't a puzzle."

"Surely," he replied. "There's another quite like it on the opposite page. It's called an Old Irish Puzzle."

Now that was shrewd, and could it possibly be true? A moment's thought, a second glance at the paper, made me quite sure it couldn't be, but then the man must be cleverer than I'd thought. Part of his tale, too, would probably be true. Where else, other than in a puzzle book, would a desert trader have come across an Ogham inscription? For that was what he was trying to make me believe it was—one of those Dark Age Irish cryptic inscriptions made by notching the edges of upright stones. They are the only inscriptions which might at all represent the "script" which edged and notched the strip of paper lying now on my desk—but another copy of which script I had seen take the shape which yielded words, words I couldn't decode, nor could Mr. Mycroft, words which I was now sure were a matter of life and death, of killing or being killed, to all the people who happened to see them.

"It's a code right enough," he said.

Safety shouted in my ear, "Stick to it: say no!"

"Why, look," I said, smoothing it out. "It's quite arbitrary. These markings are random etchings—little chance stains or at most someone cleaning the tip of a pen and trying a stroke or two to see if it has come clean."

"You forget what I've told you," he replied. "I made this copy from the book."

I couldn't resist showing my knowledge, for it seemed quite safe and it seemed also the shortest way of shutting the man up and sending him about his business, which I had certainly more than a hunch I'd be the better for knowing nothing about. I thought I could safely show I knew my business, had earned my inspection fee and that the thing he was showing me was outside my expert field.

"The only thing this faintly resembles—" I wasn't going to say a word about Mr. Mycroft's Greek knowledge, "—is Irish Ogham, but I assure you this is not Ogham. Once you know the secret of that Hibernian script it isn't really hard to read—the actual language used is generally Latin, not even Erse."

I was watching him; he wavered at that. He didn't, I felt, suspect that I had any inside knowledge. He only felt that my scholarship was in danger of exposing his little protective lie about his paper's being copied from an Ogham inscription; and, no doubt, he *had* seen such an inscription in some puzzle book—they are a common thing to find there—and thought that Sanderson's code must have been so copied also. And it might have been, for Sanderson was, I knew, a queer sort of scholar, and I've heard that Ogham inscriptions have been found in Scotland, so his loyalty to his country might have made him tie up his secret in that form. But, I knew, it hadn't.

Kerson stood irresolute for a moment. I should have risen, pocketed the ten-dollar bill, handed him his paper strip, touched the desk buzzer, and stiffly bowed him out. He acted first, though. Literally, he pounced on both bill and strip and had them both in his pocket before I had time to prevent him.

"Look here," I said—a feeble opening I own—"look here, you can't act like that."

"Good day," was his reply, with his hand on the door.

Suddenly I felt I just wouldn't be treated like that. He certainly had the power to walk out of the office, to rob us if he liked; but I still, if I chose to use it, had more power than he. I could still make him come back with a word and make him make proper restitution. And what was keeping me from doing so? Only a vague uneasiness. After all, no danger lay for *me* in this direction? Even Mr. Mycroft had never suggested that. On the contrary, the two men had seemed in a way to like each other, and even to combine in a genial contempt for me. With all his faults, Mr. Mycroft surely wouldn't put me in danger. With all his boring appreciation of himself for doing so, after all, he *had* extricated me from some danger—at least he thought so, and was coming back to prove himself right in three days' time. No, just for his own fame he would not wish me to be imperiled.

I said quickly, "That's not, I repeat, an Irish Ogham inscription as you say it is. And I'll prove my words by telling you what, in point of fact, it is."

He stopped. "Prove it, then," he said.

"First, then," I answered, for I had stopped him from going, as I knew I could, "the form," I stressed the word, "is not an Irish but a Greek code." Yes, he was caught. "Now," I said sharply, pressing the buzzer, and Miss Delamere appeared, "please hand my secretary the agreed advance fee of ten dollars. She will make out your receipt as I proceed to demonstrate what I have said."

He handed out the bill and as Miss Delamere withdrew he brought out also the strip of paper. I took a round ruler, wrapped the coil of paper spirally on it until the curl had completely papered the shaft. It did not fit precisely but closely enough, for, though a bit disjointed, it was quite clear that words were there when the edge jots and tittles came near enough to each other. I read off the inscription, for of course I had little difficulty in reciting it, and I must own I had a moment's real triumph at his startled face. Indeed, he was so startled, so taken aback by my powers that it was his turn to blurt and stammer.

"Then," he said, "that's the code—I mean—but what *does* it mean?" He was in confusion, longing to know more, and, equally, fearing to let me know something he knew. Of that I felt now quite sure.

But all I was set on was to exploit my success and make sure he didn't get away without paying every cent he'd promised.

"I've given you the first demonstration," I shot at him, "and certainly you have shown no sign of behaving like a gentleman. As, then, I've proved to you I know what I'm talking about, you can now pay in advance for the further information." At that moment Miss Delamere swung in with the receipt, "Miss Delamere," I said, "please receive from this *gentleman* a further twenty dollars and make out another receipt."

She held out her hand as though this was the way we spent every afternoon, rapidly receiving ten- and twenty-dollar bills and issuing receipts. I saw she felt I was being unusually businesslike—a back-swing from an attack of nerves and sentiment, she would, I suspected, describe it to herself. But what did that matter? I was in the ascendant; both new intruder and home critic were owning that I held the initiative.

It was rather like a hold-up, but a perfectly just one. He paid again. Miss Delamere swung out. I sat down and made a copy of the text now familiar to me. He stood looking over my shoulder as I wrote out the words: "When the flyer whose flight is not through air, sitting in his cage stretches his wing toward the left. Cloc Friar's Heel. AP. 20111318—3."

"There," I said, sitting back and looking up at him; "we are agreed that we have laid bare the text and this is precisely what it says?"

"Yes," he said doubtfully. "Yes, but what the mischief does that rigmarole possibly mean?" Then, after a pause, "Oh, heck! And it *does* mean, I know it does, if only I could make the damned words speak."

Well, it was clear that he didn't know any more than I what the real meaning could be. And why, in the name of mystery, shouldn't my guess be as good as anybody's? Anyhow, I felt sure it was good enough even if Intil wouldn't take it and Mr. Mycroft mocked it and even poor Miss Brown's "control" sniggered at it—it was good enough for this blundering trader who, I suppose, had somehow blundered on it among Sanderson's "effects." Probably he'd watched the poor old fellow, trailed him even—it would be easier for him than for us or Intil. Perhaps the poor old man had slept in this man's out-station cave and, when he'd been made a bit tipsy, had shown the secret paper, boasting that it was no use to anyone to find it for they'd never read it if they did. And certainly it kept its inner lines intact even when the outer defenses had been pierced. So I'd be giving away no real secret if I gave my own reading. If it proved a true clue, then it was "anybody's gold"—any of these desert zanies could have it, for all I cared.

It took me a moment to think that out—a moment I had anyhow at my disposal, for, of course, I knew already by heart the reading I was going to decode.

"The first part is a time reference. It is a curiously obscure way of saying the time should be twenty minutes to three o'clock. That gives the time at which a certain place should be visited—the rendezvous, the tryst, the hour of meeting." He was listening attentively. I went on. "That is made clear by the next word, a sort of signature word, as it were—the word 'Cloc' or 'Clock.' It means, 'All that goes before refers to time. Now henceforward we shall be dealing with place.' 'Friar's Heel' has, therefore, to do, as we might expect, with a route, the route. I need hardly point out to you that the only really original routes in this country are those, not blazed but rather beaten out by the sandaled and calloused heels of the friars—the Friars Minor, the Franciscan missionaries who penetrated all the way up on foot from Mexico to San Francisco, the city of their patron saint. Once we have our main points clear, as we have," I said with growing emphasis as I became increasingly vague as to that numeral-and-letter ending, "the rest is merely a matter of local investigation and a little elimination of the numerical notation until you obtain a reading which gives the required indications."

I stopped. Kerson had certainly attended carefully—well, as teachers would say. I was pretty sure he was considerably impressed. I was certain, when, after a pause, he said, "You're sure that's it?"

"Well," I countered, sitting back in my chair and trying to feel judicial, "I always say when explaining my method that there is nothing high-flown or underhand about it. It is merely an expert's way of handling evidence. Anyone could learn it who gave the time. We specialists are simply time-savers. Time is money and we save it for you—on a percentage basis."

I smiled at my little joke. He didn't, but listened with continued care. "Now, of course," and here I felt I was properly protecting myself, "there's no such thing as certainty in deduction. There's no such thing as certainty in all science. Because there isn't strict causality, strict necessity, anywhere that we can find—only probabilities either high or low." Anyhow, that was true enough. Now to underline my moral. "So I can't say, 'This is the one and only possible interpretation.' I can only say, 'Here, you see, is certainly a reading which is self-consistent, which when read in this way gives sense, gives a direction.' " I stopped again. He was no longer looking at me but was staring at the floor.

"Maybe," he said aloud to himself. "There is that trail, I've heard." Then, rousing himself and quite clearly aware that he had spoken aloud inadvertently, he added, "Well, I don't quarrel with your method—don't grudge you your big fee. But just for your information I'd like you to know I don't think you've done the trick."

Naturally he was resentful at having had to pay when he didn't want to, so I let that pass. As to his opinion of my reading, well, I knew the impression it had made on two other concerned inquirers. They'd dismissed it even more summarily. Anyhow, I was well quit of such a thorny subject. I'd had very good fortune and had survived, I suppose, very considerable risks. Two of the men on the same trail had paid me handsomely; one, I was told, had tried to put me out of the way; but now that he had failed I was safe. Mr. Mycroft was on his trail in town—and I suppose I must look upon my repayment to Mr. Mycroft of his original payment to me as a fee for his present services. If, after all, Intil was not in town, but had gone back into the desert, then this my latest client would track him there.

It looked as though all the lines were neatly canceling each other out. The way things had resulted was remarkably in my favor. I rose. "Then the matter must stand until you have proved out my deduction." I felt quite safe and certain that this client would never darken my door again.

"All right," he said absently, and, still absorbed in his own notions, he slouched out of the office. Yes, the interview satisfied me. I felt that I had won back to my natural position and in that position had carried off things in a way which was professionally creditable and which closed the whole question. I had been a good businessman dealing with difficult clients, sending them off when things might have become ugly and retaining very adequate fees.

I buzzed for Miss Delamere. Yes, she too agreed with my judgment. I could see it. She even removed the semaphore cigarette so she didn't have to speak out of the other corner of her mouth, as she handed me the letters for signing and asked whether I would approve some small immaterial changes she had made in a few of them. Usually I don't like to have my style modified. "The style is the man," and if wave and curl are admired in hair, why not a few convolutions in composition? Of course style can be too "kinky," like some hair, and then—as we were after the Euphuists—one may be glad of a "de-kinking" and everything brushed back, slick and smooth. But that's only one style. My style, like my hair, has a distinct and I believe, a becoming natural wave. Miss Delamere had adopted the patent-leather poll; her hair was a tight glossy mat. So I suppose she was all in favor of tight-cut sentences. What made me realize that she saw I had been behaving "adequately" (it was her highest word of praise because it was so meiosic; so, though long, it had always to be used and, of course, telescoped into "adqualy") was the fact that she had actually approved of several parenthetic clauses which, on ordinary days, she certainly would have cut to pieces and left them, instead of a sinuous slope of style, a series of little jolting steps.

The day, then, ended well and the next flowed as easily. The rapids, I believed, were past and quiet stretches lay ahead. Even Mr. Mycroft's visit I looked forward to with a conviction that it would simply close, safely and fast, an incident which, incidentally, might never have been quite so melodramatic as he assumed. After all, I believed what I'd said to Kerson: Every mystery is capable of several interpretations. Indeed, I often think of writing myself a detective mystery wherein, starting with the conventional corpse, the stage-property well-stabbed body, it is "proved" that no less than three different people did it and also that it was a suicide or at least a *felo de se*. Yes, my spirits were good; my heart where it ought to be, not in my boots or my mouth but safely locked in my own breast doing its quiet business. My head was remarkably clear.

Chapter X

On the morning of the fourth day I, then, gave my orders briskly. "We'll go through the mail," I said, "and get it settled. When Mr. Mycroft calls, send him in." And we had everything practically in order when the doorbell of the outer office sounded. Miss Delamere swept out like a well-shaped wave—not a billow, still less a breaker, a neat swell—and swept back again with, in her ripple, like a large piece of flotsam, Mr. Mycroft. And he grounded down on the shingle of my foreshore in perfect character.

"It turned out exactly as I calculated," was his opening, which I might have written out for him and handed to him to read as he entered. But I wasn't to be ruffled. One reaction only did I allow myself, and it was, I felt, a legitimate one. If he knew everything, or, poor, dear old man, enjoyed thinking that he did, why then, in the first case (as he would say, ticking off the points on his long fingers and keeping a stern eye on one for fear of inattention), there was no need to tell him of my visitor of two days ago, or, in the second, it would be unkind.

"I'm glad," I said with attentive interest.

"You have reason to be," was, of course, his counter. "Otherwise you'd have had to come into court to enforce what you rightly said we should see to, proper care for the public safety." He was certainly going to start on my patience early. But I was resolved not to interrupt but to get through with it all and have it over in one sitting, as at the dentist's.

"Your supposition about the envelopes was, I suppose, correct?"

"You could hardly have any doubt about that. The proof I had to bring you was in two further parts. It is now complete. I will not detain you a moment more than can be helped. I am sure you will see the significance of the brief message I have come to bring you. I found the small hotel where Intil was living. He was so sure of his method (and he might well be) that he didn't trouble to disguise himself, though he was, in the hotel register, under another name—I was a little amused that he should have chosen the name Kerson —the trader, you recall—whether out of lack of inventiveness or for some other reason, I can't say."

I felt a small inner start at that, but felt also that I showed no sign of it. And anyhow, Mr. Mycroft was so interested in uncoiling his own fine, highly-prized web that I was merely audience kept in waiting to applaud the end.

"I learned, when I had been able to make a few indirect inquiries, that he was already confined to his bed with a chill. Yes, a case of 'acute influenza.' He had had a doctor called in. As he was unable to leave his room, there was no reason why I should not be in the hotel lobby. It was quite easy to be leaving the hotel as the doctor came out and to ask whether I might share his cab. I know enough of medicine, as you know, to be able to pass for a doctor, said I had business with Intil (and this, as you know, is strictly true), said, whether it was a coincidence or no, another person whom I had been seeing on business had also gone down with the same sort of acute attack. The doctor, a nice, kindly fellow, as most are, said he didn't like the look of the patient. 'I expect,' he said, 'it's one of those acute infections which seem to be the more deadly the less they are widely infectious. So I'm not raising an alarm and having him moved yet. That might spoil his chances. Keep a patient still, that is my experience. With sulphanilamide he may snap out of it in thirty-six hours.' "

Mr. Mycroft paused. "You will have surmised the rest. The patient did snap out, or perhaps one ought to say, was snapped out: the biter bit."

"But—" I said.

"Yes, you see what happened. It has a sort of inevitability, what the Greeks called 'irony' about it. I don't think, and they didn't, that it is chance. Indeed, as I've told you, I call it the basic element, Justice *per se*. The Greeks personified it as Ananke. It is in the nature of things, so deep that if you just splash about on the surface"—I thought his eye rested on me for a moment in a coldly appraising way—"you may never strike on it. But dive down deep enough and you will. If you have dived, as some of us have, just to detect as far as we can the basis of things, then you come up knowing that there is an adamant foundation below the tides, rising up, barring certain low paths and round which the sharpest of sharks cannot dive. If you dive simply as a shark to rip your fellow fish, well, you strike that unseen rock and split your skull. It is always taking place. I've seen it too often now to doubt. It looks as though all the cunning a murderer uses actually makes him blind to quite obvious things and, in the end, he seems actually to catch himself.

"All that Intil did was to repeat, at his last move, the final mistake of those classical poisoners, the Borgias, father and son. They made ready everything. Father (who, of course, is also father of Christendom, Pope Alexander VI, 'Christ's vicar on earth,' and also king of that comfortable little country, the Papal States) still is not contented. Son Caesar has, naturally with that name, also his dreams of bettering the family fortunes. Poison has already served them handsomely. But until now it has been piecemeal work —a brother there, a fellow cardinal here. Now is the time for a grand slam—invite all one's obstacles (one is above having enemies) to a fine dinner. After which there would be an outbreak of colic and the field would have been cleared of all rivals. Everything went according to plan. The required guests accepted, and, what was more, arrived. The supply of wine for them and the supply of wine for their hosts were carefully distinguished. Yet, somehow, a mistake was made. The guests got the host's own wine and the hosts got, and unknowingly drank, the wine prepared for their invited victims.

"You see, Intil acted precisely like the Borgias. He prepares carefully a poisoned envelope for you and he has with it a normal, untreated one. Of course, only under the microscope would the poisoned one be distinguishable from the untreated one. He had to leave the gum which he had moistened when tincturing it with the anthrax culture, to dry. Perhaps then he made his mistake, when he was writing that careful little note which was to provoke you to reply. Anyhow, he took up one envelope and on it wrote his own name and address. Then he took the second and on this he wrote your name and address. He slipped his note and the envelope—no doubt very gingerly—into the envelope bearing now your name, and then, everything settled, he relaxes and licks the flap, seals it down, and mails it."

Yes, that, undoubtedly, was what had happened and why I was alive. All my old upset returned on me. How ghastly! I could now—I who a moment before had been serene, yes, nearly hard-boiled—hardly feel safe. I wanted to ask if I was really secure. But I knew Mr. Mycroft would be contemptuous of such natural self-concern and he'd also take it as a reflection on his own omniscience—for hadn't he ruled pontifically that I was secure? Well, the best thing I could do would be to make an indirect inquiry.

"Intil?" I questioned. "Is he . . . ?"

"Yes, he died last night—just like Miss Brown."

Whether it was relief, I don't know; I think it may have been. "But," I said, "you can't leave highly infectious corpses about like that?"

"I'm glad," he remarked dryly, "that you are as

actively concerned about the public health as you were over the public safety. Neither of these cases (and I don't recall your making a similar inquiry about the first when you learned the cause of that fatality)—neither of these bodies is dangerous if handled with the due precautions which are taken in all cases of death by a rapid and acute infection. Why? Well, to be precise, this was Intil's knowledge and intention—a very important part of his plan. If you will recall, I told you that he knew enough of anthrax to know that in cases where there is no natural resistance—and we have none, as do animals among whom the disease is common—the bubo, the anthrax, would not rise before the patient is dead. I believe that if it has not risen and there is no lesion, the dead body, if treated with the adequate disinfectants used in all mortuary service, can be handled with immunity."

"But his things," I went on. "His beastly little collection of poisoned gums and so on?"

"That, too, was easily dealt with. He evidently had no relatives, at least near about—a lone wolf. I told the doctor that I was probably the only person who knew much about him; I had wanted to see him about some prospecting he had been doing. As the doctor and I had got on well, he asked me, if I didn't mind, to come into the bedroom where the body was lying just after death. I had stayed about in the lobby all the time, having taken a room in the hotel. Before calling the authorities he and I arranged the body—queer, that, the wish to fold a coat hastily thrown off. As I helped him (no, we took sufficient precautions against infection), my knee struck against the jacket which the dead man had taken off when he undressed for the last time and which he had hung on the back of a chair which he had drawn close to his bedside. Something quite large and hard was in the pocket. As the doctor turned to pull down the window shades, I slipped the object, a black metal box, into my coat. My guess was right.

"After I had said good-bye to the doctor, gone to my room, and locked the door, I confirmed my suspicion. It was a box very like the one I was using four days ago here. It's a specimen box which, of course, shuts hermetically. Inside was what I had also expected—an envelope and on it only one word: 'Fur.' I took sufficient precautions, so it was right for me to give myself complete proof. Handling the envelope as I did yours here, I cut it open. Inside it was a little grayish fur to which still clung some skin. Most of the hair, too, I noticed, was stuck together. Mr. Intil was a thorough and, in his way, a daring man. He was not only content with getting an anthrax-infected animal. He had cut skin and hair, I feel certain, from the place nearest where the actual lesion had taken place. He was right to have only a small supply, for it was fully sufficient. It would have kept him from having to make another trip to the desert. There was enough 'culture' there to have killed all of us—if he hadn't muddled his envelopes when he wrote to you. There was one other object in the box—a small round ruler. I was puzzled for a moment. Then I remembered. It must have been the little rod which Sanderson probably actually had on him and round which the spiral piece of code paper was wrapped to make it legible. That explained why Intil had hold of a complete reading of the code when he came to you. He kept the rod, I suppose, as a kind of trophy, together with the other 'power,' the anthrax that he brought back from the desert. Well, I lit a small spirit lamp and held the envelope in it until it was ash. Thank Heaven, though fungus spores can resist the utmost cold they are as helpless as we before the universal purifier, fire."

There was really nothing more to say or do. I must own I had listened to the old fellow's clean-up of the business with considerable interest and not a little admiration. He was silent now. Evidently I was meant to close the proceedings. I thought out rather a neat one.

"We're British, Mr. Mycroft," I said, "so we're not effusive. We don't like it and we do like going our own ways, don't we? So I'll just say a simple 'thank you,' and good wishes to your search, and good-bye." I rose. He got up.

"Yet somehow," he remarked, more to himself than to me, "we do run across one another. By the way, I suppose you wouldn't really like to know the real meaning of the code you were working on?" I hesitated. It was a clever cast. He continued, "I should certainly have told Miss Brown, as I owed the decipherment so largely to the curious visualizing intuitions of her subconscious. And I feel, in a way, now she is gone, that I owe it to you as the man who introduced me to her to tell you, if you still wish to know?"

If it hadn't been for Kerson and his visit I really believe I should have had the good sense to say no. But the fact that I was lying low about that visit, keeping the old man in the dark, both made me feel a little guilty and also rather anxious to get any further information on a puzzle which had aroused my specialized curiosity and on my "reading" which, at the back of my mind, I didn't feel was "the thing."

"You are still sure I'm wrong!" I said, in what I felt was a challenging way, but which of course involved me in further conversation.

"As I say, I couldn't have been, but for our good friend, Miss Brown. I should like to give you, as a tribute to her, the proof of her powers."

"Well, tell me what she said," was the least I could say to that.

"You remember my hunch that Sanderson's being a Scotchman ought to give us a line as to the kind of code he'd construct? As an expert in code, you know that book codes are the easiest to make and the best for holding fast—the bigger the book the better, and best of all, a big book all divided up into chapters and verses."

I wasn't so slow as not to get it now. "The Bible," I said.

"Right: a book little known now, at least among the clever, but a mine for codes and clues to all who are familiar with it. I often wonder why people read detective novels when in all the last hundred years of 'lower' and 'higher' criticism of this set of books such beautiful studies in detection have gone on being made. But, you see, I myself had let myself become rusty there. Well, Sanderson makes his code out of the Bible—though perhaps I oughtn't to call it a code; rather, a mnemonic—a condensed, disguised set of readings to guide himself."

"But friars are surely a little later than the Bible," I rather smartly rejoined.

"That did puzzle me for a while," he answered. "But the solution of that I ought to have understood. Do you recall that on our evening visit to the old

Scotchman's house, we saw those books on archaeology? Prospectors are, I believe, often very largely unmercenary men. What drives them mainly is romance. They could make better money in a city. But they long to find, behind the veil of sand and dust, behind the site which busy men have left as being a waste-heap, the shining, forgotten treasure. In new lands that has to be ore and nuggets. Here you must work and look for what the earth's mysterious heart chooses to yield or the stars to cast down." He paused.

"Those gifts may well make all Pharaohs' hoards look like tinsel. Still," he resumed, "the prospector is a romancer wherever he is, looking to uncover some buried wonder. His real thrill is to dig, his spade to strike and there at his feet, at this moment, he is looking at some secret which 'went to earth,' was lost to men since that undated moment when the long-forgotten man or race, or natural accident made the cache and left it. Epoch beckons right across history to epoch. He feels himself on a pinnacle of time raised for a moment above the generations. Sanderson was no exception. He cared for two puzzles. His book puzzle, his 'literary' source, we now know—the Bible. His other riddle was nondocumentary history, history written not by the pen but by the spade."

"Friars aren't spade history, I should have

thought," I interrupted. I knew enough history to know that.

His reply startled me. "That was a good reason for thinking your reading of the code—though ingenious—wrong. Don't think, though, I should myself have caught onto the right clue but for Miss Brown. Directly I asked her 'control' about the passage beginning 'Cloc' she began giving a description. Her mind saw some vague image which at once, for me, laid friars by the heels."

"Did she give you the same fanciful description she gave to me and," I hesitated, "to Intil?" He waited for me to go on. "When I was with her last, in trance she said she saw a sort of circle with prongs sticking up round it." I didn't tell him how rude the idiotic little "control" had become. I thought he might suspect that Miss Brown's subconscious looked down on me as much as he did. "That image seemed to me unhelpful."

"What more did she say?" he questioned.

"Only that outside the circle of prongs was another one, standing all by itself, and that was, of course, equally unhelpful."

"Well," he said, genially enough, "we can agree, at least, on how remarkable it is that the medium's subconscious ran so accurately along the same track with two different sitters. It does look as though she must have had some real hunch."

"Perhaps so," I allowed, "but mediums, once they get an idea into their heads, generally stick to it. And certainly it doesn't make any waking sense."

"Are you sure? Certainly such a picture isn't of a monk or a monastery, but what about a megalithic ruin, a stone circle?"

"Why?" I asked, for this seemed the vaguest of fishing.

For answer he slipped his hand into one of the enormous pockets of his big, flapping gray alpaca dust coat—which made him look more than usually like a crane. Out came a small volume. He flicked a page open and extended it to me. I was looking at a drawing of Stonehenge, the British Druid monument.

"Sanderson, as I've said," he went on, "was interested in archaeology. So, at one time, was I—perhaps all detectives would be, if they had time; it's right along our line and Time is the master trail-layer. His interest, Miss Brown's control's word-picture—well, I felt, it would be no waste of time to glance at some books on megalithic prehistoric stone-circles. Here was the first, perhaps naturally so, for it is about the most famous. It's beautifully done, this little piece of detection. It's Cunnington's *Stonehenge*. And it is helpful—this chart you are looking at, as far as it goes." His long finger darted onto the page. "The circle with the prongs sticking up—the upright single stones in a circle and you see outside the ring one standing off by itself."

"That's pretty vague," I said. "The control's words would fit quite a number of other things; for example—as she said at my sitting—a birthday cake with its candles on it—and certainly that's a much more likely fancy for a child mind."

"I own I wouldn't have depended simply on that," he answered, quite uncrestfallen, "though, of course, birthday cakes don't have one candle standing out on the table all by itself and this circle emphatically has. No, that was simply a starter and made me read the book through. And it's in the print, not the pictures, that I picked up the real clue. After all, the clue here isn't what we called, a moment ago, a spade clue—something dug up. It's a pen clue or a word clue—something right in your line, Mr. Silchester.

"Listen to this," he said, taking back the book. "I'll summarize as good a piece of word detection as ever I've come upon." So, peering at the page and then over the top of it at me, he ran on: "Stonehenge: use and purpose of building not really known. Still—you see the true archaeological caution—a possible clue is given by the traditional name bestowed on one of the outstanding sarsens (the big monoliths) which stands at some distance east of the circle. A local story recounts that as the devil was building this lonely monument (all big stone circles were attributed to that hard-working liar, because they were the temples of pre-Christian peoples) there strolled up that ubiquitous gossiping 'kibitzer' of the late Middle Ages—a friar." I started. He went on. "As the old gossip wouldn't clear off, the devil seized one of the huge stones he was handling and hurled it at the nuisance who, while running away, was struck on the heel, and the stone still stands where it fell, outside the circle, pitched there by the devil's throw."

Our eyes met. "What an absurd story," I said, "but how odd those words coming in it, 'friar's heel.' "

"Absurd stories often, as you know, conceal clues. Now, what does our detective of pre-history suggest? First, that the story is evidently a construction. I think we agree with that." I nodded. "Something is being explained by someone who really has no idea what it is that he is explaining." I felt this to be a dig at me, but I had to allow its general truth. "The words which have to be explained are 'friar's heel,' and they are applied to an outstanding stone which is like neither a friar nor a heel. So, step two: Are these words really what they sound to be? The answer to that lies in another question, 'Why should they be?' Surely, indeed, they *shouldn't* be! This place, Stonehenge, we don't know much about it, but we do know it was built long before any English was spoken, when, pretty certainly, some Keltic dialect was common speech in Britain. Now, as children say, we are getting quite warm, for 'friar's heel' is none too badly recorded Keltic and in Keltic it has nothing to do with a monk's anatomy but with a celestial phenomenon."

With the glee of a child—and I must say I couldn't help sharing a little of his glow, the clue was so neat—Mr. Mycroft enunciated, "*Freas Heol* in Keltic means 'rising sun' and, final proof, *Cloc Freas Heol* means 'stone of the rising sun.' "

"I must say," I owned, "that is very neat, very."

"Yes," he replied complacently; "I think that with Miss Brown and this little book we have Sanderson's secret partly extracted."

I took my defeat in good part; I was honestly interested; but I was not wholly unpleased to be able to add, "Of course we're not a step nearer the whole solution. 'Twenty minutes to three,' which was my solution of the first part of the code, and now your fragment, 'stone of the rising sun,' still leave all the letter and number part undecoded. We're not really a step nearer to an actual practical understanding of our mystery."

"Right," he said, "right. But it will take me some time to give you the rest. I have it all. But already I have taken a great deal of your day. My real excuse for coming to see you was to fulfill my promise—that in four days I would be able to tell you you were safe. You are. If you would like to hear the rest of my reading I could call tomorrow. You should, in any case, not have returned my check, for you had earned it. Matters of, literally, life and death have prevented us from coming down to economics. But I still hope to persuade you to see my point of view in that matter of the honorarium, and if you won't, on second thought, then at least to give me the pleasure of going through this case with a confrere to whom I owe its elucidation."

Clever old fox! I was glad of the opportunity to reconsider that check, and besides, he had my interest roused, and knew it. All clues to a clue-hunter are hard to drop, and here was one which had coiled itself round my mind and feelings, had threatened my life, had killed a friend and killed my would-be murderer, had—and this was my secret—even wound itself round our desert trader. Quite apart from the fact that Mr. Mycroft had hinted at even bigger fates and issues back of the whole thing, I think it will be allowed that here was enough to make any decoder almost unable to refuse to hear more.

"Very well," I said, trying to appear the concessioner and not the concessionee, "I would be very pleased to clear up the matter tomorrow. Today I ought to finish my work."

"At ten tomorrow morning, then," he replied, and went without another word.

How well he had judged me! My appetite, my curiosity grew. Miss Delamere saw that I was not attending. She even made some remark about that "bald-eagle Britisher," but I wasn't to be drawn. I set her to go through the files ordering the card-indexes of references. I felt somehow that we had been lax. That verbal clue to the Friar's Heel, though I don't know why I should have been expected to know it, vexed me—perhaps because verbal clues are my forte, perhaps because I had been so completely wrong and had twice tied myself to an obviously superficial and mistaken rendering.

It was, then, with relief, with positive relief and interest that I heard Mr. Mycroft in the outer office the next morning as the watch on my wrist raised its long hand to the zenith and its short one to ten. I think I greeted the old fellow quite cordially, and he seemed quite pleased to see me and with everything. Without a pause, as though continuing a lecture which had hardly stopped, he began, "AP. 20111318 — 3, that's all that remains for us to settle."

"Pretty big, though, I should have thought," I said,

just to say something. "Twenty millions odd is a tidy sum even if it is minus three."

"Numbers can generally be reduced to manageable proportions if we know what they refer to," he answered. "And here we are not completely in the dark. Indeed, two lines of light focus here. Sanderson, I've said, was a Scotchman. He would, then, quite likely, make part of his code out of the book he would have known best—the Bible. Now, what did Miss Brown in her trance see at that point?"

He took from his pocket his neat notebook and read out an entry which vividly recalled my sitting with her. He recited, " 'Ever so big and it goes up and up!' She makes a staircase-like figure with her hands. 'And *everything* is in front of it.' That is all, for a time, but, on asking whether she sees anything more, the mind is switched. Now she is reporting that she sees the ocean and out of it is coming some kind of chimera." He paused. "After all, I believe that Intil, who may well have had the same Fundamentalist upbringing as Sanderson, caught onto this clue and it was because he thought you and Miss Brown together would work it out, that he decided to murder you both. I've told you that my knowledge of that book, once most studied, now largely unread, was getting rusty. So, after the sitting, I consulted the volume. I remembered the outlines of textual criticism, from my college days, at least sufficiently to know there were really only two real riddle books in that classical collection."

He stopped again and this time he pulled from his pocket a Bible. "The Book of Daniel is one, of course, and the other, the so-called Revelation, the real title of which is the Apocalypse. So AP is, you see, at once placed. That gives the book. Twenty-eleven must, then, be the chapter and verse and thirteen-eighteen must be another chapter and verse. Now let's look these up. The first is the well-known reference to the Great White Throne of Final Judgment, before which the whole creation is summoned. I think," he added reflectively, "I see the point of that," then, going on, "the thirteenth chapter ends with the eighteenth verse. It is clear from that and the foregoing description that Miss Brown's remarkable 'control,' however inadequate her vocabulary, had an amazing extra-sensory perception of the chimera in question. She told me she saw 'an awful monster, all sorts of bits of beastly animals, all come together.' "

I could confirm that at my sitting she had seemed to be frightened by some hallucination of a beast.

"Now," said Mr. Mycroft, "this is the actual Apocalyptic description of what that book calls the Beast: 'Like unto a leopard and his feet were as of a bear and his mouth the mouth of a lion.' But all this is at the beginning of the chapter. Why, then, is the reference to the last verse? That verse begins, 'Here is wisdom,' which I understand apocalyptic decoders say means, 'Here is the code-clue!' 'Let him that has understanding,' it continues, 'count the number of the Beast . . . the number is 666.' I don't think we need trouble ourselves with who the Beast is or was or shall be. For I don't think Sanderson, who, I believe, made this code, was, when he made it, any longer interested in New Testament exegesis. He was, I am equally sure, making a mnemonic code, a memo which it pleased him to work out and which he took every care should be senseless if it fell into any fellow seeker's hands. Six hundred and sixty-six, less three, is then some measurement."

I remembered that Miss Brown's "control" in our sitting had said something about losing interest in the Beast itself and seeing a lot of little squiggles. I had cut her off but perhaps she was trying to tell us she was seeing the figures 666.

"But if these are measurements," I said, "what do they measure?"

"That we shall know when we know the place of the Great White Throne," he answered.

"We'll never know that in this life," I ventured.

"I think you're wrong," he replied. "But first let us now read our code as far as we can. It runs now: 'At twenty minutes to three P.M. at the stone of the rising sun'—these are evidently very precise measurements. Because a certain spot will be indicated (as the gnomon of a sun dial indicates the hour) by the tip of the shadow of an outstanding rock—something like the *Cloc Freas Heol* at Stonehenge—falling on the ground. Then comes the reference to the Great White Throne and the whole message ends with 663 as being the major scale, or the general direction for finding the place."

"So everything turns on that term, and it seems to me completely and literally up in the air," I said.

"No," he repeated. "On the contrary, I'm quite sure this is the one reference in the whole thing which we may literally say is on the map." He shuffled in his pocket once more and produced a motoring tourist map of the great half-empty state of Utah. He opened it and pointed my attention to a patch he had underlined in red. There, sure enough, I read, "Canyon of the Great White Throne."

"The early pioneers were soaked in their Bible," he said, "and christened everything they could by biblical names. And the romantic habit remains among their descendants.

"So now we have our fixed point. And we need it," he went on, "for about one-third of the Mormon state is still unmapped in any detail. There you may look along canyons down which, as far as we know, no human foot has ever trod. Nature has defended this solitude with three great guardians, thirst, starvation, and heat."

"And," I added, "the best of all defenses—that there is nothing there that anyone could want to find."

"Generally speaking, yes," he replied. "But in this particular case I can't agree. Of course, gold might turn up somewhere in that vast area. But I don't believe it was gold that Sanderson was after and Intil hijacked him for."

"Then you believe Intil's rigmarole?"

Mr. Mycroft was silent. After a few moments he began in another tone. "We met because you could help me, I told you, in a peculiarly important search. You did help me to track Intil; that led us to finding Sanderson's body; that, in turn, to discovering his code. Intil's and Sanderson's deaths are serious matters, though neither of them will make any stir if we stay silent. Nor, indeed, will poor, dear Miss Brown's. We can leave the matter as it is, if we like. You can leave this problem as it is, if you like. It has neatly, if tragically, terminated itself. It nearly finished you off, in the same neat and leaving-no-suspicious-loose-ends way, also. But I cannot leave the matter to rest there. For me, tragic as these cases are, they are, after all, only incidents in a much larger mystery, a much more important issue."

He saw me about to say something, though I am not sure what it was that I was going to say; my mind was confused. In the night I had decided I had, anyhow, a right to the first check, but, in making up my mind to re-accept it, I couldn't help feeling under some sort of obligation to the old man!

He forestalled my slowly gathering thoughts: "I repeat, then, my offer. I am an old man to work alone. You know about this. Do you care to clear this up for good? As I have said, I am sure that my clients would not have sent me on this trail unless they had had, as I believe they have, adequate proof that what we may find is worth any expense to discover. Meanwhile, in any case, you will, of course, accept again this check about which you had some generous doubts."

I know it may sound absurd—the reason which made me finally decide to entertain again this proposal from which I had already broken away decisively enough. It wasn't that Intil was gone and so the danger of running into a very awkward rival was out of the way. It was, odd as it may seem, that I was keeping a secret back from Mr. Mycroft. I believe that the sole reason why he exasperated me was because he was always right. I was "weary of hearing Aristides called the just" and sometimes so calling himself, too. In his presence I was the little nephew who never knows and he was dear old Uncle Wiseacre who is always informed. Perhaps, I suppose, I really admired and envied him. I think that must have been it, and the thought that I knew and he didn't know, that there was now still another rival in the path, another seeker, already perhaps ahead of us on the trail, made me, unwisely no doubt, but all the more keenly, anxious to see what would happen, to watch Mr. Mycroft's growing suspicion and surprise, and all the while to be for once the wiser of the two. I wanted to detect, undetected, the detective waking up to the surprising knowledge that he had left undetected, unsuspected, an important factor in the plot.

"Very well," I said, after a deliberation which I was pleased to think he must fail to understand. "Very well, I will come along again, provided that you can give me any clear proof that we have a definite chart to go upon."

For answer, another rummage in another pocket produced another map. "This," he said, "is the best obtainable for the desert round the canyon which contains the huge rock bluff called the Great White Throne. Here is the main trail. You see, in this direction we can go into a complete unmapped desolation into which even the hardiest sightseers never go. I am sure I can pick up a trail if I have time to look out from that 'jumping-off place,' for I feel certain that Sanderson left for himself some marks to point his way back. I expect he had not visited the spot for some time; at least we know he was for some reason—perhaps for the best of reasons, for leading Intil astray—far away from his real trail when he was killed."

I couldn't resist asking, "Won't you ask Kerson the trader to come with you? He'd be better at picking up a trail?"

"No," was the reply. "I don't think we shall need anybody but ourselves and I do think that this secret should not be shared." That, then, was perhaps the reason why he wanted me—to keep me under his eye? "I've already made other arrangements and ordered the baggage we left with him to be sent down. We shall need that, but the man himself might easily be in the way."

"Yes," I thought to myself, "he certainly might and indeed even may be!"

Chapter XI

So it was that within three days I was once more off on a Mycroft meander, my office left in Miss Delamere's carmine-tipped but capable hands. He and I looked like ordinary sightseers. And we played our part, gazing at the immense rock, when we had arrived in its canyon, that Throne which was to be the starting point of our real exploration. A local worthy acted as our dragoman. We were all mounted on horses which, I am glad to say, had wisely exchanged fire and mettlesomeness for docility and endurance.

Mr. Mycroft had told our guide that we wished to do a little real exploring, to go a little off the trails altogether—just to get a real sense of the desert, after we had seen all the standard, well-photographed views. "I see," he said, "that there is emptiest country out in this direction."

"There's nothing anyone could photo out there," said the guide. "It just goes on and on. It's so much the same you can't hardly tell you're moving—till you want to come back, and then you can't find your way. It's just quiet Hell—even if you could get water, a man'd go mad out there. 'Tisn't grand or fine. It's just as near nothing as earth's ever gone. It's just a rubble world." He spoke with a real sense of dislike of this, the real wilderness—not the National Park fringe of stately escarpments. And I must say I shared it. The absolute desert is simply untidiness extended to lunatic lengths and breadths.

His next remark, however, made me prick my rather wilting ears: "Still, though, you sightseers always seem just to want to see something simply because you hope no one else has ever seen it. My father remembers when no one came even to see the old White Throne unless they jest happened to pass that way. A cornfield, and the flatter the better, was always a better sight than a canyon, however grand. The Indians still call all this 'evil land,' and it is, if it's yours and not simply something to gape at and not live off. Yet, as I say, every year more of your lot push out further and further into this jumping-off jumble land. Why, only last week there was a man up here who went right off up that there canyon and he hasn't come back yet, as far as I know. There's nothing up there, but I suppose he knows his own business or his own queer notion of a vacation."

I was riding along just behind Mr. Mycroft, but he showed, as far as I could see, no sign of additional interest at this remark. He looked, in a big-brimmed hat, dark glasses, and his long dust coat, so like faded pictures of my grand-uncles photographed in Egypt, with the valley of the Tombs of the Kings rather out of focus in the background, that I had another acute attack of nepotophrenia, or whatever modern psychologists call that respect which is the most civil but not the least intense form of dislike. And, shortly after, when we had gone some distance into a desolation which had less design of any sort in its confusion than any piece of land I've ever seen, Mr. Mycroft drew rein.

"It's interesting geologically," he remarked, "but to enjoy that one needs to be on foot. I think we'll go back now and return for a closer look round to-morrow."

The following day he haled me off alone. In the first part of the morning we had let ourselves be taken a trail ride. Then, on reaching where we lodged, Mr. Mycroft remarked, "This afternoon we'll do a little geology. We'll take along this bundle, as it has our gear for collecting specimens." Then, turning to our guide, he said, "If you will come along with us, when we reach the spot where we were yesterday we'll take to our feet and meet you again at the same place, if you'll bring along the horses in the evening."

When we were left alone we did not go far. That was perhaps the weirdest thing about this strange area—it simply had no scale. The air was so clear that there was not the slightest atmosphere to give any sense of distance. A broken rock six inches high and one sixty feet high have really nothing to distinguish them from each other unless you know how far you are away from them. Here there were nothing but broken rocks of all sizes, from one-inch pebbles to thousand-foot fragments of shattered mountains. And there was nothing else, not even a shrub. Heavens, what a desolation! So complete, so utterly unrelieved, that you had only to go round a single boulder and you were lost—you had left the known world as completely behind, you had as little sense of your bearings as though you had been marooned on the snow wastes of Antarctica.

So, after striking off the trail we were as much by ourselves as though we had been in the nothing-but-rock-strewn deserts of the moon. I was lugging along a bundle he had told me to carry. I left the direction, if there was one, to him. He walked slowly, stopping every now and then like a hound questing for a scent.

At last he seemed to have a direction or at least a fixed notion, and we trudged and stumbled over the rough ground for, I suppose, three or four hundred yards. As we advanced he quickened his pace, leaving me behind. I own I was getting bored and tired and very hot and I was stumping along not looking ahead (what was the use?) or, indeed, at anything in particular, for the prospect had no promise. I was surprised, then, suddenly to find Mr. Mycroft hurrying past me on his way back to the trail and evidently counting to himself. I mounted a boulder and stood watching him from that slight vantage point. I could then see back to where we had struck off from the trail. The moment he reached that he wheeled back and was standing by me in a few minutes.

"It was a bit of a guess," he said, "but it's worked so far, and I think we're over the one difficult hurdle or gap. That was the step between the Great White Throne and the other designated area—what we may call the Friar's Heel area. We knew that it's 663 somethings and that is all, and that is not enough as a guide, but good enough for a mnemonic, which was all that old S. himself needed. So deduction just had to be used." He twinkled at me, but I was in no counter-twinkling mood and waited dully like a mule expecting its saddle and bridle. "The White Throne is our base; our goal must be in the most desolate and untraveled area near it, for Sanderson's secret would otherwise have been blundered on by others. So this is the quarter to seek in. Next, Sanderson would use the trail as far as it went. He would, therefore, strike off at that point where the track began to bear away from this ultra-wilderness. So we strike away. When we had gone half a dozen hundred yards I looked for a clue. It was there all right. I then paced the area to be sure. It is 663 yards. Come here."

I followed him with a revived interest. Sure enough, built up against a boulder on the side we had approached from, was a little heap of stones which would, to a casual glance, have passed as a trickle of fragments weathered off the parent mass. Indeed, even when we were close to it, I wasn't sure it wasn't that and nothing more. The top stone was smooth and white.

Mr. Mycroft picked it up. The underside was not so clean; there were a few scratches on it.

"Here's clear proof," he said, pointing to the surface crackling.

"Those are simply weather crackings," I said.

"No," he replied. "They are, as it happens, Greek capital letters, which are scrawling things at best and are scrawlingly drawn here. But they show the seeker that he is on the right trail. For those Greek letters—

as was the way in Greek, as in Latin—can be used as numerals; those three letters can be read as 666."

"But, if that's so, what about the minus 3?" I asked, for this seemed to need clearing up.

"I think because our Scotch friends like scholarship—hence the Greek riddle—and they love accuracy, even in keeping their private accounts. I paced this and it is just short, I believe, by three yards of the full 666 when I walked straight from the trail to this point. This huge boulder, I take it, stood in the way, so our friend couldn't set up his sign-cairn exactly at the limit of his scale."

"But how," I said, "could you find your way over that litter of stones to as small and as concealed a mark as this?"

I asked, for though, of course, he struck at right angles away from the trail, there seemed no other guide to lead him and the whole thing was an almost uncanny piece of tracking.

"I must say," he frankly confessed, "I thought we might fail and I have been helped by something which may be fancy, but which, if it isn't, puzzles and surprises me. I don't think I could even point it out to you. Try and see now," he said directing my eyes along the way we had come; "do you see any suggestion of a trail here?"

"None," I said.

"Well," he allowed, "I may have been following a fancy but I certainly had the sense that there was a very faint track here. Anyhow, it has led us to clear evidence."

"But how do we get any further?" I asked. For answer he put the white stone back in the precise position it had occupied on the top of the small cairn.

"Look," he requested. It was naturally shaped a little like those earliest stone axes one sees in museums. "I am going," said he, "another 666 or 663 yards in the direction it points."

We plodded along counting and checking, for now I was almost as interested as he. As we reached 650 in our count the ground became a little more open, the boulders being smaller. It was slow work, for we had to round some big masses and then to be sure we had kept our line and make a deduction for our detour, in our reckoning. But, "Here," cried Mr. Mycroft as we went forward a few more paces, "here, you see, he had room to let his full scale be used."

"But where?" I asked.

"As it's in the open and so might be too noticeable," he remarked, "there's no cairn at this halt and check-point, only another of these white quartzite pebbles—not so uncommon as to catch a casual eye but clear enough for himself to pick out. See," he picked up another white stone rather like an elongated egg, and, turning it over, presented it to me. "He's put his code number on it again. Perhaps he wanted to be able to send someone else along this trail, if he ever found any-one he could trust and couldn't come himself."

Certainly, scrawled, so that it might pass for chance veining on the stone, were again the three Greek letters.

Replacing it as it had lain, he took his bearings by it and we set off again.

"Look here," I shouted to him, "how many of these hops have we to make?"

"I don't know," came over his shoulder, as he ambled ahead, threading his way among the rocks which had again become almost as big as cottages. He was counting away to himself and making his checkings as I caught up with him. It was getting exhausting. I calculated that by the time we came to and found—if we ever did—the next check-point stone, we should have tramped over a mile on this exhausting terrain. Just before we reached 600, as far as I could check by my own counting, Mr. Mycroft had gone out of sight behind some stones even higher than any we had so far seen. We were, I judged, approaching the edge where some upreared strata had once made a crest, but were now split and shattered into a rough kind of cyclopean wall. As I trotted round the base of one of these, I nearly ran into Mr. Mycroft.

"I was wrong," he said. "I was too fanciful about our Gaelic hero, may he rest in peace. He was not suffering from the Scotch form of scrupulosity."

"What do you mean?" I said, meanwhile searching the ground for another white stone.

"I mean that when he wrote 'dash three' he did not mean 'minus three' and just because his first span could not be precisely 666 yards. He meant 666 yards for three times and then——"

"I don't see the white stone to show we have reached the third span's limit," I said, still looking carefully over the ground.

"No need," he said. "As with the great architect, Sir Christopher Wren, in his masterpiece, St. Paul's Cathedral, no need for a monument when the whole place is monumental. '*Si monumentum requiris, circumspice.*' Look up and around. If you want a monumental clue, look around."

I looked, and must own that he was right and I was startled. Rounding that last immense boulder we had come into a huge circle of such stones cleft by a million years of weather and standing in a rough ring.

"Here," he said, "is the circle with the big prongs standing round it. What's the time?"

"Twenty-five past three," I said, glancing at my watch.

"Tomorrow," he said. "It is a bit too late to go

further today. But tomorrow we shall know. Yes, we can leave your bundle, as in Pilgrim's Progress, here. No one will, I wager, disturb it. Tomorrow we will start early and be here when the signal tower gives its beckoning."

We tramped back and found the trail quickly enough. The guide had, as we'd arranged, brought the horses out for us to the bend where we had left him.

"Any luck with your geology?" he asked.

"Yes," said Mr. Mycroft. "Some interesting formations in their way, at least to specialists, don't you think, Mr. Silchester?"

"To specialists, certainly, certainly," I agreed.

The next morning I was awake almost as soon as Mr. Mycroft in the small cabin which gave us quarters and we were still at breakfast when we heard the horses outside. After a silent jog, as we dismounted at the bend of the trail Mr. Mycroft said, "If you'll have the horses here again for us at sundown, that would be best. We want, maybe, to get a few rock specimens from one or two points and will make a full day of it."

We walked off slowly, Mr. Mycroft glancing at a stone every now and then and pausing even to pick up one or two, until the horse hoofs were audible no longer. Then we mended our pace. We had no difficulty in picking out our two white stone clues and, in spite of the rough going, we emerged from among the big stones into the giant circle in about half an hour. There lay the bundle just as I'd dropped it, the afternoon before.

"We've plenty of time," said Mr. Mycroft, sitting down, "so let us look to our stores."

His capacious pockets had our eatables. I carried, slung over my shoulders, our two flasks of cold coffee. We placed all these in "the shadow of a great rock" in what was indeed a "weary land." Then he pulled the bundle that I had carried yesterday, toward him and unwrapped it. Out came those objects which had surprised me so much on our first desert trip—the huge black rubber gloves.

"One hardly needs winter clothing in a place like this," I remarked facetiously.

"Oh, it can be cold enough here in winter," was his noncommittal counter. Well, I would let him keep his secret a little longer, if he wished, seeing we were really right on the goal. "Now," he said, "let's get our bearings so that at the right time we shall be in the right place." And he was right to take that precaution; I was wrong in thinking we had practically arrived.

"There must be an outstanding rock," he said, "which holds a position in relation to this huge natural ring somewhat similar to that held by the Friar's Heel to the Stonehenge circle."

"If so, it should lie east," I said.

We crossed over to that side and went through the huge rough natural columns that enclosed the area. Emerging, we saw a tumble of rocks stretching away, but sure enough, to the east there was an outstanding peak, almost a mesa, a huge shaft of stone, its sides looking as sheer and smooth as a wall. Mr. Mycroft consulted his watch and a compass.

"At twenty minutes to three," he remarked. But a thought had flashed into my mind. How had we been so stupid as to overlook it!

"It's no use our being here," I said, "whether there's anything to find or not. We'll never find it in this wilderness for we don't know the *day.*"

"You mean," he said, "that I had overlooked the fact that though Sanderson gave time of day and place, he didn't give day of month or year? No," he continued easily, "no, I noticed that, and the answer was pretty clear. Sanderson was using Stonehenge as his code system. Well, what is the whole meaning and *raison d'être* of Stonehenge? Like all megalithic circle-temples, it is built for sun worship and the Friar's Heel, which has given us a little trouble, owing to its folk-disguised name, here is literally as plain as a pike-staff. It points for one day of the year and one only—the sun-rising on midsummer day, when sacrifice was made as the rising sun made the tip of the *Freas Heol* cast its fatal shadow on the victim on the altar. Whatever Sanderson's code points to, it was meant to point by the shadow of that rock at twenty to three P.M. on midsummer day, June 21."

"But this isn't June 21."

"That presents no difficulty. A simple calculation will show where it would fall at two-forty today. The indicative shadow won't point at another angle of the horizon. At worst, as we are some months past the summer solstice, and therefore the sun's inclination is increased from the zenith, the shaft of shadow will run past and over the spot we want pointed out."

There ensued an arduous effort, as journalists like to say, or, in my own words, a long and very hot scramble. The whole scale of the place was far vaster than the area we had left behind us, the other side of the broken ridge out of which the circle had formed itself. Here rocks which seemed, when one first saw them, stones on which one might sit, turned out to be, when one came up to them after a quarter of an hour's walking, high platforms on which one could easily have put a house. After some surveying, however, and a good deal of looking back to the big Friar's Heel and getting its line, Mr. Mycroft said, "An early lunch; we have just time," and we returned to our stores in the shadow of the great circle.

When we came back to our former "furthest out" the sun was already making the mesa monolith begin to throw up its finger of shadow far out to the northeast across a desolation of smaller stone. We set out, but always the great avenue of shadow seemed to advance far faster than we were moving. At last, however, we were abreast of the monolith itself and by bearing toward it we passed into its shadow.

"We shall be late after all," said Mr. Mycroft, hurrying me far faster than I liked, for quick movement after meals has never agreed with me. "The scale of this country deceived me. Still, though we may not be exactly where we should, at two-forty, still we shall be on the road to our goal if we take the line of the shadow at that moment and mark some outstanding rock to keep us going straight." So we panted on, and at last Mr. Mycroft called, "The time is due; now we must take our line. From now on the shadow will only mislead us."

We looked ahead, but as far as I could see there were no outstanding stones to guide us; the wilderness on this side, too, was subsiding into the same chaos as it presented on the other side of the stone circle. It was as featureless as a frozen sea of ice-hummocks. Mr. Mycroft, though, forged ahead. I was, indeed, getting pretty badly winded and am glad, if not proud, to say Mr. Mycroft was carrying the parcel.

I suppose it was because my fatigue was rising that

after what seemed an interminable tramp and stumble I could not say when I first noticed that the going itself was getting better. I felt a strong feeling of relief, however, when I noticed that my old leader was not pressing the pace as he had been. His speed slackened, he almost seemed to be sauntering, and finally he came to a standstill. Then I had time to notice that not far ahead of us the boulder-strewn surface suddenly "improved"; it looked as though it were no more than a shingle beach, and still further on, I thought it might have been even sand. Mr. Mycroft, however, was not taking a view ahead or around. He had dropped the parcel and was crouched on the ground examining something in the palm of his hand through a lens in the other.

As I came up he remarked, "I think the mesa monolith has served its purpose and led us to our spot. We are arrived, or so near that we shall need only our own eyes to lead us to the actual goal."

"I see nothing," I said, looking around and then peering down at the ground from which he had picked up, I now saw, a handful of sand-grains. "And I can't see what clue you can be finding here."

"Look at these," was his reply, emptying his small runnel of silica dust into my hand, "through this," handing me the lens.

"All I see is that the grains look like pebbles, as they should under such magnification."

"Pebbles, yes," he replied, "but that's the point."

"No, I don't see."

He was just about to say something more to enlighten my mind, to give me understanding as well as information, as usual, when his eye was evidently caught by something else on the ground near by. He hurried over to it and I saw something like a piece of crystal glitter as he picked it up.

"Look at this. This is a far clearer proof than the sand, though the sand is indubitable evidence in itself." He was holding out to me what looked more than anything else like a piece of half-sucked candy dropped by a dirty child into the dust. Fortunately in this place it couldn't be that—there are some advantages in being in a wilderness and one is the absence of dirty children—so I took it from him and examined it.

"Now," he said rallyingly—that tone of his entire repertoire tried me, I think, the most—"here's the riddle: the first point is some sand and the point of that is that it is pointless."

He was in high spirits, I suppose because he felt the goal was near. But I was just tired.

"Oh, stop it!" I snapped.

"Very well. But I understood that in your branch of detection you use a lens occasionally and find evidence that way. Please look again at the grains." I was still holding them. He had taken his lens from me as he had handed me the "false candy." Now he relieved me of that and gave me his magnifier again. As under its power the sand looked like pebbles, his voice at my side said: "Silica grains have naturally very distinct and sharp edges. That's why sand is a sharp polisher and cutter. For millennia men could carve such super-hard stones as jade and porphyry only with sand. For sand is a natural glass, a hard crystal shattered into grains. But look at this stuff. It is sand right enough, but all the edges are rounded and smoothed." It was true.

"Looks like sugar lumps that have just begun to melt."

"Good," he commended. "You're right, I'm sure. That is precisely what has happened. These little cubes of silica have been melted."

I looked up. "Why, that's nonsense. I know enough about chemistry to know that."

"Well, that's the way glass is said to have been invented," he replied. "Men lighting a bonfire on the shore and, after, finding this." He held out to me the piece of "false candy."

"But who's been lighting huge bonfires here?" I asked.

"The real difficulty isn't that," he said. "It's the

chemical fact that though some sands will melt into a glass of a sort at a heat given by an ordinary big fire, they need, if they are to melt, a 'flux' mixed with them: seakale used for the 'shore glass' or beach twigs used for the 'forest glass.' Well, look around here. Where is there any weed or wood to help?" There certainly was none. "That's why," he went on holding up the "candy," "this is so remarkable. On the one hand, here are half-melted grains and here, on the other hand, is actually a piece of half-made glass. The heat required to melt sand into glass without a flux is immense. We have only just begun to be able to do so in the most modern furnaces. Yet this took place in the open desert and"—he was now walking about rapidly, every now and then stopping and picking up more small fragments of the "candy"—"over a large area. Yes, we are arrived, and the spot itself lies just ahead of us—the fused silica lumps increase in that direction."

He pointed to where the ground became progressively smoother and seemed to dip down.

"Well," I said, I must say with considerable relief, "now we are going to clear up the cache mystery for good. We have followed the indications given by the code to the letter and the minute. Though why you should think this odd little geological puzzle we have blundered on here, will help us in the human mystery, heaven only knows!"

His reply was, "In a way, heaven *has* taken a hand; indeed, it made the deal which started the game and it left its print to guide us."

With that piece of rhetoric, what should he do but go back, unpack the parcel we had lugged so far, take out the huge black rubber gloves and proceed to put them on.

"If you are coming with me," he said, "I'd advise you to do the same."

I wasn't going to be left out now, at the last. "I'm coming," I said resolutely.

"Then if you are going to accompany me, I am obliged to see that you are protected from every risk that it is possible to guard against. Please do me the favor of donning these gauntlets."

It was still hot, quite hot. The rubber gloves when I put my hands in them were clammy—"fuggy," that nasty schoolboy word, alone describes them. I hate damp hot hands.

"What's the need of all this dressing up?" I asked crossly. "Are we going to find a ring of rattlers guarding the hidden treasure of a desiccated Scotchman?"

"I beg you to act as I ask or to stay behind." He said it so earnestly that I paused. "There's just ahead of us a danger which may be much more 'striking,' if ignorantly handled," he continued, "than a thousand rattlers or Python himself."

He was evidently serious enough. Here we were at the trail's end. I might as well humor him this once and last. I pulled on the beastly things and we trudged off, down what had now become a slight slope. Indeed, as I looked about over the clearer ground we were covering, it seemed that we were in a sort of saucer-like depression which now appeared to be perhaps as much as a quarter of a mile across, a circular arena ringed with the rocks normal in this desolation. And this arena's surface seemed to get increasingly smooth as it centered down. The actual center, though, I couldn't see. Why, a few minutes' walk made clear. For the ground which had been gently sloping, now began to rise again. We were, in fact, it soon became clear, going over a series of concentric rings or what might be called huge ripples in the ground itself. These grew increasingly marked until we found ourselves on one as steep as those mounds running round a primitive earth fortress.

As I puffed up it, I asked Mr. Mycroft, "Don't you think this may be the crater of a small extinct volcano?" His "No," didn't invite me to waste more breath on making helpful suggestions. But he turned as he crested the rim, a few yards ahead of me, and modified his flat contradiction with, "That might account for the sand's being melted. But here's been an even bigger force."

"Bigger?" I asked as I struggled up beside him. We were looking into a crater, there could be no doubt. It was steep and cupshaped. And right in the middle was a hole, the beginning of a shaft, a digging. There were tools also, I could see—coils of rope, pickaxes, buckets.

"Now will you, please, follow me carefully," said Mr. Mycroft, and began sidling down the steep slope. Certainly the place was eerie enough, already in shadow and with the signs, in this utter desolation, of a secret activity which had already led to three deaths and to which my own life had nearly yielded a fourth. I therefore followed the old man pretty closely and looked to my steps as we scrambled and almost slid down toward the bottom of the cup. So I nearly bumped into him as he had come to an abrupt halt when we reached where the slope flattened, but were still some distance from the center itself.

"Still another life," were the words I heard him saying to himself. He was looking at something now nearly at our feet. I'd seen it from the top of the slope, as one piece of the abandoned and scattered gear round the central hole or shaft. It looked like a piece of tarpaulin which, maybe, had been meant to cover drilling machinery from the weather. But now, looking at it,

I saw under the edge a boot sticking out. I drew back, but Mr. Mycroft went on a step or two, bent down, pulled back the stiff black cover and exposed, stiff and brown, lying on the sand, a corpse. Peering over his shoulder, I saw that the body was nothing like so desiccated as our last desert death-find. The face, though, was turned to the ground. It was, however, with hardly any surprise that I heard Mr. Mycroft's voice saying, "So Kerson's curiosity was also awakened."

Without a word more he drew back again the black stiff covering over the stiff body and went on slowly—almost gingerly, I thought, as I followed, skirting the black pall on the ground. I came up with him as he stopped at the very center of the crater. There was a windlass hoisted over a small shaft; some considerable heaps of sand speckled with the "desert candy" lay about. We peered down the shaft. It was not very deep, I judged twenty or thirty feet perhaps. But I couldn't properly see to the bottom. The sides seemed, at some point, suddenly to open out.

"It looks," I said, to get an opinion out of my silent companion, "as though whoever dug this shaft struck on an underground cavern?"

Mr. Mycroft said nothing, but took from the remnants of the parcel which had yielded our black gauntlets, and had been stuffed in his capacious coat pocket, a line, an electric torch, and a small recording instrument of some sort. This and the torch, which he switched on, he then tied to the line and let down the shaft. I followed the slowly revolving light as it ran down the shaft until its beams shone in the cavern itself. I leaned forward to see what it would show and to prevent the daylight from getting in my eyes. It looked all black as far as I could see. Then I thought I could detect where there must be a floor of some sort, for on it I was pretty certain, though the waving light was very poor, I could see something lying that might have been a pickax. As I was straining further, Mr. Mycroft's voice said warningly, "I'd keep back as far as possible. This *is* rather a disappointment as far as danger and developments are concerned. Still, it wasn't *not* to be expected, and, on the other hand, we can't be sure there's not some considerable risk still. Wait till I haul up my line and then we'll know a little more."

He brought up his queer tackle; the torch he switched off and at once slipped into his pocket. "We're not looking for what we can see," was his enigmatic comment. The instrument he scanned carefully; he made a note of some readings it apparently gave him and then said definitely, "Yes, we'd better not stay here."

"And, and," I hesitated, "what about *him?*"

"He's past any help for himself and I must be sure

he's past any harm to others before we handle him, or what's left of him."

Though the drift of this was lost on me, I was quite scared enough of the whole place to wish to be out of it. Already in the deep hollow the clear air of the fall day was getting dusk. As we climbed the slope I looked back at that desolate pit. It seemed, where the shadow was deepest, as though an infernal glow was hovering over the pit. I felt that my nerves were getting the better of me and hurried down the outer rim of the escarpment after the old man.

"I may take off my gloves now?" That seemed a good, dutiful, childlike question with which to break the silence which had become worse than the most boring talk.

"Yes, yes," he said, and began to pull off his, which he had evidently forgotten, and, as absently, handed them to me. I felt like the page to Good King Wenceslaus, as I trotted along in the wake of the old fellow, hoping that if I kept in his footsteps the cold of fear would be less. For somehow I was quite severely frightened by the whole thing—the awful silence, the loneliness, the emptiness, that wretched dead trader, that vacant sinister hole.

My reflections, milling round that scene, broke out into a question, "Who killed Kerson?"

The reply shut me up completely: "As far as anyone, you."

We reached the great natural Stonehenge, picked up our flasks, and worked our way through the forest of geological obelisks back to the bend in the main trail. It was dusk, and the stars were out already, but our guide was waiting for us patiently enough. We saw the glow of his pipe. It looked no different from the glow of a red star which had appeared on the rock-crest of the canyon-cliff above. A thousand yards, a thousand light-years, I thought, unless we have a scale we just can't say how far anything is, just by looking at it. The guide said nothing as he untethered the horses; Mr. Mycroft said nothing as we mounted. I said nothing. We creaked and jingled along.

As we alighted at our cabin Mr. Mycroft remarked to the man, "We've had an interesting time up here; we'll be going back tomorrow."

"O.K.," like the croak of a frog, the "reflex of assent" told us in the dark that he heard.

When we were alone and, following Mr. Mycroft, I had begun to get ready our evening meal, I said in rather a beaten way, I own, "Will you explain?"

"If you will confess," was the rather grim retort.

"Well," I said, trying to show that at least I had something to contribute, "I can explain all I know. But it isn't much, and I don't see how I can have done really any harm."

"I didn't ask for a defense; I asked for facts," he replied quite harshly.

It was no use. I must get him to tell me where we stood, what we had been up against—were up against. I just couldn't—however much I hated being treated as a combination of a criminal and a silly schoolboy—I couldn't be left, as I was, completely in the dark. And this old man alone knew.

"I suppose you've guessed," I began, as we sat down to a meal I hardly relished, "Kerson came to see me. He had a copy of the code and, as you know, I find it hard for an ignoramus to treat me as one and, as you and I had not complete confidence in each other, I thought I could at least show him I wasn't a complete fool."

"And how was that proof established?" he asked cuttingly.

"Well, Kerson had a strip, like the strip you burgled out of Sanderson's desk. I only showed him, at first and after he had provoked me, how it should be wound up in order to make the words appear."

"And when you had shown him this piece of plagiarized intelligence, and had established, no doubt without acknowledgment, that you were 'knowing,' then you made your well-known wholly mistaken reading of the script?"

I let the point pass—that the first part of the reading, about the time, was mine and was right. I was now, under his cross-examining pressure, hopelessly on the defensive. I just made the feeble parry, "If it was quite wrong, then it could have done no harm? Anyhow, you can't say I sent the wretched man to his death! I didn't know the place or the way to it, and even now I have no idea how he was killed—perhaps he died a natural death—heart or something."

"No," said the inflexible voice of my judge. "He was killed; there's no doubt, and, but for you, he might well be alive."

I pushed back my plate. I had eaten all I could swallow. I drank a little coffee. It was dim in the cabin and the light was behind Mr. Mycroft's head. I turned with a sort of servile gesture and began to clear the bench on which we had eaten. I washed the dishes in the pail, cleansed the knives and forks, rinsed the cups and put them on a rack, and poured out the soiled water. I felt as though I were already doing time in a penal settlement. There was only one streak of relief in the dull gloom of my mind: Miss Delamere need never know anything of this. The old figure sat silent. If only he had smoked, but he didn't, and somehow, though I don't know why, if a person stays still smoking or just holding a cigarette, they aren't quite so unpleasantly still and waiting as if they just sit. Finally there was nothing more to tidy up. I hovered. Should I sit down, or should I say shortly, "I'm turning in," and prepare to get into my bunk.

"Now will you come outside?" said a voice, which though it may have had no welcome in it, at least had no rebuke. Almost like a spaniel petted after it has been smacked, I said, "Certainly."

We settled on the plank just outside the door. The sky looked more solid than the earth, and more active, more alive. We were in a little cup of congealed dark. That was all the earth had shrunk to; that was all our senses recorded. The hard bit of wood of the bench, the hard bit of ground under one's heels, this was all one felt. One saw only the black curve of the rock-rim opposite one, dead black and vacant as Chaos itself, and then sharp above it the dense, glittering heaven. There seemed hardly a millimeter of that embracing expanse that wasn't crammed with stars, flares that sparkled and flashed in all colors, like lighthouses and ships in a thick lane of shipping, and all the interstices filled with the wide-weltering phosphorescence of the Galaxy: stars like great cut jewels and stars like tons of diamond dust poured out in an inexhaustible cascade. And, as if that were not enough, every now and then across the glittering parade, the gala display made on a scale which makes the mind dizzy, cruised long-tailed meteors, leaving, even when they had gone, a dusty trail of brightness showing their path. Then down the sky sailed one so bright that for a moment its flash of fire almost made sufficient illumination for me to see that the earth we rested on was not merely congealed blackness.

As it faded, the voice beside me said, "Literally, we have been following a star. There's been enough mystery, too, in our search, for us little creatures not to quarrel and blame each other. 'What is man,' asked a desert poet, as, early in our history, he looked at that same ocean of light and dark which now hangs above us, hangs above us completely unchanged, while here in our dark little dell we have run through our civilizations—but never found the answer to that first question."

It wasn't very original moralizing. But then I suppose moralizing can never be. "The eternal commonplaces," weren't the great truths called? I suppose they are like that because we never really can find an answer to such obvious questions—and yet we can't get past them—there they stick, as simple and embarrassing as a fish-bone in one's throat.

Anyhow, I was sufficiently relieved that my problem and my mistake were being lifted onto a scale where perhaps we could hope, as the matter couldn't be settled, I might get off with an open verdict. Mr. Mycroft's next remark really did give me a new kind of interest.

"There's been present in this case of ours," he continued, "an element of which detectives are often aware as lurking somewhere, but which I believe they hope they will never have fully to confront."

"An element?" I questioned, for I thought I ought to say something, and I was really interested as well as relieved at the turn things had taken. Even if he were going to start making a partnership between himself and providence, the senior partner of this big firm might put in a word for me with his active "junior."

"Perhaps," he continued, "I may call it—I do to myself—The Element. It is hard to define, as are most elemental things—save by negatives. But, if that is allowed, then one might define, and yet not limit it, by saying, 'There is no chance or accident.' "

"What do you mean?" I questioned.

"I mean that absolutely true reporting of any detection, of the elucidation of any secret, shows unmistakably that there is present some basic factor moving teleologically, or, if you like, purposely, behind what seems to be chance happenings, blind hits and misses, random guessings."

"You mean all this extra-sensory perception stuff?" I asked.

"That's only the tip of the topmost fin of this vast engulfed Leviathan. For centuries, for millennia, men knew about electricity as a funny little anomaly which made grains of salt leap up and cling to a rod of amber if it had been rubbed. Now we know that electricity is the force which holds everything together, the force which makes everything we call material. Believe me, the anomalies of today are the foundations of to-morrow."

"But—" I questioned.

He completed my question, "What has that to do with us and with you in particular? All through this case, I have felt, as never before, The Element, the vast submerged drive, as being quite close, uncannily close to the surface on which we have been working. With you, as one might say, it broke through." Then I could hear that he had turned toward me to emphasize his remark: "You thought you were guessing when you gave your wrong reading, but you were not. Without knowing it, you gave Kerson a clue and that clue sent him to his death."

"How?"

"I'll deal with his death later. First, to your clue 'Friar's Heel' which you translated 'Mission Trail.' "

"Well, it might have been," I said defensively, making as it were a last stand.

His reply jiu-jitsued me. "It was! When I was

making arrangements with our present laconic friend now acting the part poor Kerson played on our earlier trip, I made all the inquiries I could. The man himself knew little and cared less, but as he, too, runs a store, I talked about the locality's history with one or two of the Indians and other wanderers. You may recall, as we left the main trail, to start off into the true wilderness, I told you I thought once that we were actually on an abandoned trail. Indeed, I am sure that to eyes more practiced than mine at that kind of tracking, there is a 'fossil trail' there, starting off from the spot where the present, used trail bends back from that outer desolation. For my informants told me that even in their time this district has 'parched out' increasingly. One also told me that there is a tradition that earlier there were actual drinkable springs in that area which we were stumbling in. The tree-ring records of Douglas show that all through this desert Southwest only some centuries ago the Indians were able in a number of places to have settlements which, later, drought made them abandon. And these great century-spanning droughts come on like glacial ages, in waves, with lulls and recessions in between. This area had such a recession or backwash of almost adequate rains perhaps a century ago. For then some Catholic missionaries, I estimate from the story I was told, actually made a trail up here. There was even a bit of a story that on their trail they reported seeing the ruins of an immense heathen temple. The stones we saw would not suggest a temple to a non-European but any cultured European—and some of the Franciscans were very cultured men—would, of course, know the megalithic 'temple ruins' scattered all over Europe from Britain through France to Greece. They would be struck by the geological formation which we have seen and would say it was like a heathen temple, while a native, not having that association in his mind, would pass it unnoticing. So you sent Kerson hunting a mission trail unknown to you and unrecorded save in a very slender local tradition."

"But how did he know that he had to start from the Great White Throne?" I asked.

"I'm certain he knew a great deal about Sanderson. He had surely watched the old man when he was through his country. It is a bit far from here by our European standards, where if you move fifty miles you may be in another nation, country, and culture. But in these huge, undetailed areas, men cover a lot of ground. Why, even in Europe, stone-age man thought little of tramping on his ten toes all the way from the Black Sea out to Ireland—and that meant two sea voyages to boot—and back.

"When Kerson learned that other people were interested in Sanderson's dives into the back of beyond, his interest became keen. Did he steal the code from Intil or from Sanderson? From Sanderson, I suspect. Intil would be harder to rob, and once he had Sanderson's code probably put it away safe until he had your help to decode it. We know he cherished the little stick on which it had to be 'enscrolled.' Sanderson would, no doubt—I expect you have come to a similar conclu sion—have been the trader's guest more than once, and the old Scotchman must every now and then have talked a little when he was holding perhaps more than he ought of the liquid 'Scotch'; small, discreet (as he thought) boasts about his own cunning. No man who is as interested in locking up secrets in clues, as was he, but wants, sooner or later, to share his cleverness with someone—someone, I have generally found, whom he likes to think of as a fool. Many a criminal has been caught simply because the detective was not clever in anything but in his power to look like a sucker."

It went through my mind that Mr. Mycroft certainly lacked that gift and, indeed, had the complementary weakness which he had just been pointing out —the need to describe his cleverness. Well, but for that I might easily be left never knowing exactly where I stood in all this tangle.

"I surmise," he went on, "that probably Kerson, on one of Sanderson's 'look-in's,' opened the old man's lips with the native solvent I've just mentioned. Kerson would copy the clue and replace it. Maybe it was coiled up on its stick in the old fellow's 'effects.' "

I interrupted, for here I actually knew more than he. "Yes, Kerson had evidently made a very careful copy and had his own idea of what the clue might be, for when he came to me he thought it might be Ogham, an example of which he had seen in a puzzle book."

"That's interesting," said Mr. Mycroft, treating me for a moment as a colleague. "That was shrewd of him. If he hadn't had to extract the clue in a hurry and could have unwrapped all Sanderson's gear he might have come straight upon the right words."

"Perhaps he had tried twisting it round," I added, "for I noticed that the piece of paper he handed me, if you are right that it was a copy, still had a tendency to curl of itself."

"Well, be that as it may, about the Great White Throne the old man in his 'Scotch'-inspired talk would be likely to begin rambling on in that biblical language which, learned by all Scotch bairns before they can understand a word of it (especially dear to Calvinists is that scene of the irrevocable Last Judgment before the Great White Throne), pours off their tongues when in 'liquor' or in delirium. The repetition of that phrase would stick in Kerson's mind; for Kerson, like most descendants of pioneers, was undoubtedly brought up on the obscurer and less ethical parts of the Old and New Testaments. He'd puzzle away at the old man's enigmatic hints.

"Of the code he would still be unable to make anything, until he decided, because he'd heard from me that you were a decoder, to take it to you. I think anyone who knows his Bible in a mechanical way, with all that chapter and verse way of handling it like a set of catch words or charms, might blunder on the clue. When you add to that the fact that any remarks about the Great White Throne would undoubtedly not only have its scriptural connotation to a trader of Fundamentalist stock, but would also, to anyone who knew this district, clearly refer to this desert National Monument—well—" he broke off.

"I suppose," I said, "he'd come up here and might learn that there had actually been a mission trail, now long lost, somewhere off the standard trail. But how did he get further?"

"The trail went at least as far as the natural stone circle, we know," he said. "From there on he'd be able, I think, to find what he was looking for, if he knew near enough what it was that he wanted."

"What was that?" I asked.

"Again he must have learned from Sanderson, either by word of whiskey-opened mouth or by examining the geological specimens the old man pretty certainly once had on him, that he was not out after gold."

"What were they after?"

"He was seeking, if not for treasure in heaven, for treasure from the heavens. But as that has been the goal of all of us, before I end with that, let me end with you."

"You mean how my guess, though I didn't know of such a mission trail, and the code didn't mean that, actually put him on such a trail and brought him to his fatal goal and end."

"Yes; it sounds strange, but it has actually happened before. It does occur, this strange insight by someone who may actually believe that he is not telling the truth." (I didn't like that, but was too anxious to have the thing cleared up even to smart much under the slap.) "The standard case was in the middle of the last century. A sound and noted scholar in Copenhagen announced to a widely interested world of classical studies, that he had found a Latin document, long lost, much desired and of specific information. He said that he had come upon the famous Antonine Itinerary, a book known to us only in quotation fragments but which originally gave the record-map (distances, post-houses, description of the terrain, etc.) of the imperial mails system of the Roman Empire. He published what, he said, were a number of excerpts. But when urged to produce the original manuscript, he demurred. Finally he was charged with having concocted the whole thing, and in disgrace, the keenest of all disgraces for a scholar, he died. A sad story, but not uncommon, alas! Poor Chatterton was a poet and so is remembered, but many who were not did the same thing and met a fate as ill. But this story only begins with the disgrace and death. Archaeological exploration went ahead. The Roman road system was excavated in all parts of Europe. Judge the surprise, the consternation, when time and again as a lost road was uncovered by the spade, its route was found 'prophesied' in the dead and discredited Copenhagen scholar's records. Then these records were actually consulted and by them it was possible to find where to dig so as to strike long-lost and buried stretches of old Roman imperial highway. Still, even today, no one thinks the poor fellow ever had an actual manuscript of the lost Antonine Itinerary in his hands. No hint of such a find has ever come to anyone's ears. If he had had that original, he could not have destroyed it, when all that was needed for his triumphant rehabilitation was to have produced it. Besides, some of his references still seem to be false. No, the only explanation is," he paused, "what happened to you. 'Free association'—I think that psychological term for this sort of tendentious fishing-and-guessing is best and most just—

suddenly gives rise to a true, but even to the mind that gives it, an unknown insight."

I must say I was relieved to find that, as it were in spite of myself, I had been accurate, reliable, acute. It seemed as good a point as any at which to leave the awkward interest in myself and my bona fides and to turn to clearing up the rest.

"By the way," I ventured, "have you Intil's moves clear in your mind?"

"Yes," he said. "He was the simplest, because the most violent. Violence is always, *au fond,* simple because it can't resist in the end those simple reactions, that crude hitting out, which ends in murder. The worst criminal never kills actually, any more than the best chess player takes pieces. He wants to win, not to show off; he wants power, not bloodshed. Intil may, indeed, have actually risked his life. I'm sure now that he trailed Sanderson and when Sanderson found him on his tracks and couldn't shake him off, they exchanged shots, probably, and Intil hit. He then relieved the corpse of everything, including the clue and the little rod that, when he understood enough, made it possible for him to get the code word perfect. You know how, once he thought he had that clue and that you two must have lit on its meaning also, he tried to be rid of you. It was neat in its way," he ruminated, "but really it showed the murderer's characteristic rashness, hurry, hastiness; so in the end he's so slapdash he actually licks the wrong envelope."

These were reflections in which, as I have already said, I could have no relish. I turned Mr. Mycroft's mind back, therefore, to where a patch of fog still lay over the center of my knowledge of this amazing business.

"But who or what killed Kerson?" I asked. After all, it was not possible to say that I, or anyone else, as far as I could see, had had any hand in that.

"What finished him off," said Mr. Mycroft, "finished our story, too, if I'm not mistaken. Here, at least, you may have my line, why I came out here and why I am returning. Some little while ago some very small specimens of ore were sent to certain people on a certain committee in a certain capital. But though these specimens were minute, they were of the utmost—I might say, incomparable—value. Beside them, gold was literally dross—a degenerate slag, a waste by-product. You must know of the hunt which is going on at present, absorbing all the energies of all the physicists, wherever they are, whichever side they are on? The search is to get a super-radium, a radioactive substance that is so active that it will set up indefinitely 'chain-reactions' in ordinary nonradioactive matter. It would cause ordinary matter to start combusting by atomic action, just as thermite will start noninflammable things burning through *its* intense molecular action."

"Then iron and rock would start smoldering like ignited wood and coal, and the world would be literally on fire?"

"That's the dream," he replied. "But at present, do what they can, the reaction, though it has been started, though the match has been lit leading to the world-mine, it won't go on. True, some progress has been made, and now the fuse burns for some nine 'sputters.' But after that, some safety catch or mechanism of the nature of things, intervenes, and the chain-reaction peters out. That was why there was such a stir, a secret stir but none the less deep for that, in high quarters when these spicules of rock, which I have mentioned, arrived—arrived in their thick lead containers. The account said, I understand, that they were of meteoric origin, and though of, until now, unknown intensity of radiation, that was not their interest. For they were not of nearly sufficient radioactive power to help set going that unlimited reaction-train—that reaction with which any possessor can destroy everyone else—"

"Himself included?" I questioned.

No answer came through the dark, but after an instant the voice resumed. "The minute rock splinters came, it was said, from the outer fragments or rind of a meteorite. The thing was not impossible. Ludblad, the Swedish astronomer, has shown that the meteorites which are always raining upon us—as we can see well at this moment (most of them are eroded by our atmosphere into fine dust)—probably come from one or even two fellow planets which rode the sky once on orbits outside Mars. They, he has given some proof for supposing, blew up after they had become mature, and, maybe, after they had given rise to life; for some researchers think that they have actually found bacterial life still lurking in these meteoric fragments. However that may be, meteorites of all sorts of geological make-up have been found: of stone and of the nickel iron which is supposed to be the composition of our own world's central mass. Traces of nearly all the minerals have been found. Yes, they were mature worlds and they utterly shattered themselves."

"How?" I asked, watching at that moment a huge meteorite, an actual spar, I suppose, of those ill-fated worlds, burst into flame above my head.

"No one knows, of course, but there are two theories: One is that all planets, this one we are sitting on included, tend—it was Joly's theory, the man who found how to date the rocks by their radioactivity—to get hotter and hotter until the radioactive layer melts the crust and, the pressure released, the liquid or gaseous center of the earth bursts out, rending this husk on which we live to fragments. The other theory is that some mad form of life must have monkeyed with matter's make-up until—" He left the sentence unfinished and in the black silence the firm earth felt to me only a dark spinning bubble ready at any moment to fly asunder.

"To leave speculation alone," the level voice continued, "if these were splinters of rock so highly radioactive—and tests proved that this part of the sender's claim was accurate—if, further, as the report went on to claim, they were not the most powerful radioactive material to be obtained, but only, as it were, the rind of this strange fruit, this apple of discord, flung by the fates onto earth's lap—well, then, this world of ours, being what it is today, couldn't let such a 'welkin's welcome' well alone. Meteorite gifts have always played an important part in man's civilization. The first iron tools, we now know from chemical analysis, are precisely that form of nickel-iron alloy which nearly all metal meteorites yield; and the ancient Egyptians and Sumerians called the metal, 'The strong thing—or the adamant—that fell from Heaven.'

"Incidentally, I suppose you probably understand that the heat generated by a meteorite, by its friction on the air, is so terrific that when it strikes the earth the sand is melted and some of it actually fuses into glass?"

"I know," I said, "that there's a company which tried to dig up a huge buried meteorite in Arizona. But I thought it had gone too deep."

"The advices which were received about what I may call Sanderson's meteorite said that it, on the contrary, had behaved like the great Siberian one of 1908. There the ball itself seems to have burst before it struck the earth and so, instead of a single mass plunging hundreds of feet into the earth, a sort of shrapnel showered down over a wide area and a core probably lighted at the center of the bombarded patch.

"The problem, however, was to find exactly where this meteorite had come to earth. It was quite likely quite a small one. Our informant, need I say, was chary. He wanted to know whether we were interested, but not to let us in on his secret, except on his own terms. I say 'we,'" he added, "a little prematurely. For it was only at that point that I myself was actually called in. There's little more to say; you'll probably have deduced the rest. Intil was our cautious informant. He wanted to get backing for what he took to be a big excavation, as it might have been. Sanderson, however, had already started excavating—though, of course, Intil did not know this. Intil had simply gained possession of some of the highly radioactive outer-ore which Sanderson had collected, and the clue, which he couldn't read. He was always rather daring but always in rather too much of a hurry."

"And Kerson's death?" I demanded, for that was the real issue, surely.

"I think," Mr. Mycroft said, "that Sanderson had exposed the main core-mass at his last visit. I believe that it must have formed round itself a kind of oxide or skin of far less radioactive material (though still, by our standards, intensely radiant). I believe that Sanderson, whom we know to have been a man of more than usual general knowledge, had the sense, when he had gone as far as that, to wait. The strange treasure was practically inert. Though it would be highly dangerous to handle, it would, unless tampered with, remain like the genie in the bottle. No doubt one day he would have asked for help. Perhaps, for all we know, his clue was not merely a highly embroidered personal mnemonic but he was working out some sort of 'agony column' message, whereby he might signal to, contact, and make working terms with a fellow explorer who, when he had tested him out, might be brought to share risks and probably profits.

"However that may be, Intil, the high-brow hijacker, got first on his trail. When these two were gone, along comes Kerson. All he knows is that there's a super-valuable ore to be found. He finds the pit, thanks, among other 'pawns of fate,' to you. He sees the mass of exposed 'ore' lying there at the bottom. He goes down and starts cracking away at the lump, the top of which is exposed. One doesn't know how long the released, or 'unscreened,' radiation took to kill him. He got as far as where we found his body, crept under the tarpaulin—violent X-ray 'burns' are rightly so called, and this must have been a furnace, the like of which no physicist has yet witnessed—and died. Now you see why I took with us the lead-impregnated rubber gauntlets, which men who work with X-rays wear—though against that charge, I doubt if they would have been adequate."

"But there *wasn't* any stone down that pit. I saw," I said.

"Not now," he answered. "When Kerson cracked the crust, the shell of that dread dragon's-egg, the core mass radiated itself away. You know they have already made in the laboratory elements higher than the 90 of uranium, the highest known natural element, but they are so unstable that they will not last. This immensely high power must have been equally unstable. The higher the power, the less it endures—a motto not without comfort in these frantic power-days! Though the electroscope which I let down into the pit showed that the whole area was still intensely radioactive"—(I thought of that sinister glow I had been sure I had seen hovering round the lips of the pit) "still the treasure itself, more deadly than the fabulous Rhine Gold, has 'melted into air, into thin air.' Well, I was bound to seek. Better in our hands than in theirs. But I must own, Mr. Silchester, that I am not sorry that Nature has once again intervened, once again withdrawn, on consideration, from us such final powers."

After a pause I felt that there was still one question to be settled. It was, of course, personal, but we had been at such a height that I felt I could raise it, we could look down on it together and I didn't much care what answer he gave.

"Mr. Mycroft," I asked, with, I think, some considerable detachment, "one small human mystery remains. Why did you ask me to come with you on this final trek? Perhaps it is because I'm a bit sobered by the scale of things on which we or you have been working, but, you know, I cannot flatter myself that you brought me along on this final exploration because you thought I should be an invaluable companion and fellow worker."

"That is frank and courageous of you," he replied, "and your frankness deserves as much openness from me. Yes, I did bring you along not because I felt you could help me out in an awkward corner but because, considering all you knew—and remember that Intil had paid you the same compliment, though in a rather pointed way—I felt I owed it to those who employed me to keep you in sight until this matter was finally cleared. I can now be sure there could be no leakage, for you are the only man alive who knew of the secret."

I was not sorry that we had had out our final personal issue and when it was laid, and it left no inflammation on the skin of my *amour-propre* in that aseptic scene, we were silent for some time. The curtain was down on the human tragedy; or rather, the little apron-stage play was over and the backcloth went up, showing the immense Void against which our pains and pleasure and opinions, I had to own, were invisible. We were silent for I don't know how long. Silently stars came up over the rock-rim, and went down silently; and silently the meteor gifts coming in from outer space and the long-wrecked fellow planets were ground to a glowing dust and their deadly power denied us, as the edges are taken off from children's and lunatics' table-knives.

Next morning Mr. Mycroft said, "I return to report the case closed: proceedings quashed by a Higher Court. The Element, as I call it, has recalled an element too high and powerful for us yet to be trusted with it." We parted, he going east and I west. Whether his lofty speculations are right or wrong, I don't venture to decide. The whole thing was too big for me. All I know is that his big check *did* turn into hard cash; all I know is that I was very glad to get back to nice, manageable human-made puzzles and to exchange for an exhausting companionship with a supermind my daily duel with Miss Delamere.

"Hope you've had a good vacation," her cigarette semaphored to me as she handed me the large and satisfying mail on my return. "Vacation," I thought, "that means a vacancy, an emptiness." I thought of that hole out of which the most terrible force conceivable had radiated itself away—where a solid chunk of supercondensed power which had punched a hole in the rocks had then turned back into nothing.

"Yes," I said, "just attending to Nothing rather opens the mind." She could not hear that I used a capital for the first noun.

THE NOTCHED HAIRPIN

TO MICHAEL

CONTENTS

Chapter I

THE RED BRICK TWINS

"DON'T touch."

"I wasn't going to! And if tact means touch, then I don't think you'd be the worse for a little of it!"

"I'm ready to apologize in advance for being so guarded, but, you see, this is quite a peculiar treasure."

"I don't see. What I do see is a very commonplace object. But I am ready to accept your apology."

Yes, it was one of the usual Silchester-Mycroft squabble-sallies. The gauge of battle had arrived by the breakfast mail. I'd paid no attention to it until Mr. M., having finished all his letters, came to the small box—the kind of thing in which you sent a wrist watch. As I had finished the paper, I let myself enjoy his attack on it—rather like the cautious behavior toward some new sort of fly in its web. When he had opened it and peered inside for a while, out came the professional lens, and then at last I was called in. I couldn't help being amused by all that preliminary ritual of inspection. For when I took a single glance, I could only conclude that the lens-play was either a mere reflex or a piece of semiconscious acting. What lay in the little casket, all dolled up with cotton wool, was a commonplace little paper knife of some dingy kind of metal. It was the sort of thing which, when Spanish was all the mode with second-rate interior decorators (a tribe which, at best, I care for very little), was described as a suitable *objet d'art* to go with stamped-and-gilded leather furniture and twisted iron fittings! Perhaps I had made some courtesy attempt to express an act of interest I couldn't honestly feel, and this, my gesture of sympathy, had simply been snubbed. And when you have labored to pretend attention, it is irritating to be accused of precipitate meddling. Therefore Mr. M.'s further defense, "But it *is* very interesting!" did nothing to mollify my feelings.

The play with so light a weapon as the lens having failed to draw me, heavy artillery was now brought to bear and provoke my curiosity. The portentous microscope was hauled into position and, to teach me procedure with treasures, the "object," certainly not "of art," was picked out of its case with tweezers and examined slowly from head to foot. Finally, while it lay in the microscope's sacred and pure grips, Mr. M. did permit himself the liberty of poking at its handle end with a pin and examining, with special care, whatever piece of dust the pin could have picked up before it was raised to the rank of becoming an "exhibit." Then, to see if by this time and all this play I had become agog with curiosity, he looked up and nodded. I saw no reason to nod back. And evidently seeing I was not to be soothed, he shut the box with a snap, carried it off like the reliquary of a newly interred saint, and locked it in his desk. Then at last, apparently becoming aware he had really been quite cavalier with my offer of courtesy, he remarked in his most ingratiating voice:

"Do you know, I believe we both may need a small summer vacation. I have lately been scanning the advertisements of houses to be let for August, and I believe I now have a couple in view, either of which might suit us very well."

At that I "perked up," as my nurse used to phrase it. And when the cunning old bird added, "The two which I am hoping you might come with me to look at are, as far as I can understand, twins—that is to say, they were both built by the same architect in the same year—built as a pair, I presume. The date, I am told, has been placed on each of them by the builder —1760." Then I couldn't help relaxing into the quite neat reply: "Perfect! Set between the French and the English Regencies, between the severity of Queen Anne and the sparse elegance of the Brothers Adam—they should be a perfect balance of taste."

Indeed, I was so mollified I was quite ready to run on with a really entertaining little impromptu essay on "1760 as the Balance of English Architectural Style." And Mr. M. actually seemed inclined to listen, when, at my saying again my key word, "balance," he spun round, went back to his desk, whisked out the little case from where he'd locked it and, disregarding all the instruction he might have had, turned over the little sarcophagus reverently, rolling out of it onto the tablecloth the object it had immured. Then, picking up a knife, he began to play an awkward game of giant spilikins, with table knife and paper knife, trying to pick up the latter on the edge of the former. He proved quite clumsy at this rather silly pastime. But at last, after a number of trials, he did get his present-by-post teeter-tottering on the blade of the table piece.

"Look," he said.

Of course there was nothing to see, or at least to applaud.

"Do you notice anything?" followed, and to my honest antiphon, "No," all he replied was, "It would be convenient, I have often thought, if only cutlers would think to make table knives and forks that way, wouldn't it?"

To my perfunctory, "Which way?" he replied, "Properly balanced; so that they wouldn't fall off the plate, because their center of gravity would lie not at the handle end but forward."

The whole subject was so trivial and dull and, I could not help feeling, done maybe to spoil my really rather generous attempt to turn his offer to be agreeable into a little piece of conversation that would have been truly instructive, that my patience again began to ebb sharply, and to avoid further provocation I asked, "May I hear more about those two houses?"

And to show that I meant what I said, when he replied, "Yes, and there's no reason why we shouldn't go and see them today," I again showed perfect cooperation.

As a result we were off in the train within an hour.

For when Mr. M. chooses to act, he can do so with a speed and precision I can often envy. When we were comfortably seated and had half an hour before lunch would be served, he took from his bag a Milton and handed me a nice little edition of Housman's Poems.

"We are going into country which these two poets illustrated. So, while I read 'Comus' and, being so much the elder, brood on the dreaming water of *Sabrina fair*, you, being of his age, can climb 'Bredon Hill' with the *Shropshire Lad*,

'And hear the larks so high
About us in the sky.' "

It was perhaps forty minutes after lunch—the right time for digestion to have reached that stage when it suggests mild exercise—that Mr. M. rose and, taking down his suitcase, said, "We shall be met at the station by a house investigator."

"Investigator?" I questioningly exclaimed. "Why go so far to avoid the obvious and not call him in common parlance an agent?"

He smiled at my rally and replied in equally good vein, "Don't you think that 'agent' sounds a little secretive, anyhow too committal, almost perhaps sinister? While 'investigator,' after all, commits us to nothing? We need not take the house if in any way you should feel that it might not suit you."

This was graciousness itself, and I hastened to assure him that all I had been told made me very much inclined to close the negotiations without further trouble.

"Well," he said as the train began to slow, "anyhow, we shall have seen an interesting piece, as museum authorities call anything that is more of the past than the present."

At the station a quiet-looking man came up to Mr. M. As only two obvious farmers and three ladies of uncertain age got off the train with us, the man did not have to use much acumen to recognize us. He ushered us out to where a delightful museum piece of a landau was waiting for us—all complete, with faded, moth-eaten cushions once royal-blue, and old stamped and tasseled leather window straps for hauling up the glass windowpanes when the cracked leather-japanned top hamper should be put up against the rain.

But today was glorious and, imagining myself the Grand Duke of Baden driving to take "the cure" with my equerry and physician, I thoroughly enjoyed it as we bowled along through the streets of the quaint little town. Mr. Mycroft, unconsciously playing up to the role of court physician in which I had cast him, entertained me, the Royal Highness, with, "Twibury is a delightful little town. It has a medicinal warm spring. On your left you see the tower of the largely Saxon church, with the characteristic 'long-and-short' work of the quoins and the 'midwall shafting' of the tower windows, while round the town itself are some peculiarly happy examples of mid-eighteenth-century domestic architecture."

All this, which would have bored me had I been listening to it "out of character," now that I was daydreaming of being a German princelet fell in so well with the whole fancy that I was already more than half in love with the place.

When, then, through orchards in bloom, we drew up by a fine, stately brick house with a flight of mellow stone steps leading up to the fanlighted and column-flanked door, I did not need to decipher, in the finely wreathed ironwork which arched over the steps and made a nest for the doorlamp to rest, the date "1760."

I turned to Mr. M. as we came to a standstill and said, "I'm won already. We may stay here as long as you please."

I should have judged that he would then fail me, and his "Well, wait," I felt, was meant to bring me down from a dream which, like enough, he saw I was enjoying. Certainly there seemed less and less to wait for, or to delay us from getting out of the small and rather stuffy quarters in which we'd cooped ourselves up in London to be in this—to quote somebody I've forgotten—"larger, serener air." For as our attendant fell in behind us as we mounted the steps, the door opened. A most efficient maid stood by it—I could see at a glance, for I am a judge of maids. And my judgment was confirmed with every step we took over the threshold: the brass was like gold; the mahogany like tortoise shell; the pieces of silver bright as mercury; not a speck of dust anywhere, still less the thread of a spider; the chintzes lately calendered, bright-stiff but not repellent.

As we passed through from the hall to the dining room, even Mr. M. was impressed and had the courtesy to say, "What a lovely polish all the woodwork has." The maid bridled with pleasure; and then, not content with having given pleasure, he must overload the whole thing and begin taking that rather absurd overinterest. He bent and looked at the grand piano we were passing.

"You use one of the new waxes, don't you?"

"Oh, yes, Sir! *Sheen* is just wonderful!"

"None of the old oils and resins now!"

"Oh, no, Sir, they was ever so much trouble, and when you'd done all your best, there they were, and never could you be sure whether the gloss would last; I'd never go back to those old things, would never let them in the house again, never!"

He had, as usual, when casually and by habit of fidget picking at the dike of some special and really boring interest, unloosed a flow of utterly irrelevant technicalities. He gave no further encouragement, but it was too late—the technician had tasted blood, or rather resin or wax or whatever it was that whetted her appetite and loosed her tongue. She followed the three of us as we moved through the dining room to a stately, tall window at the end that opened out to another short flight of steps leading into the garden. We went down these, I supposed to get a general view of the house from the back.

The garden was as charming as the house. It was of the period and as unspoiled. There were pleached alleys of beech just coming into leaf, these, with their light green, framed against a solid background of close-clipped yew, and behind that again, closing in the whole, a fine, tall brick wall and some most promising peach trees covered with bloom. At the end I thought I saw a fish pond with a statue or two, while on the right this lovely enclosure had the only outer entrance, a fine green door, serenely shut.

I was still at the top of the steps surveying this, which I already saw as my privy garden for the summer, when I noticed that Mr. M., the man he would call the house investigator, and the maid, still hoping to impart further technical tips on the polishing of furniture, had paused at the foot. There the pleached alleys met and made a kind of arbor. They went into this little bower, and I followed. It certainly was charming inside, and I became even more deeply rooted—for here, clearly, was the actual spot where I would sit, working at that very suggestive essay on "1760 as the Acme of English Taste." The place was made for such work, for in the little enclosed bay which it formed, screened from the house, screened from almost all the garden, was a sort of sanctum sanctorum fitted as a kind of shrine. I felt the owner must have used it thus, for there was a beautiful stone chair carved in lovely half-marble Hopton Wood stone that time and a small bloom of lichens had deepened, so that it was more like moss agate. This noble seat was flanked on both sides by two stone tables of the same material, and looking down on each side were marble busts, now too gone a decent duck-egg green, of two Greek worthies. I felt in my bones that I had arrived. Here was a spot so manifestly prepared that, as little as a bird can fail to lay an egg in a properly finished nest, so little need I doubt that here was the inevitable environment so apposite to my genius that I must produce a masterpiece!

Chapter II

THE INSPECTOR'S "WHO?"

I WAS just about to seat myself on this throne and see how it felt—and I was certain it must feel as good as it looked—for inspiration, when the house agent, who till then had said hardly a word, began to speak.

Not unnaturally, I felt impatience. I couldn't help dreading that this man of ledgers, rents, and "advts." would be bound to spoil quite half of my perfectly toned appreciation with sales-pressure talk about the "quaint setup" and "picturesque atmosphere." What then was my surprise, yes, shock, when I found that what he was actually saying was so incongruous that beside it the weariest clichés of the most dismal trafficker in house property would have been more apposite—and more soothing! What he was saying was not only highly disturbing but so utterly out of character with what one has a right to expect of a house agent. I felt as though one of those nightmares was coming on, when the chest of drawers begins to turn into a loquacious and voracious dragon.

"The body was there. As he stabbed himself, he fell over, of course."

Mr. Mycroft's counter, "You're certain of your . . . diagnosis?" was not answered by this utterly out-of-character character.

A further note of the odd and uncanny, a further darkening of the sudden cloud spreading over my bright day, was caused by the voice of the wonderfully prim and efficient maid taking up the tale, saying, "Excuse me, Sir, Mr. Sankey—he was murdered. I don't say that he was a man who was loved or admired, but give the dead their due and the living their rights, murdered he was, and I know it. And I know that the living ought to be protected, and not just told, against all their senses and their commonsense into the bargain, that it was just common-and-garden suicide as anyone of us might be taken with after influenza or crossed in love."

If this outbreak disconcerted me, it did not seem to have any such effect on the other two. They showed as little discomposure as did Balaam when his ass spoke and, in further likeness to that perverse if cold-blooded prophet, proceeded to enter into easy conversation with their unexpected interrupter.

"Well, Jane," said the agent, with the ease of someone asking a crony of the inglenook to cap one of his stories, "tell this gentleman your theory."

"Theories and such things, Sir, if you will pardon me, I know nothing about. Them things I leave to those who think they do–" and with this there was shot a glance that was meant to win Mr. M., who certainly had already won her heart, and defy the rival who had refused to treat her hope of the excitement of murder as being well-founded.

With a sniff she swept on. "I trust my senses and not theories, and nothing will move me not till Judgment Day, no not Judgment Day itself, that poor Mr. Sankey–as one has a right to call him whatever he may have been till he was murdered–poor Mr. Sankey was murdered, and what is more–" and here she seemed to feel the part of tragedy queen hovering over her with all its regalia–"right under my nose as I might say."

To Mr. M.'s rally, "You don't mean–as we are dealing, as you rightly claim, not with theory but with fact–that you really smelled the murderer?" she granted, as I am sure she would not to the rest of us, a cold smile of triumph.

"No, but as good as that. I as good as saw the murderer enter with my eyes and heard him with my ears. There was I, up in the dining room through which I just brought you. I was getting things ready for poor Mr. Sankey's lunch and was just by the window and suddenly I heard the garden door whine or twang. I'll be glad, if I may make so bold, to show you in a moment how it does it, and no oil will ever stop it, that I can answer for too. 'I'll be bound,' I said to myself, 'that's the trash man come to clear up those cuttings and prunings.' "

"What cuttings?" asked Mr. Mycroft, with that curious passion he has for making devious talkers deviate still more.

Of course, she rose to the question with delight, and their friendship was further cemented. "Well, after all, it was rather prompt, I remember thinking—the trash man coming so soon. For the prunings were made only the day before. Only the day before, Mr. Millum—now, there is a nice gentleman, the kind of man who can't help noticing when a house is well-kept. And indeed he might envy this one; not that I say it who shouldn't but because Mrs. Sprigg, over the way, who looks after for him—

though heaven knows I've nothing against her, save she's fonder of talk than work—well, she has neither the time nor the skill to look after that place as this is, seeing that her husbing was never strong, and then with . . ."

But that, heaven be thanked, was too much even for Mr. Mycroft. He not unneatly embanked this spreading and sprawling delta of reminiscence by giving her back her lost channel and clue.

"Mr. Millum, you were saying?"

"Oh, yes. Mr. Millum dropped in, as he's always dropping or perhaps I ought to be saying he was wanted. For poor Mr. Sankey liked it in his way. Like some cats, when you stroke them they want you to go on, and maybe would scratch you if you didn't, but nary a bit, as my mother who was a bit broad in her speech would say, nary a bit would they show that they did."

I thought we were in for country-life natural history as illustrated by the habits of the smaller felines. But Mr. Millum rose to the surface again, and with him, my rather tiring hopes.

"Mr. Millum was saying, when I was bringing Mr. Sankey his 'elevens,' that naturally the bower ought to be pruned—that was why it was getting leggy at the sides and overgrown at the top. And evidently Mr. Sankey wanted it done, in his way. Mr. Sankey hated having anything done round him. But then, on the other hand, he hated the thought that he could be seen from the house. That's why he liked the bower. Oh, he was a close one. He could sit there, and no one, not from one of our windows, could see him. That's why I couldn't actually see the poor dear gentleman . . ." (tragedy had raised her late and obviously while alive disliked master to terms of sad affection) "actually killed. Well, Mr. Millum went on about the bower being really hardly any use now and that a gardener ought to be sent for to prune it. Mr. Sankey grudged like a grating gate that he was tired of the bower. He'd move anyhow—though where else in the garden he'd find as nice a seat should have been clear as a conundrum to a one-eyed man. Mr. Millum was so patient-like, pointing out how easily the pruning could be done and quickly too, and then he'd have his privacy and the sun too. Finally Mr. Sankey said sour-as-turned-milk-like (though that was nothing to remark, heaven knows), 'Well, if you're so keen that I should stay where I am and be shaded properly, do it yourself!'

"I left them together. But after a few minutes Mr.

Millum passed me in the hall, saying, kind, good man, that he'd be back after lunch and would get to work and would see that he left everything tidy and bring no twig nor leaf in on my carpets. And he was as good as his word—always is. There he was, clipping and cutting away all afternoon till the little spot, as you see for yourselves, was neat as though it'd been to the barber's, and, need I say, seeing what I've said, there wasn't a leaf or twig or husk of an old beech-nut—and cling they do to rugs if once they get in them—brought in on one piece of my carpets!"

Perhaps even Mr. M. felt this narrative style was too exuberant. Anyhow, he took rest from its flood or gale by sinking down into the fine stone chair which I had fancied as my seat of authorship but which I now couldn't help feeling had about it an unpleasant sense of its last disagreeable occupant and his disagreeable last session. But Mr. M. leaned back at his ease and appeared only to be scanning idly the interlaced twigs that arched above us, every now and then dipping his head a little, perhaps hoping to spy a bird's nest, for the birds were fussing about up there, as they will in spring.

Jane, however, needed no obsequious attention to keep her going.

"Next morning, Mr. Sankey told me at breakfast that I was to tell Mrs. Sprigg that Mr. Millum was to come and see him at eleven prompt. Now, punctual as I am and was always, to be told to come like that would have made me late as sure as sure—just human nature, you know. But would you believe it, as I crossed the hall here on the stroke of eleven—for punctual I had to be, like it or not—there was good Mr. Millum at the door. I put down my tray, on which I had Mr. Sankey's hot chocolate and the small cup of cream and the tiny phial of vanilla, and let him in. Then I took up my tray and, like the perfect gentleman he is, he held the doors open for me. And so we came to Mr. Sankey out here together. Mr. Sankey, as I think you've learned, never thanked anyone for anything. All he said when the two of us come out was, 'Put the tray here!' And while I was arranging it as he liked—and how he liked and disliked no one could know who didn't do for him—Mr. Millum stood by cheerful and patient-like, just chatting and keeping amusing. He did glance at his pruning, but knowing well he'd get no thanks (for, as my Irish grandmother used to say, 'What'd you expect from a pig but a grunt?'), he and I went back through the house and I took him to the door and showed him out.

"And then . . ."

Jane's voice sank as she rose to her obviously oncoming emotional climax, "And then . . . I come in here as light as the day, and it was a lovely one. I pass right up to this window—" the graphic present of the seeress had now taken her style—"and I am just going out and to those steps down to ask Mr. S. will he lunch out or in, seeing what a day it was, when hearing, as I've said, the garden door twang, up I glance and surely I see the top of it opening. You can see it from the dining-room window just up there. It opened only a little, but I thought, 'Oh, he's (by that I meant the trash man) seen Mr. Sankey's out there and so'll call another time.' Most people knew Mr. Sankey was cranky, if you'll forgive the rhyme; and that their tip depended on their not upsetting him. And with that, light as air, I slipped down to this quiet place, and quiet it was and heavy as lead. For there he was, in that nice white silk suit he'd just put on that morning, flat on the gravel and stone slab that you see's round the chair, and the nice book he'd been reading flattened under him.

"Of course, I kept my head. You can't have tidied up messes half your life from a full home to a home like this full of things to be kept just right without being used to a mess and not losing your patience when it happens. I went and telephoned as straight as I'm talking to you and said to Mr. Timmins—that's our chief constable and a fine man if ever there was one—'Mr. Timmins,' I said, 'I trust you're well and would you mind stepping round, for everything shall be left just as it is until you come, strange though that may be for one like myself who likes tidiness, for Mr. Sankey's just been murdered.' "

"Thank you, thank you," broke in Mr. M. at last. "A most orderly report of perfectly correct procedure, and the rest we know."

"Thank you, Jane," added the house inspector, and she actually took their hint, thinking perhaps this was as fine an exit line as she could manage.

After she had passed through the door with a conscious sense of finish, we followed into the dining room where, too, she left us to ourselves. As that door closed, Mr. Mycroft remarked with a certain challenge in his voice, "A good case. It's murder as far as any jury or most judges would see, isn't it?"

"So I thought," replied the inspector. "And the further steps seemed at first to confirm all we've heard. First I went into the lane—I was down here within a few hours. The lane behind that wall is a very quiet place where tramps would naturally doss and doze the day off. Well, one of them, we presume, is there. He notices the door is ajar. He slips through and sees Sankey sitting, perhaps dozing, with his back to the door. He steals up the grass path, as he is hidden from the house, to see if he can snitch anything —watch, cigarette case, etc. As he's quietly turning over the things on the stone table by Sankey, Sankey stirs. Tramp snatches up the first thing, the paper knife. Sankey would stretch out his left arm to seize intruder, who almost involuntarily would strike down at Sankey's left breast and give him a heart stab, after which he would bolt quietly. I'll come to the marks on the hilt in a moment, but meanwhile the whole of that theory had been rammed fast and sunk by an awkward fact. When I came to the garden door I found . . . well, come, and I'll show you."

We went down the little grass walk to the green door. Mr. M. and our guide dropped on their knees as though at a shrine. I bent in he background, as it ruins trousers to kneel. But I could see and understand, as our guide said, "You see, there is a silt of shriveled blossom petals and small leaves packed in with light mud, splashed and pelted on by the last heavy shower. There has been no heavy rain here for ten days. That door has not been opened for that time, at the least."

The argument was conclusive and I saw Mr. M. nod.

He added, though, "But she *heard* it?"

"Yes," replied the other, "I can show you what she thought she heard, now you two are witnesses that the door has not been opened for a considerable time and could not have been opened on that day."

With this he stood up and, taking a key from his pocket, put it into the lock. With a wrench it gave, and with another wrench he pulled the door open, which, as though in protest, made an angry twang. We all looked up. At the top it was fitted with one of those old-fashioned hasps rather like giant jew's-harps, with which old doors used to be fitted to make them, when they slammed, stay shut.

"So that's what Jane heard?" remarked Mr. M.

"What she imagined she heard," he was corrected.

"Ah, but then why did she look up? What roused her attention at all?"

"Because in fact she really first *saw*, and then, having mistaken what she did see, she invented, or should I say deduced, the appropriate sound to confirm her misinterpreted visual impression."

And to prove this intriguing theory, our guide began to lead us back to the dining room. But I could have told him that Mr. M. was as easy to lead as Jane was to keep to a point. I smiled as I saw the older detective snatch at a straw of distraction, for Mr. M. is one of those who believes that at least in information it is better to give than to receive. We had hardly turned from the door when he stopped, and then, making off along the side of the garden wall, called out, "Just a moment. One more confirmation of our fully documented narrative." We waited while he rummaged over the sprays of wilted beech and finally produced quite a big one, almost a small branch, and held it up, apparently to admire it. But do what he would, he could make no further play with this distraction and after a moment consented to be led back to the dining room, still, however, absent-mindedly switching at his boots with the branchlet that he had acquired and evidently hardly knew he still retained. However, as he went up the steps he did drop it beside them. He would certainly have lost some of his gains with Jane if he had brought beech mast and leafage onto her glossy floors and velvety rugs.

"Now," said the inspector like an impatient lecturer when he had us ranged at the window, "please stay here and watch carefully that small piece of the top of the door which you can see from here." With that he left us. A moment after, we heard him, though hidden, calling to us from the door's direction, "Watch!" And as we watched, the top of the door moved some six inches or more out from shadow into light. But I heard no whine of the catch.

When he rejoined us, Mr. M. said, "That was very neat."

The other took it with a certain half-ashamed modesty. "You've had time to enjoy some of the modern painting?"

Again that almost resentful assent. "Yes, it does help us to discount the senses, doesn't it? As Constable said, 'What do we see but light falling on light.' " And Mr. M. sighed a trifle histrionically, I thought, as he added, "And shadows passing through shadows."

I am glad this kind of high-flown enigmatism seemed to fail to buoy up our inspector about the same time that my patience was thinning, and when I said almost a little sharply, "What is this all about?" Mr. M. condescended quite quickly with, "Of course, the door didn't open at all. All that was done just now was to move a branch, which let a highlight of sunbeam fall upon the upper part of the door, which made the effect as though the top of the door itself had actually moved out from shadow into sunlight—in other words, had opened."

The inspector nodded and went on, "As the door never opened, no one entered by it. The garden therefore was completely closed, no one was in it, and so the only person who could have killed Sankey was himself. We have the motive, too, which the other alternative—murder—would have left really no more than a piece of fanciful construction. I've had the routine inquiries made as to undesirable tramps. There's nothing to give us any clue there. You know that most tramps are known more or less to the police and most of them are fairly harmless—as far from the killer type as is a slug. For the other case—suicide—I have on the contrary been able to get clear confirmation. Sankey was melancholic. I have seen his doctor: growing irritability—you've gathered that from the maid; influenza this spring and its after-depression lasting on acutely. That's the general condition or state of likelihood. Have we any evidence, though, of any momentary provocation that might have sprung the mine of loaded self-disgust?"

The inspector certainly liked a phrase and I was tickled by his attempt at eloquence. But I was even more pleased when, adding, "Now, for further specific proof," he moved across to a desk and from one of its drawers took out a finely bound book. It was a delight to the eye. He held it up for us to study. I saw at once it was the beautiful Nonpareil edition of classical texts bound in pigskin and printed on esparto grass paper in that press's fine font—a treasure indeed, and a lovely addition to the décor of any room even if you never opened it. Across its broad handsome back, in finely stamped gold letters that were miniatures of the Trajan Column inscription capitals, one could read with ease the title: *Suetonius: The Lives of the Caesars. Martial: Epigrams. Pliny: Letters.*

Mr. M. took the noble volume from the inspector. "A charming selection! First, that almost unbelievable story of how absolute power came successively to twelve mostly commonplace men, with results utterly fantastic and generally fatal not only to those around them but to themselves. Then, the incomparably terse satire-comment on such a society by Epigram's father. And finally, the quiet reflections of a perfect gentleman who lived just after that too-exciting time—the ideal position for a moralist. I have always admired this way of showing Latin's Golden

Age turning, as autumn does in late October, from the gold to the silver. Here's an example: this placing of the famous Martial Epigram 1.14 on one page and on the opposite the Pliny Epistle III.16. What could be happier—each throwing light on the other! And after the horrors of the actual tyranny, as Suetonius has given it earlier, the poet and the essayist select for comment an act of heroism that shines all the more brightly against the sullen background of arbitrary violence."

I think the inspector was a little impatient at Mr. M. for having caught and bettered his taste in rhetoric. Certainly I wasn't sorry when we were brought back from comments on classical cutthroats to our actual problem.

"You will see," our informant went on, "why I have shown you this book. You are looking at the actual page which the victim was reading when the fatal impulse took him. It indicates what I feel sure any jury, without a doctor to help them, would conclude served as the 'trigger action.' "

"But," Mr. M. challenged, "how do you know this was the actual page he was reading and not merely the way the book fell when he toppled over it?"

"Look closely into the cleft of these pages. There's

cigarette ash, see, that silted down into the binding. That proves this was the point Sankey had reached when suddenly the impulse took him."

"But why . . .?" Mr. M. began; and then fell silent, reading.

His question was apparently sensed by our very informed informant.

"Reading live clues to trace dead men's motives keeps one from having time to read dead languages," he said. "But as soon as I saw that the ash had marked the last page the dead man had read, I had it translated. The vicar here, who had to come up to see about the funeral and whom I interrogated about Millum, is a fine Latinist and kindly made this rendering for me," and he took a slip of paper from his pocket. "These lines do provide us with the sudden provocation, the final proof that here we have suicide."

But before he could read his scrap or I could shift round and glance at the original that had provided such an unexpected provocation to *felo-de-se*, Mr. M.'s voice, in the best lectern manner, boomed out: " 'Taking the dagger she drove it into her own side, withdrew it, handed it to her hesitating husband, remarking quietly as she sank, "It does not hurt, Petus!" ' A fairly free translation, but it will serve."

And after paying himself this first compliment, he turned handsomely on his colleague, "Yes, that's a fine piece of deduction and a core piece in your argument. Sankey, brooding on suicide, reads how noble it is to die, and, further, in this classic case, how easy death by self-stabbing really is! 'So every bondsman in his own hand bears the power to cancel his captivity.' And to borrow another line from the same poet so much greater than Martial, the bondsman may do it 'with a bare bodkin.' "

If our guide had been a little impatient at Mr. M.'s competing with him in phrase-making, that was now all forgotten at this open appreciation and apparent conviction. He almost flushed with pleasure, and showed his friendliness with an added desire to pile proof on proof; though by now I was quite satisfied and content in every sense of the word that here we did not have a murder but simply a person who didn't seem to have been very nice, who had removed himself from the scene.

But Mr. M. seemed to want more and co-operated at once when the inspector went on, "Well, Sir, that rightly does bring us to the bare bodkin itself, as I promised. Will you now let me go over it with you?"

And, sure enough, Mr. M. brought out the little

box from his pocket. They opened it, and this time I strained to get over their shoulders a glimpse of the relic. There it lay, a dismal piece of metal.

"The fingerprints?" questioned Mr. M.

"Agree with Sankey's," the other replied, "and not a trace of anyone else's! So how could he have been stabbed by anyone else? They couldn't have grasped his hand and made him stab himself!"

"You know what this object is?" Mr. Mycroft was clearly determined to go on showing knowledge even if the case was closed, like an automatic lighthouse goes on giving out flashes of light though all the ships have gone into port.

"Oh, some sort of *objet d'art*—a fake piece, I suppose," the other answered casually.

"No, it's a real piece, on the whole. It's one of those extravagant giant hairpins, made in the form of weapons usually. This one is a miniature of a long-bladed halberd. These large skewers were used by Renaissance ladies to adorn and fasten their high-built hair. It's weighted at the blade end to keep it from toppling out of the hair coils. This one, as most of them were, is of silver. That accounts for its color. Tarnished or patinated silver, you know, is nearly black."

I did feel a little taken aback that I had dismissed as a worthless piece of pastiche not only a weapon that had just committed murder—if only self-murder—but also an archaeological object of some interest in its own right. But Mr. M., having made this his contribution to coiffeur curiosities, had gone back to mope over the Suetonius—always a danger of his mind, as much as Jane the maid's, that attraction of irrelevant interests. How strangely, I thought, extremes meet—one mind too full, the other too empty; both, therefore, caught and held by anything!

The inspector roused him with, "We should, I think, see Jane once more and ask her about this knifelike pin. Then I think we needn't keep her on call any longer nor I further detain either of you. The case will be closed."

He called Jane, who was not far off, and at once asked her about the pin-paper knife. It was a theme she fancied.

"That knife, I never did like it! You see that little pot over there, still a bit on the bright and cheery side? Well, believe me or not, that nearly lost me my situation! One day I gave it a bit of *Polisho:* it was as dirty as that horrid knife. And up the copper came as bright as the sun's self. And then Mr. Sankey came in as black as thunder and said I'd ruined all the patty something and I'd be dismissed if ever I did such a thing again!"

"Patina?" suggested Mr. M.

"Patty or putty, dirt is dirt; but of course masters can be dirty, if maids must (and like to be) clean. But I left that horrid little knife alone and, indeed, he always liked it laid beside him as he read. Often he'd play with it, spinning it about or cutting the pages of books the publishers had forgot to. And now it's turned on him."

The flow was stopped by the inspector again thanking our star witness, and once more she began to withdraw, obviously almost as pleased with her second act and exit as with her first. It was, however, her friend Mr. M. who gave her an encore.

"I wonder whether you could tell us when it was that Mr. Sankey obtained this book?" And he held out the Suetonius for her to see. "I don't see his bookplate in it, and I have noticed that it is in his own books as a rule."

I was surprised at this but shouldn't have been. Mr. M. was like a juggler and conjuror rolled into one, and for every occasion on which you observed him picking up clues you may be sure there were half a dozen when you never observed him observing—indeed, the analogy was even closer; for often I found, at the cost of being crestfallen later, that when he appeared obviously to be attending to something, in point of fact this was a blind—he was really keeping his eye on another thing that was quite unaware it was being watched.

But Jane rewarded his perspicacity with a hearty, "Well, now, Sir, you really are as sharp as the proverbial pin! True enough! It isn't—or perhaps I ought to say" (and she lengthened her round face slightly as a salute to the unmourned dead) "it wasn't his book. And I can tell you about it, too!"

"Ah, you can!" said Mr. M., somehow making with his voice a tone that ridiculously reminded me of those few encouraging chords with which a brilliant and helpful accompanist, turning round to the shy singer, will rouse his protégé to go into action.

"Yes," said Jane, throwing herself into her mood of recollection. "Now I have it. I sees it as though I were going through it all again. As I've said, I let Mr. Millum in. And he holds the doors open for me. And there I see it again. It was just like him, but today it is just a bit more thoughtful-like. For I notice —you see, being that sort myself, naturally I notice kind things that aren't merely careless kind, but cost —I notice that as he'd a big book in his right hand he'd have to open the door for me with his left, awkward-like; and I notice that he's cut his left thumb and finger while so kindly doing that pruning the day before. I remarked on it and asked if I might bandage it properly. For it was done that clumsy he must have done it himself, and men—nor, for that matter, Mrs. Sprigg—are no use for such things, are they?" We submitted in silence to the charge. "But he, so anxious never to give trouble, said of course not! It was nothing. He was being overcareful to bandage it at all and please would I not nohow draw Mr. Sankey's attention to it. As if I would! I'm a very poor storyteller if I've given the impression that *he* was that sort!"

"Then, when I was arranging the 'elevens,' Mr. Millum was, I believe, putting the book down on that other table. I'm as sure as can be he said something about having brought round 'that book, *Suet 'n Onions*.' I remember the name, for Mr. Sankey was very fond of food, but food wasn't fond of Mr. Sankey, and small blame to it, I say. He soured enough things round him, heaven knows. Not that I'd say a word against the dead; but if I did, well, I'd wager sweet food and such an acid stomach could never match or mingle. And when he couldn't eat, as when he could, then he'd read about cooking. Oh, cook had her times, as I had. A sorrow shared is a true tie, and cook and I have shared ours, and make no mistake! He'd read up new receipts in fancy cook books by people who maybe could write, but, Lord, the troubles their fancies made for cook's fingers. She'd say to me, 'Doubt if one of them ever put down his pen to handle a rolling pin. And as for washing up, why, they'd faint at the sight of a dishcloth!' Mrs. Beaton did for cook and for me. But this fancy stuff! Look at those books up there: *Second Helping*—heaven help us, what a name! And there, that white finical one, *The Gay Glutton*, and it so you couldn't put it on a kitchen table for an hour! As cook used to say, 'A cook book with a poor back is as bad as one empty in its insides.' But I must say this latest Mr. Millum lent was, you see, well-bound, sensible as all things about Mr. Millum are. And the name, too. When you come to think of it, plain and frank-like—*Suet and Onions*, both good, plain victuals."

Even Mr. M. began to flag under this drive of anecdotage and took to handling the classic author degraded to the kitchen. He began lensing its pages for lack of other interest. Jane, too, at last perceived she had had her great hour and that repetition would not add force to her presentation.

"Thank you, thank you," tolled Mr. M. like a passing bell.

And with, "So you see, murder it was and murder by some dangerous tramp," as her last line, Jane was content to make her final exit.

When she was gone, the two men were rapidly businesslike. The inspector ran through the points and Mr. M. checked them over.

"No one enters the garden on the day of the murder save Millum, and he is seen off the premises by Jane. Hence we are once more back at suicide, suicide of a melancholic prompted by reading the classic passage which says that stabbing yourself through the heart is both quite easy and practically painless, and even permits of a graceful exit and last words of an improving sort, if you wish."

We had retreated to the hall, and I was glad to go, for I was tired and disappointed. A suicide is no substitute—save to a sleuth—for a charming summer resort. But Mr. M. was not finished.

"You will, of course, now tell me about this Mr. Millum?"

I was relieved by the answer: "Oh, that, as you've

seen, is as clear as the rest of the case. He was an old friend of the deceased who lives in that twin house over the road here. He had taken great care of Sankey —who was not the kind of man with whom other people would trouble—and clearly Sankey depended on him quite a lot. He is a man—I've made the routine inquiries—liked as much by others as you see he is by the maid here. And another routine point: he is a man of very considerable means and has always lived quietly and generously with his neighbors down here. The vicar, though he said he was not what he could claim as one of his constant churchgoers, said that in all matters of charity he could always depend on his kindliness. No, even if any feature of the case should seem to point to him—and none do—the utter lack of motive would keep him clear. Indeed, he was so upset—for he is a sensitive type—that he has gone off for a few days' holiday. I may add," added the inspector, with rather a father-confessor look, "after quite rightly asking me whether it would be correct for him to do so. Yes, a likeable, open man, as you will have judged from our loquacious Jane!"

Mr. M. paused, and I thought the day might be called a day and closed. But suddenly, of all things, I was called on to prolong it!

"You see," began Mr. M. almost diffidently, "you see, I brought my friend Mr. Silchester down here almost under false pretenses. I have often found his angle on things useful, so that, though he takes no interest in my work, I value and sometimes employ his gifts—so complementary to mine—by stealth! But today we were killing two birds with one stone, or viewing a kill and also chasing another kind of quarry. We thought we might take a house in the country, and certainly the one we have seen is very choice and maybe, with the slight cloud over it, might be cheap. I myself would not be disturbed by the fact that the late owner had launched himself from the garden into the unknown. But anyhow I am glad to have seen this house and, as twins of this sort are as interesting as they are rare, do you think, before we go back to town, we might view that one opposite?"

The inspector evidently respected Mr. Mycroft and was pleased to have won him from the certainty of murder to the higher certainty of suicide—a real gain in the gruesome gain of wits these two obviously loved to play. So he replied, "Yes, I think we could. I've been in and out there these last two weeks and know the housekeeper quite well now. As our Jane said, she too is a kind woman; though it is queer, isn't it, how often kindly women don't very much like each other?"

While this was going on, he'd stepped up the flight of stone stairs that led to the hall door of this house, as a similar flight led to that we had just left behind us. The door opened so quickly that I felt we might have been watched, and we were welcomed here much as on the other shore. The inspector explained that Mr. Mycroft had been looking at the other house and had been so interested at the two being twins that he hoped she could be so kind, as he was sure Mr. Millum would wish, to show us over the place and its garden. She was a large, cheery, rather flouncy body in a copious but, in spite of that fact, tight chintz, and she bustled and chuckled ahead of us like a giant hen.

As we were led off, the inspector said, "I'll leave you in Mrs. Sprigg's good hands. I'll be down at the inn when you come back to town."

"Don't trouble to send the carriage for us," called out Mr. Mycroft. "We'll walk back; it will be charming."

We were taken over the whole house, and I fancied that Mrs. Sprigg felt a certain competitive necessity to show that her twin was as well-reared and cared for as was the rival over the way. Perhaps there was not quite the polish of the one we had first visited, but there were more beautiful things. And evidently here it was the master who cared while the maid seconded, while there it was the maid who provoked and the master who grudgingly permitted. When we had been taken to every room, I believe, save our leading lady's bedroom, Mr. M. paused and so did Mrs. Sprigg, no doubt now certain that all that remained was the small transfer of cash-loaded thanks with which such surveys always terminate. But Mr. M. had a further request.

"One of the charms of these houses is the beauty of the landscape which they serve to adorn. With their fine, parapeted roofs, what a noble prospect must be obtained from them. Do you think we might just run up 'and view the landscape o'er,' as the hymn says?"

It was tactfully put. Mrs. Sprigg was evidently what is called in that part of the world "of chapel folk," to whom an apt quotation from Isaac Watts, hymnist, is as sweet and telling as one from Horace to a classicist. "Why, of course," she beamed. "But I fear the way up . . ." and here we saw professional pride getting ready its defenses, "is not quite dusted out, as you might say. I haven't been out on that roof for ever so long and I've never seen Mr. Millum go up there neither. Come to think of it, the last time anyone was up there was last Michaelmas, when the tilers had to go up fixing down the tiles after the last big equinoctial blow we had."

"Never mind," smiled back Mr. M. "It will be worth a dirty hand or two to see the landscape."

She led us up to where at last the grand staircase shrank to attic stairs and these in turn dwindled to what was little more than an enclosed loft ladder. Mrs. Sprigg then paused, for the ascent had become steep and the way narrow. Neither her kindly but laboring heart nor her copious periphery could make the final grade.

"You'll find it ever so stuffy up there," she called as a panting farewell.

And to my surprise, when we reached the final stage and were about like chicks to break free, Mr. M. also paused and panted. Going ahead of me, he had reached the very top of the loft ladder and was about to push open the skylight door when he breathed deeply several times and bent his head. Then, recovering his wind, he pushed back the miniature glazed door-panel. A breeze came down, relieving the hot, still air which, almost like a gas, had gathered in this pocket of unventilation and no doubt was the cause of the catch in his breath.

I followed quickly, and we emerged onto as seemly a panorama as I've seen in its mild spaciousness. The Severn flowed in the distance—long stitches of silver threaded across the green. Blue Welsh hills closed the farther view, and all about was dale and orchard flowering and burgeoning, with silver-gray church towers and russet roofs of comfortable, seemly houses punctuating this easy, flowing picture-poetry of garden and field wealth.

But, after Mr. M. had hummed *Sabrina fair* and then a bar or two from the *Shropshire Lad's* "Bredon Hill," he turned back and began to peer over at the other house we had so shortly left and which I thought we had certainly viewed with sufficient thoroughness, at least for the time being. Mr. M., however, seemed in a brown study as he leaned looking over the cornice, he himself appearing not wholly unlike one of those brooding gargoyles which, with their chins in their hands, stand on the top of Notre Dame and look out over Paris. Perhaps he was thinking up some notion as to how we might possibly still get the house for our summer stay. As I wasn't quite sure whether I would like it if we could—murder is not my métier—and anyhow thought it very unlikely that even such a crafty person as my friend could really manage any such thing, I didn't pay much attention to him. The view out over the countryside was wonderfully refreshing, and I was determined to enjoy it and let the sunlight, the gentle breeze, and the obvious security and comfort of the view brush from my mind the impressions of the morning.

After a few minutes, Mr. M. came across to me proposing that, if I had taken in the topography, we go down. I agreed, but could gladly have spent half an hour dreamily gazing at that bright and reassuring landscape. I seconded him heartily when he told Mrs. Sprigg how much he had enjoyed the view. She took a motherly credit for the whole countryside as much as for her master's house.

"Shropshire born and bred," she remarked. "And though we don't take much count of those clever folk that never come back home but write clever rhymes about us, still, if I was a poet, I'd never fail for themes looking over this, our land."

We were now on such good terms because of our joint admiration that, when Mr. M. said, "Do you think I might come back tomorrow and have a second glimpse from this Pisgah? Today I didn't know this treat was in store and so did not bring my field glasses with me," she was all welcome. I must say, I felt that to peer with field glasses at a view which, if you had a real sense of landscape, should be taken in all as one—with a single stroke of the eye, as the French put it—showed, alas, in my old friend how much the scientist, with his passion for taking things to pieces, dominated over the artist, content to contemplate and become himself part of the beauty of the place.

We walked back to the little town. At the inn, where we had had rooms engaged by our inspector friend, we found him packed and ready to catch the evening express back to London. Mr. M. explained that we'd be staying a day or perhaps two more, for we were, he remarked, if not killing two birds with one stone, trying to see whether one house could prove to be not merely a neat problem but a commodious perch. I remember particularly noting his repetition of that faint pleasantry. Perhaps he himself saw that it was so thin that it required "to be applied in two coats," as house painters say. Its interest for me lay in the fact that such feeble little quips, as clearly as facial tics, prove (and I am quite as observant and able to build up a proof as he) that great power of penetration necessarily denies men like Mr. M. of a delicacy of surface touch, that sense of nuance and style which are the natural endowment of the man of taste and tact—in fine, the artist.

Our inspector simply remarked, "Well, thank you for confirming me in my second thoughts. Though less dramatic, they are, I am sure, not only better but final, and not only final but happier. I must own to you privately, as you are really a colleague, I always feel not a little relief when what could be a suicide but may be a murder reverts to its first promise! Indeed, I often wonder whether we men of skill aren't serving, in the judges and the lawyers, men who are really behind us in real understanding of crime. We should be thinking, I often think, not how it must be punished but how it may be understood and so prevented."

Mr. M. didn't seem at all surprised at this confidential outburst. All he remarked was, "I'm glad we agree, Mr. Sark, on basic principles. Even if we should ever differ on detail, I shall feel, however I think or act, we mean *au fond* the same thing, and are aiming at the same goal."

The inspector was obviously pleased at thus being

treated as a *cher confrère* and after a hard handshake went off.

When he was gone, Mr. M. remarked, "A man who is not ashamed of knowing something about Impressionist painting, and also of modern theories of light and shade and the psychophysical problems of perception, is always a much wiser fellow than his professional cleverness would lead you to expect. He can ask questions, not merely find answers; open issues, not merely close cases; and, if you have to choose and have time to watch, you will find it is the clever who do the latter and the wise who do the former."

We dined quietly (and none too poorly), he with his thoughts and I with my impressions, and a roast duck in common. The day had certainly been a queer one. But through the rather sordid story, the quiet background seemed to be re-emerging, and I began to believe that, if I could obtain the house, I might find it, in spite of the incident-accident, as pleasant, after all, as I had first taken it to be.

The next day, after breakfast, I heard Mr. M. ordering our lunch to be made up for us. As we set out on the two-mile walk he told me, "I believe that good Mistress Sprigg will let us lunch quietly in her master's garden. It will be nice to have a day out of doors."

It was. Mr. M. had his fine field glasses with him, and we took our time viewing this and that as we went, and he picked a number of points that kept me entertained. When we arrived, Mrs. Sprigg asked us to take ourselves onto the roof, and we spent a considerable time appreciating at our leisure a view that showed no signs of palling—at least for me.

But gradually Mr. M.'s unbalanced interest in the close-up—his master passion for microscopic investigation—began to draw him over to the side on which the other house blocked our full sweep of landscape. He took the glasses with him, and when I followed I actually found him looking through them down into the next garden! On my asking whether he was wishing to read the name labels on the flowers in the herbaceous border down there, he remarked, "I was studying, 'The allys trim and pleached walks: The laurelled triumphs of the topiarist: Who carves his will, but not through carnage wrought: Whose bays, themselves, yield him his victories!' Yes, yes, 'As if his only plot, To plant the Bergamot!' A garden should keep one innocent, shouldn't it?"

And then, as we had climbed so high, seeing it was obviously ridiculous that we should employ the long-distance glasses we had brought only to pore on a garden we had already viewed on the spot, he read my thoughts and offered the binoculars with, "Would you not like these, further to study the larger view? That may be Pershore Abbey in the distance, and possibly you could get a glimpse of Malvern's, too. If we come here for the summer, both, I believe, warrant a visit." And with that, leaving me to roam the leagues, he went back to brood on the narrow bound which so long had been his real perspective.

When I came back at last, having taken in quite a good deal, he had given up even this peering into the next garden. As I came toward him, he scrambled up from his knees. For a moment I suffered a twinge of alarm. Was this another attack of breathlessness, like that which had taken him just before we had completed our climb up to this, our present airy station? As I found him now, he had just risen from kneeling with his elbows resting on the parapet. But to my sympathetic question, he simply replied in that Mycroft manner, "Kneeling is today a neglected way of resting and clearing the mind. And look at this odd object I've found, actually by kneeling on it where it lay just under this coving of the breastwork. What do you think it can be?"

To that question, did I know what it was, he no doubt expected from me a refreshingly vacant but interested "No." But I was able quite quickly, and with no little pleasure at my not being at a loss, to say I did.

"It's what is called a stretcher," I remarked. "I've watched gardeners—when I've been sitting in gardens—using such things when putting up wire fences for creeping plants to grow on. It's really a jointed lever—works on the principle of a spring shoetree."

His further, "What do you think it's doing here?" didn't find me at a loss either. Looking round, I saw that the mellow old tiles, assaulted by equinoctial gales, showed the signs that Mrs. Sprigg had told us about below. They had been defended and held fast by wires stretched along their courses. Pointing at them, I remarked, "It was used for that job, I feel sure." An then, beginning to feel hungry, I suggested that we might take a real close-up and see what the hotel had given us.

"It's a bit drafty and at the same time hot up here," he replied. "Let's go down into the garden."

It was a right suggestion and I fell in with it. For a moment Mr. M. fingered the stretcher and I thought he was going to take it along with him. But finally he seemed to have decided to leave it where it was in no one's way. For when we assembled ourselves, after our climb down had brought us to the top of the proper stairs and we could go abreast, only that portfolio, without which he would feel himself as undressed as would I without my necktie, was in his hand.

When we came into the presence of Mrs. Sprigg, she was graciousness itself as he asked if we might eat in her garden, and insisted on adding to our solids a magnum bottle of the local cider to keep our liquid balance, as bankers say, on the right side. Yes, the day was going well.

But of course Mr. M. couldn't settle at once to eat in the obvious place which my eye had picked out immediately as the picnic spot. Though there was no bower, this place, like its twin over the way, had grass banks and seats set under the warm side of the yew hedges. Almost as though he were a game dog, he must smell and poke about before he could come to rest. So naturally in the end he did succeed—and serve him right—in coming on the seamy side of even this seemly place. He ferreted out the incinerator, nicely concealed behind the thickest yew hedge at the very bottom of the garden and set against the terminal brick wall. And then? Now that you know him, you will believe it, so I needn't ask, "Could you?" He poked about in the debris, "just to reconstruct," as he used to say, "the life of the place"—that horrid archaeological passion that never can see the thing as it is but always wants to pull it to pieces to see how it came to be as nice as it is, and is far more interested in fossilized refuse than in living beauty. "Dissecting the fairest complexion, To see how the blushes arrive!"

I had just thought of that rather pretty couplet—which made me less inclined to be satirical, as I myself had just produced a spray of loveliness—when Mr. M. turned to me, "Find a place in the sun. I know you can always do that, and I'll join you in a moment."

I was certainly ready to be dismissed to a happier spot. As I left him I saw that, as he had succeeded in finding nothing that even for a moment took his fancy but some old packages which had contained that far too virile tobacco, *Gold Flake*, he had taken up the big pronged stoker's fork and, like a medieval devil, had begun to poke in the depths of the still smoldering furnace.

I had, however, only had time to settle myself in, spread the lunch out, select a wing of chicken, a couple of slices of tongue and some salad, and pour myself a glass of the cider, when he appeared round the corner from his shabby retirement. Need I say, he was with a find. And once more my luck held up under the routine sentry-challenge.

"What do you think this is?"

As promptly as on the roof, I answered.

"It is what is called a laminated spring. Further, I would venture to say, with high probability that amounts to practical certainty, that it comes from one of those old wheelchairs which were so sprung —those chairs in which late eighteenth- and early nineteenth-century gout victims and apoplectics, who had had their first port-invoked strokes, were hauled about by what were called Bath-chair men. Not only do I know my cartoonists, my Gilray and Rowlandson, but, as it happens, my grandmother, though she never took port, was, if I may pun, towed to her port and final berth—like that ancient, demoded battleship, 'The Fighting Téméraire,' in Turner's somewhat hackneyed picture—in just such a Bath chair. Often, in that devious departure, I, as dutiful child and potential, if then distant, residual legatee, walked clad in sailor costume beside her equipage, at the funeral pace at which that kind of vehicle proceeded, and wiled away the boredom by fancying how I might use one of those small but tough springs that bounced her bulk up and down over the cobbles."

Again I think Mr. M. was taken aback at my luck, which twice in succession had balked him of his wish to explain, because in advance I knew. I added, taking another glass of the really excellent cider, "No doubt, one of the earlier owners of this gracious spot was eighteenth century in all his ways and, as a 'three bottle man' when bottles meant port and were crusted, himself became somewhat crusted in old age; had his first stroke; took to his Bath chair; and so made, a little later, his final journey to the parish church, where he settled down for good behind a fine slab of imported Carrara marble. The Bath chair hung about until some tidy person in this age of tidiness kindly cremated it, and sent it, Chinese-wise, to carry the old ancestor in state through the courts and gardens of the other world. This, without doubt, is its relic."

I was pleased with the *élan* of my counterattack.

Mr. M. was so rebuffed that he had to remark to cover his retreat, "Perhaps if you could spare me a little of that cider I might become almost as eloquent and your walk home possibly less devious."

But when he had drunk his share and we had munched in the silence of content till there was nothing left of our supplies but the paper that had wrapped them, all he said was, "I think I'd better take these traces of our *fête champêtre* and, like a good detective, conceal our tracks."

I stayed while he loped off round the corner to dispose of what to his mind was a possible clue.

After the incinerator had received its due, he reappeared and we ambled back to the house. We were met by a beaming Mrs. Sprigg, who, after hoping we had enjoyed our lunch and obviously registering pleasure as the five shillings passed silently from the lean detective fingers to the round fine hand that I felt sure was light with pastry and firm with kitchen maids, broke out with, "Just had a telegram and Mr. Millum is coming back! He took it so hard, you know, Sir. Just shows what a good heart he has. Not an eye in the whole neighborhood was the dimmer, I'll warrant, when our over-the-way took himself off. A good riddance, I say, and they seldom do, but this did!"

The syntax of that sentence is obscure, but I have faithfully remembered it, and its sense was not really cryptic.

"Even Jane, whom I will own is a worker, if a bit on the garulious side, and doesn't mind who she works for, as long as they lets her work as she likes—I was never that sort myself—but even Jane had her views and feels her reliefs. But Mr. Millum is that softhearted and sensitive, as you might say, that he felt it just like a shock. There he was, always running over to that side of the road, though that side, of all my time, and that's in years now, never set foot here, and that I'm glad to say. You'd have thought he'd be relieved; for Jane has so often told me that I was near tired of hearing it, that Mr. Millum would be treated as though he wasn't there, while all the while he was all interest and niceness, until something wanted being done, and then he could do it and just whistle for any thanks. Indeed, time and again he'd suggest doing some little thing and would grudgingly be let. It's all the wrong way, anyone who has brought up a brat knows that; but there, he has such a kind heart, and thank Heaven he lives with such as can appreciate a real gentleman when they sees it."

We took our leave, feeling that such a homecoming shouldn't run any risk of being run into by strangers. Besides, quite possibly the unknown Millum might prefer that strangers had not been using his house.

As we walked home through the pleasant afternoon light, although my steps were far from unsteady, I was in that ruminative mood in which enough good cider can put the mind. I did not feel inclined to interrupt Mr. M.'s silence, and evidently, as I had so successfully countered his two attempts to stump me, he had no wish to talk to me.

After dinner he was silent and went off to bed. I had thought he would suggest our going back to town; but I myself proposed nothing, partly because I was drowsy, and partly because I hadn't made up my mind about the house now without an owner. I was very much taken with it, and to discover such a place untenanted was a find. Perhaps, as Mr. M. said, since the late occupant had removed himself while outside the actual building, the unconventionality of the method ought to be overlooked in favor of the convenience of the results. If I worked in that bower, I would work there during the day and not at night.

Certainly this night passed without any untoward premonitory dreams. After breakfast the next morning, Mr. M. left me for a few moments with the paper, in which I saw nothing but advertisements of houses which just would not do. So I was in the right mood when he came back and asked would I like to have one more look at the Red Brick of 1760. Off we went, and Jane gave us the usual reception. That, too, made me feel that the place couldn't really keep on with a bad atmosphere. Mr. M. stayed on with her a moment, no doubt cementing their friendship, which I didn't regret if we might be going to live in the house and I didn't have to do the cementing. "Marble, not mortar, is my métier," I murmured to myself (for I think alliteration is too much despised today) as I strolled out to the marble-furnished arbor.

It had resisted quite successfully any sense of the uncanny. Its years of equanimity and seemly spaciousness were evidently able to deal quite well with such a small contretemps as a selfish suicide. And as soon as I was settled, out came Mr. M. to bring me to the point, I assumed. I was now prepared to be brought—in fact, had myself arrived.

"I'm quite ready," I said, when he came up to where I was seated in the fine stone chair, "to waive my natural prejudices against *felo-de-se* when it permits me to have fellowship with such a manifest sense of culture as this place yields me. I presume whoever has now become the legal owner will be only too glad to find such a couple as ourselves to sign a clean bill of health for the place. As the case is closed legally, I too am quite willing to let bygones be bygones, as far as such a small (and in this respect convenient) accident is concerned."

"But I don't remember that I ever said the case was closed."

This was not only pompous, but, worse, portentous. Was I once more—after having made a considerable effort to meet the old master's wishes and put the whole incident out of my mind—was I again to find everything being raveled, tangled, and confused, and maybe even our certainty of securing this place put in jeopardy? I was sufficiently upset to say unguardedly, "I don't understand!"

And got in reply, "I will explain, or rather I am going to bring the explanation to you. Believe me, it will interest you, and I need your co-operation."

My temporary upset began to be tinged with possible interest, for I respond to any call for help.

"Will you please get up and follow me?"

I rose. The old man took out from his portfolio a fair-sized piece of folded newspaper and, leaving it on the stone table to my right, turned to the garden entrance of the arbor. He went through this and then turned sharp right. I had dutifully followed this maneuver. We now had the high, dense hedge of the arbor between us and the chair and the two tables.

As the hedge was of beech, though the new leaves were still only partly unfurled, the old leaves, as is so nice with that species of tree when it is used for hedges, were still obligingly hanging on in sufficient numbers so that there was no visible thinning of the cover. I couldn't help thinking how like the faded leaves, still holding their post and discharging their duty, were to those old and, alas, practically extinct servants who, though due to retire, used to stay on to oblige until the new ones were sufficiently expert to take over without making any break in the ancient routine. The weave of the twigs themselves was also, at this level—in spite of the late occupant's reported grumbles—almost as close as basketwork. So I found, when we came to a pause and stood looking at this living arras, that though we were actually within three or four yards of where I had just been seated, you could no more catch a glimpse of the inner fittings of the arbor, or of the house that stood behind and beyond, than you could have seen through a brick wall.

"Mr. Silchester."

Mr. M. was using the kind of tone which he only uses to me when I have no doubt that I can do him a real service. This, you may gather, is rare, but the inflection is so impressive that I know at once we are going into action, and I must own I find it exhilarating.

"Mr. Silchester, will you do me a real favor by staying here? I may not have to keep you waiting for more than ten minutes or perhaps a quarter of an hour. If you will wait for that time completely silent, not even shifting your position, that is all I believe that will be needed, and much may turn on it."

Anyone would have felt a thrill, a tension caught from the gravity of his tone. I nodded, and he slipped back into the arbor. I heard him shifting about behind the arras of leaves but could not see a thing. While I was trying to see whether I could see, I heard Jane's voice—as playwrights say, "off," but as plumbers say of taps, full "on."

"He's out in the garden. Such a nice gentleman. I believe they'll take the house. Of course, they couldn't help hearing, but the man who was down about it all put them quite at their ease. No use crying over spilt milk, is there? Especially when it was already a bit oversour."

These sallies did not seem to awaken a response, though now I could hear another step accompanying Jane's.

A moment later I heard her say, "Why, here is Mr. Mycroft, waiting for you in this arbor." And then, "Mr. Mycroft, Sir, this is Mr. Millum, dropped over, as you wished, to see if he could be of any help and tell you anything you should know about the house and all that."

Jane was dismissed, and I heard a deep, pleasant voice say its greetings, and Mr. M. ask him to be seated, as Jane had brought a chair from the house.

"You know," said Mr. M.'s voice, "the case which has caused this house to be unoccupied is officially closed."

There was a small pause during which, I presume, the person questioned must have given a silent assent. If he was going just to nod and shrug or smile all his answers, then my position would not be as good as I'd hoped, the pleasant position of a person who has the right to eavesdrop. I began to peer blindly at the wall of brown and green leaves and twigs. Suddenly, when I had my nose right against them, I found my eye could see through a tiny space between a twig and a shriveled leaf, and there, through this natural peephole, I had a narrow glimpse of the scene which till then was only sound to me.

Mr. M. was seated quite magisterially in the stone

chair, and near him, on his right and with his back to me, was the Mr. Millum. I was in no danger of being discovered, for even had they looked at the point from which I was looking, they would have seen nothing but leaves. As it was, Mr. Millum had his back to me and Mr. M. was in profile. The stone table with the sheet of paper on it was now to Mr. M.'s left, and, as he had his hand on it as though to hold it in place, he, too, was sufficiently swung round so that he would not spy if I was, as I suspected, going beyond his instructions. But I was indeed glad that I did exceed what I had been told to do.

For a moment all was quiet and plain sailing. Mr. M. continued in his gentle, slow voice:

"That means that unless quite new evidence should emerge, nothing more will happen. The law and its investigators are contented, and rightly, with what is held to be sufficient proof of the most probable supposition. But, you see, I am an amateur, and, in the proper sense of that much abused word, that means a man who loves the work for itself and not for gain or for any ulterior motive. I am interested in understanding and am thankful to say I am no paid servant of that odd and often unscientific, not to mention inhumane, instrument called the law, and, in its hardest and perhaps least open aspect, the criminal law."

He paused, and I could see the back that was under my observation shift, and the shoulders hunch slightly.

Mr. M., perhaps to rouse his visitor, whose attention appeared to have flagged, suddenly asked at this point:

"Could you give me a cigarette?"

I was a little surprised at this request, for Mr. M. seldom smoked, and, if he did, it was an occasional and quite expensive Egyptian which he would nearly always watch smoke itself away, following its fine skein of vapor and only on occasion giving it the encouragement of a single draw.

His guest seemed relieved and at once took a package from his pocket. They were the coarse, common Virginian sort. But nevertheless Mr. M. accepted and, putting the column of weed to his mouth, asked again:

"Have you a match?"

His right hand still holding the cigarette package, the visitor with his left produced an automatic lighter, flicked open the spring cap with his thumb, and held the little flame before Mr. M., who bent his face toward it, drew on the cigarette, and then sat back. But, as I could have told him, he could not enjoy it,

There can be no question that he was a gloomy, depressed, self-centered, and, I think we can say, suspicious man. This is the type we do, rightly, associate with suicide. But usually there is some small occasion, some 'trigger action' that sets alight the deep mine of despair and launches the victim out into the unknown. Could you tell me of any incident that in your opinion might have provoked Mr. Sankey to act in that final desperate way—I mean, to use the actual method that he did? Self-indulgent men are usually timid and hate pain. A stab through the heart may be acutely painful, mayn't it?"

The questioned man roused himself at that. "Not necessarily. No, not at all necessarily, there are . . . there are cases recorded where it was evidently painless—quite, quite!"

"Even with so unhandy an instrument as a paper knife?"

"Well, that all depends on the knack with which it was driven . . . driven home. I recall that Mr. Sankey frequently played with the sharp little blade that he used—an antique—and often quoted to me the 'bare bodkin' line from Hamlet's soliloquy on suicide."

"Did he, indeed!"

Mr. M. had swung slowly round till he was facing

Mr. Millum.

"Did he?"

The phrase which had been first question-tinged with surprise had, in the second speaking, turned suddenly into challenge.

"Did he!"

It was again spoken, and this time there could be no doubt. Mr. M. meant, "You know he didn't."

The other's reply was disquieting: "Oh, yes, he really did; he really did more than once. That's what put . . . I mean, he really was a wretchedly unhappy man, he was really in a very tight place, he really was at the end of his tether."

He paused, and Mr. M. said slowly, "And so you . . . ?"

The other recovered, "And so I was not surprised when the end came."

"No," said Mr. M. "No, you were not surprised, not a bit surprised. But perhaps you will understand that I am still puzzled?"

Mr. Millum rose. "Mr. Mycroft," he said with perfect courtesy, "I am sure you had every right, on the invitation of the inspector, to act as an additional adviser, and you have every right also to view this house as a possible tenant. I would do anything in my power and, after a couple of puffs, laid aside the thing, which soon expired. Then he resumed his talk in a lighter tone.

"When a man really cares for proof just for proof's sake," he went on, "which means caring for truth for truth's sake, then he's not content with probability—he wants certainty."

Again there was a pause, and I thought that Mr. M. might be thinking that he was going to get an answer. If so, he was disappointed. I saw him glance away toward the roof of the arbor, as though waiting. Then, as the silence continued, he remarked casually: "Beautiful natural roofage the beech makes —a perfect cover. As Vergil long ago put it, '*sub tegimine fagi.*' "

I saw the other glance up quickly and evidently follow Mr. M.'s eye, turning his head also to the arbor roof, then look back at Mr. M., who still did not look at him. Finally, Mr. Millum let his head sink, and he just looked at the ground. This clearly made Mr. M. see that he'd have to go farther if he was to get any more information that this man might be able to give about his self-killed friend.

"Mr. Millum," Mr. M.'s voice was quiet but very clear, "you knew the late master of this house well.

to aid either the official inquiry or someone who might wish to be a neighbor for the summer. But I think you will understand that I see no use in our getting your two interests confused. The first issue is, as you say, officially closed. It is a subject very painful to me. Professionally I cannot expect you to respect my feelings, nor have I any right to ask that you should, even though you describe yourself as an amateur. But when even the amateur's association with the professional is closed, then surely I have a right to ask that if you, as a possible tenant of this house, wish for my services, you do not intrude upon these a grave matter that has been closed . . . in the grave."

I think Mr. M. was really rather taken aback by thus having the tables turned on him. He said nothing, but he did something. He rose. Mr. Millum rose too. They turned toward the house. But before they had taken the first step, Mr. Mycroft threw out his left arm and with the tips of his long fingers swept aside the sheet of newspaper that had been lying there on the table at his left. The paper floated to the ground. But his fingers remained pointing to the table. The other man stood pointing too, as does a pointer dog when suddenly it sees the hidden game. But with no delight. I could now partly see his face and, even if

I had not, the tension of his whole body would have told me that he had suddenly confronted something that had him held at bay. But when I looked to see what basilisk was turning him to stone, I could have laughed. There was Mr. M., in an attitude rather like that in that pompous German picture of Bismarck pointing to the map of Alsace-Lorraine and claiming it from the two cowering French ministers. But what Mr. M. was pointing at, and the other was shrinking from, was, would you believe it, the paper knife, the wire stretcher, and the old sooty spring from the long-destroyed Bath chair! To which egregious collection, which he had evidently been treasuring, he had now added, as a floral finish, the large, wilted piece of pruned beech hedge with which he had brushed his boots when we first investigated this garden.

Nevertheless, the assemblage of sorry objects did have the effect he had evidently calculated. I could only think that, as an Australian witch doctor (I remember having once been told) can hypnotize a fellow aborigine with some similar bundle of rubbish—the more efficaciously, the more absurd it is to the eye of reason—so had Mr. M. suddenly sprung this magical ascendancy over his escaping interrogatee.

It was both comic and uncanny. I found myself

caught in a giggling shiver—that queer state when you don't know whether you are being amused or frightened. But about one thing there was no manner of doubt: however inexplicable it must appear, it was plain as a pikestaff that Mr. Millum took the random grouping of junk as seriously, as dramatically, as did Mr. M.—indeed, with the deadly seriousness with which a man looks at a snake suddenly discovered in his path and coiled to strike.

Mr. M. was not slow to follow up his advantage, however oddly he may have gained it.

"You still say suicide?" he called, almost in the tone of a highwayman saying "Your money or your life."

"No," said the other, "no."

And then, recovering his voice, which had become nothing more than a husky whisper, he said with a certain quietude that was the most uncanny and finally convincing thing about all this queer drama, "I'm glad you've cornered me. I don't think I could have gone on. It did seem right . . . more, it seemed inevitable. Until . . . until it worked out. And then I saw it was no use. It was just one more mistake. Well, you have stopped it. And if you cancel me out, then the sum is even, isn't it?"

Mr. M. answered as quietly, with no drama or even emphasis now, but just like a fellow worker on a common problem. "No, it's just on that point that I'm unsure. And indeed, throughout my life this is the issue on which I've become increasingly unsure. If we now just go on according to the conventional plan in this business, then all that really happens is that, just as you took over the responsibility of terminating another life, I, in turn, take over the same kind of futile control over yours. I don't think that means balance. On the contrary, surely it means that in point of fact we have failed to stop the real thing that is running everything down and running all of us into bankruptcy, doesn't it? Granted that Sankey was in the grip of it, and that you in turn were also caught, and that you tried to cut the losses by cutting short the life . . .?"

He paused, and it was clear that he was asking a real question of the other. And the other responded with equal detachment.

"I see your point. No doubt it is the real issue. But granted that, now what are we to do about it?"

"The first thing," Mr. Mycroft resumed, as with his usual tidiness, even in the midst of what I think I may call the most delicate of negotiations, he proceeded to cover up his queer cards which had certainly taken the trick, "the first thing would be to know the 'Why?', wouldn't it? One thing I have learned about Detection. Though it is often easy enough to get at the 'How?', our science, like all the other sciences, is sadly incomplete. Very often it tends to get into stalemates because it can't get past the 'How?' on to the 'Why?' "

He stopped, and then suddenly his tone changed, became bright and sharp and certain.

"Well, then, let's start where we are. First and foremost, what do we know?" And not waiting for Millum to answer, but turning on him and watching him narrowly, Mr. M. said, with a certain lightness but with emphasis on the last word: "You see, there's no *proof*!"

Millum looked up at him, but Mr. M. sailed on: "Remember, the inspector, the official inquirer, has dismissed and dispatched his first notion and slight suspicion—it was never, I believe, strong—as quite false. His new assurance and seemingly clear proof have killed the old fancy. Theories, once they have been killed by their own parents, are very hard to resuscitate—no easier than dead men. Logical conclusions, when they have replaced false deductions, are seldom re-examined by practical minds. It takes a foot-loose amateur with all the time at his disposal to go back over his tracks. Busy men always have to go on and let bygones be bygones and mark bypaths as blind alleys. Even if I thought I could make another case, I expect I should fail to move this expert who alone can set the process moving again. Still less could I hope to persuade a good jury, faced by a good defense, to give a conviction."

He stopped again and then said slowly, "You are really free if you choose to tell me now, to my face, that the 'No' you said just now did not apply to the question I asked, and that when you said you were cornered, you were not referring to what I thought you were."

He waited, and there was a dead silence in which I held my breath for fear they would hear it.

Then Millum said slowly, again, "No, no, I don't want to go back on that. I don't want to go back at all. What I've said, I repeat: I did it. I'm sorry, but I did it. I know enough now to know that just by keeping quiet I shan't have ended this. It's got to end, to be finished. It is for you to decide how. I'll face the music if that will stop this tragic play in which I've played Hamlet and half a dozen other futile parts."

Mr. M. said nothing for a moment. He smiled slowly, and then what he did say surprised Millum and me equally. For all he did was to call out quite clearly, "Mr. Silchester! Mr. Silchester!!"

Millum whipped around, but I was so on edge that I had scuttled round just as quickly and appeared—a very dramatic entrance—at the door of the arbor before he could move.

We looked at each other for a moment and then Mr. M. said, "Mr. Millum, you see my little test. Had you denied and gone back on what you first said, you see I had a witness."

Then, before the other could speak, he went on, "Believe me, this was not done to trap you. No, even then, had you denied that you knew anything, I had made up my mind. I would not have given you over, though I think my evidence is stronger and could have been put with greater power of conviction than I have suggested. What I can now tell you is that I had decided to test you. And had you broken under the first test—why, then, I would have given you a second chance of facing the music. Mr. Silchester, you see—not at his wish, but on my instruction—was concealed behind the hedge as the necessary second witness. Had you failed, all that I would have done would have been to use this second fact to re-strengthen what I had concluded was your true will, but which, for a moment, might well have wavered and broken when it saw, even at this late hour, a door of possible escape. Then, I repeat, I would have asked you again whether you would face the issue, and I feel sure you would. But I am glad," and he held out his hand, which the other took, "I am glad you took the right way out when it looked far more likely that you could still go on taking what is really only the way further down. You answered my first bid, as I judged you would from what I had heard and then from what I've seen of you. Now let me introduce you to my colleague, Mr. Silchester. He may often have to play what seem to be rather side-line parts, as now. That does not mean that they are not essential to the play. And it does mean that because of his position he often sees most of the game."

Mr. Millum turned and held out his hand to me. His face was certainly worn. But, if I may put it sartorially and, I think, aptly, it was worn the right way. I could see in a moment that it wasn't a strong face. But that, to me, was rather a relief than otherwise—

my own rather indecisive contours always have to live, as it were, cut across by Mr. M.'s shearing profile. Mr. Millum was middle-aged, and the years had given him some grinding. But on the whole he had stood up to the pressure and taken a kindly, if not a steel-hard, polish. I was, then, prepossessed by him. Of course, it is rather a shock suddenly to be asked to take a hand which, as novelists have it, has on it someone else's blood. But I took it, for hadn't I just been called a colleague? And it was clear to me that if my partner did not show or evidently feel repugnance, neither must I. So we shook, as Americans say, and the grasp I was given added to my reassurance. Touch, as I hope I made clear at the start of this tale, tells for a great deal.

We had hardly done more than resume our places, when our conclave was added to by a fourth—Jane. Any slight sense of disturbance was allayed by her annunciation:

"Cook would like to say good morning and to ask would you three gentlemen like to stay for a small garden lunch? She would be very pleased to make it up for you, if you so cared."

Mr. M., from his consular chair, bowed finely and accepted for us. When, with her embassage successfully effected, she had withdrawn back to the authority that sent her out, Mr. M. remarked:

"That is splendid. Now we will have plenty of time. We shall need it. So now, Mr. Millum, as I said, I think we have the 'How.' But, I repeat, I have not the 'Why.' And until I have that, the case has no more than a purely legal significance; and that we have decided to leave aside in favor of the real meaning. The 'How?' can tell us nothing about the real mystery here and everywhere; the real mystery, without which we shall never understand where we are or what we are, is the mystery of motive. Will you let us know that? For until we do, we three"—it was nice of him to keep me in the team—"we can't see what we should do and how we are really to close this matter. For I agree with you, Mr. Millum, that, though we are agreed it will serve no purpose to put on this thing the false ending which the law attempts to do, we cannot leave it open. We must really try to find the true conclusion. And, I would add, when we found that, we shall know not merely more about why this happened; we shall know, if we wish, something more about why any and all of us behave as we do and become what we are."

The other merely nodded, offered me his seat, and,

seating himself at Mr. M.'s feet, where the old man magisterially presided, began. He spoke as quietly and with as clear and orderly a recollection as a good witness will begin an account of a long scene, every detail of which may be of vital importance to the court.

Chapter III

MR. MILLUM'S "WHY?"

"We met, Sankey and I, twenty-three years ago. We were both then still undergoing that lengthy and rather pointless thing called a thorough education, and were supposed, in a way, to be doing what is sometimes dignified as post-graduate work. We came across several other fellow pretenders—young, well-off people beginning to dabble in art or to play with the more refined journalism. We were, we told ourselves—I mean our loosely gathered group—the third and final flower of high-brow Londoners. The first flowering had been out in Chelsea, that western riverside suburb originally given its Bohemian tone by Turner, with his crimson sunsets and his alcohol; then retinted with Whistler's silver and lapis, his 'Battersea Bridge' and other 'River Nocturnes,' and his hydrochloric wit; and finally seared with the *fin de siècle* stylisms of the *Yellow*

Book and the scandals of Wilde in Tite Street, till it was sent to its winter quarters in Reading Gaol."

I sniggered a little at this epitome of West London cultural history. Mr. Millum, I saw at once, must in his past have been a wag, and I never can but be grateful for a little humorous relief. It helps revive my easily fatigued appetite for seriousness. Mr. M. did not need that *apéritif*, and, being for all intents and purposes judge, only bowed the narrative on.

"Well," continued Mr. Millum in his quiet, detached tone, almost as though he were reading aloud to us from a volume of memoirs, "there followed, soon after the First World War, a move out from Chelsea, a floating off of the self-styled cream from the more common human milk of talent. This trek of a self-chosen people settled right away in another corner of London, Bloomsbury—a district which once had been the home of respectability. That was part of the pose—to live as Bohemians in what had been the very center of Victorian repression.

"And then we came, the third and final phase of acidulated good taste and undercut culture. We determined we would provincialize these 'second thoughts' that thought themselves the last and best, and show that their claim to be metropolitans was merely suburban. They were only London crossed with Cambridge—a fairly good French accent, a Braque or a Picasso on their walls, and perhaps a flat in Paris and a George Moore style. We were really almost cosmopolitan. Our lot chose then as the new migration point another sad little district which we might culturize—Notting Hill. We called ourselves the Notting Hill Nucleus.

"We made a group of ourselves. We selected the peculiar characteristics which would give us distinction from those earlier efforts of clever coteries at singularity and exclusiveness. We had all been, as *Who's Who* phrases it, 'educated abroad.' We had not been to the big public schools, and we'd nearly all had part of our education at one or two of the big Continental universities. We found London delightfully stuffy. Its dreary streets and drearier hotels had for us something of the foreign-flavored squalor that a tumble-down insanitary bazaar in Istanbul has for the average globe-trotter. We lived not by action but by reaction. Our point was always to enjov what the vulgar public liked—but always for the 'wrong,' esoteric reasons. We decorated our rooms with the taste of the Edwardians—stuff which hadn't yet become antique and was simply out of date. We were delighted that we could be amused by this mélange, which, as clean bad taste, startled and shocked our clever visitors whom, to add to our sense of satire, we occasionally brought over from Bloomsbury to view us, express their disgust, and give us a further sense of our superiority. Not for us Baroque and Rococo, but the latest Gothic revival or 'Jacobethan.' We bought Alma-Tademas instead of Dalis. Our triumphs were replicas of 'The Soul's Awakening' by Sant and 'The Doctor's Verdict' by Sir Luke Fildes, which we hung on our walls instead of Modigliani nudes or dainty Duncan Grants. We shocked even the shockers. They, at least, revered their last and latest anemic, mannered art. We revered nothing, and treated aesthetics with the amused contempt and the same kind of sneers with which they treated ethics and theology. 'To find the grotesque in everything, that is the secret of life,' was one of our mottoes. We were sure we could trump everything with a laugh."

The younger Mr. M. looked up and paused. The older smiled slowly. But now, as this introduction grew, I was beginning to find it a bit overrich. The humor was turning a trifle uncanny. A note of what might be called madness was surely creeping in and tainting everything. As Mr. Millum went on, my uneasiness showed that it had strong grounds for its misgiving—rather an Irish phrase, I fear, but true.

"As such little groups will," he continued, "we felt we had the need for each other's 'moral support'—much as we would have despised ourselves for putting such a weakness into words. The fact remains that we put it into acts. We made our society quite an exclusive and definite thing. We had four rules: everyone must be at home in at least four languages; he must have no prejudices; he must have perfect manners; and, finally, he must have shockless taste. On the whole, I think we practiced what, in this queer creed of four clauses, we preached. We were rich—generally 'only' children, and most of us with dead parents: rootless creatures with really little grip or grasp but almost too good brains. Like balloons cut from their moorings. Naturally we were bored, bored stiff. Yes, to use the other old tired cliché, we were bored literally to tears when we were by ourselves. We had no emotional repressions, no financial limitations. As far as we knew, we had little sense of origin and descent, less of a way of living, and none of a goal."

"And so, to quote an author you have lately mentioned and who certainly (whatever one may think of him as a writer) did what he said: 'Who can tell to what red hell the sightless soul may stray.' "

"Before I've finished, Mr. Mycroft, I shall have given my evidence for the truth, if not the elegance, of that statement. So naturally," Millum sighed and went on, "naturally as we were bored we soon exhausted our own atmosphere as far as it could be replenished by our poor vitality. We certainly did not conserve ourselves, and we had about as much knowledge of mental hygiene or, for that matter, of physical, as most slum dwellers.

"We could, I need hardly add, only enjoy our sex life, even if it could always be seen as one more exhibition of ridiculous bad taste. It, too, had to be perfectly in keeping with the art we collected as raw material for those sneers which gave us our only purchase on life. Our sense of superiority (and without that we would have collapsed) depended solely on the fact that we could laugh at any and every feeling, however high, however low—and always prevent others laughing at us by taking care, quite a lot of anxious care, to be the first to laugh at ourselves—from our wits to our lusts.

"Hence, we had really come to the end of all our

own resources. For when everything, without exception, is ridiculous, there is nothing left that has any real interest—one is on the frontier of insanity. Having no zest, we had to have more excitement. But where on earth were we to get it? I think it was Sankey himself who suggested that we should have a dining club for queer guests. Once a month each member of our group must pledge himself to find a really original character who came from a really original underworld. And he should be the guest of the evening. By telling us about his life, he might, for an hour or two, take us out of our dead end, of collecting Tademas, Poynters, Fildes, and Stones that were no longer funny, of playing Balfe and Sousa and trying to feel how exquisitely absurd and abominably futile they were.

"We had, in the room where we used to dine, a motto written on the old gilt ceiling—it had been a second-rate dance place in the nineties. We sprawled the words in pseudo-Kufic lettering round the stucco mooring from which the chandelier depended. 'Do almost anything if it's sufficiently funny; Do absolutely anything if it's sufficient money.'

"This new idea did, for the first half year, succeed in giving a kick to our jaded life. That queer thing, luck, held, and we turned up odd find after odd find without ourselves—as we should have been—getting nipped by the kind of deep-sea fish we wanted to handle."

"Yes," Mr. M. remarked almost to himself, "it does run through its phases, I've noticed. Further, I've observed the phases are three and are definitely spaced: Luck, Fate, Doom."

The other nodded and went on. "The first fish we landed was undeniably, from our point of view, a promisingly queer one, from a sufficient depth and quite up to our expectations of blackguardism. He called himself by the generic name Limey. He'd been taken up by one of the meaner weeklies that live on dubious advertisements and more dubious competitions, sailing nearer and nearer to the wind till they are prosecuted and suppressed. He'd been writing weekly what he claimed were straight autobiographical sketches of his adventures. He asserted that he was an Englishman. Limey, I understand, is the American underworld slang for what otherwise is called a Britisher. And his boasted record was that he had made a lucrative trade as a professional killer. He was technically a highjacker, and whether or no he was the bravo he made out, he had, without doubt, striven to live up to the second line of our ceiling motto. We had read his articles—or what was 'ghosted' for him—and were delighted by their bad style and worse morality. But, however mendacious, some flavor of authentic blackguardism did get through. We looked forward to a really entertaining evening.

"He was lanky in build, acned of skin, and with a palate that rejected our wines. We were still old-fashioned as far as our taste buds went and clung to sound vintages; had we been consistent, we should have served nothing but gin and ginger beer, raw spirits, and syrups. Still, we had plenty of hard liquor for guests, and this he took plentifully. When he was sufficiently relaxed, he showed us his armory, and on the butts—for he was a two-gun man—his record of kills. Maybe they were exaggerated, but it seemed to us that here was a firm and sound basis of positive murders. No doubt he would have returned our hospitality in the way we deserved, by holding us up at his next uninvited call. But the police got him the week after. He had forgotten that in Great Britain two guns as part of standard smart dressing are considered to be in too bad taste for a young man to be allowed to go about in public so sprigged out.

"Before he left us that evening, he gave us a reference to his next possible employer. That was an Armenian who trafficked drugs into Egypt and thence into Europe. We brought him along as our next guest. He entertained us with the ingenuity of the methods —the camels whose beehive throats could be made to hold whole cargoes of heroin packages, and all the conjuror's costumes of false boots and hats and umbrellas and walking canes. He was the first to mention not merely the scandalous fun of taking in the puritan police and all the official hypocrites—many of whom, he said, were in on his ring and took his stuff —but the other little enticement: money, big money. He certainly was well-off, coming in a fine car and an astrakhan coat.

" 'Of course,' he said, 'mine's the small and respectable side of the under-the-customs trade, almost what you'd call a ladylike occupation, everything done on the petite side. The big shots carry big cargoes—not drugs for the dopees, but guns—big guns for the toughs, the big toughs. I could give you boys some names! You'd like to meet the men who have guts and laugh at the mollycoddles who bow to bishops! Well, I could arrange an introduction to one of those if you liked—if you were really wanting to dine a man without prejudices. As for me,' and he raised his flat hands palm out to the shoulders, 'what am I but what my parents were? A poor old peddler, trying to get to poor worn people a little chemical peace—the only peace there is, after all.' And he actually sighed and looked, as all Near Easterners suddenly can, more ancient and tired than the most desiccated Pharaoh.

"He went soon after, but not before we had got the name of our next guest—an Alsatian, he claimed to be. He was very discreet, and when he talked he talked with a wonderful front of emotion which we found exquisite—it was in such perfect ill-taste. He spoke of his own dear Alsatia, and hummed 'The Blue Alsatian Mountains,' of little people struggling to be free, of their need of a friend, of how easy it was for liberals to print pamphlets and shed tears and have meetings and do nothing. 'Acts,' he said, 'gentlemen, deeds—they alone show sympathy.'

"From that he modulated into an account of the secret arms traffic—no names, but just a hint of what great causes of freedom were being sustained, and how. And here again, for the second time, and with a somewhat firmer emphasis, the money theme appeared. It was a gallant trade but expensive, but, thank heaven (yes, heaven was thanked in our hearing, and again we delighted in this worst of taste), if you sowed in such a gallant trade and with a right agricultural adviser—he was gutteral in his pleasure at his little simile—you reaped. Of course, you had denied yourself recognition; you did not expect gratitude, even if the side to which you gave the help won. Hence, you had to be content just with what he would call coverage—and coverage, we discovered, was not less than two hundred per cent profit.

"I believe he would have collected our subscriptions to his crusade—for he saw we had more money than we knew what to do with—if we had not been so green that we hadn't been thinking of the money line of our jingle couplet. We had been wanting to prove we couldn't be shocked, and here we were, overlooking hot money. When he was gone, someone raised the point, but most of us were really timid rats and afraid of the police, and so decided that he wouldn't have let us in on anything anyway."

Mr. M. shook his head. "A nice point, and a good point at which to stop and reflect on a remarkable tale, if I may say so, and I have heard a few in my time. So Jane, who is now in the offing, is 'nicking the minute with a happy tact.'"

And we had a delightful lunch which whetted my

appetite for more of this odd tale that somehow—I could not make out how, but Mr. M. already seemed to suspect—led to us all being here in this place and in the spot where either a suicide or a murder had so lately been the latest incident.

"I think," resumed Millum, "that our Alsatian big-scale assassin thought we were soft, so that when he rose he said, 'I expect you find my kind of trade a bit humdrum and really almost aboveboard. I own it is; profit and patriotism are really my only interests. But you're more of the *jeunesse dorée*, so you'd really like the oddities of a luxury trade more than my straightforward hard-as-steel stuff.'

"He said it with sufficient mockery so that Sankey, who was, I think, the cleverest and toughest of us, replied, 'Well, you are really always in danger of being recognized,' and, as the other got ready to seize the opportunity to enlarge his sneer at our expense, Sankey ended rather neatly, 'and of being made the hero of the new nation, whatever it is, and of appearing with your bosom covered with its brand-new orders, and no doubt of acting as its chief ambassador!'

"Our guest saw that the laugh might be turned on

him, so he shot out, 'If you are so keen on trying to put your noses right up on what the world still rates as the worst smell, ask your own countryman Crofts, here! I mix with all if there's profit in it. And, as I see it, it's just the tough unders getting at the tough overs. That's life, it's a struggle. But beside us who do the tiger business, there are hyenas. As you want to see—as in the fairy tale—whether you can shudder, maybe you would like to see what I think to be a human hyena.'

"Perhaps he thought we'd back down. Even if we'd wished to, we couldn't. We couldn't have him leave with all the trumps. We had to get back our initiative. Sankey again spoke for us.

" 'We like our zoo to have all the contents of the Ark. With our dear vulgarian, Kipling, we call "nothing common or unclean" until it bores us.'

" 'All right,' our guest shot out as he turned to the door, 'if you have the guts, ask Crofts—here's his address. He's always wanting to use my lines for his filthy freight, but I'm not hard enough up yet to let him in on my tracks. In my world we have got to let live in order to be able to get the profits which belong to us unrecognized patriots, called by the mincing liberals "merchants of death." But I still have a nose, and I don't like Crofts near me.'

"We tittered at our guest's sudden adoption of high moral tone, and he, now quite angry, threw a card at us and left, remarking, 'Well, I hope he'll get you into a mess, as he certainly can.'

"When he was gone we snatched up the billet-doux. It was a simple *carte de visite* on which was written Mr. William Crofts and a quietly good address in Mayfair. I couldn't think why the name seemed somehow to be familiar, but we decided, on the strong recommendation we had received, to ask him to be our next guest.

"His appearance was not unpromising. His clothes were good and quiet—Saville Row without a doubt. But the face and hands that emerged from the quiet cloth were delightfully unassuring. He was heavy and no doubt brutal, but the eyes, which were large, were very vigilant—dead and at the same time extremely wary. The mouth, too, though coarse, had round it a pleasant disconcerting tension of humor. Yes, he was undoubtedly a very callous man who, under the appearance of being a simple brute, was peculiarly cunning. He was just our dish, and he seemed quite ready to amuse us.

"He began with the usual coarse stories, told with

ease and a certain finish; then introduced a slightly more varied flavor as we applauded. Finally, remarking that we were evidently adult, he began to talk of real underlife. As he began to illustrate, I remembered —and at once doubted whether his name was Crofts, and was simultaneously pleased with the quiet effrontery of the man. He had dropped the baronetcy, for that might be too obvious, but he had picked the name—or maybe the name had picked him—from the still grimmer partner of Shaw's otherwise grimmest character, Mrs. Warren. He began to talk with a lovely mixture of sentiment, business, and lechery of his 'hotels.' And before we knew it, he was offering to let us stay at one.

" 'We have to pick our clientele,' he said, airily waving his cigar like a bookie. 'Personal service, personal introduction; everything in the best taste—the apartments, the cuisine, down to the girls' dresses and conversation; perfect gentlemen on one side, and perfect ladies provided on the other. It's a large, exhaustive piece of work. There's nothing that can make for the comfort of the one and the rightful profit of the other that is not thought of by our firm.'

"We were half delighted at the disgusting hypocrisy of the man mixed with the cunning and brutality, and half feeling that we had had nearly enough. But then, none of us dared to show his lily liver to the mockery of the rest.

"Finally, as he saw we were hanging back, he remarked with a banter that nearly turned our flank, 'Well, perhaps you're too modern to care for the standard honest commodity I trade in. I ought to have guessed—being myself really only the type of man that would be happiest as an English squire, if taxes let me—that your taste would be rather too sickly for my palate,' and he took a big swig of whisky, raw. 'So, as you have your own idea of candy, and it certainly isn't mine and I don't cater in it, perhaps you'd be more interested in the capital and cash side. You could make quite a lot on quite a little.'

"He looked around to see if avarice would work where he feared lust had failed. I think someone made an appointment with him. But I did not feel, I am sure, the slightest moral prejudice, only that this cad was too near home, and that if he once got one in his hands one might find one was being squeezed by a most capable blackmailer. I'm sure that was my only reason for not going on in the direction in which now I see my tendency and events were forcing me.

"For we did go on trying to find other trial shockers, as we called them. And the next was our last. The next did, at length, bring this modern silly madness of hell-fire clubism to a head. Our secretary, who showed industry worthy of a better pursuit, went on hunting for oddities. He drew a few blanks, it is true, but one day he came in elated.

" 'Look at our list,' he said boastfully. 'Up to date our catalogue of crooks runs its roll of industries—Limey, with gin for gringos; the Alsatian, with bombs for Bengalese; Crofts, with repression-ridding for undergraduates; and our little Armenian with his 'eroin for Arabs, and in the end for all Europe. And now I can crown the list.'

"To our 'Who?' he said 'Wait.'

"Well, he certainly was right. His find crowned and closed the list."

Millum paused, and then added, "And has led, among other things, to us three being here. I can see that evening. We used to have that hideous hole in which we met lit with those awful incandescent gas mantles, over which were draped those shades just like a woman's hat in the nineties. The room was always, therefore, hot, and a slight whistling sound as of an asthmatic pug came from the lights. Our secretary was to bring our guest, and five minutes after we were all ready, the door opened.

"He ushered in a towering figure that filled the doorway with a torso dressed in fawn-gray worsted of the finest weave but rather too fine cut. At the too-many-buttoned sleeve ends, an ivory silk shirt showed its cuffs, held by sapphire and platinum links. The tie was silk of Naples yellow; the shoes of patent leather. And, perhaps you will have guessed, the hands and head coal black. He was a giant West African Negro. He bowed to us, and in that rich drawl, without waiting to be introduced, remarked, 'Pleased to meet you, gentlemen. My name is Johnstone, Odysseus Kaled Johnstone of Zimbawbee Ranch, Mid-Congo, and the Palestrina Apartments, Pall Mall." He then swept us a bow, and moved his vast frame over to us at the table. Our secretary, being able now to get into the room, began making our presentations to this black presence.

"We didn't have to put him at ease. He was easily king of his company. He spoke of Africa, and said he was sure we were interested in its art.

" 'I am no artist, alas,' he said, 'but I trust I do my little part to be a patron; and, as far as a very busy man may be, an amateur.'

"As the meal came to a close he demonstrated for us, with just the butts of two table knives, what he took rhythm to be. We all held that modern syncopation, if it was African, had demoded all classic music. Indeed, here stole in one of our inconsistencies. We had to say that the "Honeysuckle and the Bee" gave us more amusement than any song by Brahms, but this authentic savage liveliness from the Congo, we somehow made out, came under our category of delicious ill-tastes. We sat entranced, while quicker and quicker he beat out ever more complex tappings. Suddenly he said, throwing down the knives:

" 'That's merely the echo of the real thing. In Africa we still know what all the rest of the world has forgotten, that music is wonderful as far and only so far as it is the auditory aspect—or, if you will, outlet —of the whole rhythm of life. It is part of the dance and the dance part of the drama. But much as I admire our music, I sometimes think, gentlemen, I am (and might have shown I was, had I not been kept so busy as an executive) more of a plastic artist. If you will give me leave, I will ask my chauffeur to bring up for your inspection a couple of masks which I am taking on to present to one of my friends for one of your large museums.'

"Our secretary asked if he might go, and after a couple of minutes he returned with a chauffeur in lemon-colored livery with silver facings bearing a large box. It was the contrast of man and master on the one hand, and what came out of that box (a huge, white glazed cardboard thing in which are sent the floral tributes meant for a prima donna) that gave us just the thrill we'd hoped for. This evening, we now felt, was surely our best, our climax. The introduction could not have been more symbolically apt. For out of the virgin-looking pasteboard and wrappings of tissue paper came two of the most frightful examples I have ever seen of that strangest of arts—Negro dramatic carving. All the apparent exuberance of Bantu physique and rhythm has no echo or reflection in this terrifying work. The inspiration seems a nightmare obsession with blood, fear, and cruelty. True, they were carved superbly—what they wished to convey they did as powerfully as Phidias could make cold marble take on the spirit of Olympian calm. And the addition of real hair and beards, gray and clotted, did not make them comic but more terrifying. One had in its jaws a none-too-well-cured child's skull; the other's teeth were fringed with adults' fingerbones.

" 'These are authentic. So much that you have in your collections here is, as Americans would say, custom built. You will have already recognized, in regard to these, that they have been used. They are true sacrificial objects. That,' he paused, letting his hesitation give effect to the word he chose, 'that "dressing" on the beards and hair is—well, what must be employed if our magic is to operate.'

"He lifted the one whose teeth held the child's skull and put it in front of his own face. From its foul mouth came a sound which suited its looks. It seemed to breathe loathing out upon us. The appeal of these objects assaulted all the senses. For the crowning touch, *le succès fou,* was given to this show when, the warmth of the room affecting the objects, they began to yield a smell that made their showman's hints and recollections come almost tangibly to life.

"Then, turning to me as he laid aside this cloud of beastliness and his big, black, beaming face appeared again, he added in the blandest manner, 'Of course, Sir, they go too far. The artist and every enthusiast always tends to shock the practical moralist, and such, Sir, I cannot help being. Superb art, as this, has its place. But it must allow that it has no right—if I may paraphrase and convert the Latin epigrammatist—to shorten life that it may prolong itself! I am absolutely loyal to our wonderful culture. But I have, as a man of the mode—and what is that but to say a person of the current civilized mores?—to recognize that Art cannot be wholly free to be Art for Art's sake only; nor can we—however anthropologically interesting it may be—preserve the Tradition at any price.'

"We were quite at a loss as to how to take this modulation of key. But we were all too afraid of the others to suggest or show by a sign that we might be getting out of our depth in this black man's clever word-play. What in hell's name could he be driving at?

"The next remark puzzled us even more: 'So I became one of the faithful. One must move with the times.'

"It flashed through my mind that it might really prove too much for our stomachs, too violent and rapid a vertigo if, after all, this great black buck should at the end prove to be a Baptist evangelist, and under all his appearance of *outré* culture have come here to sell us Fundamentalist tracts! That would have been a joke at our expense which I doubt if any of us would have been sufficiently subtle to be able to turn to effect. For an instant I sensed our horrid fear that, in this oddest of disguises, the Trojan horse device had been employed to penetrate our Troy, and that this was the cunning master counter-attack from the 'saved' native against the 'damned' white—a revenge so exquisite and so wholly at our expense that we could not foot the bill: we should have lost face for good and to ourselves.

"But the next remark cleared us of that ghastly possibility, though still leaving us sufficiently uneasy.

" 'So, gentlemen, I joined the Faith, the One Faith of the One—I refer to Islam—Allah Akbar, Bismillah. Yes, all Africa is bowing, like swaths of ripe wheat when the wind goes over it. bowing to the Word that speaks from the Kaaba, the wind that blows from Arabia the blessed. All Africa, pan-Africa, shall rise under the green flag and the crescent.'

"A pan-Islam lecture would be a bore. But we felt with relief that we had escaped the worse fate of being asked if we ourselves were saved. That would have been, in the old, stale term, too 'shy-making.' So we settled down while our guest flowed on, as though he were the Congo itself:

" 'I do my part, I trust, loyally. At my initiation by circumcision (no casual water baptism, let me assure you, gentlemen, when performed by ritual correctitude with authentic flint instead of unorthodox steel—oh, yes, we converts pay the price for being True Believers) I took, as I've mentioned to you when I introduced myself, as my mid-second name that of him who, because he swept north with the Faith and mowed down the first white areas (I refer to the glorious conquest of Iran), was named by the Prophet himself "Kaled the Sword of Allah." And so, as I serve the Faith, I may rightly hope for houris and paradise. I say it advisedly: I am no languid convert, content to have secured only my own salvation. I spread the Word.'

"Then, for the first time, he looked us over with a sudden shrewd sweep of those great ivory eyes in that mask of ebony.

" 'Islam works with Africa as Africa understands. So it worked with my own soul. We have the so-called white man on us all the time, under the name of humanity, trying to break up African unity, so we must work quietly. We have what may be called a front. That is to say, my own business has two sides, one economic and the other religious. To give the taxation authorities the evidence they need and which I must submit for my standard of life,' and he looked complacently at his clothes, 'I have my business—large coco plantations. For some reason, that rather cloying drink wrung from black labor always appeals to the Quaker and nonconformist conscience. And behind the waving coco palm I have cover for those bigger aims which are so largely religious.'

"Then suddenly, as though he had gagged sufficiently—I think because he had made up his mind that he might do business with us—his tone changed and he became rapid, matter-of-fact, and startlingly explicit. He smiled a vast ogreish smile and hummed 'Does any little pickaninny ever really want to go to school?'

" 'That, gentlemen, is it in a nutshell. We take them to school. Education is said to be liked by the white, but only if it leads the black to serve him. Well, we have learned the lesson. Mind you, Africa is one. We have no color bar. Arabia gave us our religion and we owe Arabia some return.'

"For a moment we thought we were lost again, but he put us back on the rails with a bump with, 'My little enterprise—the first to be properly organized on a joint-stock basis with all modern office technique—is what you might call a Meet-Your-Fellow-Religionist club, or a domestic-servant agency. The Arabs up north are fine, God-fearing men, and, as I've said, the time has come for my own people to let their faith become art. So,' and he went on without a change of tone, 'for a comparatively small commission I carry out the transfers and provide the Arab homes of the north with the domestic help they need, while that domestic help gains the incomparable benefit of being brought up in God-fearing homes. Thus,' and he spoke with a complacency that awoke our rather grudging capacity for admiration, 'I am making the best of both worlds: giving my coreligionist clients in the north the economic service they require, and giving my fellow countrymen of central Africa the religious opportunities, of which they will stand in dire need when the few short years of this life are over.'

" 'Why I tell you this is not only because I realize that its anthropological and missionary interest will appeal to you, but because of quite a practical matter. My zeal for the spiritual good of my people, and for doing something practical for those who gave me my faith, has been blessed, greatly blessed. But, as you know, when a business is set up with entirely new standards of efficiency, when an old trade is completely reorganized on modern terms, then the difficulty is lack of capital. You will understand that self-interest, aping hypocritically as morality, has made it impossible for me to raise money openly on the big exchanges of Europe or America. Hence I am wondering whether,' and he waved his hand to the ceiling, 'as you have written that charming motto, as a courtesy, in sham Arabic lettering, now that the providence of Allah has put His work and a handsome profit in your way, you who have money would not aid this fine missionary work. I am ready to give you figures. But as an introduction I will tell you out of my head that we pay anything from a hundred and twenty to a hundred and fifty per cent.'

"Though nearly all our cleverness was just word-froth, we weren't quite so stupid that we didn't know what he'd told us. Under the most perfect impudence of religious zeal blended with Negro nationalism, he was asking us to come in on the slave trade. As we were mistaken often for being Leftwing because we were always mocking the Right, we were often sent some of the Left's exposures of the Right's hypocrisies. Among them, I remember getting some amusement, when I had nothing else to read—and, being a reading addict, having to read something—" (Mr. Mycroft smiled) "from reading an attack on the British coco trade, the power of vituperation making up for the lack of proof—saying that it was mixed up or letting itself be used as a blind for some kind of slave trade going on behind its plantations. And again none of us dared to show we were shocked, and perhaps some of us weren't. I know Sankey, with considerable sang-froid—but I don't think thinking he'd be taken at his word—said, 'Of course we'd have to see the actual figures and then, as the ceiling says, we're open to offers. All capitalization is exploitation and I prefer my blackguardism unblessed by the bench of bishops.'

" 'Very right, Sir,' our black tempter replied, and rose. 'I will be sending you the figures of the Mid-Congo Employment Agency, Ltd.' He bowed.

"But when he was gone, none of us could back down in each other's presence. Sankey. indeed, remarked, 'He's probably simply a wide-mouthed black boaster, but if he can live up to his word, this is going to be the most profitable dinner we've ever given.'

"It was certainly the most portentous. For everything went with a smoothness and a speed that was like some new-style story of the three wishes. The neat little brochure arrived, stating the capital and turnover of the company. Mr. Odysseus Kaled Johnstone, of Palestrina Apartments, Pall Mall, and Zimbawbee Ranch, Mid-Congo, was undoubtedly a businessman. The details were settled quietly and effectively. And he was better than his almost unbelievable word. Punctually, in six months' time, we received our first half-year dividend. It was eighty-five per cent.

"I have never discovered highbrows to be any less avaricious than ordinary men. We had put in only trial sums to begin with; a couple of thousand apiece were the amounts, as far as I remember, that Sankey and I subscribed. But, directly that six-month dividend was paid, I saw Sankey was hooked. The rest of the club—barring myself—hadn't, as it happened, much free capital. Quite large incomes, but the securities tied up in trust funds and landed properties. And you may be sure they did not save on income. We two alone had our capital free—at least most of it—to liquidate, and in less than eighteen months we had done so. For now payments had climbed to two hundred per cent.

" 'Mr. O.K.,' remarked Sankey, letting his greed make a poor joke, 'certainly is!'

"He was right—if O.K. was translated as Paying Proposition. It was clear that only lack of capital was limiting a continent-wide enterprise in a trade whose lucrativeness has been equalled only by its cruelty. Sankey, though, saw only the profit side.

" 'We've got in on the ground floor!' he chuckled. 'The dear old hymn used to seem to me to be pure, if low, poetry, when it sang of, "Where Afric's sunny fountains Roll down their golden sand." But, as it now appears, Bishop Heber actually prophesied far more precisely than he could have imagined.'

"I think we needed some bad jokes to keep the far worse taste of what we had done from rising in our gorges. I know I was uneasy, very uneasy. But there was amazingly easy money. Even to have raised the question of whether what we were doing was wrong would have been to render ourselves outcasts with our own little clique. And that would have been highly inconvenient—a kind of moral banishment. For we had made the rest of those who knew us so dislike us that without our particular cronies we should have found ourselves completely excommunicate. Self-styled Homo sapiens really never dares think wholly and solely for himself, does he?"

"Yes, Homo congruens would have been a more detached estimate," Mr. M. assented. "No doubt, many people try to think for themselves—that is, for their own interests as they take them to be. But I don't think the results are successful. Perhaps things are better as they are. But go on, go on."

"Anyhow," Mr. Millum continued, "the thing went on gnawing at me. I don't know how it was, but I kept on finding references—either through Leftwing leaflets, or sudden paragraphs in the papers, or those clever, shocking photographs in those picture papers where the most disgusting photograph is always printed so large that it can't have even a margin—references to the ugliest side of the slave trade, if, indeed, the abominable thing has a presentable aspect anywhere. I thought all these odd reminders—of what, I had no wish to think about—were merely a queer run of accidents. But now I'm not so sure."

Mr. M. nodded slowly. Mr. Millum took out his package of what we used to call—and rightly—"Gaspers," and carefully lit one of them, after offering them to us. I refused. Again Mr. M. took one and laid it on the stone table by the one already so exposed.

"And then," Mr. Millum resumed, "whatever it was that kept on showing me these pictures and putting these news items under my nose showed me a way out.

"I had one uncle, and he had always been a hard-working businessman. I knew he despised me—he'd never liked my father—and would never leave his fortune to such a nephew, not a penny of it. But suddenly he died of a heart attack, and, sure enough, he hadn't made his will. His wife was dead; there were no children. The whole estate, larger than I'd thought—enough, in fact, to get some notice in the papers—came, as next of kin, to me. Sankey congratulated me, and went on to remark that now, with it all turned over to the Congo, I'd really be a millionaire in three or four years. That led to our first quarrel. I didn't intend taking this fortune out from its present investments, I told him.

"He sneered, 'Conscience makes cowards of us all!' Then, suddenly changing tone, he said that perhaps it was too dangerous a game for anyone who could count on more 'quotable' securities—and as five grains of arsenic were as fatal as five hundred, he saw my point of view. Better get clear out, if you could. But he couldn't, so better hang for a man, even though only a black man, than for a sheep, if only a black sheep. His joking was confused, but his avarice was clear. I wouldn't see his drift, though, and he had to bring out his offer into the light of plain English. He added, truly enough, that it would be very hard to think of a less negotiable security. I told him simply that I couldn't sell to him.

" 'A higher bidder?' His tone rose with vexation.

" 'I'm not selling to anyone,' was all I would give him.

" 'I hope,' he said, 'you'll get taught by one of your smug trustees (who batten on white industrial slaves) smelling out your contraband black cargoes. I ought to have guessed you're now in the hands of respectable wardens, a remittance man, a ticket-of-leave trusty. You can draw your week's pay on Monday provided you've gone to church the day before!'

"As I watched him standing there, his none-too-pleasant face even when in repose contorted with contempt and balked money-lust, I suddenly saw him as a kind of mirror; that was what we'd become, with all our highbrow talk of superiority. I knew in a moment that I was through with the whole thing—I mean at least this filthy slave trade. I felt something like physical nausea for the whole beastly business. I got rid of him—we should meet anyhow in a couple of days, at the next club evening. I was now determined to make a break. After all, we were really a vulgar little crowd. That may explain, if not excuse, my melodrama.

"The evening of our meeting, I brought all the stock certificates—quite small, neat documents. It was a night when we'd been unable to find any guests. But, I remember, all of us were present. I began by nettling them, saying we were always boasting we couldn't be shocked. That was simply because we cared so little for anything worth caring for, and we felt safe that we couldn't be touched on the things we really couldn't do without—our comforts, our cash. Touch those and we'd surely be shocked! And with that, aping, I suppose, Cleopatra, I took out all my stock from my breast pocket, and, as we had one of those old-fashioned, open iron grate fires, I pushed them all in between the bars. Made of fine handmade linen paper, they burned up in a moment. Sankey was wild with me, and the rest took his side. Oh, yes, I had shocked them right enough, and, as I had hit them on their nerve and exposed them too, they were as sore as he. I got up and left the room. I never went back. You see, in a way I really was interested in art, and was getting heartily sick of using taste merely as a game for demoding some style that too many people had begun to find pleasure in. I was bored with the attempt always to prove that some poor fool who enjoyed beauty in any form in which it had previously been admired was just too hopelessly out of date.

"But, though I never saw any of the others again, in the end I didn't drop Sankey—at least, he kept on turning up. Why? Well, we had been brought up together. We were, as I've said, a lonely lot. We hadn't been educated with the rest of the well-to-do, and that makes a difference. It's hard to make friends after thirty, and maybe as hard to drop them. Besides, there was something about Sankey. How shall I put it? He was like a terribly damaged and grossly mishandled work of art, say a Cellini statuette which a number of slum children had been allowed to use as a Guy Fawkes doll. It would be broken, smeared, and made grotesque, and at a casual glance would no doubt be flung into the rubbish heap. But if you cared for art, you couldn't help but see that underneath, though you might never be able to repair it, it had about it real quality. Perhaps I don't make myself clear. Still I can't think I was mistaken."

"Neither can I," remarked Mr. M. quietly.

Millum seemed encouraged, and went on.

"Not long after, I left London for good, for the country—in fact, to the house over the road. This one was then occupied. But after a couple of years it fell vacant. I didn't do anything about it. It was Sankey who saw it advertised in the papers He came down to see it and took it at once. I certainly didn't ask him to. But he also seemed to feel that there was some tie between us. He had not the slightest intention of altering his way of life, but at the same time it was clear that he didn't want to wholly lose touch with me. Perhaps I seemed to be some sort of insurance against a deep, subconscious fear—I can hardly imagine a poorer one, but where else could he find any purchase of the slenderest sort?

"He settled here. I couldn't prevent it, nor did I protest. Indeed, I found him Jane. He used to send for me, and I'd come over, and though he would not come to my house and paid no attention to me while I was in his, something passed. It was an odd, uncanny, friendship—sinister, I suppose most people would say. I know I remember often feeling that we were both being kept waiting about for something.

"I thought that had happened when, one day, he asked me for a loan. I said, 'Have the investments gone badly?'

"That led to an outburst against 'those bloody hypocrites of Liberals.' Then I put two and two together, and the sum I got was correct. I had seen in the paper that there had been questions in Parliament and a fuss at some missionary meetings. That kind of detail didn't catch my eye as it had before, when I was in on the racket, but this was sufficiently insistent to revive my notice. As I've said, Sankey and I had never spoken about money—it was the one reticence, because it was the one thing that was sacred in our lot. And after our business break it would have been even harder.

"Then I saw that there was a notice of a punitive expedition and the uncovering of a big-scale slave trade run with foreign capital. I must say, it was a relief to read that when the raid on the London office took place, it was too late, and that a Negro passing under the name of Johnstone had got away and before leaving had burned all the company's files and papers.

"But my relief was not shared by Sankey. It was clear he was ruined. I could not let him go under, even if I hadn't been, as I was, more than comfortably off. So, with practically nothing said, I paid in regularly a large sum to his credit at his bank.

"Naturally, that did not make him any more gracious to me, but it made my very uneasy soul a little more at peace. I still realized that somehow I must do something more. Simply to have got out of that morass and to know that Sankey was—if unwillingly—out of it too, didn't wipe the filth off one's record.

"So we went on for some years, and, to be truthful, Sankey did not improve. On the contrary, his resentment actually grew to a pathological degree. But I stuck on, determined to discharge my debt in the only way that seemed possible short of going to prison almost for life, considering my age.

"Possibly doing this in this way to that sort of man was not the best thing for him. It was, however, surely the best way of being certain that his resentment would construe what I was doing in its own sinister terms. He naturally could only think that it was because I feared his power of blackmail over me that I must go on keeping him.

"Once or twice he as good as said so. When, in an attempt at banter, I suggested that I knew as much about him as he about me, and then, after the laugh, tried to say that what I did was a kind of amend and not without a real regard for him, his reply that my hypocrisy just made him sick showed me how sick he was. I became convinced that he honestly thought I must be helping him because I feared him. He seemed quite incapable of seeing any other sense in it. From his point of view, I supposed that seemed the only way of making a meaning that would leave him any sanity about himself and any power to feel—as he had to feel—superior to me."

Mr. M. nodded and said, "Spinoza gave us the classic formula for that: 'Man imputes himself.' "

"Well, I've proved in my case that that was true," Millum continued. "For a couple of years we went on deadlocked—a couple of years of his deepening gloom and my seeing that we were getting nowhere and yet not seeing any way out of it. For I would not yield to his maniac construction of things. I could have gone abroad and left no address. But I would not, for the sake of recovering my own integrity, give up this chance of helping him because he hated me. In one way, it made my effort at reparation more sensible, more valid."

Mr. M. again nodded.

"And then, would you believe it, his spirits began to recover. He actually became almost courteous to me, if not friendly. Jane noticed it. We shared a certain relief, for this house had become a gloomy place, and it ought to be so serene and sane. I attributed it to virtue working through at last. How the disbanded club and myself of some years back would have laughed at this gull!"

Then, in a graver tone, "Well, I learned that reparation isn't so lightly made, nor the way out so easily found. His spirits went on improving, and I was almost certain that we were going to be on a really genial level, if not one of confidence, when the whole house of hope went up like smoke.

"He asked me over one day to meet a couple of young friends. How he'd made them I don't know, or perhaps I ought to say that the first glance showed they weren't made—they were strangers whom someone unknown to me had sent along. They were just what we had been fifteen or twenty years before. Rich, well-dressed, intelligent, traveled. But all they had gained was the loss of their own tradition and the power to cancel out the power and force of any other. They had keen heads, but no roots or stance. And soon the conversation was in the old mold. What was more, after a little, it modulated still further. Perhaps I was alarmist. Even now I can't be sure I had any real evidence at that stage. But I thought that there were references being made that could only bear one meaning, and I thought that in some way I, too, was being sounded by all three. What I did was, no doubt, a mistake. I got up and left. I was far from enjoying myself, and if Sankey was going to be such a criminal fool as to boast of his past in front of these two young blasé immoralists to see if he could shock them I was determined not to be present at the exhibition. It was not only because he would probably drag me in, but because—I again have to say it—I had this oddly deep, if futile, affection for him; for the more you do for a person the less he likes you and the more you like him—a queer rule, but almost invariable. So I rose and left. But when I'd gone I felt my uneasiness grow, not lessen. An irrational feeling kept on telling me that there was something worse in this than the none-too-pleasant reason I had given myself.

"The next evening he sent me a message that he'd like me to come over after dinner. I did, and found him in a nervous state that seemed to rise to a point when, after some hints and a certain amount of not-too-good-natured banter, he seemed on the point of taking me into his confidence; then he sank back into a suspicion that became more and more veiled and sullen. All the while he was smoking heavily."

"And Latakia is not the tobacco indicated—to use the medical term—for that mood."

"How do you know he smoked Latakia?" Millum asked, turning to Mr. Mycroft.

Before he could reply, I intervened. "Mr. Millum, when you know Mr. Mycroft well, you will never ask that question. He will reply, 'Just by using my eyes,' which leaves you, and is meant to leave you, in the dark."

"Not quite so bad nor quite so simple as that," Mr. M. chuckled. For some reason, in spite of the sordidness of the story, he seemed in rising spirits. "I'd prefer to say, 'By cross-examining all the senses and, as a good cross-examiner should, separately.' But more of that later. Meanwhile, we must get on with your story."

"Finally," said Millum, resuming, "Sankey got up without a word and left the room. He tried to slam the door behind him but it bounced off the latch and stood ajar. I therefore could hear him calling for Jane, and when she came I could not help hearing that he was ordering her to get her hat and cloak and go out with some letters—letters which he must have had in his pocket when he left the room.

"It was an unpleasant night—one of those nights when the west gales from the Atlantic meet the eastern wind from the steppes, and on this borderground we have slush and sleet and a wind both boisterous and piercing, a rain both soaking and freezing. It was not the night to send anyone out, but there was a small mailbox on the main road half a mile away that was cleared first thing in the morning, and evidently Sankey had made up his mind that he must catch that mail. Now I am sure some die had been cast in his mind and he was going to act quickly and secretly. I heard Jane say, 'Well, Sir, I'll have to change my shoes and things,' and pause, hoping he d relent. But all he said was 'Well, hurry up.' With that, he came back into the room.

"I didn't stay for more than five minutes after that. I was feeling both sore and uneasy. He paid no attention, huddled over the fire—didn't turn his head or say anything as I said a short good night. I shut the door and had just wrapped myself up in my coat and opened the hall door when Jane came into the hall from her side of the house. It was a shame to send her out in this, for the wind blew in like ice, making a sound like a trumpet. Without a word I took the letters from her hand, left her standing there, and closed the door behind me.

"Then it crossed my mind: why should I, any more than she, tramp in the mud and slush just to catch an earlier mail for a selfish beast? There was a fanlight you have seen over this door, and, as the hall lamp was hung high, you could see to read as you stood on the top step. Just to assure myself that the letters didn't look too urgent—say an overdue income-tax return or something of that sort—I looked them over, deciding that if they appeared to be simply social letters they could wait stormbound till tomorrow. I ran them through my hands. There were only three: the first two were addressed to the two young men I had met just previously in this house; the third was to an address in Africa, a postal station given as being on the upper Congo. Perhaps it was totally insufficient evidence to go on. Pretty certainly, I should have done better to have left possible ill alone.

"I went down the steps, and by the time I was at the bottom, my mind was made up. I went across the road and straight into my own house. My Mrs. Sprigg had left a kettle steaming on the hob by my sitting-room fire. I held the envelope backs one by one in the jet of mist, and one by one the gummed flaps curled back. I put them down carefully, drew out the letters, and read them over. The first two were almost identical in what they said. You have guessed. He was asking them to come in on the Upper Congo Agency which had been reconstituted, and he was demanding that, as he had put them on to so profitable a thing, they should purchase for him a considerable block of shares. Evidently he had sounded them out enough to know they would close with his offer, and the certainty that they knew he had put them in the way of making big money was shown by the size of the commission slice he demanded for himself.

"The third letter, therefore, was no surprise. It said that he had obtained further capital, that he would require at least a considerable percentage of liquidation profits for his past shares which had gone with the old company, and that on a commission basis and at what might be called a disgracefully handsome figure, he would be ready to raise more capital. So that explained his shifting behavior with me! He wanted more money still, and, as he could not believe I was other than the sneak he'd always known, he still thought I might yield another substantial sum. But, like most amateur interceptors of mail and other such subterfugists, having got my information and had my worst suspicions confirmed, I found that I had not thought out what my next steps would be."

Mr. M. nodded. "That's always the point, if you would like to know, where a good detective looks for his breakthrough. To start with, he can seldom be as wise as the man who first thought out the first steps of the crime. It is where the criminal begins extemporizing that his tracker finds the gaps in his defenses and the holes in his tunnel. The 'tangled web we weave, when we practice to deceive' is not, as the moral poem says, at the first step, but at about the dozenth, when the variables begin to get out of hand."

"Well, I hurried and felt I ought to cover my tracks. Besides, I should have felt a beast if I had got Jane into a row. So, on that kind of impulse, choosing to convenience the person we know, at the much worse cost of thousands we don't, off I went in the snow and rain, at least feeling I was doing what I didn't want to."

"Which is also," chimed in Mr. M., "far from the best of guides."

A sentiment with which I could concur.

"As soon as they were dropped into the mail," Millum went on, "and I couldn't get at them, all safely re-sealed and in the sacred keeping of the postmaster general, I had the natural revulsion. But the matter was out of my hands, however heavily it was on my mind. And Sankey, having determined not to try whether I would come in on the racket again, evidently had as little wish to see me as I him.

"Soon, too, I had signs that the abominable thing was working. I realized that he was spending money far more freely than the handsome allowance he took from me could cover, and when I made discreet inquiries, I found it was not on credit, but on cash. One of the young men turned up also. I was not, I am glad to say, asked over. But whereas the two of them had come the first time in a nice enough sports car, now this one appeared in a large Rolls-Royce, with a sealskin-and-gray-liveried chauffeur, and even a similarly clad footman—all the possible evidences of a sudden rise in what we used to call the standard of living. I felt a rising disgust at the sheer ostentation."

Then he added, after some hesitation, "I expect you'll think that I can't be giving you a straight report here and that I'm becoming, at best, subjective —trying to make out consciously or subconsciously that things just ran into me and not that I planned them."

"No, not necessarily," Mr. M. reassured him. "Indeed, I'll say for your encouragement that I am now sure that, when we are on the lookout for something, it will, more often than the law of chances can explain, come part of the way to meet us."

That seemed to reassure Millum, and he went on. "That's exactly what I found. I found I couldn't get this beastly business out of my mind or see any way out of it. I wasn't prepared to go to court and make a clean breast of my part and go to jail for a long stretch just to get Sankey there. I didn't want him in jail, really. I only wanted this thing to stop. Besides, said my bewildered mind to itself, if you put yourself and the other three in jail, would that stop what is going on on the upper Congo? Pretty certainly O.K. Johnstone is now keeping well out of the hands of European police.

"And, as it happened, the first step out of the deadlock and on to a new problem took place when I was trying to take my mind off this worry which now engrossed a great part of my time and made me often hate Sankey with something like loathing. I used to go up to the big curio sales in London, at Christie's and Sotheby's, for I had found a real anodyne in art collecting. I did not buy nearly as often as I went, for those places were great educational centers in their way. You could learn the cultural history of most of the West and a good deal of the East if you went regularly, and the study did take the mind off the present, which to me was now almost uniformly unpleasant. For to my moral worry was added the further one that I did not know how long Sankey would allow me even my present immunity and would not push me to go in with him. I had become convinced that he was now of that unpleasant, very dangerous, and none-too-uncommon class, the mad-and-bad, the cads who think they can always win, and that their power of damaging others gives them complete immunity from counterattack.

"It was one of those big mixed sales—several remarkable collections from small but good collectors had come into the market. There were a number of small examples of the great second-rate Baroque artists' works, some fine ironwork, a couple of really good tapestries, a fine set of majolica, and a half dozen pieces of early Murano crystal; and with it the usual pieces of brocade, stamped leather furniture, and some fine weapons—the usual equipment of seventeenth- and early eighteenth-century Italian houses of the rich.

"Everything went for good prices till one piece came up and, to my surprise, didn't seem to rise. It looked to my eyes as good, if not a better, museum piece than most of them. But the bidding began to fail at a ridiculously low figure. I turned to the dealer who used to handle the bids I made and whispered 'Why?'

" 'Reconstructed,' he whispered back.

"But it was a lovely piece of work in line and finish and inlay and—" Mr. Millum faltered a moment for a word and then said lamely, "though an instrument, as decorative as any piece of furniture. As the auctioneer said for the second time 'Going,' I nudged my professional friend, and he nodded, making the bid only ten shillings above the last. Once again the auctioneer went through his threefold ritual, but this time was the last for that, and it was knocked down to us.

"My agent remarked as we took it over at the end of the sale: 'Worth the price, of course, though it would have fetched ten times that, if sound all through. The trouble is that some old fool a generation ago replaced the original working part with another. Why can't people leave things alone? He surely can't have wished to use it '

"But I am not sure, myself.

"Of course, such playing about with toys can't stop a real worry. It only suppresses it for the time being—and it really didn't do even that for me."

"No," said Mr. M., rising to the surface of the conversation like a large trout at a fly. "No; this incident comes under the category you mentioned a little earlier. It wasn't a sedative, but one of those mysterious irritants. Like taking an aspirin and finding that by mistake we've taken *nux vomica*."

I had no idea of what they were talking about, but Mr. Millum nodded and went on.

"You're right. And what's more, after that everything went—I almost said smoothly—but perhaps I ought to say . . . inevitably."

"'*Facilis decensus Averno?*'"

"Yes, Vergil knew human nature, even if he was ignorant of vulcanic geology. The down gradient took a sudden dip by my making two discoveries—no, observations. The first was over here, at Sankey's. After a considerable period of sulking, he suddenly called me over. I guessed the interview wouldn't be pleasant. It wasn't. He wanted to know whether he could come over whenever he liked and use part of my place. Why? Absurd reason: this bower, in which it was his habit to sit whenever it was fine, had now become too overgrown, dank, and dark—it kept the sun from him and yet did not screen him from the house. So he had come to think that he'd like my garden better—though, in fact, he'd hardly ever caught sight of it.

"For a moment I thought the whole thing could be disposed of—all this arbor needed was pruning; it was hopelessly overgrown. I pointed that out. No, he couldn't have a man fussing round. Besides . . . besides . . . I gave up trying to persuade him and cleared out. He was fool, knave, and egoistic paranoiac. I wasn't going to have an outbreak with him—as I knew he was really only trying to pick a quarrel—over some goddam silly little thing such as pruning a hedge. When things are on edge with the unstable, anything may make the break, and I still had enough good sense, caution, and a general notion that I didn't know where I was going to know that, when the break came, it must come on a clear issue and one I had thought out.

"But he wouldn't let me alone. I ought to have known that. Just sidestepping the particular point was not even treating the symptom. Back he came—or, to be exact, I was again sent for. Now he was demanding that I sell or give him part of my garden, so that he could cut it off, build a wall across it, and make it part of his—a complete fool's fancy anyway, for that lane that runs between the houses is a right of way. If he was so insane about his privacy, he would have to build a covered bridge, or make a tunnel underneath the road—like the absurd eccentrics of the eighteenth century used to do.

"On getting back to my house, I ran up to the roof, just to see how his insane notion could possibly work out if he forced me to it—like Naboth when Ahab was after his vineyard—and, glancing over in this direction, I could see how the spreading of the latticed branches of this arbor had spoiled it as a 'sun trap,' and how easily even unskilled pruning could put it right. As I was standing there, my foot struck against some object that was lying in the small parapet way that runs between the tiles themselves and the actual parapet. It was obviously something which the roof repairers must have left behind when they finished their job. A little while before I had had to have some tiles replaced. I picked it up idly and began to fiddle with it, wondering, with the surface part of my mind, what it actually was, and how it had been used—while my deep mind was just worried to exasperation by feeling that I was really being trapped.

"My fears were well-grounded. I ought to have foreseen this fix. Of course it was inevitable. Sankey was determined to show his complete power over me, and this occasion gave him an opportunity.

"I had hardly been five minutes in my study before my Mrs. Sprigg knocked at the door to say that Jane had been sent over to ask whether I would 'step round' again. Yes, the moment I came here to where he was sitting, it was clear that he was now acting the part of the dictator. He looked up at me and repeated almost exactly the words that he had used before, except this time he omitted any reference to purchase! It was an ultimatum. I was to do precisely as I was told. All the time he was making known his intentions, he made his points with his paper knife, like a schoolmaster with his cane to a stubborn boy. I felt so angry I could have snatched it out of his hand, except that I was sure that a burst of temper now would be fatal. Finally, with an air of triumph, he tossed the paper knife into the air, caught it as it turned and dived down, and, waving me to the door, told me these were his terms."

Millum paused. His breath was now coming fast as he recalled the scene in which he had been so shamed. I noticed that the story was a little different from Jane's. But this was the fuller and better account. She did not suspect the drama that had been going on between what she took to be two of the gentry, at least one of whom had too much money and too short a temper.

"Then," Millum resumed, "I had the final proof that he was really mad. He gave me a sidelong look and, as I simply nodded, he suddenly remarked in quite a perky tone, 'Well, haven't you anything to say, any further counterproposals?'

"It flashed into my mind that this might be—what do you call it—one of the sudden rises in the manic-depressive fluctuation?"

"That will do as well as any other 'program note' for what a poet has called 'The ghastly music of the madman's mind.' Go on," said Mr. M.

"I said to Sankey, with a not-too-ill-simulated chuckle, 'you may have my garden, of course. But there's no arbor in it.' He actually paused at that. Do you know, I don't think he'd thought whether there was one or not. That made me think I might win time.

And, sure enough, when I said, 'Look here, let *me* prune your arbor roof and then see if that won't serve,' he actually nodded his head. He was evidently playing the part in his mind of a judge granting a reprieve. It was a nice warm day, and he was comfortable enough in his own garden.

"Finally he said, 'Very well, very well. You may try. Trial by ordeal, eh? And if you fail—and you probably will—then the forfeit is your garden. In the old days it would, of course, have been your head!' and he, in his turn, chuckled.

"I got to work that very afternoon. And while I worked (you know how often the mind will work freely on some problem and the answer come up all of itself while the hands are busy), while I was pruning, I suddenly saw what that roof repairer's gadget was for."

Mr. Mycroft put out his hand casually and, picking up the withered branch among his collection of debris, switched the table a couple of times.

The other said, "Yes, yes."

"Then something chimed in your mind?"

Millum again said, "Yes. Just like a chord!"

"But a chord can have four notes?" questioned Mr. M. still further.

Again Millum agreed. But their continual agreement only left me more completely in the dark.

"The fourth was a kind of trigger, though," Millum went on. "I was trying to rest my mind that evening when suddenly, in the book I was reading and which I thought would be just the thing to get my mind off my troubles—the last place in the world where I would find them popping up—a phrase, a very well-put phrase, struck out at me."

"As Quakers put it, 'It spoke to your condition?' " Mr. M. suggested.

"I don't quite know if you would put it that way if you knew what it actually was," replied Millum.

"I'm not sure I wouldn't," replied Mr. M., very sure of himself.

But this was such a common state with him that I ventured out of my humble ignorance and its need for enlightenment to take his usual response and say, "Please go on!"

"What I saw seemed to make the thing not only simple but to get rid of my last hesitation. Anyhow, after that I felt under a real compulsion at least to try. I had to, if I may use the term, cast the die. Whether I failed or no, I now had the sensation that

I was simply a tool, a surgical instrument, a lance being used for medical purposes . . ."

He stopped, almost started again, thought better of it, and then said briefly, "There, that's my story," and was silent.

"A very incomplete one, if I may say so," I started up.

Mr. M. waved me down. "No," he remarked, "no, the only omissions I can see are two, and quite small: the incident of which Jane has told us, that in one of your kindly efforts to distract the almost insane Sankey you lent him that charming collection of classic literature that opens—to give the *mise en scène*—with the extraordinary crime stories of a family, six of whom became masters of the world, five of whom went off their heads, and four of whom were murdered. The other small omission, and I think perhaps more important, is the second visit which you made to your own roof."

Millum nodded, adding, "But do these matter? It was motive you were after; method, by some reason best known to yourself, you knew. After all, I threw in my hand, didn't I, when I saw your exhibit? And I think you may allow, all the more because of what

I've told you, that I was ready enough to surrender to anyone who could bring it home, and," he paused, "more than willingly, to one who brought it home in the way you did."

It was Mr. M. who now was looking at the ground.

Then, after quite a long silence, during which my patience was not improving (but neither of the others seemed to care or think of me), at last Mr. M. said, "Now for our third problem, that third act, up to which it is so easy to write the two pointing acts, but which is itself so hard."

But there Mr. Millum broke in and, to my pleasure, was on my side. I was in the dark, and whether Mr. M.'s idea of a denouement was as interesting as he fancied, for me to judge I must have some notion of what had actually taken place; and I still had only the foggiest. To find, then, that Millum, with whom I had grown impatient—he seemed so blindly to back up all Mr. M.'s hints at it all being clear as daylight—to find him on my side and bewildered after all, made me feel a fellow sympathy for him, whether he was or was not a murderer of a man who certainly was a most unpleasant person.

So when Millum said, "May we go back a little?"

I joined in with a hearty, "Hear, hear."

"I've put my cards on the table," he continued, "and I don't want to make out that it is anything but a pretty grim hand. And I repeat that I am ready to pay the stakes, even if that should include hanging. I have given you the motive. It is for you to judge whether you think I have been truthful and, if so, would human life be safer if Sankey were alive or if I were hanged. I can now say I really and literally don't care a hang. I can't see that he had not become a kind of human cancer, but equally I can now see that so cutting him out was a false stroke. I'm at the end of my tether, you see. But before I go, just to get that surface part of my mind at ease and leave it free for the main problem, which is, of course, motive and whether means do cover ends, I would be grateful if you'd tell me the steps by which you came to—" and he pointed at the table, "to collect that bouquet of such telling arrangement that the moment I saw it I knew the game was up. I have given you the motive, the 'Why'; now, show me how you found the 'How.' "

Chapter IV

MR. MYCROFT'S "HOW?"

MR. MYCROFT rose and stretched himself. He seemed wonderfully at his ease; indeed, had he been that sort, I would have said he was almost in a kind of high spirits. He seemed quite ready to fall in with our wishes—perhaps flattered that we wanted to know. It crossed my mind, too, that maybe he wanted to use the back of his mind in the way in which he and Millum had been speaking of it, while he ran through with us the past moves he had made. He could not, however, avoid the traditional cliché at the start, that "patter" opening of all these old hands at juggling.

"Quite simple, really. 'Quite obvious,' you'll say, when I've put the cards out. Yes, I'd like to run through the steps of the approach with the two of you. For, in the first two acts is always the secret of the third, or there's no secret at all. All we have to do is to understand what has been put before us. And there you can help me as much as I can help you.

"But once more, refreshment. We took your 'Why' in two helpings, with lunch sandwiched in between. Now permit me, in vulgar British parlance, to wet my whistle before I give you my *obbligato* on the 'How.' "

He turned to me, "Mr. Silchester, I, as an amateur detective, am going to make an olfactory deduction. I am certain I scent muffins on the afternoon air. I deduce that they are preparing for our tea. Will you, acting on that clue, see if your eyes can confirm my flair?"

I did not, however, have to move. For on looking toward the dining room I heard a sound, and a moment after, like a richly laden ship, Jane sailed into view complete with what the French call *thé complet*, but, if I may be provincial for once, only the English can really equip. Millum and I rose to relieve her, and there was enough to load the three of us. For accompanying the muffins Mr. M. had scented was a dish of some excellent light pastries and also on a noble platter an equally good, massive plum cake.

"Tea," pronounced Mr. Mycroft, when I had given each of us a cup, a fine oolong made more fragrant because drunk from fine Spode, "tea is the most social of all meals. It puts us at our ease, as all meals tend, but being the lightest of all meals," and he took a muffin and eyed the cake appreciatively, "it leaves the mind free. Tea is always so important to English people because they need this, the gentlest of the drug stimulants, before they can relax."

Certainly China tea always showed the master at his best, and, as I only had to listen, I saw no reason why I should stress the meal's liquid against its solid side.

We were well on the way to a threesome friendship by the time it closed, and Jane was carting back the relics to show in joint triumph with the cook what devastation we had made of her munitions. Millum proved quite delightful, and time and again gave me fresh points for my essay, now almost a thesis, on "1760, the Climax of Our Culture." So I was really ready to rest my mind and give my whole attention to Mr. M. when he leaned back, fingered the "Gasper" which again had been offered, and launched so swiftly into his narrative that once more he never lit it.

"I'll begin at that part of the story where it began for me, that morning that Mr. Silchester recalls—so little a while back, but so much has taken place in between—when I received a small package by mail. With it had come a letter from a professional friend of mine, to say that he had been sent here on duty to clear an issue on which a little doubt had been raised. He added that he had looked into it, and, after seeing the grounds on which the superstition had grown, he had by a full and thorough investigation come to the conclusion that there were really no grounds, only an ingenious fancy, for disturbing or doubting the coroner's verdict at the inquest. The whole matter had turned, he concluded, on the one piece of material evidence which he was pleased to say he could send by mail. Should I reach his conclusion by an examination of it, then would I return it with my confirmation. Should there occur to me any further details on which I might require more information, would I come down and see him on the spot. He would be there one day more anyhow, seeing the local authorities so as to conclude the matter properly. 'Anyhow,' he added, 'the country is now at its best, the place itself has real quality, and an accident of such a sort does not spoil permanent charm for either of us old hands!'

"I like that about Sark: he is a highly placed specialist who has never let his specialized professional interests spoil his sense of the whole, but rather aid his work. He will retire well and then, I hope, employ that fine natural talent for painting which you saw, Mr. Silchester, he could, like all general talents, deploy in the service of his vocation.

"I asked Mr. Silchester to view the little problem with me. He agreed with the expert." (This was certainly a mellow way of putting my rather hurried reaction, and one which had proved evidently to be wholly mistaken.) "He saw in the object nothing but what it appeared to be, a piece of old-fashioned decorative metal, now being used—as modern poor taste loves to do—for another purpose than that for which it was made. My lens confirmed him and Inspector Sark. For on the handle of this *soi-disant* paper knife were copious fingerprints, all of the same pattern and all vouched by Sark to be Sankey's. They were well-marked, and there was not a trace of any others. The handle had been gripped firmly.

"But as I studied them a doubt arose in my mind. Well-gripped, yes, but gripped what way? The pad of the finger is a wonderful device for gripping, because, like the tread of a motor tire, it is toughly elastic. When a car turns a corner too quickly, you've noticed that the treads make marks on the road not of a rightly formed impress, but distorted. They are pulled away toward the direction in which the car, by its momentum, was lunging, as they grip the road to save the car from leaving it. Now, it was precisely for that effect that I knew I ought to look. I ought to find in miniature that same displacement-effect on the butt of this handle."

Mr. M. raised up his bundle of relics to the table —whence tea had for a time denied them pride of place—and laid them out again, picking up the paper knife.

"That distortion of the fingerpad whorls would be quite clear, if Sankey . . . the last time he used this, used it with such effect. To change my simile to make my meaning quite clear, if the knife had been used only as a paper cutter and for no other purpose, never as a dagger, then the finger whorls would appear like a series of ripples on a still pool. But if the paper knife was ever thrust home not between the pages of a book, but between human ribs and by a human hand, then all these ripples would be as though a wind had blown them and they were swaying away from the point and direction toward which the point of the dagger was being plunged. I hope I have made that plain!"

Millum turned away and drew hard on his cigarette.

"That was enough to make me wonder whether I could know more. And then, as I looked up and down this small shaft or haft, I did catch sight of something else. This little handle has on it two metals, a common device of silversmiths to vary the appearance of their work. And this was an authentic piece, undoubtedly, a small Renaissance toy, one of those fantastic hairpins from that fantastic age, made of silver when the silversmiths counted among themselves artists as competent as Cellini. The shaft of now almost black silver—we know the late master of this house respected patina, if nothing else—has had added lengthwise, you see, to its upper part, three small flukes or flutings which no doubt add to the design. But the odd thing was that, when I touched this other dulled metal, which you see is a deep gray, not black, the small file mark showed that it was aluminum—a metal which Cellini and his peers might well have loved but no one had seen till he and his had been in their graves some four centuries.

"But all that proved nothing. It did, however, make one's mind all the less inclined to sit down and say ditto to Mr. Sark. I felt no more at this point than that I could ask our inspector some questions which would amuse him and no doubt rouse him to a fairly matched argument such as we unravelers love. So I went on studying this piece till Mr. Silchester—who is an intuitional type—became almost vexed. For I had to bring out my heavyweight piece, my large microscope, which always appears to him, as I dare say it must look to any novelist's eye, a piece of drama rather than a necessary process of detection. It repaid me. For on working my way along the stem I found, on reaching the end, if not one more clue, at least another challenge to the authoritative verdict.

"You see, the top of this hairpin now turned paper knife is a flat capital—the conventional Renaissance conclusion to any such little columnar composition. I was looking at that to see whether I could find any faint, half-obliterated traces of the thumb, which might and ought to be there if this knife was driven home by a man striking at his own breast. There weren't. But then, such traces on such an exposed area might possibly have been wiped off or never have made a clear impression. And, moreover, I had to allow that the blow could have been given without the thumb being in that position. But while I looked and failed to find what I was looking for, I was rewarded by another doubt. Across the top, you see, is a shallow groove."

I certified that was so; Mr. Millum did not. It did not seem important to me, I must say. Mr. M. read my thoughts.

"And why not? you rightly ask. Yes," he allowed, "it wouldn't have held me, if I had not seen in the magnification of the microscope that this groove was holding something. Again, nothing of note. But in case of suspicion, everything must be made to answer who and what it is, even if what it says is quite above-board. The groove was clogged; natural enough in an old object and one which, as we happen now to know, was never permitted to be cleaned, but which might be touched unintentionally by duster and cleaning rag. I picked out the contents of the groove and had little difficulty in recognizing them as common gum—resin. I cleared the whole groove and stored my minute specimen on the chance that it might prove helpful. But when I had done that I found I had raised another little question—again no answer, but a fresh query from the groove itself. When it was emptied, I noticed that though the silver was darkened, it was much less dark there than the silver of the rest of the piece. In other words, that cleft looked unmistakably as though it had been made much later than the rest of the workmanship and its chasing. So I was certain of two things: the groove and the aluminum fluke fittings were additions to the piece and lately made. Now, why someone should so trouble to toy with such a toy—that, certainly, was a small mystery.

"But my work in the groove had given me another indication. It began to point to the sort of man I might be needing to find and, further, it told me he would be one possessed of no little antiquarian knowledge.

"So, putting my witness again under the microscope's penetrating eye, using the finest point I could handle, I made a series of small scores on the groove's sides. Then, under the power of magnification I was using, the verdict stood out, plainly written.

"One of the most active and lucrative fields of detection—for the sums of money involved are high—is in the judgment of ancient bronzes. The market is large, because so many cultures wrought their most enduring works in this metal. 'Perennial bronze'—the phrase itself is now a venerable antique. More lasting than iron, less likely to be melted down than gold. The prices are often very big because such work is not seldom of supreme mastery. And where there's money value there'll be sharks to prey on gulls. The forgers, it must be owned, have done wonders and, on the other hand, the detectors of forgeries have been as resourceful. It has been a worldwide underground battle, both sides using all the science they can summon. The great triumph of the forgers was their discovering how to make that patina so prized by collectors and so puzzling to Jane. Between the two, I, a mere scientist, have no wish to judge. *De gustibus* always closes such controversies for me.

"But what did catch my attention and was laid aside in my memory for future possible use was the reply of the museums to this attack on their treasures, this subtle flooding of their market. They found that though to the keenest naked eye a patina of yesterday chemically produced looked indistinguishable from one which two or three thousand years of quiet burial were needed to produce naturally, yet, under the microscope, a touch of the file (unnoticeable to unaided sight) showed up the lie. As the oxidation of the copper (which is, of course, the patina) proceeds, fine fissures of decomposition eat into the metal, making patterns like a tree and hence called dendrition. But the important point is that if time and nature produce such tree patterns they are wild, like forest trees; while when man produces them artificially and hurriedly, the patterns look actually artificial—they are stiff and mechanical, like trees from round a doll's house! And the same is true of silver. What I saw under the microscope were these small formal tree patterns.

"It was while I was trying to put these two or three small anomalies together with the doubt that I had about the fingerprints that I was helped by Mr. Silchester, who thought I ought to close the act I was playing and put on another. As you may have gathered, he is developing a theme of which I hope we shall hear more—'1760, the Climax of Culture'—and in running out his first bright ideas he fell upon the word 'balance.' Then, as so often happens with him and me, his repetition of the word gave me an idea almost before I could see what it would mean, an idea for an experiment. While I gave him another form of provocation, which no doubt will prove as stimulating to his creative faculty in the field of history, I took the paper knife from the field of the microscope and began to judge its balance. As it showed where its center of gravity lay and toppled over toward its pointed end," and Mr. M. illustrated it for us, "something went into place in my mind. Of course such pins are, as we have said, weighted in that way so as to keep them from toppling out of the coiled hair of their wearer. I knew also that I must not jump to conclusions. And the best way not to do that is just not to look at what is forming in your mind, and the best way to do *that* is to jump up and do something else. So I suggested to Mr. Silchester that we should catch the train and come here.

"On our arrival, Sark made fine play with his conviction based on evidence. Several times I felt that I would look pretty foolish if I ventured to go against him. But I still felt it would be safe for me to check up on every one of the doubts which I had. First, that admirable Jane, admirable in her loquacity as in her other services—believe me, it is not that people talk too much that bores us, it is that we listen too little—Jane told me that she never used any of the resins as a polish. Whence, then, had the resin in this groove come? Next, when we were in the garden, we were shown how impossible it was for anyone to have entered by the garden door—and indeed it was—and how the notion that one could was all an illusion of sight, a thing which only an artist combined with a detective would have noticed. That's exactly the kind of proof that knocks a jury flat with admiration—showing, as they always wish to believe, the uselessness of all evidence. For remember, juries are always against the court. That's the strength of the system and the safety of democracy—the common man let in to watch the experts at their game and to have the ruling voice if the experts overplay their clever hand so that it becomes pure sleight of hand.

"But I mustn't run on. We were shown, as I've just said, how the illusion of sight built up the proof which really wasn't there. Just because Jane wanted a murder—for murder is always more appealing to active people than suicide—she found the proof. She didn't want it to be suicide because you can't catch a suicide—he's slipped through your fingers. But you can have a hue and cry after a murderer, especially if he's a tramp—someone who won't work when the rest of us do. Yes, Jane's motive is clear enough, though . . ." and Mr. M. paused and the younger Mr. M. shifted uneasily, "had she seen clearly enough then, I feel sure even she would have preferred suicide as the explanation.

"Still, to return to the facts, to my mind Jane stood her ground. I'd seen that she was a really good reporter, and though she was caught by the trick or play of the light on that door (not being a careful student of the Impressionists. those great questioners of what we really see) yet she did not only see: she heard.

"Now I know that hearing can be more of a nuisance than seeing. If seeing is a shaky sort of thing on which to build belief, the ear is even more flimsy. We know that even courts of law don't allow hearsay! But here we come to the real problem of all the senses which Mr. Silchester raised some while back and to which we can now fruitfully return. Our great Ionian father of detection and analysis, Heraclitus, said, 'The senses are bad witnesses.' He put them all in a bunch. I think he was mainly right. But, if I may patronize one of the source thinkers of mankind, I would venture to go a little further. I'd certainly agree that the senses may be pretty poor guides on the immense trail of detection on which Heraclitus and the first Greek scientists were setting out. They were seeking the prints of a hand as ubiquitous as it is invisible. But in the humdrum matters of lying, murder, and theft—in short, in what goes on on the surface of life—it is not so much our sensory witnesses, our expert reporters who are at fault, but ourselves, as cross-examiners. Beside the mistakes they make, ours are monstrous."

Mr. M. paused and laughed. "I am sorry to seem to be getting my second wind in the far past. You will think that I am like the classic French lawyer who could never begin placing his case before the court without going back to the Fall, and finally made as a concession a datum line with the Deluge. But, Mr. Silchester, you raised the point, and in point of fact—it is a tribute to your unanalytic intuition—the case largely turns on it. At least, if that seems too much for me to claim yet, I can tell you that at that point my vague questing turned into what I believe is called, in hunting circles, a breast-high scent.

"Let me, then, say one more thing about the senses, and then we'll get straight back to the story. When we sense something, experience anything, I believe that nine times out of ten the sense which calls our attention gives us a perfectly sound report. The mischief is that we are in such a hurry and so careless that we don't distinguish between what it actually tells us and the 'sense' we want to make of it. The worst judge on the bench, dozing and bored, hardly handles evidence so carelessly as we do matters of life and death being given to us by our only messengers, the senses. For they alone can tell us of what we call the world round us through which we are running blind.

"Now, the basis of good cross-examining is to take

one question at a time and one witness at a time. So as soon as I'd talked to Jane I saw, as I've said, that she was a good reporter—vivid, alive, interested, observant. You say she was caught out by the door seeming to move, and I have granted that. But I ask myself what made her first think that the door had opened, what called her attention so that she looked down in that direction? Quite another sense: hearing. Now, hearing is a most troublesome sense, but it's mainly because we really won't give our attention to it when it is speaking to us. We immediately turn aside and ask our eyes to go and see what hearing is talking about. That's no way to treat a witness, and we get what we deserve—a muddle. That's what Jane did. Unfortunately it's become the standard human reaction; our eyes have run away with us. That's why we say seeing is believing—and sight has treated the rest of the senses with a contempt they do not deserve. It is quite amazing how much, how intensively and diagnostically, people can hear, if they try and notice that they are hearing and are not just getting ready to see. And then there's scent too, even more neglected and one which I have found, as I hope to show in a moment, a useful tracker also. After all, the French say of a man of great artistic acumen, one who seems to go beyond sight, that he has a flair—he has some kind of power to smell out a masterpiece under a disguise that would throw sight completely off the track.

"Well, I maintain that Jane heard *something*. Our inspector friend could explain away her misinterpretation of sight. But having done that, he was content. He did not try to explain *why* she thought she heard the door open as well as saw it. Having shown that it couldn't have been opened that day, he left that other little problem, which was really the big clue, lying neglected. He could see, being an artist, that there was a sight; she did see something, which she misinterpreted. Perhaps had he been instead a musician he would have asked: 'Even if she misinterpreted it, what could she have actually heard?' If he had asked that, I believe he would have known as much as I learned."

He paused and added, "Considering how things have turned out, I think it was providential that his hobby was painting and not music. Of course, I had one advantage to start with. Being an amateur, I have been able to pursue detection just because of its interest and not as part of a social system for catching criminals. The police can never become real artists at their task," he sighed, "because it is at best a weary effort to stop things when they have already gone too far, to kill because you can't cure, to overthrow but not to understand. They can't prevent because they are not really interested in the great problems of all detection—human motive, human desire, and the greatest of all tragedies, our vast desires and our mean, inadequate, hopeless means. I know this sounds like rambling moralizing but, believe me, it is because these were my premises when I began to take an interest in the problems of detection that I have on a number of occasions been able to see deeper into a problem than my official colleagues. And, moreover, that point of view was precisely what gave me the viewpoint from which I was able to oversee the whole of this problem.

"In my interest in the pure problem of detection I had noticed this matter—over which we have had to take all this time because all the rest turns on it—the problem of the senses, how easily we let ourselves be confused when we are trying to decode their messages. And sound is the first that I started with, because of its notorious difficulty. Bats have a perfect system of biaural hearing—that is to say, they use their ears as we should, but as a matter of fact as we only use our eyes. They judge where an object is by echo sounding, by sending out their incessant squeak and judging with such precision that they can fly blindfolded through a maze of wires and touch none. We judge the place and distance of an object by the same triangulation done through our eyes—binocular vision. We could do the same with our ears no doubt, if we chose. But we are lazy. Hence we hear but don't really attend, and, not giving right attention, we are self-deceived.

"So years ago, seeing this gap in our power of detection, I made a small dictionary for myself, like those dictionaries of synonyms—but mine was what I rightly called a dictionary of symphonies."

At that, even the obedient Millum looked up, his face showing as much polite protest as mine.

Mr. M. smiled.

"Don't be puzzled thinking that I made a catalogue of all the big works by the great musicians! I'm using the word with more accuracy than they. My catalogue shows the unsuspected similarities of sound that can be given by different, utterly different, objects and so lead to completely mistaken identification. You'd hardly believe how like, indistinguishably alike to the untrained ear which most people are content with, sounds are—sounds which are taken to be quite different because, when we look, we *see* they are caused by objects that *look* quite different. Do you know that some crockery, when it is being washed in soapy water, will emit a note so like a growling dog that people will look out of the window thinking that the watchdog has been roused?

"Once I had a case which turned on whether someone had gone down a passage to kill a man at the other end. Someone swore that someone had so gone. Under examination he recollected he did not see him, but heard him. On further examination he allowed that he did not hear the actual footsteps but heard the boards of the passage creak. On the carpet being raised in the passage, it was found there were no boards underneath, but flagstones. The case fell through—I'm glad to say. For I came in at the end and was able to find the man, to save him from hanging, and to get him to make a lifelong reparation. For the witness I've quoted, and on whose evidence everything turned, was discredited not on his sense of hearing but on his wrong and rash interpretation of what he heard. What he was ready to keep on swearing to, even when discredited, was that he had heard the creaking of boards as when they are stepped on and he added, 'I heard that creaking regularly go along that passage. I am sure that someone did walk down it.' And he was right, flagstones or no flagstones. But they don't creak. Then what could give the same sort of sound? I went to my catalogue, thinking I would find boots—which wouldn't be helpful. Boots I found correlated with the sound made when a cork begins to be drawn from the neck of a glass bottle, and much else of other examples but none to my point. But as I went through the creaks I found correlated with boards—what would you think? That hard cloth called corduroy—generally only worn by gamekeepers, and that, at one stroke, gave me my man.

"Now we are ready to strike. Jane heard—she says —the door open. What Jane actually heard, but misinterpreted in the terms of her unexamined wish, was a twang. As she wished the sound to come from the door, she was certain that it did so. She gave evidence that this was not only possible but probable. And we ourselves sounded that catch or hasp above the door," he pointed over his shoulder toward the garden wall behind him, "that reacted aurally like a giant jew's-harp. Further, she did see the shadow made by the spray of branch above swayed by a gust of wind. So, putting a further false deduction to her first wishful mistake, she added up her findings and was convinced that the door had opened. She heard, I repeat, a twang. She was in the position least suited to use our only method of detecting place by sound, biaural hearing. For she was glancing out into the garden, and the sound, as it happens, originated from a source not on her right, but on her left."

"Excuse me," Millum interrupted, his tone quiet and his comment to the point, "excuse me, I don't follow just here. Surely, if her left ear was toward the . . . the source of the sound, she was very well placed to judge the direction?"

"A good objection," allowed Mr. M, "but you have overlooked the echo. In acoustics, as in painting, each source of sound or light throws back part of its radiation until we often, as here, think the echoing surface—in this case the brick wall behind us now—is the actual source of the sound wave. The sound wave that we are tracking was sent out above and behind Jane's stance. Naturally, then, she first heard and perhaps heard only the echo that glanced back from the wall and so came first to her right ear!"

Millum bowed, and I nodded with growing appreciation.

Mr. M. went on: "It was the fact that Jane *had* rightly heard a twang and yet had wholly mistaken whence that sudden buzz of sound came from—it was that thought that suddenly, like a note resolving a chord, made the whole thing begin to take shape in my mind. And then, as happens when once you are in line, everything began to fall into place.

"When we were in the arbor I had noticed that it was an odd time to prune trees, with the sap rising. I suppose we can now say that as Sankey was mad enough to have killed a goose," he smiled gently at Millum, "that laid him golden eggs, why should he not prune trees just when they are about to yield! But I didn't know that then. And the more I looked about, the more I was puzzled, and therefore the more hopeful of coming upon a very remarkable story. For I next noticed, as I looked at this arbor, that though the pruning had certainly not been done incompetently, there was one place where an ugly cut, a complete break through the canopy, had been made. When we were down by the door I therefore looked over the cuttings which had been taken over there, and saw at once this one considerable branch that had been amputated. Before that I had observed the skylight which the amputation made, while I was sitting in this chair. I saw then, as I see now, that it permits one to have, as through a porthole, just a glimpse of the upper part of the corner of the house over the road—but not quite up to the parapet. To be able to see the parapet itself," and Mr. M. crouched in his seat, "you see I have to double down until my head is now where, a moment before, when I was sitting up, my heart was!"

I watched the demonstration, but again Mr. Millum turned away.

"And then came a further point, really a very nice one—one that gave me hope." Mr. M. looked across to Millum and repeated, "Real hope! But first for proof. After this I had only to look where I was now pretty sure I'd find. Our source again was our highly educated inspector, once more showing that a man's keen power of observation must always be distinguished from the use to which he puts that power, the meaning he attaches to the finds he makes. And, further, just because he was so well-read, when he made his mistaken misinterpretation he was further out and off than Jane herself. About the volume of Suetonius *et al.*, both he and Jane were agreed. The inspector was sure it clinched his case for suicide, and I was sure it reopened it and gave me a new conviction and a new hope—for, as I shall show in a moment, it gave me not only the direction in which I was to look but also a first light into the motive and into the character I was to discover. That is why," and Mr. M.'s voice became gentle, "that is why I used the word 'hope' advisedly and why I was not merely amused but glad that the very intelligence of the highly educated inspector had thrown him off the scent. And here, in another and actual sense, came in that sense, the sense of smell.

"My further little volume, which will be a companion to the first I have mentioned on Similar Sounds, will be on Similar Scents. But this collection of synolfactorics, if I have to coin a rather ugly neologism, is still in a very rudimentary condition. I have, though, been able to find some associations which the ordinary person would say at first sight, but not at first whiff, have nothing in common—for example, that cooking red peppers (a delicious dish with veal Milanaise) give exactly the same smell as that disgusting fume, burning rubber!

"Naturally, what every student on this subject would start upon would be the tobaccos. The first thing is to train the nose until it can tell at the first whiff what tobacco a man smokes or has smoked. As soon as I entered that room up there," and Mr. M. pointed up the steps to the house, "I knew that here we had a Latakia smoker, and a Latakia smoker is, as one might say, out on the end of the branch. By that

I mean, as it is the strongest of all tobaccos, he is very unlikely ever to go back to the weaker, as a man who has taken to inhaling will never willingly enjoy the finer taste given by a good tobacco when flavored simply on the palate. And Latakia is an end of the passage in another sense, for, as you probably know, many of the types are highly impregnated with opium. The man who takes to the strongest of all the Asia Minor tobaccos is already more than halfway to the smoke that has suffocated half of all Asia—the poppy latex.

"So I know by my nose that the late owner of this house smokes and, more, that he smokes only one brand. Then, once smell has given me that information—for that pungent tobacco hangs about, as maids say, very long—then I can set my eyes to look out for traces, should they be needed to lead me further. That's when, Mr. Silchester, you will recall with what rightful triumph the inspector produced this book which, unlike Jane, he knew well enough and could use as evidence for his theory of suicide. For he found the passage about painless *felo-de-se*, and found it because it was marked by the silt of tobacco ash—which happens when a careless smoker or an engrossed reader studies a passage and, unaware, lets the burned-out ash fall and settle in the crease and groin of the leaves. Of course the ash itself, especially when crushed between the leaves, would not have been enough for me to work on, however much it may have been depended on as a guide by the master of masters of our craft. All honor to the ashes of our great eponym, but between you and me I have always had my doubts as to whether even he could read, translate, and detect through tobacco ash as infallibly as he is said to have asserted. Perhaps he was a medium and acted clairvoyantly, the ash acting by its chance patterns merely as a provocatant to his mystic insight —as with the ladies who divine from stranded tea leaves! Or perhaps some subtle fume from the ash acted on his superfine olfactory sense and raised him to vision, as the laurel leaves' smoke at Delphi soothed and uplifted the Pythian Sibyl!

"But these are speculations into an almost sacred past. Let us return to the profane present. I did find with the ash something I could go on. In the crevice of the page I found with my lens—while Jane's narrative generously gave me time—not only ash, but fragments of the actual tobacco. It was Virginian—a thing a smoker of Latakia would never use. In the crevices of the first couple of pages I found further ash—not so much as in the deposit in the later pages, but with it a crumb or two of unburned tobacco, and that tobacco was Latakia. In other words, when I had reached that point I could say definitely the following things: that Sankey had read the earlier few pages but had not reached the Petus passage, for before he could get as far as that he fell struck through the heart while he held the book; secondly, I could be sure that someone who smoked Virginian tobacco had been reading, yes, and brooding, over that Petus passage before Sankey was given the book; and thirdly, that no one had had that book since, for the inspector had locked it up as soon as it was handed to him by the chief here, who himself had taken it from under the undisturbed body.

"Nor, while I studied the book with my lens, with some profit, as you see, did I fail to keep on listening to Jane's bright flow. And I was again rewarded because of her vivid visual sense—simple minds are often photographic in their memories. In describing that last day, she had really let nothing escape her. You recall her account of her bringing in what she called Mr. Sankey's 'elevens'—his chocolate, and how the visitor from over the way, coming at that moment with this book (which she claimed, with an understandable misreading, for cookery) still, though carrying this large volume, was able to open the doors for her even though he had to do it with his left hand. And she noticed that this left hand had both thumb and first finger heavily bandaged. Naturally, as soon as I could—in point of fact, today—I examined that thumb and finger, persuading their owner, in lighting my cigarette for me, to show them. I could see on them no sign of lesion. But if, that fateful morning, they were to pick up quickly and unnoticed a paper knife on which their prints must on no account appear, it would be a wise and an obvious precaution to bandage them, would it not?"

During this recital Millum had sunk still lower as he sat on the ground. Mr. M. turned and put his hand on the bent shoulders.

"Please," he said, "don't take this part of the tale tragically. When we come back to motive then it will be time to be grave again. And here I shall be able to show to Mr. Silchester, here is a point very much in your favor. Now, to go on with the means: well, I find them showing finish. It might be considered by some people that here was so subtle a false clue, planted so deeply to put a sleuth off the scent, that it would fail to tell. But you see, it was right and paid off just because the police in the higher ranks have now become so intelligent and even scholarly. It illustrates the old advice: it always pays never to talk down to your audience, never to despise your foe, never to patronize the police.

"Now you see, Mr. Silchester," said Mr. M., for he had now turned to me, as his attempt to keep Millum's mind interested in the means, and the Mycroft way of retracing them had failed to rouse his patient, "you see, Mr. Silchester, why I proposed to you, after the inspector had closed the case, that we look at the other house. The venue of the trial we were holding had to be changed. The real interest no longer lay here in this garden: this was simply the end. The start of the course we had to trace lay, I was sure, over the wall—where the book had come from.

"I had a pointer, too, like the sign of a gun. Indeed, not *like* a sight but, as it happens, an actual sighting line which pointed the way I must go tracing back the source of the mystery. It not only pointed to the house over the way—it actually pointed to the exact place on the house. So we visited Mrs. Sprigg, and you recall I asked that I might 'view the prospect o'er,' and that quotation and the fact that I wanted to enjoy her countryside made her glad we should have our Pisgah view. And you enjoyed it."

"And you didn't!" I cut in.

"But wait a minute," Mr. M. said, "we are still on the way up to our mount."

"That," I replied judiciously, "may supply the reason why you were not as full of interest in the landscape when you got there as you'd thought you'd be. Yes, I remember when we came to the final climb and Mrs. Sprigg had faltered and left us—when you reached the top of the last ladderlike flight and you were just going to push open the small glazed door leading out onto the leads, you had to stop to get your breath. Though I must say, the air up there was stifling as an anesthetic."

"Good memory and fair observation, while deduction, I am glad to say, is as wrong as I'd hoped!"

After that little flourish, which I let pass and forgot in the interest of what he next said, he went on quickly, "As I paused, and hoped you and Mrs. Sprigg—if she were still keeping track of us—would think I was finding my breath, I was lensing that little door. You recall it was made with two leaves so it opened down the middle, and Mrs. Sprigg had said no one had been there since the roof repairers, months ago. But I saw at once clear evidence of almost the date on which someone had but lately gone ahead of us!

"Spiders' webs! We of the 'tec trade are always talking about the web and all that. But why hasn't anyone till now seen that here we have a fascinating trail marker—yes, and even a fascinating colleague!"

At this rhapsody I asked with more than a smile, "Master, are you simply spinning a tale or following a clue?"

"Wait, I beg," he answered, "for I must tell you that someone has actually written the very book that for years I wished I might have had the time and skill to write. For six years Dr. André Tilquin has watched and noted *La Toile Géometrique des Araignées.* He gave up two rooms of his house that they might demonstrate how they build their gossamer traps, trapezes, and hammock homes. And gradually, from studying this, the finest of lines, he made out from these faint but strictly geometric patterns the shadow of the strange mind that cast this print. You can't, of course, do much with spiders. But what you can, goes like clockwork. That was one of the most interesting finds made by le grand Tilquin. He found that if you put the right kind of species of spider in the corner that was rightly proportionated to its 'geometric sense,' then it had straightaway—or as soon as it got over the shock of your being about—to weave you a web as quick, sure, and firm as though you had ordered it. No, alas, I didn't come on this find myself. I had to hear of it through crime. A French criminal, following up that old story of how the Protestant family escaped their pursuers by a spider providentially weaving a web over the door they had so lately slipped through, learned that he could so hide his tracks from any casual police pursuit.

"Yes, quite a lot might be done with insects. There's no slacking or moodiness about them. You are, in fact, directing a machine by knowing the exact setup which sets its electromagnetic switches going. But I can say that once my mind had been put on this track I saw that I must study the real nature-made web, and it has yielded me something more useful—at least on my side of the crime game—than just knowing how to hide myself. Threads, after all, have been used for a long while to mark whether someone has passed along a passage. The spider's web is far the best. It's obvious, then, how useful it is to be able to make them spin across gaps you wish to have marked in that way.

"But not only will they tell you if anyone has gone by. I have found they will tell you—within a number of days—how long ago it was that the passer passed.

They notice and mark the track of a trespasser, however light-footed and hand-padded. The neatest cat-burglar housebreaker, who breaks in so gently and in such gentlemanly fashion that he would never call without his gloves on, can't help breaking a cobweb and can't know when he has done so. The web has, on each of the transverse bars—not on the radials, only on the laterals—those smears and spots of gum in which the fly is caught. My discovery was to note that when the web has been ruptured and the radials and laterals mixed up, the whole web, perhaps because the gum contains a strong acid (of this I am not sure) rapidly begins to decay. I am pretty sure from this work that I can tell within a day or two, by study of the collapsed web, when it was ruptured.

"I saw, then, that we had had a forerunner of a few days ago, and one that went there without even the housekeeper knowing of it. After that I was free to recover my breath, and we could start taking bigger views. But here you were again a little disappointed in me, for I gave most of my time to what you took to be the poorer view. You were right, if contemplation was your end; but mine was to unravel action. So you find me once again kneeling and pausing. But believe me, while I was so kneeling and, as

I said honestly, thinking, I was also getting the view which brought everything else into view. For now, from the broad gutter behind the parapet, I was looking down into this garden so that I was precisely reversing the view we can have from down here."

Mr. M. pointed up to the gap in the arbor roof.

"I was looking through that gap, and even if I had not known what to look for, my eye would have been guided, would have been sighted, right onto this seat."

"But, dear master," I interrupted, "you forget that I looked down here too and saw nothing in particular. Indeed, I doubt whether that hole does really show up from there; for this seat, which you say you could see, is itself mottled green. Honestly, I don't believe it could be clearly detected from there."

"Right again," he allowed generously enough; but then added, "If the seat was empty, you could hardly see it. But if it was filled with a white object, say a white silk suit, then it would show up like a white bull's eye in a dark-green target—a very fine mark indeed."

"Still," I came back with some force, "what you are really suggesting is that someone went up to that point on the roof and, crouching there, threw that paper knife with such power and aim that it struck home right down there—right into the heart behind that silk suiting! Why, not the most competent of knife throwers with a really fine weapon would think of attempting that. I have seen what they can do at vaudeville shows. It's good, but to claim that for even the most expert is simply drawing the longbow."

"But bow is precisely the wanted word," he replied.

Again I was quite ready. "Of course only a bow could do it, but here again, unfortunately, I know something, and what I know doesn't help your clever theory. I once belonged to an archery club. The longbow, the pride of England, has, you may not know, been brought back. It is not only a very graceful weapon but a very powerful one. I was never very competent at it, but I have seen men who were, and they could certainly do the job you suggest. But not at all in the way you imagine. Nor with the weapon you suggest. The longbow depends for its firing upon a proper stance being taken." I took the position to show. "You see: the whole body has to be swung from the hips and shoulders, as the string is pulled and the arrow discharged. So not only do you have to be standing up and with space about you, but you have to have, for a bow of proper strength and stretch—

say a five-foot one (and that at least would have been needed, with a few hundred pounds of pull)—you have to have the cloth-yard arrow of something nearly as long. That wretched paper knife or pin—why, the finest archer in the world couldn't send it more than a yard or two and then he wouldn't be sure it would hit anything at which he aimed."

This fine counterbattery was met with the unyielding defense of, "Right again in all that you know about."

And then, with a slow smile, "But being so British and athletic, you naturally forgot that the bow is not a purely British preserve. Men went on thinking about its problem of ballistics long after the longbow was demoded. Indeed, that progress went on until, without a break, the bow turned into the harquebus—you see, the very word has the same root.

"Soldiers were always seeking for a more scientific, less artistic, weapon—one that would permit perfect aim, settled sighting, not just hit or miss, and also more strength. They exhausted the tensile resilience of wood and then they took to steel. But there they came up against a check, the limit of human muscle. You may remember Ulysses' bow (if Odysseus is just now too odious a name for us) that none of the Suitors could draw? It was an approach to the small steel bow. We know it was not the longbow. Its great strength was due to the fact that it was not made of wood but of the horns of certain wild goats. But not Ulysses himself could draw a bow of steel. So they made gears and loaders to stretch the cord to the trigger, and that required a stock and barrel on which the bow could be fixed and strung. Then on this stock there was grooved a channel in which the arrow could lie.

"Don't be surprised that you failed to appreciate the force of this device. Our earliest European blue-stocking, the Byzantine princess-authoress Anna Comnena, remarks about this invention that 'It is a barbarian weapon, entirely unknown to the Hellenes' and 'For ingenuity of construction, length of range, power of penetration, and deadliness of effect, a really devilish contrivance!'

"The inventors of this sire-of-a-gun—if I may coin a name—found that they need no longer use the clumsy, quiver-filling long arrow. In fact, this new weapon called for something much more like a bullet. These last arrows are sometimes called billets, sometimes quarrels, but usually bolts, for they went like bolts from the blue, almost too fast to be seen. In shape they were almost exactly like this." And Mr. M. held up the paper knife. "This, that fell like a bolt from the blue onto the doomed man in the arbor.

"So you see why, when I had this in my hand, my mind had been opened with this key so that I could find the further lock that this key finally fitted! And recall, I had not one, but several suggestions given me by this bolt that unlocked the door. Three of these were: first, the flukes which had been fitted on it to give it true flight. These, I saw, could be easily and quickly fitted along the haft, just before firing it; second, there was its own rightful forward, or salient, balance, required to keep it front-end on while in flight; and finally, the fact that at its other end was a groove, and in that groove I had found impacted resin! What is resin chiefly used for even now? To make strings that are under very great tension able to keep strong and not fray and burst. You know violin strings are treated with resin, and bow strings are regularly rubbed with it. So it was hardly possible for me to avoid suspecting that this bolt had been shot from a crossbow.

"Then, to judge the range, and whether the weapon in question would serve at the distance from which it had to strike, I crouched in the parapet of the house over the way, at that corner which allows a glimpse down onto this spot in this garden. There I could see what perfect concealment and what perfect rest for the weapon, and, finally, what a perfect aim all were given. It was a part that practically played itself. There was something about the whole thing that reminded me uncannily of the old folk tale of the weapon that actually makes whoever touches it carry out the avenging deed with which the long-dead wizard had charged it."

He was silent a moment, and certainly Millum did not look at all inclined to comment. But a point did occur to my practical mind, more concerned with getting things into the clear light of fact than tracing fanciful connections in myth.

"Master," I said, rousing him with the playful courtesy-title, "Master, you speak of the bow practically going off of itself—the manner in which Jane, should she be capable of breaking a piece of porcelain, would fall back on the immemorial defense of all her tribe: 'Why, Sir, it came to pieces in my hand.' But this crossbow which we shall never see, and for whose actual nature we have to depend on your incomparable powers of reconstruction and historical imagination, Master—can we really assume that such a piece of antiquity remained in such terribly efficient working order right down the centuries? It might well have hung on some baronial walls, but I doubt if for the last few centuries it could ever have been used even to shoot a mud pellet to knock off an archdeacon's top hat! And I don't believe any of . . . of us," (I thought this was a courteous and protective way of including Millum) "any of us could have put such an almost-gun into . . . well, changed it from an antique piece of decorative furniture into something really deadly."

"You're right. You're right on two of your points," he allowed, looking across at me with his head quizzically on one side—a way he has of looking when he does not want to appear surprised at someone else's acumen. "The third point, however, you overlook."

And, having once more put himself back into the saddle of superiority, he continued, "The bow itself had pretty surely been properly repaired as lately as the nineteenth century, perhaps even later. It was that—as we have been told the dealer said at the auction where it was last bought—that spoiled its value for any museum or any real collector of antiques. You are naturally not a careful student of that epoch—the last century—which for you has neither the charm of antiquity nor the interest of modernity. It lies in that dark valley called the out-of-date. But for me it will always be my home of first memories. And I recall, when looking through that very accurate and often amusing history of mores, the volumes of the London charivari, *Punch,* with which we used to beguile not unprofitably pre-cinema evenings, that when that paper was almost radical, it had a cartoon censuring the young Queen Victoria because she and her ladies were charged with having seated themselves in a kind of grandstand and thence to have shot at driven deer. And since, as you have demonstrated to us, they could not draw a long bow, and the sporting guns of that day had enough 'kick' and made sufficient noise to provoke female vapors and bruise 'lily shoulders,' the royal and titled ladies are shown shooting with this silent but lethal weapon, the crossbow.

"So you see, with a weapon of such precision and force, from such a coign of vantage and seclusion, shooting right down on the . . . prey, as sportsmen do from concealed platforms in the jungle, why, the whole thing was so near a certainty that it was, as we say, foolproof. You simply had to put yourself in place; look down the stock and barrel of your weapon; see your line of sight kept true for you by the sighting hole cut in the arbor roof; see the white coat showing up, and showing just where the heart lay (and, I would add, with the face of the man about to be . . . to be executed mercifully hidden from you); and then all you had to say was, 'It does not hurt, Petus,' and press the trigger. Then you return the paper knife to its owner, from whom you had borrowed it when you placed the Suetonius on his side table while he was fussing at this other table about his chocolate, the drink that was to prove his viaticum."

"But," once again as a fact finder I insisted on full information, "you've described a weapon of such force with this monster steel spring; you've said it couldn't be drawn by hand. You've got still to explain how the . . . man loaded it."

"That," he replied, picking up the roof repairer's wire stretcher, "that was the final clue. This is the actual type of lever used to string these smaller bows—the bigger had a crank. All I needed now was to find the bow itself. Of course, whoever used it would destroy it at once. Indeed, his speed to get rid of the greater clue kept him from doing the same with this stretcher, though it should not have awakened any suspicion in anyone's mind, for its purpose and how it got on the roof were both known. It was pretty safe to leave it up there. Hence we visit the garden, and naturally all was gone of the bow itself but the spring. And that was so sooted, and its temper so gone in the fire, that it also would be safe from suspicion should it be found. You would have been supported by any investigator in your theory that it was the spring of some old Bath chair. No other conclusion would have been possible—unless all the other evidence had not pointed to its real purpose and aim."

Mr. M. paused, and there was the longest silence we had yet endured The shadows were beginning to draw across the garden. It was getting cold, and I felt a whole gaggle of huge gray geese going over my grave.

After some time Mr. Mycroft remarked to me, "There was only one small point I would like to note here. Now that I have brought back your mind to the incinerator from which I know you winced, you will recall the old empty packages of *Gold Flake* cigarettes that lay around the mouth of the furnace?"

"That put—" it was Millum speaking at last, "the last golden nail in my coffin!"

"No," replied Mr. M., "no, I would not call it your coffin. I'd call it your husk. It cracked your shell out of which you'll now have to make a breakaway—for

I mean to give you one. Anyhow, now we can go back to the real interest in all human action—not means, but motive—motive, without which we often can't find even the means. I can see the role that opportunity—what we call a queer run of chances—played with you. 'O Opportunity thy guilt is great!'

"But what I see further is that you stood, you didn't budge until with Opportunity there came up its great and subtle ally, Casuistry. It was the suggestion-temptation that, after all, the blow would not really be felt, that the dispatch need not hurt—it was that, wasn't it, that suddenly made you resolve to try, that was your trigger that fired you to your deed. You remember a little while back I said there was a point here that gave me hope? I thought at this point of my tracking (and now I'm sure) that I detected a double motive, a double motive in the use of the Petus passage that had first served its purpose by rousing you and provoking you to the brink of action. No doubt it seemed desperately necessary that every possible suggestion and clue should be left about to persuade the philosophic police that there was adequate provocation to suicide at that moment—as Sankey sat within bow shot. But also I believed, and believe, there was a hope, a wish by the bowman, to point out not only to the police and himself but even to Sankey that death by heart-stabbing was painless. Muddled, you say? Certainly. For that's what makes for the real mystery of murder—muddled motives. There was the wish to be out of an intolerable situation and, blended inextricably with it, as our motives always are when under tension, the wish to believe that no wrong is really being done—indeed, that one is doing a service to the obstacle itself as it is pushed over the edge out of the way. Muddled, yes. Of course, Sankey might never reach the passage as he read—you might not be able to let him have the time to do so—and, in fact, you didn't. Besides, his only possible weapon has been taken from him. Petus is not simply to be told that stabbing doesn't hurt, he is to be stabbed. To save him further trouble of making up his mind he is to be flung out of the body. Precisely, precisely! don't you see, the whole thing is a perfect example of the psychology of confusion, of murderer and murderee inextricably involved."

He turned once more to Millum. "You would employ what is called in China 'the happy dispatch.' And you would do it by means so easy, so light, that Shakespeare marvels that so much of consequence, and with such power of pain as a human soul, can be let out of its prison with nothing more than what you would use, 'a bare bodkin.' And the bodkin, you see, with its long delicate handle and its shorter lance head, might suggest a model of that dagger which in the Middle Ages was called a misericord, an instrument of mercy with which to release from life one who had lost honor, lost the fight, and could now only suffer.

"Well, before taking the risk and having this strange unsatisfying success, it is a pity that you did not come to me. I think we could have managed the whole affair. Not that I think we could have done much with Sankey. I judge that was a case where a higher court would have had to handle the problem—some complexes refuse any form of reduction that we can employ in this life. But as to you, I can say, though it is late, it's not too late. That you've been given this second chance—considering the risks you took and also that in Inspector Sark you had against you one of the best detective minds in Britain—shows, I think, that you were meant to go on till you solve this problem. I'm no sentimentalist. I believe in justice and only venture to differ from the law when it follows its own idea of rigid consistency. So now, as I stand for justice, I must act!"

At that I started up. "What! Are you going to call the police after all?"

All Millum said was, "I'm ready. The case, as you see, is out of my hands."

Then Mr. Mycroft said slowly, "I arrest you."

Then, as though to be more precise, "I should say, I have arrested you. For that is what arrest is—it is not judging people, but leaving that to a higher authority. But it is, in the name of that authority, telling them to stop, to wait, to prepare their case and consider their future. So I have arrested you. You have been brought to a standstill, and I don't see how, placed as you now are, you can do anything more. You are at a dead center. Adding your physical death to this wouldn't make things any better. We are always saying two blacks don't make a white, but the law, which is so fond of wise saws and modern instances, never seems to have heard of that one. So, as I have brought you to this pass and can see that you can't do anything about it, but equally can't be left where you are, I must do something about it. I don't see any way out of it (or believe me I would take it) than for us to take it together. I must and will go surety for you."

Turning quickly to me, he said, "Mr. Silchester, I wonder whether you would go and talk with Jane. I find that I shall have to take this house if it is at all suitable, for I shall have to spend the summer down here detained by the development of a case. You are a much better judge than I as to whether the house would be suitable for us. Would you, therefore, go and look it over? And if you come to the conclusion that you would also wish to spend the summer down here with me, I shall find that as useful an alliance, I believe, as I have in the past—unexpected as our contributions to each other's interests generally are."

And with that drop of subacid put in at the close of his compliment—as bees put formic acid in their honey—I was sent off to wait like a junior while the elders talked. But though I felt at the beginning I was just being got rid of, when I found Jane I must say I found some pleasure in cutting Mr. M. out in her good graces. She was far better company than I had suspected, having really a good natural wit. Several times she broke out into loud laughter at my remarks and had to own that she had 'really quite forgotten herself.' So by the time we had seen the whole of the house—and it was worth seeing, every part being most expensively furnished and as equally well kept—

the dusk had begun to fall fast, and guide and explorer were mutually won over.

On going down I thought Mr. M. might think I had been too long, but when I reached the garden, now moonlit and looking much more romantic than sinister, there were the two M.'s walking up and down like old friends who had just met after a long separation. They were actually arm in arm, a liberty which Mr. M. has never taken with me.

Within a week we were settled. By some odd accident—Mr. M. says it is not uncommon in men like that because of an unconscious fear that the very thing may increase the closeness of death—Sankey had never made a will since he was at college. Then, as he was about to make a journey into Anatolia, he was told by his lawyer that he ought, to save possible trouble, make a brief will against contingencies. So he had scrawled half a sheet of paper and had had the hotel boots- and the desk-reception clerk sign it as witnesses. But it was quite valid, and the lawyer had rung through to say that they were holding it, and what did Mr. Millum want to do about it, for he was sole beneficiary under the will, and the lawyer was the executor.

So Mr. Millum provisionally was able to tell us

that we could move in as soon as we liked, and I must say I found Mr. Millum quite an asset.

It's said that two's company, three's none. But it's not true when two companions are really as far apart as Mr. M. and I—the scientist and the artist. I used to call Mr. Millum the hyphen, for his gift, which was mainly that of a collector and an antiquarian, neatly linked the two extremes on which Mr. M. and I stood. Gradually, too, I noticed he had a nickname, or title, for Mr. M. He used to call him Mr. P.O. When he had got into the way of doing that pretty regularly, I stopped him one day when Mr. M. was out of the way and asked him what he meant by it—for I didn't want to be laughed at for not being able to see some obvious point and manifest relevance.

"P.O.," I remarked, "stands, I understand, for post office in all customary abbreviations by initials—a habit I dislike, but one which seems to delight the alphabetically rudimentary mind of our present bureaucrats. But that attribute of office applied to Mr. M. seems to me singularly inept. For a post office distributes the mail and other information sent to it. I cannot imagine a worse receptacle into which to put information you wished distributed than the mind of Mr. Mycroft. Granted that his ear hears most things, his mouth gives less away than ever did Elwin, the classic eighth-century miser."

I thought that opening was pretty good and would show I was no ignoramus for not having found out what the real meaning of the appellation could be.

"Yes," said Mr. Millum with courteous agreement, "yes, I agree that no title for our honored friend could fit more oddly than that of post office. And of all ministries, that of postmaster general is the last I would imagine his taking—though, if he did, I believe our postal service would be improved, for a more varied and competent mind I never met."

"Yes, yes," I intervened, "I think I can appreciate his powers as well as any man, and even the blind spots he has at times don't make me underrate the keenness of his insights at others. But if not post office, what can P.O. mean? That was my question."

Mr. Millum hesitated a little longer this time but, seeing I was not to be put off, continued, "I agree that it is a good thing that Mr. Mycroft has not got the distributive mind, as you happily put it. Considering that my life is in his hands and yours, you will have no doubt that I agree it is a good thing that he is not interested in publicity. And please never forget that I remember my debt. Though I know people of your caliber of discretion carry it so far that some things are never mentioned even among ourselves. Forgive me for doing so, but the opportunity being given by you, I felt I might take it."

This was all a little shy-making, to use that dear old-fashioned phrase of my childhood. So I shifted back from dangerous ground by asking again. "But what does P.O. stand for, if not for post office?"

His answer rather deepened my embarrassment instead of lessening it, and made me sorry that I'd raised the issue at all.

He said, "P.O. stands for probation officer."

Then, when I was at a loss as to what to say, he added even more quietly, "But the initials go even better when expanded in Latin. That gives an even more precise description of the office, the difficult office that remarkable man chooses now to spend his time in carrying out."

He stopped, and so I felt bound in courtesy to ask further, "What is the title in Latin?"

When he answered, "*Pastor Ovis*," I was no wiser —I have let my Latin get rusty. Besides, I felt a certain relief that I didn't know and was protected by what someone has called that defense against a shock to the feelings which is given by the obscurity of an ancient tongue.

I didn't feel I needed to say I didn't know and so bowed, and remarking, "Well, I suppose it's apt," slipped off and consulted a good Latin lexicon that was in the house.

Inexpert as I am with that kind of heavy reading, I soon deciphered the code words and saw at once how sound, as usual, had been my intuition that warned me that we were on the verge of something that might prove positively sentimental, a thing to which my natural good taste has always given me a vigorous aversion. I'm not saying that there's any actual harm in that sort of thing if it helps you, and you happen, as poor Millum had, to fall into a position in which you have to be in the hands of someone else, however sound those hands may be. If Mr. Millum felt safer when penned, that was a matter for his feelings. After all, this was a better pen than the only other place which goes in American slang under the same name. And as he had to choose one or the other, naturally I approve his choice. No doubt Mr. M.'s "rod and staff" were much more comfortable than a warder's truncheon. But if Mr. Millum thinks that the role of the successfully bleached black sheep suits him, it certainly isn't mine. Black or white or a charming gray with mottlings of fawn, I intend to remain in the team not as the hero worshipper nor the reformed rake but as the candid kid.

But I don't want to end on a captious note. Both the summer and the team proved most propitious. Millum could, and did, talk metaphysics to his heart's content with Mr. M., and when he'd got this off his chest and the master had withdrawn to his endless studies and what people actually do and the mess of it and what they ought to do and the neatness that would result if they did, as they never will, then Mr. Millum would come and discuss matters of fact with me. I found him charmingly well-informed on what I now called My Period and ever so helpful in assisting me in ordering my material and adding to it for my opus.

As the days have gone by and this remarkable work has grown under my hands, I cannot help feeling increasingly that, maybe before not too long, the whole of this queer case may be seen to fall into its proper proportions. It will appear at last inevitably as the accidental and dramatic occasion or provocation that led to that definitive study, *1760, the Co-ordinate Acme of British Culture*, by Sidney Silchester. And I think, as I shall have it printed in a face of type of that date just to show that we cannot improve even on the print, I shall concede to the good taste of the period and add my rank, as it should be, in Latin—*Armiger*. If Mr. Mycroft chooses, he can take it as a far more sensitive compliment than being called P.O.! For then he can imagine, and I shall not in courtesy dispute it, that he is the Knight—if something of a white one—of whom I am the Esquire.